7 ELEMENT LIFEFORCE HEALING

Dr. Harry Elia

Fulton Books, Inc.
Meadville, PA

Published by Fulton Books 2020

FDA DISCLAIMER: Any statements or treatments in this book have not been evaluated by the FDA and are not intended, diagnose, treat or cure any diseases or conditions. Also, consult your physician before starting any exercise programs described in this book.

ISBN 978-1-63338-382-1 (paperback)
ISBN 978-1-64654-999-3 (hardcover)
ISBN 978-1-63338-383-8 (digital)

Printed in the United States of America

DEDICATION

This book is dedicated to my parents, John Rocco Sr. and Anna Elia, whose dedication and love for their family can be seen in the eyes of their children's children's children, making them truly immortal.

CONTENTS

ACKNOWLEDGMENTS

The following people were instrumental in the formation of this work:

Shelly Gioffre—for all her support of my work
Vincent Ferrau—my backyard Chi-Gung buddy and best friend
Ron Diama—my first Taoist teacher
Dr. Art Joseph—my most ardent supporter
Dr. Marcie Prisco—for saying, "Next week, Harry, we'll talk on elements."
John and Cherilyn Elia—my children for gifting me with their lives
John Rocco Jr. and Camille Elia—for their financial and emotional support
Dave Brown—for graphic art and illustrations
Andrew Izzo—for illustrations
All the Taoist Masters who walked the different path of the *Tao*.

INTRODUCTION

We live in an age of technology and science. Tremendous amounts of information are at our fingertips. Anything that happens anywhere in the world is at our breakfast table. We identify with what we believe to be solid irrefutable fact. We govern our health with clinical scientific analysis. Our greatest scientists build a ten-billion-dollar atom smasher with the hope of identifying the smallest solid building block of life. They search for the "God" particle and hold to the belief that the secret to our existence is palpable and can be measured definitively.

After billions of dollars have been spent and the best scientists have poured over the data of the smashing and separating the smallest particles that make up our universe, what is their findings? Well, they had a hard time explaining their findings. One of the overriding theories that has been offered to explain the results is supersymmetry (also called string) theory. Simply stated, there is a field of energy that serves as a background (Higgs field), which gives all particles of the universe their relative mass. This energy field makes everything relative. In essence, it is the energy field that is necessary for all particles (solids) to have mass.

I have my own Dr. Harry Elia unified universe theory, which states, "The universe is as etheric (energy) as it is solid, and it is the etheric that gives meaning to the solid." I cannot give you the mathematics to this theory nor can I take complete credit for it, because it is derived from a philosophy that is over two thousand five hundred years old. That philosophy states that man and the universe are made up of Yin and Yan, matter and energy, and energy directs and rules the matter (solids) while matter gives energy its base and support.

What does this have to do with health? Everything.

Up to now, medical science has studied health only in the solid, physical tendon, bones, organs, and chemistry, all parts of the physical body. Our modern health science has all but ignored anything that cannot be perfectly proved in a laboratory or make money for its developers. What about mental health? Most of our mental health science still deals in chemistry, not energy. Remember, it is Love that creates the chemicals, not chemistry that creates Love. Try and put Love in a test tube and measure it definitively.

Think of this as an example of solids and energy. Right now, I am writing this introduction on my kitchen table. I perceive the table as being solid and feel it solid. Scientific physicists will tell you that it is the arrangement of the molecules that make it solid and that in reality there is more empty space than solid particles in the table. Sounds ridiculous to you, doesn't it? But that is an accepted fact in physics. Your perception of the hard and solid is not really all that there is to life. Scientific physicists have accepted that fact, but medical science still ignores it and holds only to what can be done with chemical drugs when it comes to health.

Our medical science has been capable of great things, and I do not stand here to degrade the progress of the scientific medical community. What medical science has achieved is absolutely amazing. What I sincerely want is to open up our eyes to the wondrous other half of our existence, our etheric energy or, better stated, our Lifeforce. I propose the Elia health principle, "The human body is 50 percent physical body (solid) and 50 percent energetic body (Lifeforce), and it is the intelligent energy of the Lifeforce that directs the physical body, and the physical body supports the energetic Lifeforce body." Our exploration and study into the function and balance of our Lifeforce does not negate medical "solid" research but can only add to and double our healing ability and our health.

This is my purpose in writing this book. I want to introduce and further the recognition of the beauty and functionality of an ancient philosophy of energy that may become more beneficial to your health than the latest pharmaceutical. We will search for the meaning of life and health by looking at the whole picture and the overall function and balance of the body rather than trying to describe life by breaking it down to its smallest particles. It is my sincerest hope that by opening the door to the energetics of *you*, you will see more pathways to improve your health and your life.

PART I

Health

CHAPTER 1

The Two Bodies and the Immortal Chi Crystal

The greatest mystery is our own life. The most fantastic journey is the inner voyage. Seeking the truth about ourselves and discovering who and what we are is our destiny.

Have you ever stopped to think about what you are? Are you your personality or your ethnicity? You are. But what makes you up? It is easy to see the physical body with its trillions of cells, organs, bones, muscles, etc. What else makes you up? Are you a sophisticated bag of chemicals? Oh, wait a minute, a sophisticated bag of chemicals with a brain and a soul. What coordinates the whole system? The physical brain is responsible for some of the coordination of reflex function, chemical balancing, memory, and movement, but can it run all that is you?

I often ask my patients, how does a single cell work? How does it thrive? How does it metabolize? How does it grow? What is the key to when and how it does these things? Most of my patients can hardly muster an intelligent answer to even one of these questions. So I ask them to explain to me one chemical reaction in one of their cells. They seldom have an answer. Let's go a step further. How much serotonin does your individual body require exactly at this moment for perfect function? Do you know? Does anyone know?

If we could get the greatest minds of all time in one room together, could they tell you exactly what your personal serotonin levels should be at this *exact* second? All the scientists of the world cannot answer that one simple question for your individual body. How about the perfect balance of all the neurotransmitters, hormones, enzymes, and other secretions that happen in the body millions of times a day simultaneously? The liver produces over fifty thousand biochemicals and processes over thirteen thousand biochemical reactions in the body. At this precise moment, your liver is doing thousands of biochemical reactions *simultaneously* to the *perfect* micro-milliliter. Do you know the structure of one of those reactions? More significant is the question does anyone know when and exactly how much your personal individual body needs and when it needs more or less? Who is running your seventy trillion cells right now? It's not a cascade phenomenon. It cannot all be explained by feedback loops, and the physical brain's capacity—even considering the percentage of the brain we supposedly "don't use"—cannot handle that much function. Again, what is running your body and where is it?

The answer is your *Lifeforce*. All living things have Lifeforce. When one or more living cells exist, they have Lifeforce energy. Put cells together with organized tissue and organs, the Lifeforce of that being connects and combines to a much more complicated form. Lifeforce is the all-intelligent and all-powerful force that is the underlying presence of all physical life forms. A great illustration of this all-intelligent Lifeforce energy is in a simple flower. We all know the phenomenon of the plant that comes up from the ground, grows around obstacles, and turns its flower, petals, and leaves to face the sun. How does it know what to do? How does it move to turn and face the sun? These flowering plants have no muscular system, no nervous system, no brain, and no muscles to move it. The plant is a living organism and thus has all-intelligent Lifeforce energy. Lifeforce energy will always direct the living form to do whatever it takes to keep that living tissue alive and thriving. Whenever one or more cells of living tissue exist, they exhibit a natural intelligent energy. That intelligent energy is the underlying and the directing force for that single cell or the trillions of cells that make up the human body.

Another example of the directing Lifeforce is the phenomena of the body's gut flora. Over forty thousand strains of different bacteria have been identified as part of a healthy gut flora. That means you have billons or maybe trillions of bacteria in a healthy gut. This bacterium is vital to the absorption of nutrients and the elimination of waste. Without these bacteria working within your body, you would die. Medical science is now seeing the importance of this bacteria and even its vital role in your immune system.

Now what happens to a body that dies and is left for a few hours in the sun? That's right, that dead body would soon start to swell and stink as the trillions of bacteria in the gut would start eating away the body tissue, destroying the body and causing it to stink. Remember a few hours ago while that body was alive, that same bacteria were functioning in total harmony with the body. Remove the all-intelligent Lifeforce and that bacterium goes wild. Without the Lifeforce directing and controlling it, the bacteria in your gut flora attacks and destroys the same tissue it was benefiting just a few hours before.

Aha! It is DNA you say. DNA is the thing that runs our body. I'm sorry to disappoint you. DNA is only a template for reproduction. A few seconds after you die, all your DNA is intact. In fact, we can extract DNA from dead tissue thousands of years old. DNA has an important place in the human story, but it is not the underlying intelligence that directs life to do the perfect action for that living creature.

Where is all the research on Lifeforce? If it is the underlying intelligence behind all life and it runs the body's functions, why don't we know more about it? We have lifetimes of information and research on the physical body, its chemicals and organs. We have libraries full of physiology and psychology. There is nothing in modern science about why and when a neurotransmitter is created and used. Who decides how much of a substance needs to be created and when is the perfect moment? What if any has Western science researched about the energy that is really you? You are not your organs or your brain or the billions of facts that you have acquired (only to forget).

You are the Lifeforce energy that is inside and around your physical body. It holds your emotions, higher thoughts, and spiritual essence. It has a vast network of communication not only within the physical body but also within the etheric field that is inside and all around your body. Your consciousness, or "soul" if you want, is also found in and around your physical body. One thing is certain: when your physical body dies, it will stay here. With no intelligent Lifeforce to direct it and give it the power to live, your physical body will be buried and will decay.

Einstein taught us that energy never disappears; it just changes form. Your Lifeforce, consciousness, or soul or whatever you would like to call your energetic spiritual "*you*" separates from the physical body and goes on its new journey. When I was about six or 7 years old, my namesake grandfather, Harry Tavernia, died. I always remember looking at the waxen figure in the casket and knowing something was not there. The body looked familiar, but what was missing was the *Lifeforce energy* that was my grandfather. The person, who was hard and stern at times yet could break into laughter that would fill a room, was not there. The shell or vehicle of my grandfather's physical body was there, but who he really was was gone. I don't have any idea where we go when we die, but I know for sure that we do not stay here attached to a physical body.

Lifeforce energy with its universal intelligence and consciousness is the *real you*. If the Lifeforce energy is the real you and the directing energy behind your body's function, what do we know about it? We know it has a superintelligence because it is the underlying force of our survival. We also know that this intelligence is far more complex and complete than our physical brain can conceive. We know that when it is weak or disturbed, we get sick. We also know that if it gets too weak or disturbed, it will separate from the physical body, and the physical body will die.

Thousands of years ago, a group of Chinese shamans, philosophers, and thinkers started wondering and experimenting with this mystical force that is the underlying directive force behind physical life. These early Chinese shamans and philosophers are generally called Taoists. Taoist shamanistic mysticism can be traced back in China over five thousand years.

The Taoists observed the perfection and balance of nature and sought to see the connections between man and nature. They called this fantastic unseen force the great Tao.

> The Tao is like an empty bowl,
> Which in being used can never be filled up.
> Fathomless, it seems to be the origin of all things.
> It blunts all sharp ends.
> It unties all tangles.
> It harmonizes all lights.
> It unites the world into one whole.
> Hidden in the deeps,
> Yet it seems to exist forever.
> I do not know whose child it is;
> It seems to be the common ancestor of all, the father of things.
> —*Tao Teh Ching*, number 4, Lao Tse

The first written works of Taoism date back some five thousand years ago, during the reign of the Yellow Emperor. These texts had to do with experimentation of the most powerful of physical energies, sexual energy. The *Pillow Books* were conversations between the Yellow Emperor and his three female sexual advisors. Unencumbered by rigid religions or ideologies, the early Taoists saw the sexual energy as a microcosm of the Yin and Yan balance of the earth and the heavens. They practiced methods to develop, store, and use these powerful sexual forces for health and spiritual development.

A few hundred years before the great Western philosophers Plato, Aristotle, and Socrates on the other side of the world, there was another group of Chinese philosophers. Among these were Confucius, Lao Tse, and Mo Tse. The Taoists call Lao Tse the "father of Taoism" because of his popular *Tao Teh Ching* writings. Most scholars agree that the philosophy in this two-thousand-five-hundred-year-old book is based on many older shamanistic sources. The sciences of acupuncture, herbology, martial arts, meditation, and even Chinese Traditional Medicine all had their basis and roots in Taoism.

> Thirty spokes converge upon a single hub;
> It is on the hole in the center that the use of the cart hinges.
> We make a vessel from a lump of clay;
> It is the empty space within the vessel that makes it useful.
> We make doors and windows for a room;
> But it is these empty spaces that make the room livable.
> Thus, while the tangible has advantages,
> It is the intangible that makes it useful.
> —*Tao Teh Ching*, number 11 (John C. H. Wu, translator)

> Those who see what is to be seen are wise men.
> Those who see what is not able to be seen are companions of the universe.
> —Hua-Ching Ni, *Attaining Unlimited Life: Teachings of Chuang Tzu*

Taoists were far ahead of Western science because they concerned themselves with the concept that *what is unseen is far more important than what can be seen.*

> Taoist thought is permeated with the notion that Man and Heaven are a unified whole; that the entire universe is contained within Man, that they are in essence one and the same.
>
> —Stuart Alve Olson, *The Jade Emperor's Mind Seal Classic: The Taoist Guide to Health, Longevity, and Immortality*

The shamanistic Taoists view mankind as a microcosm of the greater macrocosm of the universe. They see mankind as connected to all of nature around them. Not a separate entity but a part of a great whole. We are infused with the same Lifeforce energy that moves the earth, brings the season changes, and is embodied by the inner intelligence of all living things. This power of the Lifeforce is unseen and cannot be put in a test tube or chemical laboratory. Try to put Love in a chemical lab. Of course, we can say that when Love is present, certain areas of the brain are stimulated and certain neurotransmitters are produced, but it is the *Love energy that creates* the neurotransmitters, not the neurotransmitters that create Love. The "unseen" emotion creates the physical chemical properties, not the other way around. You can artificially put into the brain, chemicals that can change emotions, but like my early school experiments of electronically stimulating a frog leg to make it move, that is just recreating artificially what the *live* frog did naturally. The unseen and immeasurable Lifeforce is the *directing* force of the chemistry and function. Lifeforce energy *is you*. The facts you have gathered up are parts of your brain and will cease to exist when your brain dies along with your physical body. Your insight, "personal Chi," and higher awareness are part of your Lifeforce Chi body. They are part of your Spirit energy, and they will continue in some way after your death.

In our modern society, we often prescribed drugs for what we say is a chemical imbalance causing a mental problem. The real cause is the physical and emotional imbalances that the patient has experienced and has had over time in their life. Put that together with the thousands of harmful chemicals that we come in contact with every day in our environment and that "mental instability caused by a chemical imbalance" is a person out of balance for so long that their brain chemistry has changed, causing the irrational behaviors. There are of course circumstances that mind-altering drugs are helpful, but that is because the person has been so severely out of balance for so long, creating a crisis situation. Much like an alcoholic after thirty years of drinking has destroyed his liver tissue so much that he may need drugs to help his liver and kidney continue to function. What about kids? Our modern society is so full of chemical toxic stress, drugs, radiation, vaccinations, and emotional imbalance, even DNA-altering fetal chemical stress, along with constant connection to electronic devices (cell phones, microwave transmission, video games, TV, computers, etc.) that it is not hard to see how our children's brain chemistry can be in a state of imbalance, even in a short time. In Traditional Chinese Medicine, there are no problems attributed solely to mental illness, just problems of energetic and physical imbalances that need attention.

Taoist thought is unique, but many shamanistic practices from other parts of the world also echo the connection between man and his environment and the unseen "spirits" or energies that make up our existence. Taoism is a vast historical, scientific, and philosophical volume of knowledge that is far more than we can cover in this one small book. The concepts of Taoism however are vital and important in our exploration of health and the human body. The following are my interpretations of some of the foundation principles that are important to our journey toward better health and happiness.

I. Spiritual growth requires a healthy body, serene mind, and longevity.

> The Shen (spirit) depends on life form;
> The Ching (physical body) depends on sufficient Chi (Lifeforce).
> If these are neither depleted nor injured, the result will be youthfulness and longevity.
> —Stuart Alve Olson, *The Jade Emperor's Mind Seal Classic: The*
> *Taoist Guide to Health, Longevity, and Immortality*

The Taoists saw a man as a sacred trilogy of essence (physical body), energy (Lifeforce Chi body), and Spirit(*shen*). A good example of this is a flower. The deep roots represent the physical body or essence. The roots must be strong and pull the matrix of earth and Water into the plant. The stem of the plant represents Lifeforce or Chi, which distributes the raw physical energy upward. Finally, we have the culmination of essence (physical body) and energy (Lifeforce Chi body), the flower (spirit). The flower cannot be vibrant and healthy unless the roots are deep and solid, the stem strong and unbroken; then the physical energy can be transformed into Spirit energy. This is why the ancient Taoist ways are so important for our health journey. They have been experimenting in the human laboratory for thousands of years, not only finding external elixirs, herbs, supplements, and food to enhance the body but also experimenting with internal methods such as breathing practices, meditation, and movements of the body to enhance the Lifeforce.

The Physical Body

Matrix
This fragile body
Is matrix
For mind and soul.

> We cannot afford to neglect our Physical Bodies, even if we recognize that we must not identify with them exclusively. Actually, in our search for our true selves, our physical existence is the best place to start. We can alter our lives by how we eat and exercise, and we can expedite our search by keeping ourselves healthy. If we are free of physical blockages and pain, we can identify our inner selves much better.
> In the search for the mind and soul, it is wise to understand that the body is not the true self, but it is also wise to maintain the body. They should be neither denial nor mortification of the flesh, but it takes a wise person to both maintain the body and look beyond it.
> —Deng Ming-Dao, *365 Tao: Daily Meditations*, number 238

Taoism is one of the few philosophies to emphasize the importance of physical health to spiritual development. Most of the Eastern martial arts have come into being because the Taoist philosophy had a physical connection to spiritual development. Taoism started with the physical body. They thought to refine and train the physical body and use the physical energy for spiritual growth. Most Western religious practices demonize the physical body and sex. Taoists see the physical body and sexual activity as a part of the Yin-Yan balance of the whole. Therefore, the physical body and sexual activity is not negative or to be ignored nor is it to be abused and used for negative purposes. It is to be trained, controlled, enjoyed in moderation, and used for the positive. Physical and sexual energy can be important energy for spiritual development. There are even some specific Taoist sexual practices for the increasing of physical and spiritual energy. It is always important however that the *hun* spirits of man (spiritual nature) directs the *po* spirits of man (physical nature). This arrangement benefits the whole and allows for spiritual growth. Excess in anything is seen as destructive in Taoist philosophy.

> To destroy something, lead it to its extreme.
> To preserve something, keep to the middle.
> —Deng Ming-Dao, *365 Tao: Daily Meditations*

Moderation and balance are the keys to health and spiritual growth. This is the wisdom of the middle ground.

Serene Mind

> When the mind is poised and well concentrated, the supreme Self of man becomes visible. At other times we do not see the real man and the apparent man thinks himself all in all. The Seer or higher Self is there, but we are not conscious of it. When, however, the mind becomes clarified, the Self appears in Its true state and we do not have to make any effort to perceive It.
> —Swami Paramananda, *Concentration and Meditation*

> If you correct your mind, the rest of your life will fall into place.
> This is true because the mind is the governing aspect of human life.
> If the river flows clearly and cleanly through the proper channel, all will be well along its banks.
> —Brian Walker, *Hua Hu Ching: The Unknown Teachings of Lao Tzu*, number 45

Meditation and stillness are important parts to the whole of spiritual development. I've often said to my patients "a little bit of stillness balances out a great deal of chaos and stress." Our minds are *on* all the time. Our modern technical lives require us to be constantly figuring out and solving problems. We also spend a lot of a useless mind time on idle thoughts, fantasies, and trivia about the latest pop star. Bringing stillness and calmness to our minds reduces the stress and constant activity that is so prevalent in our modern lives. It is said, "If the lake is calm, the dirt will settle to the bottom, and the Water will be crystal clear." We need to spend some time *being*, not *doing*. One of the goals of the practices in this book is to help with that clarity. Meditation is the shutting down of the physical thinking brain and connecting to the spiritual intuitive Lifeforce. Chi-Gung and Tai Chi are active forms of meditation and will help calm the mind and balance your energy.

Longevity

> The sages awakened through self-cultivation;
> Deep, profound,
> Their practices require great effort.
> —Stuart Alve Olson, *The Jade Emperor's Mind Seal Classic: The Taoist Guide to Health, Longevity, and Immortality*

Spirituality to the Taoists is like walking ten thousand stone steps up a steep mountain trail to the monastery at the top. It is a long arduous journey, and there are many obstacles in our lives to spiritual growth.

Life offers many challenges. The challenge of making a living, having food, shelter, and security are difficult and time-consuming. The stresses of family life, such as being good family members, and the challenges of raising children can also be taxing. So the time for spiritual growth is limited by life's necessities. Experience is also a necessary ingredient for spiritual growth. So you can see the importance of being healthy and living a long life. It would give you adequate time to achieve the spiritual development necessary. Just getting old was not the goal. Being youthful in your old age was vital. The physical practices of Taoism are essential to spiritual development. Their exercises were for the purpose of moving and balancing the vital Chi (Lifeforce) to improve health and for the adept to raise spiritual potential. In later sections of this book, we will draw from their knowledge with breathing exercises, meditation, movement, and stillness practices to replenish, store, move, and balance the physical body and the Lifeforce Chi body.

II. The concept of Tao.

> It lies in the nature of Grand Virtue
> To follow the Tao and the Tao alone.
> Now what is the Tao?
> It is Something elusive and evasive.
> Evasive and elusive.
> And yet It contains within Itself a Substance.
> Shadowy and dim.
> And yet It contained within Itself a Core of Vitality.
> The Core of the Vitality is very real,
> It contains within Itself an unfailing Sincerity.
> Throughout the ages Its Name has been preserved
> In order to recall the Beginning of all things.
> How do I know the ways of all things at the Beginning?
> By what is within me.
> —*Tao Teh Ching*, number 21, Lao Tse, (John C. H. Wu, translator)

The Tao is the universal, all-intelligent, and all-powerful force behind the universe and all living beings. This force is unseen and cannot be grasped totally by the human brain.

> The Tao that can be described is not the real Tao.
> If you try to hold it, you cannot find it.
> —Lao Tse, *Tao Teh Ching*, number 1

To the Taoist, this intelligent underlying force is something that you must align yourself with to survive. The best example of this is nature. Nature has a will of its own. If we attempt to control nature for our own selfish needs, there are always dire consequences. If we try to control nature with science, there is always that "Oops" moment when a mistake is made and chaos occurs. One can only look at the beginnings of nuclear power, X-ray, even offshore drilling to see a few of the oops. Only when we align ourselves with the Tao can we have peace, harmony, and health. This is why Chang Tse, an ancient Taoist, said that "the unnatural must not be brought into the natural."

Although this force of Tao is unseen and mysterious, we can align ourselves with it by following the example of nature. Seeing natural balance in all things and balancing our own lives. Paddling with the current is far more effective than fighting upstream. With meditation and Taoist exercise practices, we can begin to connect to this all-powerful and all-intelligent force that is part of us.

The same intelligence that is behind the growth of plants, the changing of the seasons, in fact the beauty and intelligence of the entire natural ecosystem and the universe, is an example of Tao. That same all intelligence resides in and around each one of us and is not only a part of you; it is the *"Real You."* Instead of trying to have absolute control over our lives and environment, we need to follow the path of our lives, changing what we can and working in harmony with what it is.

A good example is frustration. Frustration in our lives is basically events that happened that are different than we expected or pictured them in our physical brain. Your physical brain is a limited organ; it is not the universal brain. Whatever the universe does is reality and must be accepted as such. What we decided we wanted to have happen down to the smallest detail is often different than what the universe has planned. Being open to the myriad avenues available to you, not just the small picture your physical brain has formulated, is a start to being in the flow of Tao.

III. What is outside is also inside.

> Unseeable, unrecognizable, the Tao is beyond any
> attempt to analyze it.
> At the same time, its truth is everywhere you turn.
> If you can let go of it with your mind and surround it
> With your heart, it will live inside you forever.
> —*Hua Hu Ching: The Unknown Teachings of Lao Tzu*, number 33

Man is not separate from nature or the universe. We are all connected to our earthly environment. No matter how much we try to separate from nature, we cannot. This is one of the most important statements for our later discussion on 7 Element Lifeforce Healing. Using the ancient Taoist concepts of earth, man, and heaven, we will be able to see the balance of energy and function that is the 7 Element Lifeforce Health concepts.

These basic concepts led the Taoists on a five-thousand-year research journey on internal and external elixirs that would support and strengthen the unseen Lifeforce in the human body. It helped create the concept of Chi, the Lifeforce of the human being. These early explorers also focused on breath as a means to move and circulate this vital energy. They understood that our Lifeforce energy cannot be stagnant; it must circulate to be healthy and vibrant. They developed and practiced daily regimes of meditation, breathing, and exercises to move and vitalize this precious Lifeforce energy. Thousands of years ago, they were far ahead of our modern science in focusing on this Lifeforce energy as a key not only to health but also for the adept, a pathway to spiritual development.

The Taoists were able to do so much more because they started out with knowing that what is unseen is more important than what can be seen or measured with our normal senses. This invisible and all intelligence is the directing force behind all physical life. All healing is directly related to this *innate intelligence*. A simple cut is a prime example of the innate healing power. A knife crosses the knuckle of your finger. You wash it out and sanitize the cut. You put a Band-Aid on the area that helps slow the bleeding. Your innate intelligent Lifeforce goes immediately to work. It "knows" where clotting must occur, and it starts immediately to lay down tissues to start the healing. Muscles in the area have already begun to contract to help close the wound. Then it begins its magic of regrowing the perfect tissue for the area. With the old dead tissue cleaned out and within a week, depending on the severity of the cut, the area is completely healed. Cut into a dead body and there is obviously no healing. It is not just a cascade chain reaction; it is Lifeforce intelligence at work. The "scientist" in you will still cling to the chemical reactions and the unconscious brain to explain this mystery; but it is the why, when, and how much in perfection that is the innate intelligence. Lifeforce does the *perfect* action for each circumstance.

> The natural healing force within each one of us is the greatest force in getting well.
> —Hippocrates

The chemical reaction to a cut and brain reflexes are like your house alarm. Yes, the pain causes a chemical signal of inflammation when you are cut. This is the alarm. The person in that house is the one who thinks about the cause of the alarm. If it is an intruder, you arm yourself with a sword (I don't like guns) and proceed to the site of the alarm. Then finding out what set the alarm off, you act appropriately. As the person in the house, you represent the Lifeforce. If there were no you (Lifeforce) in the house, the burglar wouldn't care about the alarm. Consequently, using our example of a cut, the chemical signals of inflammation would be totally ignored, just like cutting a dead body. Because without you, the Lifeforce, there would be no perfect action.

There is no doctor on the face of the earth, no matter how intelligent, that can accomplish that simple feat of healing a cut. Medical doctors can do fantastic things—repair lost limbs, do skin grafts and transplants—but not one of them has the "all-knowing" and healing ability of your own body. You will need the assistance of a skilled doctor in an extreme accident, trauma, or health crisis. Even with their help however if your Lifeforce intelligence is not functioning, you will not heal. Many people with pneumonia die in spite of the antibiotics and the tireless work of great doctors. If your Lifeforce is too weak or confused, you will not heal. *In essence, you heal yourself.*

There have been rare instances of patients who have been given only a few weeks to live. The patient then makes some peace with their past, family, and their life. They draw family together to express their Love and regrets, and they get ready to leave this world in peace. In some rare instances, this balanced, forgiving, and peaceful state allows the patient's Lifeforce to come alive and become powerful. Grapefruit-sized tumors disappear. Medical tests are completely reversed, and the person comes back from the brink of death and back to health. Doctors are baffled and call it "spontaneous healing." The word "miracle" is thrown around. Now I'm not saying this will happen to everyone, and I admit that these are *extremely rare* circumstances. But they do happen, and even if it only happened once in history, it still proves the power of the same Lifeforce that is your birthright.

If health is your concern, then you must not ignore its most important component: Lifeforce. The physical body is only half of the health mystery. The Lifeforce body or, as the ancient Taoist called it, "Chi" is the other half. Since Lifeforce is the underlying intelligence behind physical function and healing, it is the *more important half* of you. Just think how much better your health quest can be if you double your efforts by doing health practices that balance your Lifeforce. The focus of this book is to acquaint you with the force of Chi and give you some tools to circulate and strengthen your vital energy. Concentrating on this vital energy is a pathway to improving your health and vitality. Lifeforce or Chi must be strong, must circulate, and must be organized (unconfused). Focusing on strengthening, organizing, and circulating this vital Lifeforce is a way *to heal from the inside out.*

IV. Individual growth and physical, mental, and spiritual development is the only hope for mankind.

The Taoists saw little chance that mass religious movements would change the world for the better. They realized that as an organization gets bigger and more powerful, it sometimes loses its roots and its way.

You can go to church every week and feel uplifted, but if you do not bring that spirituality into your everyday life, then your development will be stifled and limited. Our goal should not be to have a separate spirituality once a week but should be to make all our actions be of a spiritual nature.

Also, we do not have control over others, and when we try to force our way of thinking on to others, we usually fail miserably. You do not have the power to change others. The only power we have in changing the world is to change ourselves. This concept is directly from Lao Tse two thousand five hundred years ago. "The only hope for mankind is for each individual to work on his or her own spiritual development." In fact, our only hope in the betterment of mankind and ourselves is for each of us to constantly work on our physical, mental, emotional, and spiritual evolution. As my first Taoist teacher and dear friend Ron Diana said, "You are instrumental to the evolution of the whole universe." I hope the thoughts and practices in this book will give you some guidance in your personal evolution.

Lifeforce Anatomy: The 7 Element Lifeforce Crystal

What is the 7 Element Lifeforce Crystal?

The 7 Element Crystal is the spiritual geometric representation of the Lifeforce Chi body. It is the "formless form" that holds our consciousness and is the underlying all-intelligent force that directs the physical tissue. It includes a spiritual brain that is the counterpart of our physical brain. It is the geometric, energetic information that is passed through the crown, down the falx cerebri, and recorded by the hypothalamus and pineal gland. The hypothalamus and pineal gland then translates this complex spiritual, energetic, sound, light signal to the physical body.

To understand the Lifeforce Chi body, you must be able to "see" that you are more than your physical body. Remember, a cadaver has every piece of DNA and tissue that a live person does. It has brains, blood, organs, and all the cells. What it is missing is the Lifeforce Chi body. We know that as a person dies, his physical body ceases to have Lifeforce. The innate intelligence that once ran the body is gone. Think of this example, if you are driving your car and you get to your destination, you would stop the car and get out. If the car represents the physical body, then you the driver represent the Lifeforce Chi body. You can see that the driving or directing intelligent force is not the car; it is you the driver. As soon as the driver (Lifeforce) gets out, the car lies dormant or dead. When you die, there is a separation between the physical body (the car) and the Lifeforce Chi body (the driver). Kirlian photography has proved that the surrounding energy of a person, which can be photographed, disappears when that person dies. This energy is the *real you*. It animates, directs your body, and stores your consciousness. It is the 7 Element Crystal structure that infuses the physical body with intelligent Lifeforce energy.

The Lifeforce Chi body is similar to sound. There are sounds that the ear can hear and sounds that the ear cannot hear. The frequency of sound is what allows us to hear certain sounds and not others. It doesn't mean that the sounds that we cannot hear do not exist. It just means we can't hear those frequencies. The human body is of a denser frequency, so we can see it and touch it. The Chi body is of a higher frequency, so just as with sounds that we cannot hear it exists; we just can't see it or touch it.

I have a great example of the two bodies and the importance of the Lifeforce Chi body to your health. For our example, let's agree that global warming is caused by earth's carbon pollution, which then causes the "greenhouse effect." Much of our scientific research bears this out, but let us just accept this model totally for my explanation. If we discovered that the earth was warming and we wanted to find the cause but were limited to just doing research *on* and *inside the earth, no research in the atmosphere at all*. For our example, let's assume that we have no concept of the atmosphere, only what we could touch, feel, and experiment with here on earth. If this were true, we would find the results of global warming: the earth drying up, higher temperatures, glaciers melting, etc. We could even do some damage control by irrigating crops and turning seawater into fresh water, but we would still not know the cause of global warming unless we did *research in the atmosphere*. In this example, the earth represents the physical body and the atmosphere the Lifeforce Chi body. All our medical research confines itself to the internal physical body. Over 80 percent of all our diseases are listed as idiopathic, meaning *we don't know the cause*. We can see the results and try to help the organs concerned, but we can't tell a person *why* they got their disease and *what caused it*. Looking for the cause of allergy, autoimmune disease, or many more of our modern diseases by researching just the physical body is the same as looking for global warming by researching just *in* the earth. Man is more than just his physical being and physical makeup, but our Western science is not "comfortable" doing anything that cannot be put in a test tube and fixing anything with something other than a chemical drug.

A good example of this is a recent patient that we helped in our office. The background is as follows: a healthy ten-year-old male suddenly collapsed into spasm and passed out in the middle of a school day. He was rushed to the hospital on oxygen, and doctors began running a multitude of tests to see what caused this seemingly healthy child to pass out in spasm and be dangerously close to dying. All they could find was an extreme drop in the boy's calcium levels. They immediately started him on intravenous calcium, and after a few days in the hospital, he was released with his calcium levels being close to normal. In the ensuing months, his parents brought him to a series of specialists to solve this problem. The only thing the specialists could tell them was that they thought he had some sort of autoimmune problem causing his parathyroid (the calcium transport gland) not to be functioning. But they could not come up with an adequate diagnosis as none of the tests matched up to any known diseases. He was prescribed large doses of Tums as the medical doctor said that Tums "was the most absorbable form of calcium."

The patient presented in my office eleven months later after his incident, after multiple medical doctor visits and his Tums prescription were not working. Over the course of eleven months since the incident, his calcium absorption levels continued to plummet to dangerous low levels. In my first visit, I found three energetic glitches in the Lifeforce Chi body, caused by use or exposure to refined sugar, vaccinations, and electromagnetic radiation (see glitches in chapter 2) that were short-circuiting parathyroid function. I energetically cleared the three glitches of the parathyroid and had the patient remove all refined sugar from his diet. I also put the patient on whole food supplementation with two products: Cal-Mag (calcium and parathyroid desiccate) and Cataplex F (omega 3s and a small amount of iodine), both Standard Process Company products. The patient was tested one month after his first visit in our office, and his calcium absorption numbers had improved from a dangerous low of before our first visit of 7.3 to normal levels. Following our treatment and checkups in my office once every two months, it has been almost two years, and every subsequent blood test has revealed normal calcium levels. If the medical doctors that treated this patient saw me energetically remove glitches of the parathyroid using Applied Kinesiology, Total Body Modification, and 7 Element Lifeforce Healing methods, they would have thought I was from Mars, but a healthy young patient is the reply to that.

For thousands of years, Taoists Chi-Gung Healers, Acupuncturists, Traditional Chinese Medicine Practitioners, and countless Shamanic Healers have been researching and treating the Lifeforce Chi Body. Modern Alternative Chiropractors, Applied Kinesiologists, and other energetic healers have provided new inroads into the solving of many disease problems of their patients. Even this author's ability to *eliminate* allergies, not by avoiding the allergen or using drugs to block the reaction but by alleviating confusion and short circuits in the Lifeforce (see chapter 6), can be repeated over and over again but would still draw ire and scorn from the pharmaceutical-backed medical scientific community. It is inevitable that we combine our healing, joining Eastern and Western systems together, just like the two parts of our being, the physical body and energetic Lifeforce Chi body. It is a chance to increase our ability to solve disease problems by stretching our horizons and doubling our healing potential. Just as the physical body and the Lifeforce Chi body does, we have to work together.

Try to predict the weather without looking at the atmosphere, but only looking *in* the earth. Many things in the earth influence the atmosphere, the rising mountains, the sea currents and temperatures, the topography etc. They do work together, but it is by looking in the atmosphere that the weather can be predicted. What happens to and what you do to your physical body will have a great deal of influence on your Lifeforce Chi body, but is the Lifeforce Chi body that directs your physical body, much as the atmosphere directs the weather.

The future of healing lies in our investigation into the power of the human Lifeforce. There is a master in Java that can set paper on Fire by pointing to it, hold a Ping-Pong ball suspended in air between his palms without touching it, and easily move objects without being close to them. He has demonstrated these and other "skills" in an open setting created and observed by scientists and engineers, with all possible "tricks" ruled out. He is a master Mo Tzu Taoist who has spent most of his life in the ancient internal study of the human energy field. Because of his lifetime of study and discipline, he has also been able to perform countless miraculous healings. If you want to know more, pick up a book called *The Magus of Java*.

He is not the only one. There is a simple farmer from South America called "John of God" who, without any medical training, performs what experts call "miracles of healing." These two examples are only a few of the many in history that have achieved the level of healing power beyond medical science's ability to even explain them. This is an example of the potential of the Lifeforce power that is an inherent part of *you*. Working internally and externally, you can heal, focus, and strengthen *your Lifeforce*.

7 Element Lifeforce Crystal Anatomy

To understand and use the principles of the 7 Elements Lifeforce Crystal for our health, we must first look at the energetic Lifeforce Chi body anatomy. A human being is made up of half physical body and half Lifeforce body.

illustration 1

The Chi body is made up of layers of energy in a geometric form. Each layer is slightly different so that when viewed as one, they are a three-dimensional crystal.

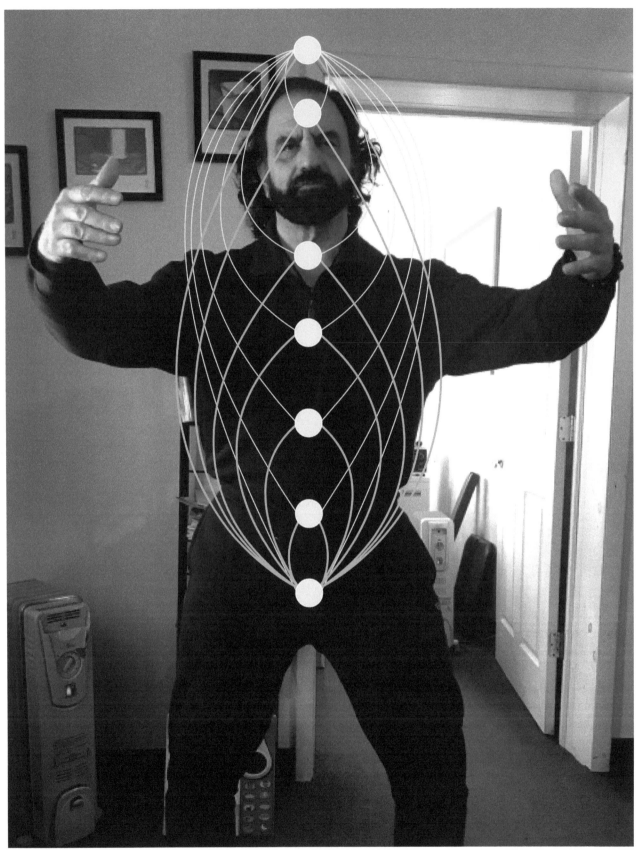

illustration 2

In this Crystal, hundreds of triangles are formed. As in all crystals, if the form of the Crystal is *distorted* in any way, the tiny triangular faucets of the Crystal will be uneven and compromised. When inspecting a diamond, the jeweler looks for a tiny flaw inside the diamond. If the geometric cuts were imperfect, then the light refraction of the diamond will be flawed. This is one of the ways diamonds are graded. If the geometry of the cut is perfect, then there will be no small "smudges" of darkness inside any of the many internal triangles. The diamond will then reflect the full beauty of the light. The light that passes through the diamond will be reflected and enhanced so that the diamond will sparkle and give off a characteristic color.

Our Chi body or 7 Element Lifeforce Crystal is no different. It is a three-dimensional energy form. When balanced and illuminated by the subtle and all-powerful universal (or God) energy, its illumination is like a perfect diamond. With each breath, we "pull" universal or God energy through the geometry of our Chi body matrix and into our physical body. If the Chi body Crystal is balanced and even, the light refracted into the physical body will be one of pure harmonious energy. If the Chi body has imperfections or any imbalance, the physical body receives imperfect and cloudy messages. The imperfections of the Chi body form caused by the hate, anger, stubbornness, and pain distort the matrix. This will cause small dark shadows in the faucets of our diamond. It also creates imperfect function in the physical body. Every exhale will also pass back through the field of either perfect form or distorted form, then reflect that light out to the universe. This will in turn send Love or angst out to the universe.

Illustrations 3, 4, 5, and 6

The most important concept of this relationship between the physical body, the Lifeforce Chi body, and the universal or God energy is that the Lifeforce Chi body's geometry can be changed. We can change it *from the inside out*. Putting real, undistorted life-giving food into the physical body can make positive changes to the Lifeforce Chi body geometry. Having balanced emotions and manifesting Love from the inside out can balance and positively change your Lifeforce Chi body's geometry. With your next breath, your physical body will reap the benefits of that change in balanced and positive energy. This concept of balancing the Lifeforce Crystal is why I believe the healing work that I have done in eliminating allergies and helping patients with autoimmune diseases actually works. With each breath, we can change the human body. If we refine the physical tissue and limit the chemical toxicity but also balance and circulate the Lifeforce, each breath will bring more harmony to the physical body. Conversely, if we fill the physical body with toxicity and allow destructive and unbalanced emotions and thoughts, it will affect the crystalline structure of the Lifeforce Chi body. With each new breath that comes through our Lifeforce Chi body, we can be healthier or sicker. The theme of this book is to help you restore balance and harmonize the Lifeforce Chi body to create a healthier physical body and hopefully a more evolved and harmonic universe.

The Lifeforce Chi body directs the physical body, and the state of the physical body is also reflected and supports the Lifeforce Chi body. So poisons ingested into the physical body can create breaks in the energetic geometry of the Lifeforce Chi body. This is easily seen on the cellular level. All living cells have Lifeforce Chi energy.

Illustration 7

Put cells together into a group, and that group creates its own Chi field.

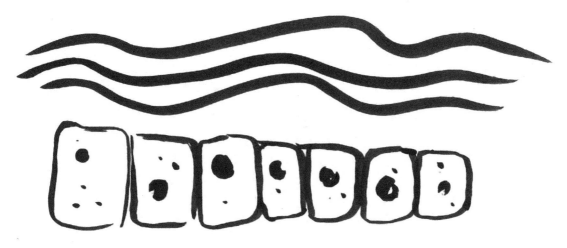

Illustration 8

Complex tissues and organs have complex electromagnetic or Chi fields of their own. Put them together in a complex organization of tissue and organs and you have the human Chi body or the 7 Element Crystal. Let's go back and take a look at the group of cells in illustration 8. If one of those cells becomes toxic, by let's say the hundred different caustic chemicals we breathe in on average with every breath* or a pesticide preservative or any of the thousands of chemicals we come in contact with every day, the result will be a short circuit or breaks in the electromagnetic field that these cells have.

Illustration 9

Every cell's health and vitality contributes to the vitality and health of the Chi field. On a larger level, putting emotional or toxic pressure on an organ will weaken the overall Chi body. That gap or distortion in the Chi field will weaken a tissue, organ, or a system's ability to fight off viruses and bacteria. The best example of this is shingles. Shingles is the herpes zoster virus or chicken pox. Once you have chicken pox, the herpes zoster virus lies dormant in the dorsal nerve roots of the spine. It can stay dormant for the rest of your life and never cause a problem. The combined energy of your Lifeforce Chi body keeps it that way. However, if your Chi body is weakened by stress, shingles will then break out in the skin of that particular dorsal nerve root. Medical doctors all agree that the only scientific link to the outbreak of shingles is high emotional or physical stress. The reason is that the Chi body's energy geometry is weakened, allowing the otherwise latent virus to destroy tissue. We all know that the bacterium in a body goes berserk after death, causing bloating and a foul smell. That exact bacterium was in the body before death. While alive, it is the Lifeforce that kept the bacteria under control and doing positive things for the body. When the Chi body separates from the physical body, which is death, there is no directing or restraining force; this allows that bacteria to go berserk eating up the body's tissue, causing the bloating and smell of a dead body.

There was a very recent one-hundred-seventy-three-million-dollar research study funded by the National Institute of Health and included two hundred eighty top scientists from eighty research institutions around the world. The final result of this enormous scientific study was that *healthy human beings coexist with at least ten thousand different species of dangerous and pathogenic microbes* (bacteria, fungus, virus, etc.). The study goes on to say, and I quote, "It turns out that nearly everybody harbors low levels of bacteria and pathogens that are known for causing specific infections. But when a person is healthy, those bugs quietly coexist with benign or helpful microbes, perhaps kept in check by them." Or perhaps kept in check by a balanced and fully functioning Lifeforce.

Back and Forth

We speak in this chapter about the two bodies. We have to remember that when you are alive and living, there is no separation of the two. They function in complete synchronicity. If the two were to separate, you would be dead. The good way to imagine these two parts in harmony is to imagine a lake of Water and the air around it. If we could make that lake and the air above it a closed system, we could observe an interesting phenomenon. The Water in the lake would continually evaporate into the air above, and the air above would condense back to the Water. The two forms would continue to change density back and forth. The lake of Water represents the physical body and the Air, the energetic or Lifeforce body. The lake, being a more solid form (physical body), can be touched and felt. The air is more of an etheric form (Lifeforce Chi body), harder to touch and quantify. When a person is in a spiritual and emotional growth period of their lives, it is like putting heat under the Water. There will be more evaporation. The energy (steam) will rise, and air will become full and denser. This is like having more spiritual energy and insight. Conversely, if a person focuses strictly on the physical and shuts himself off from any spiritual development, it would be like putting a plastic cap right on the Water and not allowing any Water to evaporate. The more "evaporation" or energetic spiritual development during your lifetime, the more balanced your Lifeforce and the more you equip the spiritual body for its next journey.

It is possible through common sense, health, nutrition, balanced lifestyle, combined with ancient practice, wisdom, and active physical practice to increase, circulate, and balance your Lifeforce. Connecting mind, breathing, body positions, and movement, you can change the very Lifeforce geometry of your Chi body. You have the power to help the all-intelligent force that directs and runs your physical tissue. The ancient Taoists have a great saying:

> It is said that he who knows well how to live
> meets no tigers or wild buffalos on his road,
> and comes out from the battleground untouched by the weapons of war.
> For in him, a buffalo would find no butt for his horns,
> a tiger nothing to lay his claws upon, and a weapon of war no place to
> to admit it's point.
> How is this?
> Because there is no room for Death in him.
>
> —*Tao Teh Ching*, number 50

Filling yourself with Love and life creates a powerful balanced and circulating Lifeforce, which leaves no room for sickness or disease.

The Nature of the Chi Lifeforce

Chi is an elemental and powerful force. Its existence cannot be denied, but its nature is elusive and extremely difficult to quantify. The Chi Lifeforce is in every cell. Just as the cells make up tissues and organs, the elemental Chi Lifeforce of the cells combines to make up an organized intelligent energy, which is the perfect directing force for that living organic organism. Chi must be in constant motion, but it must also be in balance to function properly. How is this possible: movement and balance at the same time? We can use the example of the balance board (a board place over a hard round cylinder). To maintain equilibrium on a balance board, we must slightly shift the weight back and forth over the center. The constant movement of back and forth (Yin and Yan) creates an energetic power. If there is too much movement to one side or the other, you will fall off the board. This slight back-and-forth movement in an equal and balanced way creates a dynamic vibrational energy. So the first characteristic of the Chi Lifeforce is that it must move or oscillate but be in balance.

Illustration 10

The second principle of Chi Lifeforce is that it must circulate. Circulation of the Chi allows for Chi's refinement and increased power that is apparent in the serious practitioners of the Taoist arts and the martial arts. The health of the physical body depends on the circulation of Chi to every area of the body, but it also must maintain balance, meaning no area must slow down or block the circulation of Chi. For a simple example, if you cannot release or control your anger, Lifeforce Chi will sludge or stick in the liver organ and in the liver area of the Lifeforce Chi body. This will hold up circulation of the Chi and cause the Lifeforce Chi body to be out of balance. Imbalance of the Chi Lifeforce will cause the signals from the Lifeforce Chi body to be dissonant, which will affect the perfect function of the physical body.

So we know that the Lifeforce Chi must move and circulate but always be in balance. The closest physical thing that we can relate to the Lifeforce Chi is Water. One of the properties of Water is that when Water stays stuck in one place too long without circulation, it stagnates. We also know that running Water actually cleanses itself or purifies. The third principal of Lifeforce Chi is that the more it circulates, the purer it becomes. If we can increase the circulation of the Lifeforce Chi, we can increase its purity. Taoist practices such as the microcosmic orbit, Chi-Gung, Nei-Gung, and Tai Chi all work to move, balance, circulate, and purify the Lifeforce Chi.

A fourth characteristic of the Lifeforce Chi that is similar to Water is that circulation will increase the self-perpetuation and power of the Lifeforce Chi. Let's look at the example of a pool of Water. When the kids were little, we had an above-ground pool in our backyard. Once a week, I would take a long skimmer and use it as a paddle. Walking around the outside of the pool and using the skimmer inside the pool, I would create a whirlpool. This whirlpool would take out all the dirt and deposit that dirt in the center of the pool where I could vacuum it up easily. So the whirlpool helped cleanse and purify the Water much like circulating Chi purifies it. However, another interesting thing happened when I created a whirlpool. As I pulled out the skimmer and stopped the circular action, the whirlpool continued for extended time by itself. The whirlpool effect became self-perpetuating. This self-perpetuation phenomenon may also account for the increased power of a whirlpool-like affect. The circular swirl of Water, wind, or Chi increases its power. The best example of this is tornadoes and hurricanes. If the winds matched up exactly evenly against each other, the energy would create a stalemate.

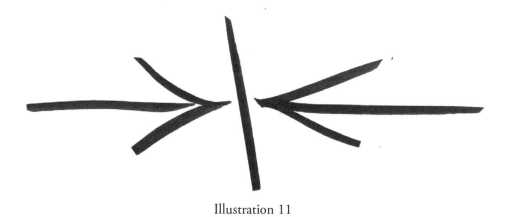

Illustration 11

However, if the winds folded over, one going under one going over or one going left and one going right, the created whirlwind would increase the power hundreds of times. This is the powerful phenomenon of tornadoes and hurricanes. It is also similar to the earliest Taoist symbol known.

Illustration 12

Let's recap. Circular movement in balance creates purity and increased power. Lifeforce Chi is always moving (vibrating) back and forth in balance. It must also always circulate. If we can increase the circulation and yet keep it in balance, it will create purity and power. Your Lifeforce Chi can be purified and increased in its power by the circulating effects of Chi-Gung, Nei-Gung, guided meditation, Tai Chi, etc. Couple this with balancing your mental and emotional state, you will increase your function and health. Add to that a refined and balanced physical body (organic whole nutrition and exercise), you will not only increase your health, physical power, and longevity but you have the potential to draw in energy and create a more spiritual being. This is the last important principle of a balanced open physical body in conjunction with a balanced circulating Lifeforce Chi body. The two acting as one become an organic organism magnet for all the energies of the earth and heaven. How do we make a magnet? We take a solid base of Metal, wrap a wire around it, and send a current into the wire resulting in a circular energy pattern.

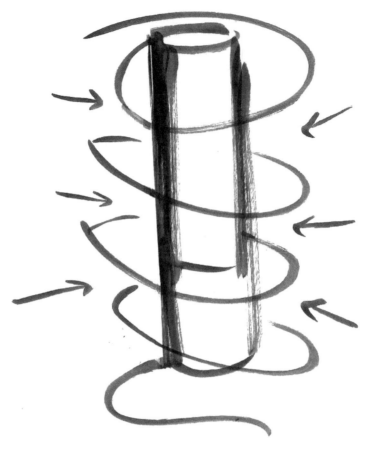

Illustration 13

The resulting circulating electricity creates a magnetic force that energetically attracts other Metals from the outside. So if we take a physical body then circulate the Lifeforce Chi energy in a circular pattern as illustrated below, we create a magnetic force that energetically attracts and pulls into the Lifeforce and physical body energy from the other living organisms, the earth, and the heavens. We literally become a magnet for spiritual energy.

Illustration 14

The Lifeforce Chi can also increase in circulation inside the physical body. There are many "rivers" of Chi inside the body. Chi, like Water and electricity, is better conducted through certain types of tissue. Muscles and joints that are stretched out and open allow for better Chi circulation. The denser the tissue, the harder the circulation of Chi. Fluid-filled areas of the body allow for greater Chi flow. The fluid-filled spaces of the ventricles in the brain along with tiny membrane spaces like the falx cerebri allow for movement of Spirit Chi. The areas of the cerebral spinal fluid around the brain and down the whole spinal cord allow for easier transmission of Air (brain) Chi. The lymphatic system found throughout the entire body allows for easier Metal Chi movement. The open spaces of the bronchioles and lung alveoli also easily transmit Metal Chi. The heart and circulation system, which travels to all sections of the body, moves Fire Chi more easily. The more Yan organs of the gallbladder, stomach, and intestines move Wood and earth Chi more easily. The bladder and bone marrow allow for better transmission of Water or kidney Chi. It is easy to see that when these areas are jammed up, overloaded with food and waste products, or sluggish from sedentary existence that the internal rivers of Chi are slowed or blocked to the detriment of the physical body.

We know that Chi moves both inside and outside the physical body. We also know that areas of fluid or more open space allowed Chi to flow more efficiently. The body has denser areas where Chi vibrates and moves slower and "rivers" of Chi where the movement is easier and quicker.

Illustration 15 Circle with two types of tissue and Chi movement

Let's focus for a moment on the two major internal rivers of Chi: one being the heart and circulatory system and the other being the closed system of the cerebral spinal fluid circulating around the brain and up and down the spinal column. Both these systems are circles. The blood flow and cerebral spinal fluid continue in a circular pattern.

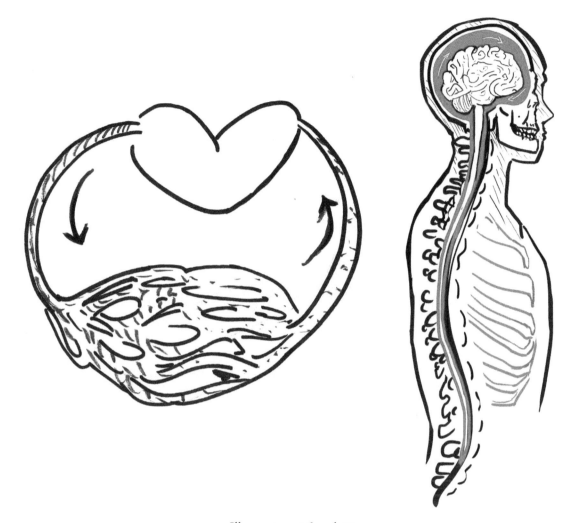

Illustrations 16 and 17
Illustration of circulation and cerebral spinal fluid circles

If these cycles of circulation are free of minor blockages and increased, then the circulating Chi Lifeforce inside the body will be purified and increased in power. We know that even light exercise will increase blood circulation up to four times. This means that the cells of the blood system will pass the same spot four times instead of once. We also know that the Chi Lifeforce travels easily through the fluid circulatory system. Increasing the cycle of blood flow (physical aerobic exercise) therefore also increases the cycle of Lifeforce Chi inside the body.

Cerebral spinal fluid is also a circular movement of vital fluid for the brain and central nervous system. It is important that there be no turns or twists in its vital channel. As we get older, stiffening of muscles and arthritis of the spinal joints can make the spine stiff and crooked. Keeping the spine in balance and open allows for greater circulation of cerebral spinal fluid and also greater circulation of internal Chi Lifeforce. I often tell my senior Chi-Gung class that you are "as old as your spine." Keeping the spine and body loose and flexible is another way to increase physical and energetic health. Through exercise, we can create a more efficient circulatory system. Practices like stretching, yoga, and Chiropractic can help us have a more balanced, open, and flexible spine helping increase circulation of cerebral spinal fluid. This helps us increase the inner circulation of Chi in these two areas.

Remember that increased circulation of Lifeforce Chi does three things:

1. Cleanses and purifies it
2. Increases its power and self-perpetuation
3. Creates a magnetic effect drawing in universal energy

Keep in mind that the physical body and the Lifeforce Chi body cannot be separated in life. So increasing the internal rivers of Chi by greater circulation and/or removing blockages will not only increase the inner cycles or circulation of Chi in the physical body but will also influence and increase the external cycles of Chi in the Lifeforce Chi body. The opposite is also true. If we increase the external circulation of the Chi Lifeforce though meditation, balanced emotions, and Taoist Chi-Gung, we will enhance the physical body's health.

Exercise, yoga, and movement increase flexibility and circulation. Massage that moves muscle waste opens up the lymphatic system. Chiropractic and proper posture allow for smooth flow of nerve and cerebrospinal fluid. Better circulation in all the internal rivers of Chi will increase the health of the physical body.

We can also increase the movement of Chi in the Lifeforce Chi body. I believe that acupuncture, which works at the skin level, uses poles that conduct energy (needles, fingers, or lasers) and is manipulating and allowing for better flow of the Lifeforce Chi body. Because of the surface tension of the skin, the energy of the Lifeforce Chi body flows more easily along the skin surface in the acupuncture meridians. Taoist practices like the microcosmic orbit and other sitting and standing meditations also move Chi in the Lifeforce Chi body. Remember that the two bodies are not separate; energy flows back and forth between them, and when we increase the circulation of Chi inside the body, we also increase the circulation Chi outside and vice versa. It is these movements of Chi that are vital in balancing and increasing the perfect energy of the Lifeforce. The later chapters of this book will include simple and more moderate methods for increasing the perfect all-powerful energy of the Lifeforce that is the *real you*.

Taoist Trilogy

> Humans have Ching (physical essence) and Ch'i (Lifeforce energy), which
> results in them obtaining the shen (spirit); if the Ching and Chi disperse,
> this will cause the shen to perish.
> —Stuart Alve Olson, *Ta Ping Ching* (Great Equaling Classic), *The Jade Emperor's
> Mind Seal Classic: The Taoist Guide to Health, Longevity, and Immortality*

> Perfecting the ching (Physical Body)
> results in perfecting the ch'i (Lifeforce Chi Body);
> the perfecting of ch'i results in the perfecting of shen.
> —Stuart Alve Olson, *The Liu Ching* (Classification Classic), *The Jade Emperor's
> Mind Seal Classic: The Taoist Guide to Health, Longevity, and Immortality*

I wear a symbol that illustrates these concepts and the Taoist idea of trilogy. The symbol is a smaller version of a tsuba. A tsuba is the guard on a samurai sword that is between the blade and the handle protecting the hands in battle. The tsuba designs were often very elaborate with tigers, dragons, or family crests. This particular one was designed by one of the most famous samurais, Miyamoto Musashi. It is said to look like two sea cucumbers.

Illustration 18: *namako-zukasi*

It represents to me the Taoist trilogy of essence (solid physical body) one half, Chi (etheric Lifeforce Chi body) other half, and *shen* (spirit) in the middle. If we refine and purify the physical body, circulate and strengthen the Lifeforce Chi body, then the Spirit that is inherent inside will become apparent.

If Lifeforce is the all-intelligent energy behind all life and is the directing force of your physical being, then how can you heal and strengthen your Lifeforce?

Balancing and circulating the Lifeforce Chi is the key to strengthening and healing your physical body and health. There are five ways that I know of for any individual to balance, heal, and strengthen the Lifeforce Chi body.

1. Open up your heart: Love unconditionally.

    Love yourself, Love the people close to you, Love your enemies, Love the world, and Love your life, without exception. An open and completely unconditional loving heart allows the two parts of your being to connect. Your Love (Lifeforce Chi body) and your physical heart (physical body) are the two connectors between the more physical you and the more spiritual energetic you. This phenomenon of Chi balance is described at length in chapter 6 (fields of existence) and chapter 7 (being one with the universe). Opening your heart will also greatly help balance your emotions and, in doing so, balance the Lifeforce Chi body.

2. Breath: Breathing is the pump of the Lifeforce.

    With the breath as a driving force and the mind as a directing force, disciplined breathing practice makes it possible to build up, move, and circulate the Lifeforce Chi. Chapter

4 of this book has detailed instructions for developing your breathing practice using the 7 Element principles.

3. Open up the physical body: By opening up joints, muscles, tendons, ligaments, fascia, and, in ultimate practice, the bones, you will allow the Chi that is inside the physical body to more easily circulate and move, thus enabling better Chi balance. All stretching practices, yoga, soft Eastern exercises, and martial arts can help in this process. Some of the stances and practices in chapter 5 of this book should also be helpful in opening up the body.

4. Open up the Lifeforce Chi body: Nei-Gung, Chi-Gung, Tai Chi, Ba Gua Zhang, and other Taoist practices put the mind and breath together with the body through stillness or movement to move Lifeforce Chi though the meridians and the physical body. Chapters 4 and 5 will focus attention on some of these practices.

5. Getting help from others: Acupuncturists, Chi-Gung masters, energy healers, shamans, body workers, alternative Chiropractors, massage therapists, emotional healers (mental health therapists), and others can help balance your Lifeforce Chi in times of crisis or when you need help with blockages.

Origin of the 7 Element Lifeforce Crystal

When it comes to elements, there are many perceptions. The ancient pagans used earth, Water, wind, and Fire to describe and connect to their environment. Acupuncture and Traditional Chinese Medicine use five elements to describe the workings of the human body: Water, Wood, Metal, earth, and Fire. The Eastern traditions of Ayurveda and Buddhism use 7 chakras or energy vortexes to explain the body's energy fields. Seven Element Lifeforce Healing is a three dimensional fusion of these perceptions into a balanced form that allows for the functional connection of the physical body and energetic spiritual form that is a human being

I Ching

In earlier times, people lived simple and serenely.
Sensitive to the fluctuations that constantly occur, they
were able to adjust comfortably to the energy of the day.
Today, people lead hysterical, impulsive lives.
Ignoring the subtle alterations of yin and yang which
influence all things, they become confused,
exhausted, and frustrated.
Like the cycle of day and night, everything is a Tai Chi
incorporating movements between yin and yang.
If you do not see the patterns in these movements,
you are lost.
But if you consult the I Ching with an open mind,
you will begin to see the patterns underlying all things.
Knowing that daybreak will come,
you can rest peacefully at night.
When you accurately perceive the fluidity of things,
you also begin to perceive the consistency behind them:

the creative, transformative, boundless, immutable Tao.
—*Hua Hu Ching: The Unknown Teachings of Lao Tzu*, number 64

The *I Ching* is an ancient Chinese text. Many scholars place its origin anywhere from five thousand to 7 thousand years ago. This ancient Taoist wisdom is connected to much of ancient Chinese philosophy, Traditional Chinese Medicine, Eastern cosmology, and divination and is an integral part of Chinese civilization. It proposes a universal creative order and a flow of life events and change. It is literally translated as the "Classic of Change." Using the parts of the universe—Earth, Mountain, Water, Wind, Thunder, Fire, Lake, and Heaven—the *I Ching* uses trigrams or three lines to describe the various parts of the universe. Putting these trigrams together, the *I Ching* describes and predicts states of change and balance. The 7 Element Lifeforce Crystal fuses these concepts into a usable and predictable pattern to describe the workings of the human body and Chi energy field. It will also help patient and practitioner predict the subtle imbalances in the flow of Chi. These concepts originally developed from the shamanistic Taoist philosophy and studying and learning from Nature, our great teacher. The *I Ching* used for the 7 Element concept is more closely related to the "old" or original *I Ching* (there are two), and it does have some elemental changes, which will be discussed. This perception of the *I Ching* will allow us a language to interpret, balance, and improve the function of the Lifeforce Chi body.

We start with the four powers of the universe: absolute (full power), strong, weak, and middle. All three lines being the same signify the absolute power. Absolute Yan is three solid lines. Absolute Yin is three broken lines. Strong Yan, meaning more Yan than Yin, is two solid lines in the upper (Yan) position and one broken line. Strong Yin is the opposite, with the Yin lines in the Yin position underneath. Weaker Yan still has two solid lines, but they are in the lower or Yin position. Conversely, weaker Yin is to broken lines in the Yan position above, with a solid line below. The middle Yan position has two solid lines again, but they are split by a broken one. The middle Yin is again opposite.

Man is between two great powers, the power of heaven and earth. The heavens above and the earth below, with the man in the middle. If we use these concepts to explain our universe, then there would be elements of heaven, elements of earth, and elements of man. Looking at heaven, we can divide it into three elements: (1) the heavens (spirit); the stars, planets, sun, and cosmic energy, (2) the Air, the atmospheric covering that is unique to our earth, and (3) the forces that come down to the earth: rain, storms, thunder, and lightning, which we will call Metal.

The earth has three elements also: (1) Water, (2) Earth, and (3) Wood (all things that grow up from the earth). Using diagram 19, we can see the hierarchy of these elements.

Illustration 19

The Taoist universal trilogy is heaven above, earth below, and man in the middle. Man has two polarities, male and female, with the male polarity being more Yan and the female polarity being more Yin. Picturing the universe with these trigrams looks like this.

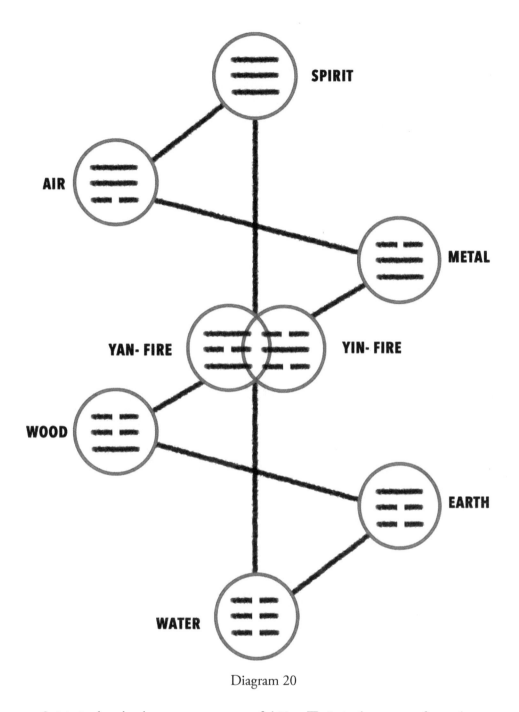

Diagram 20

Heaven or Spirit is the absolute or most powerful Yan ☰. It is the energy from the stars, planets, the sun, etc. Its direction is one of straight down from the heavens. Its opposite absolute Yin is Water ☵. Water lies the lowest. It always seeks the lowest place. Water is the most east central element of life. When we travel in space, we look for Water as evidence of our type of life form. Water your garden, and the Water will disappear, sinking into the earth. If you are not near an ocean or lake, where do you look for Water? You dig a well. If you dig deep enough, you will find the Water under the earth.

The next pair of elements are strong Yan, air ☱, and its opposite strong Yin, Earth ☷. The round Earth serves as a tabletop for man's existence, and Air,—the atmosphere and wind—surrounds the Earth.

Wood ☳, which includes all things that grow, is directionally up from the Earth. And Metal ☴, which represents the forces of rain, thunder, and lightning, come down into the realms of humankind.

43

In the middle, we have the Fire Element. If we were looking at the entire universe, Fire would represent humankind whose position is between heaven and Earth. Humankind has two polarities: male and female, Yan Fire ☲ and Yin Fire ☷. Later in this book, we will discuss all the elements thoroughly, including their relationships to one another and their functional aspects in the human body.

To understand the 7 Element concept, we need to look at the human body and compare it to the universal picture. Remember the Taoist concept: *"What is outside is also inside."* The human being is a microcosm of the macrocosmic universe. We can also divide all that exists into Yin and Yan. Some areas will be more Yan, but all will have Yin inside and vice versa. The human body can be divided into a spiritual upper half and a material or more physical lower half. The three main spiritual "or closer to heaven" elements of man are Spirit, Air, and Metal. Water, Earth, and Wood represent the bottom or closer to earth half.

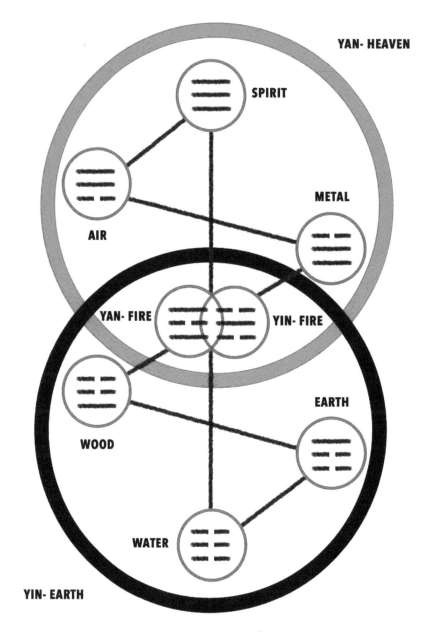

Diagram 21

The Fire element in the universe represents humankind. The corresponding Fire organ in humans is the heart. The heart is truly the essence of a human being. It is between Yan and Yin, physical, earthly man, and spiritual man. It is the great connector of the body. The heart circulates one of the physical aspects of Chi, the blood, to all parts of the body. Fire is also the great transformer. In elemental aspects, Fire turns Wood into heat and light energy. Fire molds the Metals of earth into useful tools and vessels. Spiritually, the heart (Fire) is man's great transcendence. Combine any physical action of a human being with Love, sincerity, and compassion, the emotion and virtues of the heart and that action becomes elevated to a spiritual purpose. For example, growing food is a physical action for survival. Sharing that food with someone who is hungry and in need makes it a spiritual action. Even sex can be just a physical action, but when combined with sincere and unconditional Love, it becomes a spiritual connection between two people. The elements are arranged with spirit, Air, and Metal above, Water, Earth, and Wood below, and with Fire in the middle. The corresponding organs, systems, endocrine glands, emotions, purpose, belief systems, etc., can be found on the 7 Element Chart in chapter 4.*

> To understand the universe, you must study and understand these things…
> the eight great manifestations: Heaven, Earth, Water, Fire, Thunder,
> Lake, Wind, and Mountain, the combinations of which reveal the subtle
> energetic truth of all situations, as taught in the I Ching.
> Understanding these things, you can employ that internally to leave behind what
> is old and dead and to embrace why is new and alive.
> Once discovered, this process of internal alchemy opens the mystical gate to
> spiritual immortality.
> —*Hua Hu Ching: The Unknown Teachings of Lao Tzu*, number 61

I do not think there are any real discoveries in the human experience. There is only "remembering," making new connections and perceptions, and things that existed already; but the body of human knowledge did not include them yet. We all have been here before, if not in our physical form, at least in part of our spiritual form or in our genetic memory. I have studied Taoist philosophy and healing for over twenty-five years. I've always been drawn to and felt a strong connection to Taoist thought. Being a practicing Chiropractor and naturopath, I know that my healing is my contribution in this lifetime. I feel that I have remembered something and have made certain perceived connections differently than others. Years ago while I was doodling during a Taoist course on the five elements with my first Taoist teacher and friend Ron Diana, I scribbled the following picture representing different organs and glands.

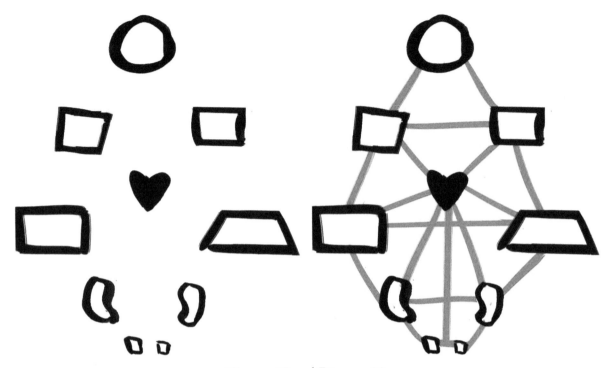

Diagram 22 and Diagram 23

I started fooling around with the interconnection between all the organs. I was searching for communication systems between the organs other than the brain and nervous system. I was looking for a higher communication system to explain the almost automatic action of chemical production and function of the organs, also to explain the changes of emotions and thoughts make to the physical body. Putting this together with my knowledge of some modern energy healing techniques, combining Taoist thought, the *I Ching*, and not being afraid of challenging age-old perceptions, the 7 Element Crystal took form.

The 7 Element Crystal is a representation of the whole human being. It shows the major energy relationships between the organs and glands. It helps represent the body, as it should be seen, as an oscillating energy crystal. We can easily note the crystalline structure of many tissues in the body. Look at trabecular in the interior of our bones. The compartmented tissue structure, even the pineal gland, the "grand crystal," which when x-rayed is often seen as a calcified area in the center of the brain. The entire physical body and the entire energy body are crystalline structures. Have you ever wondered why there is foot reflexology, Korean hand acupuncture, or ear acupuncture? They exist because any complete piece of a crystal is a complete microcosm of the whole Crystal.

7 Element Lifeforce Healing

© 2013 DR Harry R. Elia   Diagram 26:   7 Element Crystal

The Two Brains

Each of the two bodies, physical and energetic, has a directing force. The physical body has the physical brain, which is extremely complex in its function and action. The Chi body or energetic body also has a brain. For lack of a better name, we will call it the spiritual brain. The concept of a tactile form physical body and an etheric Lifeforce Chi body is similar to particle and wave theory. We have "a solid type" particle energy theory, which is easier to experiment with and predict. Then we have wave theory, which is harder to grasp.

The Physical Brain

The physical brain is extremely complex. It coordinates body action (movement), which in itself is an extremely complex process, with millions of muscle cells contracting and relaxing in perfect harmony. It is driven by the pulses of billions of nerve messages, *all* absolutely perfect. All this for one simple movement of an arm, leg, or hand. It also reacts to body signals and balances hormones and body level of all sorts of biochemicals. It stores millions of memories and experiences.

As complex as our physical brain is, it is like comparing an ant to human when compared to our spiritual brain. The spiritual brain for example "knows" which ones and exactly how much of those thousands of biochemicals are needed at the right millisecond. It "knows" to the exact milliliter the perfect amount. It is the underlying all-knowing force behind the perfect function of up to seventy trillion cells of the body. It is even the "behind the scenes" energy of physical brain operation. The physical brain is our "hard wiring." It is exactly like the computers that we have today, tremendously complex and useful for our daily lives. The spiritual brain however is akin to the programmer who writes the software for the computer's function. Without the software for guidance, the electricity for power, and a person operating the computer, your computer hardware is inert and useless. Just like the physical body and brain, without the Lifeforce energy of the Chi body and spiritual brain. Death is just all that hard wire with no power or software.

The function of the physical brain is just like a computer. That is why we have them. We "invented" something that functions along the same lines as our physical brain. It is generally agreed that computers run on a binary system. Some will say zeroes and ones; I like ones and twos better as zero is a starting point in my mind and doesn't function like a number. But it is agreed that it is binary, comparing two things, the multiples of those two things, then making a decision, and filing that decision.

Our physical brain works the same way. We compare two things. We have sensory input from seeing, hearing, or touching and compare that input to our memory files. Once compared to our memory files, we then make a judgment or memory and file it. The brain can get a little more complex by a combination of hearing, seeing, smelling and then comparisons, judging, and filing; but it is essentially still comparing two things. We see our world in a binary code, Yin or Yan. The physical brain is extremely comfortable with this binary function. Did you ever wonder why everything is good or evil, black or white, Republican or Democrat, conservative or liberal, "I Love it" or "I hate it"? When we are faced with the "grays," the physical brain is uncomfortable. Ever watch a candidate debate when there are twelve candidates? It's very confusing. We try to narrow it down to two choices to feel more comfortable and capable of making a decision. And yet we are always comparing one to the other, eliminating and continuing to pair a decision down to two. We are not able to focus on all twelve at once. We are glad and comfortable when it is all over, and we only have two choices. We feel much more comfortable and confident in our choice. Sometimes we will say, "I'm not wild about that candidate, but he is better than the other one." This makes our choice easy because it's one or the other. Our physical brain can occasionally entertain more than two thoughts or things at a time, but its operation of judgment and storing works efficiently and comfortably when it is in a binary function and never when it is five or more at once.

The Spiritual Brain

The main difference between the two brains is that the physical brain mainly functions in a binary capacity. See, hear, touch, smell, taste, compare the new sensation to past files, then make a judgment or comparison and make a new file. The difference here is that the spiritual brain can coordinate and function on a multilevel of unbelievable complexity *simultaneously*. Thousands, millions, billions, and even trillions of decisions and functions at the same time. This is hard to comprehend because you are using your physical binary brain. Let me give you a few examples. See if you can imagine one hundred million light years. Count all the stars in the sky and hold their positions in your mind at once. For a moment, I want you to try to comprehend and have a realistic perception of the whole universe. The vastness of space, the complexity, and variation can be talked about; but your brain's picture can't compare to the real thing. You can study all about the galaxies you want, but you cannot comprehend the whole picture in your mind. It is beyond your physical brain's capacity.

The spiritual brain can coordinate thousands of functions of different systems, tissues, organs, glands, and cells at the same time. More unbelievable is that this function is perfect down to the tiniest millimeter of biochemical substance or the exactness and perfection of the tiniest adjustment to function. What keeps multiple systems, millions of chemicals, billions of nerve impulses, and trillions of cells functioning perfectly all at the same time? The spiritual brain does, as part of the spiritual or energetic Lifeforce Chi body. As an example, let's compare the physical brain to your home. It is a complex structure, electronics, heating and cooling systems, living beings, etc. The computers in your home can store countless pictures and information. The view from your home is very restricted however. You can only perceive what is outside of your windows or inside your home. If your home is the physical brain and in comparison the spiritual brain would be the whole earth and solar system. The spiritual brain would be tens of thousands of times and more complex. We can have glimpses of the sky from our window, but the complexity and intricacies of the whole earth and solar system make the workings of even our complex home insignificant in comparison.

Sometimes a little bit of the spiritual brain energy can seep into the physical brain. When in deep meditation or absolute stillness, we can sense and sometimes understand information from the spiritual brain. We can call that our insight. I believe that sages and some of the many psychics and "mind" readers have accessed tiny bits of information from the spiritual brain, allowing them to "see" pieces of the great complex net of information. I also feel that exceptional geniuses, such as Mozart, could somehow access the spiritual brain in their medium. Most composers work off a theme and use a piano to compare the harmonic chords of each instrument one at a time. Supposedly, Mozart could "see" all parts of the symphony in his head at once. Mozart could write down all the parts of the symphony right from his head with perfect pitch, without any rough copies, but just in one final copy. This ability to see many things in your head at once and make complex judgments about many things at one time is a spiritual brain function. Many geniuses in mathematics and science along with chess masters have been able to connect in a small way with their spiritual brains. It may be the future of our evolution to have complete contact and use of the same mystical, magical, and insanely complex part of our Lifeforce.

Communication

How does the physical and spiritual brain communicate with the body? The physical brain communicates with significant linear and chemical systems: the nervous system, the endocrine system, and the circulatory system. These systems are very complex and can function somewhere near the speed of light. They need vessels, wires, chemical secretion, and receptors to function. It is a magnificent and complex hardwired system. It keeps levels in checks and balances and reacts to imbalances fostering homeostasis.

The spiritual brain communicates with a vibrational signal that is instantaneous. It uses no lines or linear transport. Its signal is received instantaneously to all the body's living tissue, with each section getting *different* and *perfect* messages at the *same time*. How is this accomplished? Using my meager physical brain to explain such a higher-level function is difficult. I perceive it like this: visualize the Lifeforce energy body as an energetic crystalline structure similar to the 7 Element Crystal on the cover of this book. The physical body is a denser crystal form in the center of the nonvisible form. Now imagine a constant vibratory force of sound-light combination, oscillating through the energetic Lifeforce Crystal all the time. It would set up a frequency of vibration through the outer and inner Crystal. Now if we alter the balance or "cut" (as in a diamond) the form of the outer nonvisible crystalline structure even in the slightest way, then the constant background universal God vibration would alter the vibratory frequency immediately. This would change the signal to all parts of both crystals (Lifeforce Chi body and physical body) at once. The signal would be a symphony of information. If this crystal structure holds the information of your Lifeforce, changing and hopefully balancing the crystalline structure will send balanced, sophisticated information to all the solid living tissues of the physical body.

As an example, I believe in and use my practice that your emotional energy is part of your Lifeforce Chi body and is in and around your physical body. If you can let go, release, or balance overemotional energy, change your thoughts from negative to positive, you change the Lifeforce Chi body Crystal. You can also use reflexes, intention, and physical practices to alter the Lifeforce Crystal. When you are in a positive attitude of Love and acceptance, you are balancing your Lifeforce Crystal. This will immediately change the Lifeforce vibrational signal. The body organs and glands will then react to this positive change with *perfect action* by producing the right chemicals for physical body harmony. The same process can be reversed in the negative. Negative emotions and thoughts can cause imbalance in the Lifeforce Crystal, resulting in incomplete or imbalanced (off-key) messages to the physical body.

This is why positive thoughts and emotions change the physical health of the body. Practices of Chi-Gung, yoga, and other Eastern exercises, along with meditation, help balance the Lifeforce Crystal, allowing the oscillatory vibration of the Lifeforce Chi body to be in harmonic alignment. This harmonic alignment and balanced messages to the physical body radiates positive physiology, increasing all systems, including the immune system. In 7 Element Lifeforce Healing, we can also use vertebral and other reflexes to enhance the Lifeforce Crystal. Chapters 4 and 5 are full of ways that can be used to balance your Lifeforce by yourself. Chapter 6 will give insight to practitioners in ways that they can positively influence the Lifeforce Crystal of their patients.

When the hard wiring of the brain or body is destroyed beyond repair by stress damage, neglect, or serious disease, it may be too late to change and fix the physical plant (body). If we smash a computer severely, no amount of software will change its function. The reality of our existence however is that we have the ability to heal the damaged tissue and parts of our "hardware" physical bodies as long as the damage is not complete. If our physical body is still functioning even minimally, we can make changes in the vibratory messages of the Lifeforce Chi body and bring about changes and healing in the physical body.

Healing from the Inside Out

There are many layers to the physical body. There are also many layers to the Lifeforce Chi body. The *I Ching* or 7 Element Lifeforce Crystal or Chi body is multidimensional and uniquely complex. Many healers can work with problems in the outer energetic or spiritual layers and "clear" them before they entered the physical realm. I have seen this work and do wholeheartedly feel that this is true. However, if we only work from the outside in the spiritual tug-of-war, it makes us similar to Greek mythology where man is just a plaything of the gods and there is a spiritual chess game being played without man's ability to change the outcomes. The 7 Element Lifeforce Crystal is the closest structure that I can imagine of the all-intelligent, all-powerful formless Lifeforce. Using breathing practices, meditation, Chi-Gung, visualization, and unconditional Love, we can balance and harmonize the Lifeforce Chi body Crystal from the *inside out*.

When your Lifeforce Chi body Crystal is in balance and harmony, outside negative spiritual or other negative energies cannot deform its shape or disturb its perfect function. Add to that refining and supporting the physical body with real Lifeforce energy from Mother Earth's bounty of organic, complex, and live food and Water along with whole food supplementation when needed, we can change the frequency of the physical body and in turn further balance the Lifeforce Chi body Crystal. Like a warrior who engages a powerful enemy and summons his deep internal power and drives his opponent back, our internal power, if developed, can drive imbalance and illness away *from the inside out*.

There are times in our lives that we all need help in staying true to our way or path. In these times, friends, partners, or professionals can help us come to our own realization of why we stay "stuck" or travel in the same loop of negative action. Spiritual intuitives, energetic healers, and spiritual guides may be able to take away negative spiritual energy and help us heal. But the true movement back to our "path," conquering and fulfilling our life's purpose, resonates from the *inside out*.

Whatever your health status is, you can *start now*. Change your thoughts to Love and harmony. Practice kindness and goodwill to all. Refine the physical body through exercise and nutrition. Eliminate toxic chemical and emotional stress. Work on balancing the Lifeforce Chi body with meditation, prayer, breathing practices, and movement exercises; you will change the course of your health. The focus of the rest of this book is to give you enough information and direction to change your life and health to harmony and happiness.

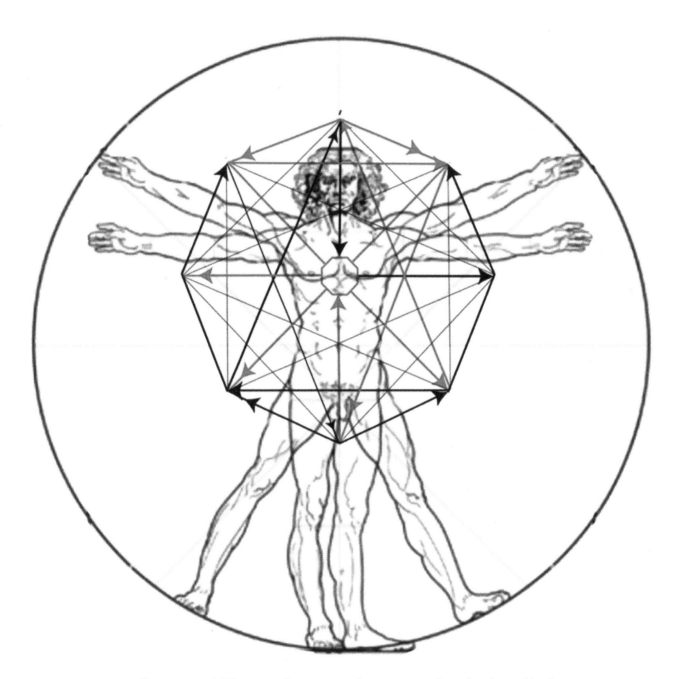

Illustration 24: The seven element crystal superimposed on the physical body

CHAPTER 2

The Cause of Disease

Disease, or "Dis-Ease" as D. D. Palmer coined it, is a lack of balance and interruption of the smooth working and flow of energy throughout the body. Health is the body in balance, the opposite of disease. The body in balance is like the flow of a great river. The river courses on and can create great power. The balance of rain and winter snow melting in the spring and the evaporation of the Water in the summer is the great universal cycle. The body is the same. When the creation and flow of Chi (Lifeforce energy) is in balance with the loss from activity and body functions and the gain from nutrition and rejuvenation, then the cycle makes for great power and wonder. When the body is blocked just like a dam in the river, it builds up power in one area but loses it in another. If energy is wasted or used up like it is in a drought, the river and streams dry up, and the plants will suffer as the life-giving Water is absent from nature.

There is a third interference in nature, and that is man. When man tries to manipulate the river and causes other natural disasters by his disconnection or attempt to control nature, then nature's expression is confused and aberrant. These are the three ways that a river is distorted. One, no rain (empty); two, a blockage or imbalance; and three and lastly, a distortion of nature by man's attempt to control it (dams and toxic waste). These are exactly the same as the causes of disease. There are three causes of disease: depletion of the Chi Lifeforce, blockage of the Chi Lifeforce, and miscommunication or distortions of the natural Lifeforce function. All three causes of disease can overlap and many times do.

I. Lack of Chi Lifeforce

Chi is the vital force or Lifeforce that living things possess. But Chi is more than just energy; it is *intelligent* energy. The Chi Lifeforce is inexplicably connected to the ultimate intelligence of the universe. You may call it God or Tao, but by any name, Lifeforce has an undeniable intelligence. In the early 1900s, chiropractors called it the body's "innate intelligence." It is the same "magic" in which roots of trees grow deeper in times of drought; grass and weeds grow around and through any obstacles; animals change their fur and even their color to adapt to the seasons, and they evolve and survive no matter what the circumstances. Our vital Chi Lifeforce is the key not only to our survival but also to our health and well-being.

Lack of Chi Lifeforce means not having enough Lifeforce energy to run all the functions of the human body. The body can be compared to a great cruise ship. There is a huge crew (energy) that must see to various jobs on the ship. These include keeping people safe, feeding them, entertaining them, cleaning the ship, getting rid of garbage, protecting the ship, and directing the ship to its destination, etc. Think of all the jobs done by the crew as systems of the body. Let us imagine that there were not enough crew due to budget cuts or sickness; then the crew would have to do two jobs and work round-the-clock. Suppose a crew that is steering the ship has to leave to clean up the garbage. The ship would go aimlessly and could easily run aground. If there isn't enough crew and we prioritize the jobs and keep the ship steered correctly and protected against pirates but left the cleaning and the garbage details alone, the ship would stink, disease might flourish, and the function of the ship would degenerate from the inside out. Any time the jobs of the ship of the body are not taken cared of one hundred percent, the health and safety of that ship is at risk. With lack of full energy, the body starts prioritizing the jobs, and some areas will be lacking.

For example, the body may make less of the complex digestive enzymes needed for digestion. Have you ever wondered why lactose intolerance usually starts as a person reaches their forties? As a person gets older, we use more of our energy reserves. Milk is a very difficult substance to digest. Pasteurization robs the raw milk of all the enzymes you might need to digest it. If the body does not come up with the complex enzymes needed to digest milk due to a lack of energy, then you may develop lactose intolerance. That is why when the same person was twelve, milk was okay, but when they get to be forty or fifty, they are lactose intolerant.

Follow this logic and compare it to the immune system. The immune system protects us from disease; it also stops and removes cancer cells, which are always being formed. Even babies have cancer cells. These are cells that have a reproductive malfunction and grow unrestrained. The immune system constantly recognizes these cells, isolates them, and removes them. Just imagine if the energy concerns of your "ship body" only allowed for 70 percent function of the immune system; in the long run, you may be more susceptible to disease and cancers than if your immune system was 100 percent energized. *Energy is health.*

Here is another way to think of lack of Chi and your health. If in your family finances you spend more than you make, after a while, you would be looking at a higher and higher deficit. You could exist for quite a while "robbing Peter to pay Paul." Sooner or later however, there would come a crisis, which would stretch you beyond your ability to borrow or pay. If you could not obtain a loan to get you past the crisis, your financial house would collapse. Health is no different. When energy is overused, your body must start to shift Chi back and forth to cover deficits. Sooner or later, there is a crisis, and without adequate energy reserve, there will be a collapse. Disease, sickness, and possibly death can follow. Contrast this with you "saving money" each month by doing something positive for your health every day and handling the stress of your life without "running out of gas' at the end of the day. The positive energy you generate will help the body escape disease and give you the needed energy to conquer a health crisis. Give any surgeon the choice of operating on a person who is out of shape and has various health problems or a person who is in great physical condition, and the surgeon would choose to operate on the latter. They know that the healthier a person is, the better the chance of surviving the surgery, having less surgical complications and recovering and healing from surgery much better and faster than the person whose health and energy is already in jeopardy.

Why is your Chi Lifeforce not at 100 percent function? Because you are spending more than you are making and saving. The "Yuan Chi" battery of Lifeforce energy, infused at birth by your parents, will fail later in life if you draw too much from it. Yuan Chi is the battery of life instilled at birth (genetic Lifeforce); this compares in our financial example to an inheritance. Even if you have a large inheritance (good genes) but you are careless and overspend, you will still falter at some point. If your parents give you a good set of genes but you squander your health and energy, you will still run out of "health money" or Chi, leading to a health crisis no matter what your genetic makeup. Contrast this with someone who receives almost nothing from his or her parents (poor genes) but works hard, spends less, and "saves" more of their "health money" (Chi). They will be healthier and probably outlive people born with a "richer" genetic makeup. A recent study has borne this out. Extensive genetic testing was done on a couple that both passed their hundredth birthday. These scientific geneticists expected to see a near-perfect set of genetics. What they found shocked them and left them baffled for an explanation. They found that the male partner had horrible cancer genes. They would've predicted him to have colon cancer in his forties. He had markers for all sorts of cancers. The female's genes were even worse. Had she done genetic testing in her thirties, she would have scored in the group where they would have suggested removing her breasts to avoid future breast cancer. Yet both these people were healthy and functioning past one hundred years, without any extraordinary medical procedures done to extend their life. The point here is that your genes give you a "potential" strength. What you do with your Lifeforce energy and your physical body will determine your health and longevity.

This brings us to the leading drain on Lifeforce energy, *stress*. What is stress and how does it affect our health? Stress purely means any stimulation that causes a reaction. So literally, stress is everything. Anything that causes a reaction is stress. The key word here is *reaction*. Yes, all physical movement is a reaction, so is that stress? Yes. We cannot avoid stress. The most important thing about stress is the total Chi or energy loss of our *reaction*. We must look at stress that way. For example, eating is a stress. Food must be chewed. The liver and pancreas have to make enzymes to break the food down. The stomach churns, and after absorption, the colon must push out the wastes. All stages of digestion are reactions to eating that use up energy. Again, it is not the stress, but the total gain or loss of Chi energy of our reaction that measures our stress. If we are eating fresh live food with lots of Lifeforce in it, the energy we receive from that food and the complex life-building blocks it gives us will more than compensate for the energy used in digestion. So the total energy gain will increase your health.

Now let's look at eating processed foods with carcinogens, pesticides, additives, refined sugar, and little or no real nutrition. The liver must first detoxify the poisons. The pancreas and adrenals must handle the shock of refined sugar, and the lack of real nutrition or Lifeforce leaves little positive energy. So the total energy gained or lost from eating Standard American Diet (SAD) food might actually be negative in some cases. Overall, we might lose Chi energy rather than gain it. The way to deal with stress is to limit the energy drain of action or reaction and to find ways to add energy to our being.

Emotions

Emotions are the easiest way to lose our valuable Chi. "Anger is like sticking a knife into your side and letting your life blood flow onto the ground" (an old Taoist saying on anger). Emotions are so important to our health, and we should examine them closer. Emotions are part of our being. It would be easier to walk around without a head than to separate human beings from emotions. Feeling emotion is one of the unique experiences of this form and part of the overall journey that is human life. Emotions, like stress itself, are not the problem. The problem happens when emotions cause inappropriate *reactions* that drain energy. How does this happen? Emotions become supercharged by connecting to past events or belief systems that we have fixed into our brain's file banks. It is the same difference as having a small campfire that is cooking food and keeping us warm versus a raging forest Fire, which is engulfing and destroying everything. They are both Fires. One is controlled and useful and the other out of control and destructive. Emotions are just part of our being that need to be felt and experienced or released in a positive way. When they hook into a distorted belief system, they become huge and can be not only destructive to others but also disastrous to our own energy and health.

If we were to play a beautiful melody on an electric guitar, the experience might be pleasant and beneficial. If I plug the guitar into enormous speakers, that same melody would blow out your eardrums and disturb your whole physical body. The cord represents our connection to a belief system. If that belief system is developed with Love and respect for everyone, then the speaker that it is connected to will enhance the guitar melody. If the belief system is distorted with hate, spiritual separateness, prejudice, and uncomfortable memories, etc., then it will cause an overblown reaction, which eventually will negatively affect your health. Have you ever had strong negative emotional situation? You can almost immediately feel the drain in your energy. Work with your emotions and introspectively deal with your core issues and belief systems so that there will be no out-of-control raging emotions.

Having balanced and realistic emotional reactions to life's situations is essential to preservation of vital Chi and Lifeforce. Through 7 Element Healing, we can help you identify these irrational belief systems and their connection to your health. Look at the 7 Element Chart and identify the emotions, core issues, and belief systems that are your particular stumbling blocks. Then see the organ or systems they can disrupt. In chapters 4 and 5, there will be specific breathing and Chi-Gung exercises to help you clear and change the energy of the core issues and belief systems that may be your individual stumbling blocks.

Adrenal Glands

No discussion of stress and lack of Chi would be complete without talking about the adrenal glands. In the thirties, a medical physician named Hans Selye was one of the first to investigate the adrenal stress connection to health. He compared his autopsy research with cadavers to the medical history and cause of death of his subjects. He found clear connections with a person's general health and the resulting shape of their adrenal glands. If a person was "sickly," suffering from respiratory ailments, asthma, a poor immune system, and other diseases, which led to an early death, Hans Selye discovered that these sickly people had shriveled-up adrenal glands. He then compared them to the cadavers that came from healthy robust people, who died by accidental death and were not diseased. He found that the cadavers from the people who were healthy in life and died by accidental causes showed healthy full-sized adrenal glands. His research suggested that the health of the adrenal glands correlated to the overall health and immunity of that person.

The reason the adrenal glands are so connected to your health is that they are the great "adjusters" of the body. As a survival instinct in times of danger, the adrenal glands create a fight-or-flight reaction, pulling energy from all body systems and pumping the brain and muscular system full of blood and energy for your survival crisis. This reaction is the same for any crisis in the body including the false crisis created by fear or irrational emotional pressure. Even a chemical stress crisis can cause an adrenaline reaction. The prime example of this is refined sugar. Refined sugar is a purified chemical substance. It is not found in nature in that form, and because it is so purified, it has a druglike reaction in the body. Recent brain mapping studies show refined sugar to brain map exactly like cocaine. When you eat any refined sugar on an empty stomach, it immediately raises your blood sugar levels. Raising your blood sugar levels is like a five-alarm Fire in the body. If the blood sugar goes up radically, you will pass out. The adrenal glands are called immediately into action to pump up the function of the pancreas. The pancreas then oversecretes insulin to allow the sugar to enter the cells quickly and lower the blood sugar levels. This happens with every candy bar or sweet that you eat on an empty stomach, thus stressing and draining your adrenal and pancreatic energy. Shocking the pancreas constantly causes the pancreas to hypertrophy in reaction to the stress. Over time, the pancreas will burn out, which is the cause of late onset diabetes. For proof, check the medical records before the 1900s before refined sugar was prevalent; they show almost no one with diabetes, which is almost in epidemic proportions now.

Using up your adrenaline stores to adjust to the refined sugar stress will leave less adrenal ability to adjust to your other health needs. The adrenal glands also act like a SWAT team for the immune system. As an example, when criminals with armor and high-powered guns and equipment hold up a bank, the local police just surround the bank and call for the SWAT team with its training and equipment that is a better match for the well-armed robbers. This is similar to having immediate availability of adequate adrenaline at your service. It is the adrenals that "pump up" the immune system's reaction to a strong invader. If your adrenaline is depleted from any type of stress, then your immune system may not have the pumped-up power to repel a strong invading virus or bacteria. This is just one example of many of how your diet can directly affect your immune system and overall health.

Toxic Stress and Cancer

In our lifetime, toxic stress has become the number one obstacle to a healthy and long life. Chemical pollution created by technology is the big white elephant in our living room that no one wants to see. Chemical pollution is the creator of that dirty six-letter word *cancer*. The industrial, agricultural, and chemical revolution of the early twentieth century has pitted man's spiritual energetic and biological wonder we call a human being against a man-made onslaught of toxicity and poison. Cancer is the cumulative effect of toxic stress on our being. Science tries to downplay toxic chemicals by insisting on a one-to-one relationship of cancer and pollution, never daring to test the thousands of toxic chemicals we breathe, drink, absorb though our skin, and eat in our food *at once* and *over time*. In recent years, science has actually found many one-to-one relationships between cancer and specific toxin. However, they still insist on setting "safe" level of toxic pollutant and chemicals. What is a safe level of poison? If I offer you two glasses of Water, one with pure distilled Water and another with a "safe" level of arsenic in it, which one would you choose? Would you choose the one with poison? Of course not. Safe levels only mean that that particular chemical will not kill you today.

The "magic bullet" of cancer is the *cumulative* effect of all the caustic and carcinogenic chemicals we deal with in a lifetime. One such toxic is chemical pesticides. Most of our chemical pesticides work as nerve toxin. They work just like a nerve gas binding up the cholinesterase that helps regroup and clear our synapses. Without clearing the acetylcholine in between stimulation, excess acetylcholine will build up in the synapses until a tetany affect causes a total muscle spasm, then death. Almost all bug sprays, crop sprays, and lawn treatments work in this manner. Our homes are also loaded with formaldehyde and caustic Fire retardant chemicals. These chemicals are found in our rugs, upholstery, and drapes. Our food has preservatives and additives. What is a preservative? It's a chemical that kills bacteria and mold so that a product can have a longer shelf life. These things are not natural parts of food, so upon ingestion, we must also detoxify them.

The wonder drug of the century is antibiotics. They have helped save thousands of lives, but do you know how they work? Most antibiotics disrupt and destroy the genes of bacteria, causing the bacteria to create mutated bacteria with defective cell walls, thus stopping that bacteria growth. What is the closest thing to a bacteria cell? A human cell. Think about that. There are no scientific studies, and it is doubtful there will ever be, about the possible link between modern-day overuse of antibiotics and increases in cancer.

The onslaught of pollution in our Air, Water, and food over the last one hundred years has a direct relationship to the epidemic growth of the number of cancers in this century. In 1850, the statistics show the main cause of death as pneumonia. Cancer was almost unheard of. If you were a doctor in the 1800s and had a cancer patient, you could use that case for a dissertation study because it was so rare. The only common cancers happened to coal miners, and it was so specific to coal miners that they named it black lung disease. It was not found in any other part of the society. Today, lung cancer is the number one killer. The rates of all types of cancers are skyrocketing. In the fifties, breast cancer was found in approximately one in fifty women. Now it is one in 7. That increase has nothing to do with genetics or longevity.

Science would have you believe that cancers have always been around, and people just live longer now. In 1850, the average lifespan was thirty-eight and a half.* Now the average is seventy to seventy-two, depending on where you live. You must remember however that this is the *average* from birth to death. In 1850, over twenty-nine out of one hundred babies never made it to year one. Now less than 2 percent of babies don't make it to year one. Think about that mathematically. If we take out the 25 to 29 percent of zeroes, meaning babies who did make it to year one, the average stats for longevity in 1850 would rise up to somewhere between sixty-three and sixty-five years old. Not far off from what we are now. Factor in the number of young women dying in childbirth and young men dying in huge numbers in war (some battles in the civil war killed over a hundred thousand sixteen- to twenty-five-year-olds) and our modern medical miracle myth of longevity doesn't look so good. So although the average longevity statistics have gone up, it does not mean that people did not live into their eighties, nineties, and one hundreds back in the 1800s. It just means that a lot less made it to forty. Couple this with the fact that we now have more diseases and more diseased people than ever in the history of man. Multiple sclerosis, lupus, amyotrophic lateral sclerosis, myasthenia gravis, diabetes, rheumatoid arthritis, and the list goes on and on. Diabetes is a phenomena and epidemic of the last one hundred years. It was not ever recorded or heard of in 1850s. That is because there was no refined sugar in any great quantities until the early 1900s. Figure it out. The overwhelming evidence and sheer number of diseases that did not exist before, coupled with the myth of longevity now, compels us to point the finger at the man-made toxic environment.

Let's look at toxic stress in the terms of energy and what we can do about it. Remember, you are a physical and energetic spiritual being. You are an organic living entity. As such, you align with what is organic and unrefined from nature. Any man-made chemicals are aberrant to your nature. The spiritual brain and energy field are aware of every toxic molecule you come in contact with. The beauty of the body is that it has a great detoxification system. With the ridiculous onslaught of toxic stress we deal with, it's surprising that we are not dead in a couple of years. Your body works tremendously hard to detoxify every man-made chemical you come in contact with. However, this takes up energy. The constant detoxifying of your environment's pollution is a drain on your Chi.

Let's take you through your morning and count the toxic insults you most likely encounter. First, you wake and rise out of bed. You have been sleeping on a mattress, pillows, and bedsheets that have been treated with caustic Fire-retardant chemicals. To prevent mold, your drapes, rugs, and upholstery are all laced with formaldehyde, one of the chemicals I have found in my practice to be closely linked to indoor allergies. You head for the shower; remember the shower Water that is absorbed through your skin is saturated with chlorine, fluoride (both severely toxic chemicals), and also possibly copper and lead from the pipes (depending on the age of your house). Recent studies have shown a multitude of caustic chemicals including prescription drugs in tap Water. You grab your shampoo. Have you ever read that label? You use your antibacterial soap. Now regular soap kills 99.9 percent of all bacteria; antibacterial soap has added poisons to kill more if that's possible. Remember, the closest thing to a bacteria cell is a human cell. Okay, you are out of the shower, and we are going to brush our teeth with saccharine- and fluoride-laced toothpaste, both have been linked to cancers. The FDA doesn't regulate toothpaste because it's not a food. Are you getting the picture? You haven't even gotten out of the bathroom in the morning, and you have contacted and consumed or absorbed a multitude of man-made caustic chemicals. This is not counting the nearly one hundred different caustic and toxic chemicals that you breathe with every breath.* Our modern theme of "better living through chemistry" should be altered to be "better cancer through chemistry."

There have been studies done on pockets of people around the world that have a much greater longevity than in America. Three of these areas are in the remote northern mountains of China, a seashore village in Japan, and the remote Ural Mountains in Turkey. The researchers are always trying to find the magic potion that created the longevity of these people. In the Ural Mountains, it was yogurt and goat's milk. In Japan, coral calcium was going to save the world. They have all missed the real reason for the longevity of these people. All these small societies are isolated from the pollution of the world. They live in pristine environments devoid of the chemicals and toxins that most of us endure. They also live without a great deal of technology. They ate "real" food unprocessed, unpasteurized, and devoid of chemicals.

In a study done on this small tribe of people in northern China, it was found that they had eighteen times the number of one-hundred-year-olds by ratio to America. This population lived an agrarian lifestyle, which would be similar to the early 1800s in this country. Many of the houses had no running Water. There was very little use of modern machines. The most amazing fact was that there were no hospitals for hundreds of miles. The people took care of their illnesses in traditional ways, and yet they lived longer than in America and were functioning and working in the fields at one hundred to one hundred ten years old. Cancer rates were negligible. The scientists looked for some genetic superiority, which they never could find. They overlooked the obvious. A pristine environment, outside work and exercise, "real" food, and unpolluted Water, without the benefits of technology and its chemicals, may be the secret to a long, healthy, and cancer-free life.

Where does that leave us? We can't regress to the 1800s. Our only hope is to use technology to cure the destruction it has caused. If we can focus our technical knowledge on cleaner Air, cleaner Water, and a more natural life-filled food without additives, preservatives, and genetic modification, we may be able to turn the tide. We must develop better use of local organic farming and reverse the trend of growing here, processing, and shipping it there. If we can focus on the vitality and nutritious complexity of our food and not on its shelf life, then there is hope. It is my opinion that if we used all the money that is put into cancer research to clean the Water, Air, and food, the cancer rates would start to decline within two decades. Our "war" on cancer should be turned into a focused purposeful goal of returning our planet and environment to a clean, chemically free habitat for our children and their children. We can't stop progress, but we can change its direction. Man's brain, when put to a use that is not totally selfish in nature or purely capitalistic, can produce great things. If we can shift our perceptions, we can use the very thing, technology and science that have caused our sick Earth, to help heal it. It is a priority, not a choice because time is running out.

How does this toxic environment actually cause cancer? The main problem with our toxic environment is the *cumulative* effect of pollution. Science always wants a *one-to-one causative factor*. In many cases, like asbestos and mesothelioma or cigarette smoking and lung cancer, they can find their one-to-one causative factor. However, as I mentioned before, one of the keys to how toxins cause cancer is the *cumulative effect*. Remember the example of the glass of "safe levels" of arsenic-laced Water versus the glass of pure distilled Water? What if there were one thousand glasses of Water with "safe" levels of arsenic in it, would you drink all of them? Of course not. Now let's take one glass of "safe level" arsenic Water and put it next to a thousand of other glasses of "safe levels" of various other toxins and carcinogens. Drink them all in a day and your health might be affected in some way. Drink them every day for weeks, and the effect would probably be noticeable. Drink them for years and years, and in many people, they will cause a cancer. Yet scientists would not be able to identify one chemical as the chief cause of your cancer. So they would draw no relation to the chemical toxicity and your cancer. This is exactly how we live every day in our modern environment. Small amounts of toxic chemicals are breathed in, eaten with our food, and found in our Water. When you get cancer from the onslaught of these toxins over the course of forty to sixty years, there will probably be no way to link your cancer to one specific carcinogen. When detoxification becomes a full-time job over sixty years' time, the amount of Chi lost can be devastating to your health. It also keeps you from running all systems with 100 percent efficiency, which can lead to other diseases and ill health. The individuals with greater longevity from the pristine environments we discussed previously have not had to detoxify nearly as much and have saved a lifetime of Chi, which has been used for running their bodies and immune systems at one hundred percent.

We have already discussed the loss of vital Chi from the body, detoxifying every caustic chemical it comes in contact with. There are however some nasty chemicals that do not even detoxify. Pesticides used from the twenties to the fifties, including Pentachlorophenol, can be found in modern women's breast tissue and will not be broken for thousand years. They can also be passed on through the mother's breast milk.

This factor of retaining toxic chemicals forever in our systems can lead to breakdowns in the energetic immune system. Each cell has many parts including cell walls, plasma, genes, nucleus, etc. It also has an energetic structure created by the Lifeforce of that cell. Cells have an energetic field when put together in a cohesive tissue, and they form a larger coordinated energetic field (see the illustrations in chapter 1). This shield of energy prevents bacteria and viruses from "taking over" the cells. Just like a fort in the old movies, it allows the inhabitants to keep invaders outside the walls, preventing them from destroying the protected inner workings of the fort. Toxic chemicals that are never eliminated completely from certain cells help short-circuit the energetic defenses of that cell (illustration in chapter 1). A short circuit can render bioelectric energetic defenses of a whole area powerless, just like having breeches in the walls of a fort. Chemical problems from past decades can still haunt our health.

There is another way I believe toxicity causes cancer. Up front, I will tell you that I have no research to back this up and only theory and experience. I believe strong exposures to very toxic chemicals when we are in our formative years ages zero to twelve or fetal exposures can seriously corrupt parts of our genes. These corrupted genes stay with us our entire life and may be passed on to our children. Our immune system and our intelligent energetic Lifeforce keep these genes from acting. However, constant exposure even to small "safe" amounts of toxins may turn on these corrupted genes. This helps create small cellular cancers of only a few cells in size. The incredibly complex and beautiful physical and spiritual being that we are finds these small cells, walls them off, and rids the body of them. The problem is that during our life, the toxic pollution of the cells continues and continues. At some point, the body's reservoir of Chi and Lifeforce can no longer keep up with the constant toxicity. Certain groups of these negatively encrypted cells grow into tumors. I have known people who seem relatively healthy and do not have exposures to high levels of carcinogens at the time of their cancer diagnosis, but many of them had high childhood toxic exposures to chemicals that are currently outlawed as carcinogens; thus, another sad connection for us to think about.

Electromagnetic Stress

Our modern environment has seen a tremendous increase in electromagnetic radiation. This includes atomic radiation, radio and TV waves, microwaves, and other communication waves, high-power electrical power lines, and electromagnetic radiation from home electricity and electrical mechanical devices. Since the discovery of X-rays, our lack of appreciation for the energetic protection of our two bodies has led to countless deaths and destruction. With the dropping of the Hiroshima and Nagasaki bombs, the devastation to human tissue that atomic radiation could cause became apparent. Atomic radiation has become part of our lives, whether it includes diagnostic testing, the carbon monoxide detectors in everyone's homes that emit low-level atomic radiation, or atomic plant mishaps that spread radiation all over the world.

Radio and TV waves were developed in the thirties and fill our environment with thousands of frequencies. Microwave ovens are in everyone's home, along with all the microwave communication devices, including cell phones, police radios, and short-wave and other microwave transmitters. High-tension power lines along with large conjunction boxes within one hundred feet of our homes have been proven to be detrimental to human health. If you are as old as I am, sixty (a dinosaur), you will remember when every home had only one TV, a stereo system, and possibly one or two transistor radios or small record players. The electromagnetic radiation of the modern American home is many times higher than what it was in the fifties.

What does all of this have to do with our health? Conservative science continues to tell us that cell phones don't cause cancer and that there is no evidence that the modern world overloaded with electromagnetic radiation has any relationship to the rise or creation of thousands of diseases that shorten and destroy modern human life. Remember, conservative science saw nothing wrong with X-ray when it first came on the scene or cigarette smoking in the thirties, forties, and fifties. In the twenties, fluoroscopes with high doses of X-ray radiation was used in shoe stores on children as a sales gimmick. Why are all these types of radiation harmful? To understand, you must look through different eyes than the eyes of conservative science. Remember, a certain percentage of what we hold as sacred scientific fact today will be overturned and proven wrong in the future, just as it has in our recent past.

Conservative science has no knowledge or understanding about the half of your existence, which is the spiritual energetic Chi body (Lifeforce Chi body). All types of electromagnetic radiation can affect your Lifeforce. Any type of waveform energy field affects it. Constant blasting by a microwave cell phone held against your head has to disturb and damage the sacred geometry structure of your energy field. If your Chi is abundant and balanced, it will repair the temporary disturbance. It is easy to see however that constant energy field disturbances cannot be a good thing for your health.

An interesting example of this is in the study of certain "cancer pockets." These were studies done on areas with unusually high cancer rates. Love Canal where toxic chemicals were dumped was one of these studies. A recent study of another pocket in Toms River, New Jersey, revealed a startling fact. The researchers discovered two links to scientifically related causes of the high cancer rates. The first seemed logical to them. There was a very toxic chemical found in the Water supply that was being dumped in the river by a leather-tanning factory. The second thing that was scientifically and statistically connected to the people who got cancer in that area was the use of electric blankets. This baffled most of the mainstream scientists but makes perfect sense to me. Put a field of electrical energy, which is a heavy gross energy compared to the subtle human Lifeforce, into contact with the Lifeforce Chi body over long periods of time, and that field of disturbing energy will interfere with the matrix of the energetic spiritual geometry that is you. Electromagnetic stress may be "unseen," but it is definitely another drain of our precious Lifeforce caused by our modern environment.

Physical Stress

Physical stress is the loss of energy caused by movement and posture or the lack of movement. In the past, agrarian cultures exercised their bodies with long and hard hours mostly outside. Although it was a hard life, this work was actually physical exercise. Our modern-day life is a sedentary one, usually devoid of any physical exercise. Moving the body moves the Chi. Sitting for long periods of time stagnates the blood circulation and the Chi. Sitting for hours at a time can actually shorten your lifespan. Modern life demands that we do some sort of exercise to balance out the hours we spend sitting.

Physical stress is impacted by the efficiency of our movement and posture. Movements and postures that are inefficient, which means they cause joint friction, and activities that completely exhaust the physical being over time will wear the joints of the body down. In my practice, I have seen many shoulder problems due to tightness in the mid and lower trap muscles and instability in the upper and middle thoracic vertebra. If you were to have someone squeeze your trapezius muscle, applying slight pressure (the "Mr. Spock" area next to your neck), then if you were to move your arm and shoulder, you would see a good example of abnormal joint friction. Abnormal tightening of muscles in any area of the body can cause joints to wear prematurely. Our poor postures, especially poor sitting postures, contribute to tight muscles and an unbalanced physical structure. A good Chiropractor can help with structural alignment and posture. Modern shoes can also cause inappropriate gait mechanisms wearing hips and knees out and causing foot bone distortions.

Our whole Western approach to exercise can also be self-defeating. In the Western world, we have to achieve. We have to show improvement with every workout. We have to push ourselves beyond our physical capabilities. For example, jogging or walking can have a positive health benefit. The increased cardiovascular efficiency, the movement of Chi around the body, and the overall effect of moderate muscle movement can cause an overall increase in Lifeforce energy. What do we do with that? Instead of enjoying the exercise and going at your own pace, we decide to get together and compete in twenty-six-mile races. I always wondered what possessed people to compete in a race that is in honor of the first Greek to run twenty-six miles to deliver an important message, but upon delivering that message, he dropped dead.

In the West, we walk on mechanical treadmills checking our watch for heart rate and pulse while watching the angst on the TV news. I've even seen someone walking in the woods reading the newspaper, talking on his cell phone through an ear mike, and smoking at the same time. Walking can be a wonderful experience of not only exercising but also enjoying and connecting to nature and to the neighborhood that surrounds you. Our exercise should also be adjusted to what is going on inside us. On a particular day, if we don't feel that great physically, we should do a little less, on a better day maybe a little more. We should focus our attention on the experience of exercising—concentrating on how we feel, our breathing, and our surroundings rather than how much we accomplish.

Competitive sports have their place. They play a great role in discharging and balancing the Yan energy of youth. They can help in the physical and emotional development of both young men and women. Competitive sports can teach teamwork and sportsmanship. They become detrimental when they don't adhere to the principle of respect for all participants. If the competitors have humility and respect for their opponents, the game becomes fruitful fun and athletic competition. When the ego dominated, a "win at all costs even if you have to cheat" attitude is adopted; the pressure of competitive sports can create negative physical and emotional consequences, especially for children.

As we start to mature, there is a natural transition from warrior to sage. Activities that we once were able to do may no longer be appropriate. Understanding that fact and having the ability to make smooth transitions over the course of our lives is an important life skill. In fact, we are different in almost every decade of our lives. Making the right changes to fit our physical and emotional life situations helps keep our Lifeforce Chi balanced and even. Professional athletes who never learned those same lessons are the ones whose careers are shortened, and their health is impacted. Many professional athletes die before their time due to the rigors of professional sports and the damage done to the bodies. This—coupled with the common use of steroids, growth hormones, and painkillers all too common in professional sports—leads to broken bodies. Some athletes have a hard time adjusting to "life after sports" and can turn to drugs or depression. Life is like a long-distance race. You must pace yourself and adjust to each part of the race if you are to finish well.

So our first cause of disease is the draining and wasting of our vital Chi energy from the combination of physical, emotional, and chemical stress. If we continue to overuse and drain our vital resources, it is like using up your *Lifeforce* battery. When the Lifeforce battery gets weak and can no longer be charged enough, debilitating disease and death soon follow. If we can slow the draining of this battery and do positive things to continue to charge it as much as we can, it may never reach the power that it had in our youth, but it will slow the decline of our body and allow us to be "young in our old age."

It is easy to see how we grind our bodies down over the course of our lifetime. There is overwhelming physical, emotional, toxic, and electromagnetic stress. What do we do? Dealing with stress must be a twofold effort. We must do our best to reduce all the different forms of stress that affect our body. It is impossible to go backward or give up some of our technology. However, every little toxin, physical stress, emotional stress, or electromagnetic stress that we eliminate is one little bit of energy that our body doesn't waste, saving us valuable Chi, Chi that can be put to the energy of keeping all systems, including our immune system, running at full steam instead of sixty or seventy percent. In the famous words of Father Guido Sarducci from *Saturday Night Live*, "If you had to pay money for all of your sins to get into heaven, masturbation would be a little one, only worth about a quarter. But, *oh man*, do those quarters add up."

The second thing we can do about stress is to strengthen ourselves from the inside out. We can do exercises and practices along with fortifying nutrition to add energy to and balance our two bodies. Picture the example of Atlas holding up the world. We must reduce the weight of the world (stress). But we can also build up our strength so that the weight of our stress world is much easier to manage. Doing both may help us live longer and, more importantly, healthier and happier lives.

II. Stagnation of Chi

The blockage or stagnation of Chi is the second cause of Dis-ease. When Chi is blocked in any one area of the physical or Lifeforce Chi body, it will create shortages in another area. Just like our earlier city analogy, if a thoroughfare of the city is blocked, vital goods and services cannot get from one place to another. This causes regional shortages. Any time Chi is shortchanged in one area, organ, system, or tissue of the body, health is at risk. The blockage doesn't have to be complete. A partial blockage can slow the efficiency of the system. Compare this to a bend in a stream. If the bend gets too clogged with garbage on its way down the river, the increased viscosity due to the garbage will slow the flow of the stream. Think about a slowdown in the circulatory system. Blood must be fully circulated to all areas of the body. This allows for full oxygenation and nutrition to the cells. The more times the blood circulates, the better chance the disease-fighting white blood cells have of ridding the body of viruses, bacteria, cancer cells, and parasites. Thus, the slowing down or stagnation of the blood can lead to a greater chance of disease. This is true because where the "blood goes, Chi follows." The unobstructive momentum and maximum flow of Chi and blood around the body is vital to health.

Another simple health example of stagnation is overeating. Clogging the digestive system with too much food or food that is hard to digest diverts energy from the rest of the body. The slow passage of the lumps of food through the digestive system slows down the whole body. It also causes toxins to stay in the system too long, causing irritation and damage to the intestines. Most of our diseases in the Western world are diseases of too much and excess, not too little. Stagnation in the physical body can result in stagnation of the Lifeforce Chi body, interrupting the balance of the 7 Element Crystal.

There are few main areas where Chi is blocked or slowed down. Number one area or cause of Chi stagnation is emotions. We have already talked about how emotions can drain Chi in the first section of this chapter. However, strong emotions that a person holds on to will coagulate their Chi in one area. Through 7 Element Healing, we can locate the blocked emotional Chi and identify the emotion and the area of life that is causing stagnation. Different emotions can cause blockages in different areas. Using the 7 Element Chart, you can match up the emotions to the organ and locate the life area or belief system causing the problem. Chapter 6 has an outline of the 7 Element Lifeforce emotional technique for practitioners. A good therapist, Chi-Gung master or alternative healer can help you release blocked emotions. Always remember that you are in charge of *your being*, and with work and practice, you can be in control of your emotional reaction to a situation.

Another common blockage of our Chi is structure. The physical structure, especially the human spine, is of paramount importance to the balance and flow of energy. A balanced and supple physical structure will enhance that Chi body just as a balanced Lifeforce Chi body field will enhance physical body function. In all ancient practices, whether it be yoga, Chi-Gung, or any of the martial arts from any corner of the world, the balance and flexibility of the human spine is prized due to the importance of the flow of vital Chi. D. D. Palmer, the father of Chiropractic, was well aware of this principle when he researched problems caused by blockages in the spinal column. He came to the conclusion that the misaligned vertebra, which he called subluxation, created interference in the flow of nerve energy. His research and discovery about spinal balance created a whole new area of healing science called Chiropractic. Structure affects function. A balanced and flexible spine and body helps focus a balanced and healthy Chi body. Chi-Gung and other Eastern exercise practices along with Chiropractic can help remove structural Chi blockages and restore health.

Holding on to an issue can also block the flow of Chi. A life issue is one of life's challenges that you must deal with. Your "issue" is usually some sensitive or past conflict that raises the Fire of emotion once it is touched upon. For example, some of us have issues of fairness or injustice. When a life situation centers on fairness or injustice, it will have an inflammatory effect on your emotions. Holding on to an issue or any inflammatory emotions attached to that issue is another way that Chi stagnates. Our focus and mental attention to whatever issue plagues us keeps Chi stuck in certain areas of the Lifeforce Chi Crystal and may result in blocked Chi of a specific organ. Issues of fairness or injustice will block energy at the liver area or Wood Element. Each element has a specific issue and belief system that is related to that element. Using the 7-Element Chart, you can find your troubling issues and belief systems and match them up to the elements, organ systems, and glands that they affect. It is important to know "your issues," the things that push your buttons. They will be easy to recognize because the universe will continually present you with situations concerning your issues, until you resolve them or let them go. You must be able to see "the big picture" where all things even out. If you only concentrate on the unfairness of your personal life situation or "story," you will create shadows and thick areas in your Lifeforce Chi body. These will darken the light of your Lifeforce and transmit weak and negative signals to the physical body, hampering the full function of a physical organ or system.

Belief systems are basic statements that you have developed from your past history. They are usually created between the ages of birth and 7 years old. Between these ages, children are not well versed in reality. They have versions of reality that are "bigger" than life and not necessarily real. These are the ages where we truly believe in Santa Claus and the Easter Bunny, easily suspending reality for our childhood perceptions. As children, we can form hard rules that are implanted in our subconscious brain. When we form these rules, we do not have a full grasp of reality, so these belief systems are not 100 percent true. However, they can become "larger than life' and so implanted as to direct our thoughts and choices when certain life situations connect to them in our adulthood.

Our emotional environment can also affect belief systems when we are aged zero to 7. A household that is fraught with strife or fear can transmit negative belief systems to the children. For example, one of the most powerful beliefs that is associated with the Water Element is the statement that "life is safe or life is unsafe." A fractured, violent, and fear-filled upbringing can develop into a belief system that says life is scary and unsafe. When faced with a challenge in life, a person with this type of belief system will look to the negative and will be fearful in facing their challenges. This can also lead to an overall negative outlook on life in general, always waiting for the "other shoe to drop." We all know people who will give a negative spin to even the good things that happened to them. Change will usually frighten these people. For example, even a person who is out of work and finally gets a better brand-new job might find it panic attack threatening and anxiety producing. However, not all people brought up in a hectic or scary situation develop these fears, and your work in self-development and improvement of your life will be helpful in changing a negative belief system. It is imperative for your health to change a negative outlook on life to a positive one.

If you believe that life is unsafe, you will always have your adrenaline use up a notch, and you can be fearful of even regular living activities. This fearful attitude is sometimes justified by a person's horrible childhood situations. Children of incest, war, starvation, and abandonment may have justifiably developed a fearful continence. However, if you do not release and realistically face your fears, your energy, Lifeforce, and health will be affected negatively. Examine the 7 Element Chart in this book and identify where you have issues or belief systems that are impeding your energy balance. You can use the specific Nei-Gung, Chi-Gung, breathing, and meditations (found in chapters 4 and 5) along with positive reinforcement to overcome your fears and reestablish new realistic and healthy belief systems.

III. Miscommunication

The third cause of disease is miscommunication or confusion. The body has many communication systems. The physical body communicates via the nervous system, the endocrine system, and the circulatory system. These systems form a checks and balance function. If a hormone level is too high, the body's brain and nervous system will signal a gland to slow down production. When food is tasted and chewed in the mouth, glands are already secreting hydrochloric acid and enzymes to break the food down. These actions are vital to the body's function. If the body's response is blocked and the messages misconstrued, it can be catastrophic. Many of the debilitating diseases we have today are called autoimmune diseases. That means that the very system that is supposed to keep us from disease, the immune system, is causing the disease. Autoimmune diseases and allergies are the best examples of miscommunication as a cause of disease. If the body is fully communicative and has the ability to heal itself (which it does regularly), then we should be much healthier than we presently are.

The main physical body communicative systems are the nervous, endocrine, and circulatory systems. The nervous system connects all parts of the body to the brain. It is easy to see miscommunication when it happens to the physical nervous system. Toxic chemicals and heavy Metals—such as mercury, lead, and aluminum—have all been found to disturb the nervous system directly and cause aberrant function and serious disease. Even our simple example of a spinal subluxation can cause nerve impingement, resulting in severe pain and restriction of movement along with possible organ or gland malfunction.

The physical nervous system can be damaged directly by our toxic environment. A simple example of this is acetylcholine. Acetylcholine is the main neurotransmitter, which jumps across the synapse of our nervous system. Have enough acetylcholine secreted in the synapse and a message will speed along that nervous system line. Another neurotransmitter is cholinesterase. Cholinesterase does the job of clearing the synapse of leftover acetylcholine. This is like a teacher erasing a chalkboard to clear the board for more writing. If acetylcholine is not cleared from the synapse, it will build up, causing unwanted and continued stimulation of the synapse. Continued stimulation of the synapse will cause muscle spasm and tetany, a complete and contracted state with no relaxation. This is how the nerve gas works. Most bug sprays, lawn pesticides, and mosquito repellents also work in the same manner. They bind up cholinesterase, which keeps the synapse active, causing death by spasm. Small amounts of these chemicals are deemed "safe" for humans. We have already discussed the cumulating affect and its cancer-causing scenario. This is only one of thousands of chemicals, heavy Metals, and toxins that can affect nervous function directly confusing the physical brain and nervous system.

It is a little harder to see malfunctions of miscommunication in the Lifeforce body. Let us look at a simple example of a single thought connected to a simple movement. There is an amazing volley of neurochemical transmission, something in the effect of a million stimulations per millisecond, to perform a simple movement. Multiple muscles contract and relax in sequence. Joint sensors are proprioceptive, and there are thousands of tiny adjustments and synchronization from other body parts and senses.

For example, the action of picking up your coffee might require nine hundred ninety-nine thousand nine hundred ninety-nine stimulations per millisecond, and if your nervous system was interfered with so it gives only nine hundred ninety-nine thousand nine hundred ninety stimulations per millisecond, then that action might make you knock over your coffee cup rather than grab it smoothly. Even a "supercomputer" cannot replicate all the sensation and perfection of that one simple movement. If we try to track that message back to the brain, we would find an area of activity, but we would still not "see" the thought energy behind the movement. The thought creates the chemicals and the physical movement. A thought is a combination of Lifeforce energy and the physical computer of the brain, like a software program and hardware of a computer working together. Even physical movement, which we can track through the nervous system, requires an unbelievable amount of balance and coordination between both the physical body and the Lifeforce Chi body.

The Lifeforce Chi body is many times more sophisticated and more superintelligent than your nervous system. Keep in mind that your Lifeforce works in coordination with your physical body. How do I know this? Ask a dead body to move or fight disease. Also, keep in mind that things that jam up the physical body also affect the Lifeforce Chi body's function and vice versa. Some toxic exposure can create what we call "glitches" in the Lifeforce Chi body. These glitches create confusion in the Lifeforce Chi body structure, which then create confusion in the signals to the physical body. Glitches and confusion in the Lifeforce Chi body can create bizarre and aberrant function in the physical body. Think of a glitch as a short circuit loop that once started continues to short out. Working to balance and untangle the Lifeforce can help turn around unexplainable and bizarre function of the body, including allergies and autoimmune problems.

Here is an easy simile about glitches. A while back, my personal computer got loaded with spyware. So much so that when I tried to goggle an address to get some information, my computer took me directly to my eBay account. Knowing very little about computers, I was totally baffled and confused about this bizarre occurrence. Looking at the screen, there was nothing that I could do or think to do to fix it. An experienced IT guy would come in and get "behind the screen" so to speak, clear out the spyware, and as if by magic, my computer would function normally. Miscommunication of the Lifeforce can cause problems that are random and unexplainable. If you are just looking at the computer screen or, in our case, the physical body, the malfunction does not make any sense. If you could look at the balance of the Lifeforce Chi body (or let us say a glitch in the software), you would see the imbalance or malfunction, fix it like the IT guy does, and the body's function would return to normal, just like my computer.

This is the foundational cause of an allergy or an autoimmune disease. They are malfunctions caused by a confused Lifeforce Chi body and consequent reaction of the physical body. Pollen has been around for millions of years. No pollen, no food. Why should anybody be allergic to pollen? Search medical history before the 1900s and you will not find widespread evidence of allergies. If pollen does not get into the bloodstream, how does it cause a chemical histamine reaction? Because the Lifeforce Chi body is distorted and imbalanced, its miscommunication causes an abnormal reaction. Allergies are malfunctions of normal physiology. They are not in your "genes." This is clearly evident by the fact that people's allergies change during the course of their life. Some people's allergies start in their adulthood. Others have childhood allergies that change and go away. This should be an obvious clue that the problems of allergies are not caused by genes or the allergens *but are distortions of normal human being function*. Untangle the Lifeforce Chi body's miscommunication and it is like getting spyware off your computer. The aberrant function of the physical body will become normal function. I have seen this happen in my practice many times, and I have been able to eliminate many types of allergies including anaphylactic peanut allergies, using only 7 Element Lifeforce Healing techniques, without the use of shots or drugs.

The biggest problem with this form of disease causation is that it is unpredictable. Exposures of different toxins may cause different "glitches" in the Lifeforce or none at all depending on the individual person. These glitches will be different in each person and may cause different diseases or different levels of the same disease. Because of this, healing these diseases is where alternative healers excel. The conservative medical profession is interested in categorizing and standardizing all disease and treatments. They become baffled by problems that are different or don't occur at all in people with the same exposure. There is almost never a one-to-one cause of disease. Diseases, even simple headaches, are multicausal. Even more baffling is that people with the same disease may have different causes. The medical profession also has limited their means of discovering causes because they have no knowledge of the Lifeforce Chi body, the all-intelligent energy that directs the physical body. Don't get me wrong; the medical profession is excellent at crisis care, and they are superb when a person has a severe health crisis. If you should find yourself in a severe health crisis, seek out *their* help because the medical professions will function superbly well in helping you. What they have difficulty in is knowing how that person *arrived at their disease*. This is because *each individual may have arrived at their disease in a different way, and people who have the same disease symptoms may have different causes*. This frustrates the scientific medical doctor because they want to have a *one-to-one* cause for each disease and also *one* treatment for each disease.

Autism is a great example of this concept. Autism shows itself at different ages and has multiple and varied effects. These range from completely antisocial disconnection to mild forms of ADHD. Trying to come up with one cause baffles science. Ask many autistic children's mothers and they will swear that the symptoms of autism started right after a vaccination. However, that child may be at the culmination of many glitches and malfunctions, making that last vaccination reaction the one that put them over the top. Test just one vaccination and you get no causative factor. The vaccination may be a causative factor if you included the combinations and bundling of vaccinations, overuse of antibiotics (which cause a rise in *Clostridium botulinum* and other toxic bacteria), and exposure to nerve toxins, pesticides, preservatives, toxic chemicals, and sugar reactivity. Not to mention the hundreds of new drugs and chemicals the gestational fetal child may have been exposed to. Another problem is that many of these insults are at the time when the baby's systems are young and undeveloped. No one would give a baby an adult dose of any medication nor would you give a one-month-old adult food or a couple of shots of Jack Daniel's. Their digestive systems are too immature. Vaccinations intended for a mature immune system may cause different problems when given to someone under two years of age. Why is it such a mystery that the combination of modern toxic environmental and medicinal insults including twenty to thirty-two different vaccinations before the age of two can cause serious developmental problems? Just because a majority of children develop normally with these insults does not mean that these insults do not cause problems in some.

While on the topic of vaccinations, let me enlighten you to two monumental facts that are not discussed in our vaccination-happy country. This information comes from a mentor of mine, Dr. Michael C. Gaeta, whose information on the subject is eye-opening and can be researched at www.gaetacommunications.com.

Fact number one, human babies are incapable of making their own antibodies until at least the age of one to two years of age depending on the child. The only way human babies can get antibodies is through their mothers' milk. Vaccinations are *not* antibodies. They are protein combinations that allow the body's natural antibodies to recognize a specific viral invader. Since it is a medically accepted fact that babies less than a year old *cannot make any antibodies, that makes any vaccination given before the age of one to two years old useless in fighting disease*. The medical profession is well aware of this fact but continues to assault children with multiple vaccinations before they are even capable of making their own antibodies.

Fact number two, the gold standard of modern medical science is the double-blind study, where one group is given the drug and another group is given a placebo with the results compared and studied to prove that the drug or treatment works and has no side effects. *There are no double-blind studies done on vaccinations.* However, when it comes to the relationship of ASD (autism spectrum disease, which includes autism, Asperger syndrome, and pervasive developmental disorders), there is a natural double-blind study, it is called the Amish, who are *not* vaccinated due to religious exemption. In the Amish of Lancaster County of Pennsylvania, there is *one case of ASD in every four thousand eight hundred seventy-five children*. In the Amish community of Northeastern Ohio, there is *one case of ASD in every ten thousand children*. In the highly vaccinated state of New Jersey, the current rate of ASD is approximately *one case in every eighty-eight children*. For those of you who want more proof, research www.gaetapublications.com and any other sources not connected to the profit of vaccinations.

Please understand I am *not* against all vaccinations. I only think that it is about time we did *real* research, unbiased and unconnected to the billions of dollars in profit, on vaccinations and their positive and negative impact on our children, without fearmongering and Gestapo tactics.

Alternative healers may offer your best chance of solving some of the more illusive and difficult problems resulting from Lifeforce disharmony. As my healing mentor and master healer, Dr. Victor Frank, the developer of Total Body Modification Technique, would say, "You must work backward from the disease and untangle the different causes in each individual patient." Another healing giant, the father of Applied Kinesiology, Dr. George Goodheart, always said, "Fix what you find," which meant to me, fix whatever you find in that individual that is not functioning at one hundred percent, even if it does *not* seem related to the disease. The overall improved function may be the key to the inherent innate intelligence of the body solving the disease conundrum. These giants of alternative healing used muscle testing, reflex work, dietary changes, and nutrition to help their patients with difficult diseases. As Chiropractors, they felt their work was an extension of the Chiropractic philosophy of organizing and clearing the nervous system of interference. But it was much more than that. Through their organ and vertebral specific reflex work, they were actually changing the Lifeforce Crystal. 7 Element Lifeforce Healing builds on these principles and combines their healing work with ancient Taoist concepts and arts of Lifeforce energy such as Chi-Gung. One hundred percent Lifeforce function depends on the energetic balance and perfect communication between the major organ systems. Reducing body pollution and balancing the Lifeforce body can turn around problems that baffle our narrow Western scientific thought.

In my personal practice, I have found nine different causes of miscommunication of the Lifeforce Chi body. If a patient comes to me with allergies, autoimmune problems, or developmental problems like ADHD, the first step in healing would be to untangle these Lifeforce glitches. These blocks to health are exposures to refined sugar, vaccinations, heavy Metals, solvents, molds, electromagnetic radiation, neurotoxins, pharmaceutical and recreational drugs, and emotions. Remember, not all people exposed to these chemicals develop a glitch. Remember, a glitch is a continuing short circuit loop that affects the function of the Lifeforce. Each person is an individual and may or may not react to an exposure. I will explain each briefly the technical work for practitioners with individual patients, which can be found in chapter 6 of this book.

Refined Sugar

Refined sugar is one of the most common damaging substances of our modern world. Refined sugar is a man-made processed chemical. Refined sugars as we know it now in all its forms—corn syrup, high-fructose corn syrup, fruit syrup, sucrose, dextrose, etc.—have only been used for about one hundred to one hundred twenty years. Before that time, diabetes was unheard of. Refined sugar (this also includes commercial concentrated fruit juices and apple juice) shocks the system. Refined sugar gets into the bloodstream quickly and raises the blood sugar rapidly. This is like a five-alarm Fire in the body. The body reacts to this stress by using any adrenaline it can muster in a flight-or-fight reaction. This adrenaline then shocks the pancreas into producing insulin to rapidly lower the blood sugar levels. This stress reaction is like "punching your pancreas" with every candy bar on an empty stomach. Type 2 diabetes is nothing more than the wearing down of your pancreas from years of shocking it into action. Some people have genetically stronger pancreases than others, and so it seems like genes "cause" diabetes. Nothing could be further from the truth. Medical history before the 1900s shows absolutely no diabetes. With the commercial refining of sugar and adding it to almost all commercially made products, we now have epidemic levels of type 2 diabetes even in people in their thirties and forties. Hardly a genetic or longevity cause.

The problem with refined sugar is that *it is a drug, not a food*. I will explain my point by using the example of alcohol. A beer is 6 percent alcohol. Drink one beer and the body is not shocked or affected too radically. The body can easily adjust, and the liver can detoxify the alcohol in one beer. Now let's take that same alcohol and refine it to 100 percent pure (as refined sugar is). This is sometimes referred to as Woodgrain alcohol. If you were to drink one very large glass of 100 percent alcohol of the same alcohol that is only in a small percentage in beer, you could die on the spot. Still not convinced? What if I challenge you to stay away from steak for three weeks? You could eat any other protein source, just no red meat steak. Even if you are the biggest steak Lover, if I made it worth your while, it would not be too hard for you to stay away from steak for three weeks. Now let me challenge you to three weeks with absolutely *no refined sugar, none at all*. Most of you would be climbing the walls in three days, "Jonesin" for your drug fix. Recent studies have found that refined sugar similarly affects the same brain areas as cocaine. In a recent study, the brain mapping of cocaine was *exactly* like the brain mapping of refined sugar. I believe refined sugar is a little sister to cocaine. A white powder that stimulates the body to frantic energy, a delightful "high" feeling, then causing an energy crash and leaving you addicted and wanting more.

Depletion of your adrenaline stores due to the sugar-adrenaline-insulin reaction, explained above, connects the high-refined sugar lifestyle with increased illness due to weakness of the immune system. The immune system needs adequate stores of adrenaline, which kicks it into hyperfunction in response to a virus or bacteria invading your body. So a long-term and regular diet high in refined sugar can directly weaken the immune system because the sugar-pancreas-adrenal drain takes precedence and depletes adrenal stores. Energetically, the sugar-adrenaline-insulin shock also overwhelms the energetic circuits, causing energy drainage and miscommunication in the energetic Lifeforce Chi body. In my thirty years of practice, I have found refined sugar consumption to be linked to glitches that help cause allergies, ADHD, and emotional disturbances.

What is the difference between refined sugar and natural fruits? It's all glucose, isn't it? The human being is a tremendously intricate and highly organized spiritual energetic and physical entity, not just a bag of chemicals and cells acting at random. Being an inseparable spiritual and physical being, it is uncomfortable with any man-made product. Processed food refined sugar, and any other distortion of natural food will always react poorly with the body. Recent scientific studies note that carcinogens are caused when food receives *any* processing. The more it is processed, the more problems your body has with it. Your collective energetic and genetic body has had millions of years to adapt to the bounty of natural foods and substances on the Earth. Man-made chemicals and processed "food" products have only been around one hundred or so years. The all-intelligent energetic Lifeforce Chi body will always reject man-made and flourish with nature made.

Vaccinations

We have already discussed some possible vaccination side effects, but glitches caused by vaccinations in the energetic communicative system of the body, even in healthy people, can contribute to asthma, allergies, and other confusing diseases. Past vaccinations, even from many years before, can contribute to the energetic spyware of a present disease. The best explanation I can give you is the example of a fuse in your house. If you overload one set of electrical lines in your home, you will blow out a fuse. If no one resets or fixes the fuse, a certain part of that house network would not function properly. Now imagine millions of these electrical energetic networks in a gigantic house the size of America. If we keep overloading and blowing fuses, sooner or later some functions of our gigantic electrical system will no longer work properly. If someone could go inside that great house and fix those fuses, electric circuits would breathe life into functions that were aberrant because of those past blown fuses. Toxins, refined sugar, vaccinations, and poor diet, etc. blow our Lifeforce Chi body's energetic fuses, causing imbalance and confusion. Over time, the cumulative effect of these blown fuses creates the same spyware with the energetic Lifeforce body that we talked about with our computer analogy. Fix the specific glitches that the individual patient presents and you are a step closer to untangling the knots that have caused their aberrant function (allergies, immune system disorders, etc.). In review, vaccinations given when a person is two years old can be a small part of the tangled web causing their disease. Muscle testing and energetic frequency reflex work connected to specific organ glitches can reset and fix the energetic problems caused by past vaccinations. These procedures and information are found in chapter 6.

Heavy Metals

All physicians should be aware of the damaging effects of heavy Metal toxicity to their patients. Mercury, lead, and a host of other heavy Metals from our toxic environment can directly damage the physical nervous system. Severe toxicity must be dealt with quickly with physical detoxing methods; however, in my practice, I have found that nontoxic level exposures to heavy Metals can cause glitches and miscommunication in the Lifeforce Chi body of some patients. No matter how much detoxing we do, there will always be a trace of heavy Metals that will stay in our bones. Again, this slight trace of certain heavy Metals may cause glitches and again only in some patients. Using Applied Kinesiology muscle testing to identify the Metal and the connecting organ dysfunction, along with Total Body Modification energetic reflex work, we can eliminate these heavy Metal Lifeforce glitches. The more glitches that are eliminated, the closer the physician and the patient are to a solution to their health dilemma.

Solvents

Solvents are very nasty benzene ring compounds. These toxic chemicals can be found in paint, lacquer, paint thinners, nail polish, hair spray, Wood stains, glue, and many other compounds. Heavy exposure to these compounds can cause direct physical brain damage. Nontoxic levels of these compounds will cause miscommunication in the Lifeforce Chi body of some patients. These compounds usually interfere with the energetic function of the liver, adrenals, and nervous system as a whole.

Molds

Exposure to molds usually causes corruption to the Lifeforce Chi body's communication in regard to the kidneys and the integument system (skin). Molds also are so commonly found in our homes and also in plastic packaged bread products. It is impossible to be completely free of some mold contact. Because molds are living organisms, they have a wide frequency variation. When harmonizing mold, we often ask the patient bring in a little bit of the specific molds they may have come in contact with.

Neurotoxins

Neurotoxins are also very damaging toxic chemicals in our environment. In large exposures, they can easily cause death. They include almost all bug-killing chemicals, herbicides, and bug pesticides. As with all man-made chemicals, they can energetically glitch almost any organ system. We find that neurotoxins more frequently affect the pituitary and pineal glands along with the reproductive system. In chapter 6, there is a frequency chart of glitches and the organ and systems that they commonly affect.

Electromagnetic Radiation

Electromagnetic radiations can be damaging to the 7 Element Lifeforce Crystal of our energetic Chi body. Lifeforce energy is subtle and powerful but no match for harsh disruptive man-made energies like electricity, microwave, and atomic radiation. These harsh energies can easily kill in large amounts. However, small electromagnetic radiation—from high-tension wires, computers, electric motors, cell phones, microwave transmission, etc.—also cause miscommunication glitches and malfunction to the body. Remember, your Lifeforce Chi body is a subtle but formed geometric energy structure. Harsh man-made and unseen energies can disrupt and interfere with the subtle Chi body. I find in my practice that electromagnetic radiation glitches most commonly affect the thyroid and Metal Element including the immune system. Through 7 Element Healing Techniques, we can clear these Lifeforce organ-specific glitches.

Prescription Drugs

Prescription drugs have become a very common glitch of the Lifeforce. It seems that in our modern drug-happy environment, many people are on a shoe-box full of different drugs. Remember, there is no health in drugs. All prescription and recreational drugs are usually just taking away pain or a symptoms and not solving the underlying health problem. One of my first 7 Element Healing patients was given two strong steroids to relieve the symptoms of a problem she was having. After her drug treatment, she found herself having anxiety attacks, crying at the drop of a hat, and being far more emotional than she was before her drug treatment. We were able to help her by removing the Lifeforce glitch caused by the drugs and using neurotransmitter harmonization with the adrenals and liver (see chapter 6). We have since seen that prescription drugs most often affect the adrenals and liver. The systems most commonly affected are reproductive and endocrine.

Emotions

Emotions do cause tremendous drain and are a major cause of health problems due to the blockage of Chi; however, as a miscommunication glitch, they are not as common. Due to extreme fear issues however, it is important to note that in some severe anaphylactic allergy patients, emotional harmonization must be done before final allergy elimination is complete. All nine glitches can affect any organ, gland, or system; but emotional glitches of fear seem to favor the Water Element, which includes the kidneys and adrenals.

Enhancing Your Lifeforce

We have spent a good part of the first two chapters talking about the Lifeforce Chi body. We have seen that Western medical science has all but ignored this magnificent, all-intelligent energy that directs the physical body and health. We have also been centering on the negative factors of our current toxic, stationary, and technological lifestyle that lead to disease and weakness especially as we get older. What can we do to enhance, circulate, and balance our precious Lifeforce energy? I have briefly listed below 7 ways that you can positively alter your Lifeforce Chi body energy. They are simple, natural methods to fortify your Lifeforce and increase your health. Chapter 4 will contain more in-depth strategies to help you heal. With just some time and mindful practice, you can balance and empower your Lifeforce energy. The second part of this book should give you enough tools and information to help you live healthier, happier, and longer.

Change Your Lifeforce

I. Change your breathing

Breathing is the bellows of your Lifeforce Fire. Making changes in how you breathe can alter such things as the acidity or the alkalinity of your blood. We have all heard about the relationship between acidity of the body's tissue and its connection to disease and poor health. Just mindfully changing your breath changes your energy field. Using your diaphragm and bringing your breath to the lower parts of the lungs moves energy down and back up your body, creating a circulation. Western breathing or chest breathing separates the two parts of the body causing anxiousness and dissociation and contributes to blood acidity.

Chapter 4 will illustrate the 7 Element Lifeforce Healing breathing exercises to strengthen the Lifeforce of each of the individual organ systems, thus strengthening the whole of the 7 Element Lifeforce Crystal. There are advanced breathing exercises later in this book that will allow you to circulate Chi by your breath alone.

II. Change your "inside gut reaction" from negative to positive.

Go from fear to fearless. If your inner reaction to events is generally negative, your Lifeforce Chi body and physical body will receive negative energy messages. The belief systems that you have created from your past experiences can actually impede your health. *Expect good things to happen.* Remember, *positive attracts positive. Negative attracts negative.* Even saying to yourself "I don't want this thing to happen to me" helps bring what you don't want into your life. There are some great books on the law of attraction, such as *The Law of Attraction*, written by Ester Hicks. These books along with anything written by Louise Hay and Dr. Wayne Dyer can be helpful in changing your negativity and drawing positive energy, people, and things into your life.

III. Balance your emotions.

We have spent some time in chapter 2 discussing the power your emotions have and how overemotional reactions can drain your Lifeforce. Emotional reactions that are reasonable, realistic, and direct your energy to solving a problem harmoniously and spiritually do not upset the vital balance of the 7 Elements of your being. There are volumes of psychological information to help you cope and work with your emotional balance. Two of the best sources that have helped me are two books by Elkhart Tolle, *The Power of Now* and *The New Earth*. Other books by Dr. Wayne Dyer and Dr. John Demartini can all be helpful. If the traumas of your past are dramatic, you may need some professional help in overcoming their power. Seeking a reputable counselor or therapist can help you move past emotional obstacles. Keeping the passionate Fires of emotion burning smoothly and slowly helps you hold on to your precious Lifeforce energy.

IV. Balance your life's activities.

All our activities can be categorized into work or family or responsibilities or play or growth or rest. Most of us spend a great deal of our waking time working. If your job allows you to grow, develop, and evolve, then you are among a lucky few. For many of us, this is not an option. We have to spend a great amount of our energy working to economically survive. Remember, however, that for our health benefit, we should bring some simplicity and saneness to our own personal "dog-eat-dog rat race." "Less is sometimes more." "Simplicity is golden."

Recently, I played a board game called *The Game of Life* with some friends. The winner of the game was determined by the person who ended up with the most money at the end of the game. Marriage, having children, and life growth experiences were meaningless compared to amassing money wealth. Some of us sadly go through real life this way without a spiritual purpose and ignoring the connections to those around us.

In a conversation with my best friend and shaman, Vinny, he made a point about how most people don't really connect to their surroundings or to one another. We spend our time in idle conversations, "small talk," never really engaging another person, even the people around us who we are supposedly close to. Our time is filled with schedules, appointments, and activities; and yet we seldom find even a few minutes to simply sit and enjoy whatever nature has put in front of us. Balance is the key to our Lifeforce energy, so balance is also the key to our activities of life. We must find time to have enough rest and recuperation. It is also vital to pursue emotional, mental, physical, and spiritual development. I often say, "A little bit of stillness balances a great deal of chaos." We must do our best to bring harmony and balance to the different areas of our life.

V. Reduce man-made toxic chemicals and support the body with whole food nutrition.

It should be obvious that every little bit of energy that we spend detoxing from our environment is energy that can be better spent running the body systems one hundred percent. Remember, your body must detoxify every toxic molecule of the Air, Water, and food that we consume. A study in California found the average person breathes in approximately one hundred five different toxic chemicals in each breath. It is upsetting that our entire environment is grossly polluted. Our only path is to reduce our exposure as best we can. Toxins that pollute our individual cells and organs can also short-circuit the Lifeforce Crystal.

Whole food nutrition can be an answer to help fortify the physical body. The current organic food movement is a momentous step in a right direction. Getting the complex nutrients that were apparent in our food before the agricultural and pesticide revolution of the twenties is one reason why many of the diseases we have today were nonexistent or extremely rare before that time. There will be more information on this topic in chapter 4.

VI. Exercise. Move the Chi.

All exercise and movement helps the blood of the physical body and the Chi of the Lifeforce body circulate. Aerobic exercise and resistance training can help build and refine the physical body. Yoga, stretching, and soft Eastern exercise practices like Tai Chi open the joints and make the body supple to allow precious Chi to circulate. The Chi-Gung exercises in chapters 4 and 5 will help you connect your breath, your mind, and your body, to balance and fortify your Lifeforce Chi body. All exercises that are not too strenuous, depending on the individual person's conditions, will help Lifeforce Chi energy body and the physical body. Regularity is the key issue in exercise. I often say, "In exercise, it's not what you do that's important; it's how regularly you do it." My favorite Taoist saying is "Anything that a person does for one hundred days in a row will change their life." Exercises must be done properly to avoid injury, but the most important part of exercise is regularity.

VII. Love.

Love yourself, Love your partner, Love your family, and Love your life—regardless of your or their circumstances. Love is the connecting heart force. Just as our physical heart connects all the parts of our physical body, opening your emotional heart and loving actually connects the two different halves of our being spiritual and physical. With passion and purpose, there is always enough energy. Love is the transcending force, transforming and elevating man's actions from physical to spiritual. The energy of the survival, nurture, and material more Yin Elements of man must pass through and be transformed to reach the nonmaterial and harmonious Yan spiritual Elements of man's potential. The spiritual energies of man must also descend through the heart to function compassionately in man's material pursuits.

All deteriorating diseases (not counting accidents or specific-from-birth genetic defects) are brought about by a draining (overuse), blockage, or miscommunication of the Lifeforce energy. Understand the flow and relationship of the physical body and the Lifeforce Chi body, which means that *the physical body supports the matrix of the Lifeforce body, and the Lifeforce body directs the perfect function of the physical body.* Even a person born healthy with wonderful genes must spend time, effort, and focus on his health to live a long and healthy life. Please remember if you are already facing a severe and serious health care crisis, you should see a medical doctor, as medical doctors are the experts in crisis care. If you are concerned however about living a long and healthy life, you can seek the knowledge and spend the time and effort to balance and understand that the key to health is the sacred gift of an all-intelligent, all-powerful Lifeforce, inherent in all human beings.

CHAPTER 3

7 Element Principles

The 7 Element Principles and concept is a way to connect to the all-knowing power that runs your body and being. In our time, modern science has achieved tremendous technological success. This success is still only half of the complete picture. Looking for life by tearing life down to the smallest particle is one way to try and understand the Lifeforce energy. Another way to view the Lifeforce is to see the whole functioning energy at once.

Increasing Lifeforce energy by increasing the circulation, balance, and clarity (no confusion) is the other half of the journey to healing and health. This view and focus is not in contraindication to scientific fact but is the counterpoint that completes the whole of health

The principles in this chapter and in the remainder of this book when applied have the ability to answer some of the unanswered questions about Lifeforce itself.

Remember, if your Lifeforce is 100 percent strong, fully circulating in balance, and without confusion, then disease and cancer cannot exist. If your Lifeforce energy is at 80 percent function due to wasting of the precious energy (overuse) and blockages (both cause imbalance) or confusion by toxic insult, then disease and cancer can find openings to destroy your health.

Water

Water is the absolute Yin. In humans, it is the primary necessity for life. If evolutionary Darwinism is correct, then all the animals on the Earth including man evolved from the sea. Even in our human fetal stage, we are aquatic. We exist in a Water-filled bubble. In our fetal state, we do not breathe Air with our lungs. Our oxygen and nutrients are provided through a fluid-filled umbilical cord from our mothers. Hence, Water is our first "world." Water is birth. It is the void from which we ascend and return. Water seeks the lowest place. Water is synonymous with human life. When we search the cosmos for human life, what do we look for? Evidence of Water. We know that there cannot be humanoid life without Water.

Water is the ultimate Yin for many reasons. In many Taoist traditions, Earth is seen as the ultimate Yin, because man stands on Earth and is between Earth and heaven. Although we exist on Earth, Earth's surface is covered by more Water (ocean) than solid ground. Water your garden and where does the Water go? It seeps into and under the Earth. In a dry desert-like area, where do you find Water? You dig deep under the Earth, and you will find Water lying underneath. Even the Earth's core is a moving molten liquid, which has more in common with Water than Earth. The hardest rocks of Earth cannot keep Water from seeking the lowest place. Given enough time, Water will cut through the hardest rock proving that the "softest (Yin) overcomes the hardest." Most scientists agree that the human body is made up of 70 to 90 percent Water. Dehydration will destroy the heart (Fire Element) faster than malnutrition (food, Earth Element). We can survive many days without food but only a few days without Water. Because of all these reasons, I have placed Water as the most Yin element.

Water represents physical survival, and it is connected to many of the physical and structural parts of our body such as the bones. It is the foundation of our physical presence. It is concerned with and represents our physical survival instincts. Fight-and-flight adrenaline activity is associated with the adrenals and the Water Element. The Water Element includes the kidneys, bladder, all reproductive organs, adrenals, pelvis, sacrum, legs, and feet. Sex is also in the realm of the Water Element due to its connection with the physical sex organs, reproduction, and survival of the species. Sexual orgasm is a "Water event" for both men and women.

Drinking Water helps all ills. I often tell my patients, "Water is like a priest; it can give absolution to all sins." What I mean is if you overeat, if you have too much sugar or alcohol, drinking Water always helps. When you have a cold or flu, consuming liquid food like soup and drinking lots of Water is always helpful. The easiest way to avoid a hangover is to stop drinking alcohol and start drinking Water. The main emotion connected with the Water Element is fear. Fear freezes all body activity and system functions and can be devastating to your health because of its power to drain your vital Chi. The following is a chart of the Water Element's connections:

	Water
Organs	Kidneys, bladder, and sexual organs
Glands	Adrenals and sexual glands
Systems	Reproductive, skeletal, and urinary
Meridians	Kidney and bladder
Area of the body	Pelvis, sacrum, reproductive organs, legs, and feet
Points	Posterior—sacral hiatus, GV 2
	Anterior—pubic bone, CV 2
	All physical point—CV 1
Time of day	Bladder—eight to ten o'clock in the evening
	Kidney—ten to twelve midnight
Month of year	December and January
Purpose	Survival
Core issues	Change, support, and will to live
Life areas	Sex, financial survival, physical survival, and safety
Breath	Reverse (back) breath
Emotion	Fear (all fears)
Belief systems	Life is safe or life is scary.
	I want to live or I want to die.
Food	Water
Virtues	Yan—perseverance
	Yin—gratitude
Sound	Chooo
Number	1
Color	Black
Age	Birth

Earth

Earth, the second element, represents security and solidness. It is the matrix of compounds from which all life receives its necessities and nurture. Earth's link to the nurture of our existence connects it to family, motherhood, and ethnicity. As Water is the spark of life, Earth gives us substance and sustenance. The Earth can be solid, firm, and unyielding; but it also can be soft and yielding. The Earth can be as hard as granite or as soft as a muddy field. Like all mothers, it has a Yin and Yan side. It is in the nature of all mothers to defend their young with ferocity. Yet they can be the very softest, most caring, and femininely tender beings with their young. The area of the body connected to the Earth Element is the belly or abdomen. The point for the Earth's element is the umbilicus, our connection again to motherhood and nurture. Earth gives us our tabletop, which supports our activities and forms the solid base of our existence. Your tribe, family, and ethnicity are where you get your social matrix and early identification from the ages zero to 7. The system and organs connected to the Earth Element is the digestive organs and system, another connection to our sustenance and nurture. Earth's emotions include guilt, worry, and anxiety. Earth's virtues are selflessness and gentleness (respect for all things). Here is the chart for the Earth Elements connections.

Earth

Organs	Stomach, spleen, pancreas, small intestines, and large intestines
Glands	Pancreas and stomach
System	Digestion
	(a) food breakdown
	(b) absorption
	(c) elimination
Meridians	Spleen and stomach
Area of the body	Abdomen, digestive organs, and low back, lumbars 1, 2 and 3
Time of day	Spleen, twelve to two o'clock in the morning, Stomach, two to four o'clock in the morning
Month of year	February and March
Points	Anterior—umbilicus, CV 8
	Posterior—meng mein, GV 4 (lumbars 2&3)
Purpose	Nurture
Core issues	Self nurture and nurture of others, and abandonment
Life areas	Family, motherhood, and ethnicity
Breath	Belly breath
Emotions	Guilt, worry, and anxiety
Belief systems	I am worthy of Love or not. I feel secure or abandoned.
Food	Complex carbohydrates, whole grains, and root vegetables
Virtues	Yan—selflessness
	Yin—kindness (respect for all life)
Sound	Fuoooo
Number	2
Color	All shades of brown to tan
Age	Birth to 7 years

Wood

The Wood Element is the third element, and its associated organ systems serve two extremely important functions in the body. There is no element that is more important than another; all the elements need to be in harmony for our maximum health. The Wood Element is vital to the human form as it coordinates the systems of metabolism and detoxification. The Element of Wood is best represented by the example of tree. Trees combined Water and the matrix of Earth, and grow to reach up to the heavens. Wood's direction is up. In fact, all of nature's natural food bounty can be considered part of the Wood Element. The main Wood Element's organ is the liver, sometimes called the "second brain," and it is the chemical production plant of the body It is estimated that the liver produces over fifty thousand of the body's biochemicals and that the liver also performs over thirteen thousand different biochemical reactions. The Wood Element energetically is also the site of collection of one of the body's most dangerous emotions: anger. It is a common Taoist saying, "The over emotion of anger is like taking a knife to your side and allowing your lifeblood to drain from your body." Unrestrained anger is one of the most draining of all the emotions. The Wood Element represents our personal growth, our individual achievement, our material success, our connection to material things, and our desire and drive to succeed. Our relationship with responsibility and our connectedness to the issues of fairness and righteousness also fall under the category of the Wood Element.

	Wood
Organs	Liver and gallbladder
Glands	Liver and gallbladder
Systems	Metabolism, detoxification, and part of digestive breakdown
Meridians	Liver and gallbladder
Area of the body	Solar plexus and lower ribs
Time of day	Gallbladder, four to six o'clock in the morning and liver, six to eight o'clock in the morning
Month of the year	April and May
Points	C V14 (one-inch under the xiphoid process) GV-5 (lumbar 1)
Purpose	Growth
Core issues	Fairness, righteousness, and responsibility
Life areas	Achievement, job (career), material wealth, and individual growth
Breath	Lateral rib breath
Emotions	Anger, frustration, jealousy, and resentment
Belief system	I can handle or not handle the load (responsibility). Hard work is good or foolish.
Food	All above-ground vegetables.
Virtues	Yan—frugality Yin—humility
Sound	Shuuoo
Number	3
Color	Green
Age	7 to fourteen years

Fire

Each element has a Yin and Yan meridian and organ. The Fire Element's Yin and Yan parts are particularly important in light of the 7 Element perception. If you view the 7 Element Crystal as the universe, Fire represents mankind, which resides in the middle between heaven and Earth. So although Fire is one element, because of its position in the center of the 7 Elements, its Yin and Yan parts are more important. Yin Fire represents women, and Yan Fire represents man.

Fire is the great connector and transcender. The Fire Element is at the center; thus, it is the bridge between the three physical or more material elements of the body—Water, Earth, and Wood—and the three more spiritual or etheric elements of Spirit—Air and Metal. Fire connects the physical man to the spiritual man. It is the secret of transference for physical to spiritual activity. Love, the emotion of the heart, is our savior. Take any physical work activity, no matter what your job, focus on how your job helps others, and infuse compassion and Love for your fellow man into your everyday duties and your work becomes a spiritual practice. Love, compassion, and the realization that we are all connected on this journey transforms our ritual work and activities into a higher purpose.

In the body, the Yin energy of the lower body must ascend and pass through the heart (Fire Element) while Yan energy must descend also through the heart. Yin Fire represents the heart's inner feminine compassion while Yan Fire represents the outer more male passionate part of the heart. Because of its connection to all things in the body, the heart and Fire Element represent our relationships with others. The Yin or Earthly Fire is our relationships to family, friends, and Lovers. The Yan or heavenly Fire is our relationship to the entire universe around us.

Love is the most intriguing of all human emotions. All the other emotions have their place as long as they are not "over emotions" that cause overreactions. They also can have very opposite and negative sides to them. Love is the only emotion that has no opposite. When you truly Love someone unconditionally, it is impossible for you to hate that same person. Hate is an emotion of the air Element and the mind. Pure Love from your heart cannot be negative. If you connect too much in an unhealthy way to a person or thing, that is not Love; that is obsession, another emotion of the mind and the physical brain.

As an example, if you have children and you truly Love them, even when they had done something horribly wrong, you may be upset, angry with their actions, but no matter what, you will still Love them. Even in a jilted romance, if you truly loved the other person, you may be disappointed. You may feel sad and grieve the lost relationship, but there will be no hate for that person. If your Love for someone turns to hate, then you never truly and unconditionally loved him or her. There are many people, including myself, who feel that striving for and experiencing unconditional Love is the entire reason we are here in this Earthly existence. Here is the Fire Element Chart and its connections.

Fire

Organs	Heart
Glands	Thymus
Systems	Circulatory and muscular
Meridians	Heart, circulation, and sex (pre. card.)
Area of the body	Hands, arms, and chest
Time of day	Heart, eight to ten o'clock in the morning and circulation-sex, ten o'clock in the morning to twelve noon
Month of year	June and July
Points on the body	Anterior—CV 18 (the angle of Louis) Posterior—GV 5 (T4–T5)
Purpose	Connection
Core issues	Connection to others and to the world around you and awareness
Life areas	Relationships with people and your environment
Emotions	Love
Breath	No breath (in between)
Belief systems	I deserve or don't deserve Love. Open heart: People are kind. Closed heart: People will hurt me.
Food	Spices, citrus fruits, bananas, strawberries, blueberries, etc.
Virtues	Yan—sincerity Yin—compassion
Sound	Yan—haaaa Yin—hooooo
Number	4
Color	Yan—bright red Yin—deep red
Age	14 to 21 years

Spirit

Spirit, being the absolute Yan, is the most etheric of all the elemental parts of man and the universe. It has the least amount of physical parts that can be touched but is vitally important to the whole. Spirit represents the connection between the inner physical self and the outer energetic self. The spiritual organs are small parts of the brain including the pineal gland, hypothalamus, falx cerebri, ventricles, limbic system, and other highly developed brain systems. All elements are found both in the physical and Lifeforce Chi bodies. Spirit also serves as a connection between the physical body and the Lifeforce Chi body. A thin slice of tissue called the falx cerebri relays complicated super frequency light and sound energy messages from the outer energy body to the center of the brain. These are picked up by the crystalline pineal gland, which refracts and interprets the signal sending those complex messages to the hypothalamus area. The hypothalamus then directly signals the nervous system, the endocrine system, and other parts of the brain. The signals are symphony of messages that enable the brain to keep the body in homeostasis. This, coupled with the instantaneous and automatic frequency, changes the signals of the immortal Lifeforce Crystal due to shifts in its balance and structure. When balanced, it gives us perfect action for one hundred trillion cells.

The three central elements in the Lifeforce Crystal—Spirit, Fire, and Water—have a unique relationship. They represent the two absolute positions along with an exact middle position. This creates an interesting relationship for the two bodies. The Fire Element is suspended in the middle between the two opposites. So if either of those opposites are drained or blocked, it will immediately affect the middle Fire Element or the heart of the body. Running your adrenals to the ground, weakening your kidney energy, which is the core of the body's energy, will unleash its control balance of the heart energy, inflating heart heat and pressure along with straining Spirit energy.

Conversely, blocked or compressed spiritual energy (closing to your spiritual self) pushes heart pressure down, weakens kidney, increases material focus, and slows down the physical body.

Keeping a good balance between the spiritual and the physical parts of your being keeps the heart healthy and fully functioning. The Spirit Element core issues are purpose of life, spirituality, peace, and harmony. The Spirit virtues are acceptance (Yan) and patience (Yin). Here is the Spirit Element Chart.

	Spirit
Organs	Hypothalamus, ventricles, falx cerebri
Glands	Pineal
Systems	Limbic and higher brain function
Meridians	Governing vessel
	Conception vessel
Area of the body	Inner and upper central brain
Time of day	GV—noon, CV—midnight
Month of year	At the beginning of the year (New Year)
	End of June, beginning of July
	(between yin and yan)
Points of the body	All spiritual man, "crown," GV 20
	Anterior—third eye, GV 24
	Posterior—external occipital, protuberance, GV 18
Purpose	Oneness
Core issues	Purpose of life, spirituality, peace, and harmony
Life areas	Spirituality, purpose in life, insight, and "sixth senses"
Breath	Lateral abdominal (sides expand)
Emotions	Shame

Belief systems	Peace and harmony are or not attainable.
	I am one or disconnected to the universe.
Food	Air (breath as nutrition)
Virtues	Yan—acceptance
	Yin—patience
Number	7
Color	White
Age	At or around twenty-one

Air

The Air Element is the Air, oxygen, and atmosphere we vitally need for life. It can however also be the tremendously destructive force of the winds of hurricanes and tornadoes. The Air Element in the body is connected to the physical brain, nervous system, and endocrine system. The physical brain is the driving and directional force of the physical body. Our physical brain, when properly influenced and balanced with the other elements, can solve complex problems for the good of mankind. However, without the heart's compassion and the spiritual element's influence, the physical brain can become the instrument of great destruction and tragedy. Just think about how some of the greatest minds in history used their intellect for death and destruction. The Third Reich is a prime example of intelligent physical brains disconnected from the heart's compassion and spiritual awareness, which used intellect for destructive and detrimental purpose.

The Air Element and Earth Element are opposites. Earth is solid and dense while Air is transparent and etheric. In Western culture, the air Element has a greater importance. Westerners value the physical brain and problem solving as a solution to all life. They also live "in their head." In the West, we are constantly overwhelmed with volumes of information. Our physical brains are taxed to the max with work and life situations. Any spare time we have is still filled with facts that are mostly trivia. We find it impossible to sleep because our brains are on automatic and will not shut down. Most people in the Western cultures find it impossible to meditate and still the mind for any period of time. Obviously, the physical brain is important to the function of mankind and civilization. It is said however, "You cannot think your way to heaven." This saying illustrates the importance of the balance of all the elements and how problems occur when one element is overemphasized. Here is the Air Element Chart.

Air	
Organs	Brain
Glands	Pituitary
Systems	Nervous and endocrine
Meridians	Triple warmer and small intestines
Breath	Chest
Area of the body	All parts of the physical brain, except the pineal, hypothalamus,
	and other spiritual parts
Time of day	TH, twelve to two o'clock in the afternoon
	SI, two to four o'clock in the afternoon
Month of the year	August and September

Points of the body	CV 24 ("dimple" of the chin)
	GV 16 (the jade pillow)
Purpose	Thought
Core issues	Control and judgment
Life areas	Organization, problem-solving knowledge,
and rational thought	
Breath	Chest breath (anterior)
Emotions	Hate, obsession, and prejudice
Belief systems	My life is in control or out of control.
Food	Nuts, seeds, oils, and fats
Virtues	Yan—adaptation
	Yin—tolerance
Sound	Heeeeeeeee
Number	6
Color	Gold
Age	Twenty-one to twenty-eight

Metal

When counting from the bottom, Metal is the fifth element. In the flow of energy however, Metal comes after all the others (see the elemental flow chart later in this chapter). The Metal Element should be the culmination of the energy of all the other elements. As an example, think about the production of a fine samurai sword. First, the Metal ore has to be dug out of the Earth. Then using a Wood and Fire to mold it and Water to cool, a craftsman combines his physical and mental skills along with his spiritual ability to create a masterpiece. The Metal Element represents man's true creative ability. Because it is at the end of the energy flow, it draws from all elements to arrive at perfect creation. Much like the harvesttime of the months of October and November, it is the culmination of the efforts of the whole year. Being the lesser Yan ☰, it represents the heavenly functions of the physical human being existence. Art, culture, and creativity are the true culmination of the physical man and a spiritual man together. The Metal Element is connected to man's expression and creative endeavors. It also represents openness, with the essential movements of allowing in and letting go exemplified by breathing. When properly balanced with the other elements, the Metal Element represents mankind's achievements in anything that we build or create. The organs of the Metal Element is the lungs, and it is also the general of the immune system. The thyroid is the gland of the Metal Element. The emotions connected to this element include grief, sadness, sorrow, and holding down or on to a particular issue. Here is the Metal Element Chart.

Metal

Organs	Lungs
Gland	Thyroid, tonsils, adenoids, and parotids
Systems	Respiratory and immune
Meridians	Lung and large intestines
Areas of the body	Throat, neck, upper chest and shoulders
Time of day	Lung—four to six o'clock in the evening
	Large intestine—six to eight o'clock in the evening
Month of year	October and November
Points of the body	Anterior—CV 22 (the jugular notch)
	Posterior—GV 14 cervical 7 (*shen bei*)
Purpose	Creativity
Core issues	Being your true self, being open, and letting go
Life areas	Communication, expression, and keeping secrets from the world
Breath	Reverse chest breathing
Emotions	Grief, sorrow, and sadness
Belief systems	It is okay to speak out and be my true self or I will be ridiculed if I speak out, and I am my true self.
Foods	All meat and poultry
Virtues	Yan—forgiveness
	Yin—openness (to new people and ideas)
Sound	Sssssssssss
Number	5
Color	Blue or gray
Age	Twenty-7 to thirty-four

#	VIRTUES YIN	VIRTUES YAN	LIFE AREAS	BELIEF SYSTEM POS.-NEG.	CORE ISSUES	EMOTION	PURPOSE	ELEMENT	BODY POINTS	TIME OF DAY / MONTH	AREA OF THE BODY	SYSTEMS	ORGANS / VERT.	YIN/YAN MERIDIANS	GLANDS	#
7	PATIENCE	ACCEPTANCE	PURPOSE OF LIFE / INSIGHT / HARMONY	PEACE HAPPINESS AND HARMONY ARE OR ARE NOT ATTAINABLE / I AM ONE/OR DISCONNECTED TO THE UNIVERSE	SPIRITUALITY PEACE HAPPINESS HARMONY	SHAME	ONENESS	✳ SPIRIT	SPIRITUAL BODY CROWN ANT.-THIRD EYE / POST - GV - 18 (I.O.P.)	CV-MIDNIGHT GV-NOON / JAN 1 JUNE 30 ALL EQUINOXES	CONNECTION TO LIFEFORCE CHI-BODY FALX CEREBRI VENTRICLES HYPOTHALAMUS PINEAL	LIFE FORCE BRAIN / INNATE INTELLIGENCE	HYPOTHALAMUS / CRANIAL BONES	CONCEPTION VESSEL / GOVERNING VESSEL	PINEAL	7
6	TOLERANCE	ADAPTATION	ORGANIZATION PROBLEM SOLVING KNOWLEDGE RATIONAL THOUGHT	MY LIFE IS UNDER CONTROL / MY LIFE IS OUT OF CONTROL	CONTROL JUDGEMENT	HATE OBSESSION PREJUDICE	THOUGHT	AIR	ANT-CV-24 (CHIN DIMPLE) / POST - GV - 16 (JADE PILLOW)	TH- 2-4PM SI- 12-2PM / TH-SEPT. SI-AUGUST	ALL OF THE BRAIN (EXCEPT FOR THE ABOVE)	NERVOUS / ENDOCRINE	BRAIN / JAW C1 C2	TRIPLE WARMER / SMALL INTESTINES	PITUITARY	6
5	OPENNESS	FORGIVENESS	COMMUNICATION EXPRESSION KEEPING/OR NOT SECRETS	IT IS OKAY TO SPEAK OUT AND BE MYSELF OR I MUST HIDE MY TRUE SELF AND "HOLD MY TONGUE"	BEING YOUR TRUE SELF LETTING GO ACCEPTING	GRIEF SORROW SADNESS	CREATIVITY	METAL	ANT-CV-22 (JUGULAR NOTCH) / POST. CERV. 7 (VERTEBRAL PROMINANCE)	LUNG 4-6PM LARGE INT. 6-8PM / LUNG OCTOBER LARGE INT. NOV.	THROAT NECK UPPER CHEST SHOULDERS	RESPIRATORY / IMMUNE	LUNGS / C3-C7	LUNG / LARGE INTESTINES	THYROID	5
4	COMPASSION	SINCERITY	CONNECTION TO OTHERS AND THE WORLD AWARENESS SINCERITY	I DESERVE LOVE /OR NOT / OPEN HEART- PEOPLE ARE KIND / CLOSED HEART- PEOPLE WILL HURT ME	RELATIONSHIPS WITH PEOPLE AND THE ENVIRONMENT	LOVE	CONNECTION	FIRE	ANT-CV-18 (ANGLE OF LOUIS) / POST - T4-T5 (MING MEN)	HEART 8-10AM PERICARDIUM 10-NOON / HEART JUNE PERICARDIUM JULY	CHEST ARMS HANDS	CIRCULATION / MUSCULAR	HEART / T1-T7	HEART / PERICARDIUM OR CIRC./SEX	THYMUS	4
3	HUMILITY	FRUGALITY	JOB (CAREER) MATERIAL WEALTH ACHIEVEMENT INDIVIDUAL GROWTH	I CAN OR CANNOT HANDLE THE RESPONSIBILITY / I JUST CANT WIN / HARD WORK IS GOOD/ OR IS NOT	FAIRNESS RIGHTEOUSNESS RESPONSIBILITY	ANGER FRUSTRATION JEALOUSY RESENTMENT	GROWTH	WOOD	ANT-CV-14 near heart (1" BELOW XIPHOID) / POST - GV - 5 (T11)	LIVER 6-8AM G.B. 4-6AM / LIVER MAY GALL BLADDER APRIL	SOLAR PLEXUS TRUNK RIBS	METABOLISM / DETOXIFICATION	LIVER GALL BLADDER / T8-T12	LIVER / GALL BLADDER	LIVER	3
2	KINDNESS	SELFLESSNESS	FAMILY MOTHERHOOD ETHNICITY (TRIBE)	I AM WORTHY OF LOVE OR NOT / I FEEL SECURE OR ABANDONED	SELF NURTURE AND NURTURE OF OTHERS ABANDONMENT	GUILT WORRY ANXIETY	NURTURE	EARTH	ANT. UMBILICUS / POST - GV - 4 (BETWEEN L2-L3)	SPLEEN 12-2AM STOMACH 2-4AM / SPLEEN FEB. STOMACH MARCH	ABDOMEN INTESTINES LOW BACK	DIGESTIVE-BREAKDOWN ABSORBTION ELIMINATION	STOMACH PANCREAS SPLEEN SMALL & LARGE INTESTINES / L1-L5	SPLEEN / STOMACH	PANCREAS	2
1	GRATITUDE	PERSEVERANCE	MONEY (FINANCIAL SURVIVAL) SEX SAFETY	LIFE IS SAFE LIFE IS SCARY / I WANT TO LIVE I WANT TO DIE	CHANGE SUPPORT WILL TO LIVE	FEAR	SURVIVAL	WATER	PHYS. BODY CV-1 ANT. CV-2 / POST - GV - 2 (SACRAL HIATUS)	KIDNEY 10PM-MID. BLADDER 8-10PM / KIDNEY JAN. BLADDER DEC.	LUMBO-PELVIC SACRUM LEGS FEET	URINARY REPRODUCTIVE SKELETAL	KIDNEYS BLADDER REPRODUCTIVE ORGANS / SACRUM COCCYX	KIDNEYS / BLADDER	ADRENALS	1

The 7 Element Laws

There are many universal laws. There are laws about gravity, the atmosphere, geology, etc. Laws are relationships between two things. This relationship affords balance and produces function. The characteristics of one partner of the relationship influences and helps balance the other. It is sort of barter, one partner has certain capabilities and is responsible for those parts and another partner has a different set of capabilities and uses those to foster balance. So the relationship is not always even; each partner brings to the table a different ability, which when traded with another creates the balance. When you go to the store, you exchange the money you have earned from work for groceries. The grocer gets the money he needs, and you get the food that you need. If the trade is balanced, then there is harmony. The elemental laws are the same.

There is a Yin and Yan to the balance of each partner. The Yin element is responsible for the *support* of another element. Support can mean providing the matrix for the proper function of the other partner or literally support, such as the physical body gives the Lifeforce Chi body a supporting structure. It also means to build up the energy of another element's organs. A supporting element is one when stimulated will help generate Chi in another element organ system. The more Yan Elements are more responsible for *directing* and *dispersing*. These are controlling responsibilities. Directing means to stimulate another element (or organ system) to action. Dispersing means to reduce the buildup of energy when one element, organ, or system is blocked and slowing energy flow. Each element organ system, except Fire, supports and directs other elements and in turn is supported and directed by another set of elements and organ systems. This "barter system" among the elements makes for constant movement and direction of energy. As long as there is balance in this movement, the body, physical and energetic, will be in harmony. Harmony and balance are the keys to full function and health.

There are many connections between the body's organs and systems. Looking at the one-dimensional 7 Element Crystal, you can see many triangular lines that connect one element to another. The real-life three-dimensional energetic Crystal has multiple connections between all organs and systems. The 7 Element Laws are the main highways of connection and interrelated function. When the body is out of balance, there is always at least one element that is "full" and another that is "empty." Once we understand the 7 Element Laws, we can use that knowledge to transfer energy and balance the Lifeforce Chi body.

7 Element Lifeforce Healing

We are a microcosm of the universe. From the Taoist perspective, "What is outside is also inside." What is universal is also part of us. The 7 Element laws use universal or elemental principles, which apply not only to the universe but also to the functioning of you, the human being.

7 Element Laws

Support	Directs or disperses
Water supports Earth.	Spirit directs or disperses Air.
Water supports Wood.	Spirit directs or disperses Metal.
Earth supports Wood.	Air directs or disperses Metal.
Earth and Fire supports Metal.	Air directs or disperses Earth.
Wood and Fire supports Air.	Metal directs or disperses Wood.
Wood supports Spirit.	Metal directs or disperses Water.
Air supports Water.	Earth directs or disperses Spirit.
Spirit supports Fire.	Water directs or disperses Fire.

	Supports	Directs or Disperses
Water	2	1
Earth	2	1
Wood	2	0
Fire	0	0
Metal	0	2
Air	1	2
Spirit	1	2

7 Element crystal.

Each universal law can be exemplified with the interactions of the organ systems in the human body. So as an elemental law, such as the rain from the sky, Air *element* fills or supports the *Water element* and has its duplication in the physical body. These physical connections serve as clues to the energetic connections in the 7 Element Crystal. Knowing these relationships from the 7 Element Crystal Chart will allow us to realize and fix imbalances of the Lifeforce. Below are some simple examples.

Water Supports Earth

This law is sometimes hard to visualize because we stand on Earth. Water however is the most supporting substance of humanoid existence. When we travel to other planets to seek out extraterrestrial life, we search for any evidence or past existence of Water. Underneath the thin skin of the Earth lies a viscous moving sea of molten liquid. Also, dig down deep enough on any place on the Earth and you will at some point strike Water. Water, the absolute Yin, always seeks the lowest place. In the body, the Water Element represents the kidneys, bladder, and adrenal glands. The adrenal glands support all the systems of the body. Adrenal energy is what is used to pump up the function of many of our systems. Get too hot or too cold and the adrenals adjust the blood supply to balance the heat. Raise your blood sugar rapidly and the adrenals will stimulate the pancreas (Earth Element) to produce extra insulin quickly to lower the blood sugar. The adrenals come to our aid when any system needs to work quicker and harder for body balance.

The Water Element also represents the kidneys. In Traditional Chinese Medicine, the kidneys represent the body's core energy, sometimes called your Yuan Chi or birth energy. It is the Lifeforce battery of your physical body. So as your core energy, the kidneys (Water Element) supports all elements, including Earth. The Water Element also connected to the bones and the skeletal system. The abdomen (Earth Element) is supported by the pelvis physically.

Upon ingesting a meal, all the body's energy is needed to digest the meal. Digestion becomes a priority of the body, which is why you are sleepy and sluggish after a big meal. You would never eat a large four-course meal immediately before running a marathon nor would you have a huge meal right before a football game. The body's energies would be directed to digesting that meal, and if not, digestion would become a problem. Having adequate adrenal energy is the driving force for digestive action after a large meal.

In taking care of the survival necessities of shelter and safety (Water Element, see chart), man then turns his attention and energy to the making and being part of a family, tribe, or community (Earth Element). If the necessities of survival and safety are not met, then the security of family and community cannot be realized. Water supports Earth.

Water Supports Wood

The Water Element, being the most Yin of all the elements, plays two supporting roles. In addition to Earth, Water also supports Wood. In nature, it is easy to see the lily pads floating on the Water and growing right from the lake. Hydro phonics is the "newest" oldest way making a modern comeback to grow healthy, robust, organic vegetables and plants directly from the Water with no Earth support. In the body, the Water Element is connected to willpower and adrenal energy, which is the force and power behind the drive for achievement, material wealth, and self-development, all things associated with the Wood Element.

Adrenaline (Water) from the adrenal chromaffin cells increases the catalysis of glycogen in the liver (Wood) helping the breakdown of lipids in fat cells.

Earth Supports Wood

Elementally, it is easy to see Earth's support of the Wood Element. Where does Wood sprout up from? Earth is the matrix from which all vegetation springs forth. Earth is the solid tabletop that all growth comes up from. Developmentally, our Earth years from zero to seven allow us the security and self-assurance to begin to explore our own identity and individual growth (two functions of the Wood years that follow seven to fourteen. See chapter 7).

Earth also supports Wood by:

1. Cholecystokinin secreted from the duodenum (Earth) causes release of bile from the gallbladder helping the gallbladder (Wood) break down fats.
2. Glucagon secreted by the pancreas (Earth) causes glycogenolysis in the liver (Wood).

Nutritional fuel helps support the entire body including metabolism and detoxification, which are two functions of the liver (Wood Element). Close investigation of our organ anatomy will show that the stomach, pancreas, intestines, and spleen (Earth) all lie slightly lower in the body than the liver and gallbladder (Wood), Earth physically supporting Wood.

Earth with Fire Supports Metal

Where do we find Metal ore? We dig into the Earth. The combination of Earth (mining) and Fire forges the Metals we make our tools from. With Metal, we create.

The physical body's thyroid, which is included in the Metal Element, is responsible along with the liver for the body's metabolism. Without the nourishment from the Earth Element's digestive system and delivery in connection of the Fire Element's circulatory system, metabolism would not be possible. The supporting nourishment allows the thyroid and liver to promote metabolic role and, in the case of the thyroid, direct puberty development.

Earth Element's digestive function is a supporting cast member in both metabolism and detoxification. The Earth Element (digestion) is the cornerstone and support for the functions of the Metal Element organs, thyroid and lungs, and also the Wood Element organ, the liver.

Wood with Fire Supports Air

Almost every spiritual tradition calls for the burning of Wood, incense, or sacrificial offerings. The smoke from the burning of Wood rises into the air. The released energy and smoke from anything that we burn on the Earth ends up in the Earth's atmosphere that represents the Air Element. The liver (Wood Element) is responsible for detoxification of all poisonous and noxious chemicals. It also detoxifies drugs, both pharmaceuticals and recreational. Alcohol is also detoxified by liver. Alcohol and other solvents have a direct and rapid effect on the brain's (Air Element) capacity to function normally. By detoxifying these brain-altering drugs, the liver in effect supports the full function of the brain.

The liver is also sometimes called the second brain. It is the chemical center and factory of the body. The synthesis of chemicals allows the body brain to coordinate and balance the physical body through chemicals, many of which come from the supporting liver.

Wood Supports Spirit

We can see a dual example here. In a common shamanistic practices, we write our concerns, problems, wishes, or dreams on a piece of paper (Wood) and then burn them to release them to spirit.

This elemental law is one of the hardest to envision in the physical body. If we can look at the functions, core issues, and virtues of the Wood Element, we may be able see its connection and support to the Spirit Element. The core issues of the Wood Element are fairness and righteousness. It is also concerned with the life areas of growth, individual achievement, self-improvement, and responsibility. When these three areas are in good balance, it is easy to see that they will foster a more spiritually balanced person, hence supporting spirit.

Air Supports Water

When the Air condenses, it forms clouds; the clouds rain down on the Earth. This fills the rivers, streams, and even the oceans. Elementally, Air supporting Water is easy to envision; rain comes from the air. This elemental principle is also easy to see in body function. In the body, the pituitary gland, which is the gland of the Air Element, produces vasopressin, which stimulates the kidneys (Water Element) to contract its tubules and increase blood pressure when needed. The pituitary is also the stimulator of the adrenal glands (Water Element). The adrenal glands come into play whenever the body needs to adapt in many ways such as temperature changes, blood pressure, a rise in blood sugar, or in flight-or-fight reflexes.

The anterior pituitary (Air Element) is directly responsible for secondary sex characteristics of the reproductive system and sexual organs (Water Element). These are only a few of the many connections of the Air Element's organ and gland, the brain and pituitary, to the Water Element's kidney, bladder, bones, and adrenals.

Spirit Supports Fire

What builds the passion of a person? Spirit. When a person is filled with a higher purpose, their actions have passion (Fire). Our feelings of oneness with all things, which is a Spirit Element purpose, helps fuel compassion and connection with those around us, which is a Fire Element characteristic. In the body, the pineal gland is a spiritual receiver and transmitter of the Lifeforce messages to the physical body. One of the few responsibilities that science has been able to isolate and contribute to the pineal gland is to regulate sleep and our rhythmical cycles. These rhythms put us in touch with those things around us, connecting our physical bodies to our surrounding environment. Connection is a Fire Element purpose.

Spirit Directs and/or Disperses Air

When the atmosphere builds up with fog and clouds, what is it that disperses the clouds? It is the power of the sun. The Air Element represents the physical brain and mental processing. When the brain is over-loaded, obsessed, or just plain thinking too much, which is a common theme in our Western culture, having a spiritual connection, meditation, and seeking a sense of life's purpose puts the thinking brain in its place. Compared to the Internet and the TV dribble that fills our brains, a spiritual question like what is our life's purpose or dealing with death will disperse most of the garbage that fills up 90 percent of the Western mind. In the physical body, the pineal gland (Spirit Element) acts as the "supreme commander" gland sending stimulation and messages to the "general of glands," the pituitary (Air Element), which connects directly to the endocrine system and autonomic nervous system.

Air Directs and/or Disperses Metal

What is steel's natural enemy? Air. Sooner or later, through oxygenation, Metal will rust. Our finest structures and our best car creations will at some point rust from air. If the pituitary gland (Air Element) is the "general" of the glands, then the thyroid (Metal Element) is the "sergeant" of the body's glands, taking the general orders and directing and dispersing them among the working soldiers of the body. The pituitary directs the thyroid in both metabolism and secondary growth changes. In most cases, the thinking brain (Air Element) must be engaged and directs speech (Metal Element), but as we all know sometimes, we are out of balance. And in that case, our brain does not always direct our speech.

The anterior pituitary (Air Element) secretes thyrotropin, which directs and stimulates the thyroid (Metal Element) to release thyroxine and triiodothyronine. It also stimulates iodine absorption by the thyroid.

Air Directs and/or Disperses Earth

A sandstorm is a good example of Air dispersing Earth. Wind is capable of wearing away mountainsides and sanding down the stones of Earth. Even the great pyramids of Egypt will at some point be worn away to dust by the Air and the wind. There are many direct connections between the brain (Air Element) and the digestive organs (Earth Element). When you start to chew your food, the brain is already stimulating the stomach and pancreas to produce the acids and enzymes to break down the food. Stomach (Earth Element) motility is directed by the brain (Air Element). These are again just simple examples of the directing or dispersing connection between the Air Element and Earth Element.

Metal Directs and/or Disperses Wood

When we need to clear the forest, you will hear the sound of the axe, the saw, and the machete. Wood is cut and dispersed by Metal. In the physical body, the thyroid (Metal Element) directs the liver (Wood Element) in the function of metabolism. Emotionally, there is a clear connection between the Metal Element and the Wood Element. The liver, the body's Wood organ, is associated with the emotions of anger and frustration. One of the easiest ways to release anger and frustration is by communicating and expressing your frustration (in a positive way). The functions of communication, expression, and creativity are all associated with the throat or the Metal Element. So in effect, positive expression (Metal Element) "cuts" or disperses anger and frustration (Wood Element).

Metal Directs and/or Disperses Water

Elementally, Metal is sometimes used to contain Water, but it doesn't always make the best containers or restrainers of Water. We can also look to the Metal-reinforced concrete of great dams that direct and restrain Water. In the physical body, the examples are numerous. The following are just two clear connections between the Metal Element and its relationship to the Water Element. The thyroid (Metal Element) through hormone production is the director of the secondary sex characteristics (Water Element) of puberty. The parathyroid is also connected to the Metal Element, and it is essential in calcium absorption, which supports a healthy and strong skeletal system (Water Element).

Earth Directs and/or Disperses Spirit

Without Earth, there is no place for man to stand and appreciate the heavens. Earth gives us the solid framework of our existence. It has a restraining and directing function when it comes to our spirituality. My shaman tells a story about practicing intensely with a famous and accomplished martial arts master. While they were in a critical place in their practice, the teacher's wife yelled in from the other room to the master that he had neglected to put out the garbage that morning and she couldn't make dinner till it was done. He immediately paused the practice and took the garbage out (his family obligation). This story illustrates the fact that things of the Earth Element—family, motherhood, etc.—always keep us spiritually "grounded." No matter how spiritually high or lofty spiritual place we are in, the baby crying for diaper change, the teenager acting out, or any family emergency or tragedy always restrains and directs our spirituality, putting it in perspective as we attend to the right-now Earthly important family things.

Water Directs and/or Disperses Fire

What is easier to see elementally than the dousing of Fire with Water? In the physical body, the kidneys and urinary system (Water Element) have a direct effect on restraining or dispersing blood pressure and heart function (Fire Element). Congestive heart failure disease is directly caused by failure of the kidneys to function. The kidneys (Water Element) also act as filters for the cleaning and full function of the circulatory system (Fire Element).

Some of the above examples may seem contrite and not very scientific. However, they point to relationships between the organs, glands, and elements. It is the *relationship* that is important. In chapter 6, we will focus on the ways that you as an individual or as a health practitioner can use the relationships of the 7 Element Principles to increase health and function. Remember that health is vitally dependent on the *balance and clear communication* between the 7 Elements and their respective organs, glands, emotions, purpose, etc.

7 Element Chi Time Flow Chart

The Chi time flow chart discerns the approximate time schedule for Lifeforce differentials in the Chi flow throughout the body. Chi remains inside of every cell. However, we also know that the overall Chi or Lifeforce cannot be stagnant and still; it must circulate and course around the organs and meridians. Energy ebbs and flows through the areas of the body in a cyclical pattern based on the 7 Element Crystal. The ideal time for each element is a time of healthy natural increased energy of those organs and glands associated with that element. If that element has deficient or blocked energy, then it will be magnified at the ideal time. So the two-hour time period (see chart) for each element, organ, meridian, or gland will be a time of great vulnerability if weak; or if in excess, it will become too full or blocked.

Practitioners and lay healers may use the chart in various ways. First, it will accent the treatment of any element organ gland meridian if treated at its ideal time. It can also be used to figure out energy imbalances and bring them into balance. For example, the chart can be used for people who have problems waking up in the middle of the night. Suppose a person wakes up every night at two o'clock in the morning. Two o'clock in the morning is the transfer time between the spleen and stomach of the Earth Element. Because two o'clock in the morning is at the height of energy of the Earth Element, which is responsible for digestion, a reasonable hypothesis would be that the person is eating too much, too late, and including refined sugars, which would pump up or energetically overfill the spleen and stomach meridians, waking that person up. This hypothesis can be easily muscle tested out. One answer is to stimulate the element that is the disperser of the Earth Element from the 7 Element principles in the beginning of this chapter, which would be to stimulate parts of the Air Element. This will disperse or restrain the extra energy in the Earth Element organs and meridians. This can be done before bed to avoid the overload and again if you wake up during that time so you can get back to sleep quickly. If you look at the Chi flow chart, the correct stimulating element will be on the opposite side of the chart. In this case, it would mean stimulation of the element from opposite the chart at twelve o'clock noon to four o'clock in the afternoon, which is the Air Element time and meridians.

Another way to use the chart is to "pull" blocked energy. For example, if the problem is between two o'clock and four o'clock in the morning like the above problem we mentioned, you can use the next element on the chart. For example, if the stomach meridian and organ is the location of the excess energy, then stimulating the gallbladder meridian and Wood Element can help "drag" the energy on its path to the next element. Having a map of the energy movement throughout the course of the day can be helpful to the challenges of figuring out energy imbalances. More insight into using this and other methods for healing will be outlined in chapter 6.

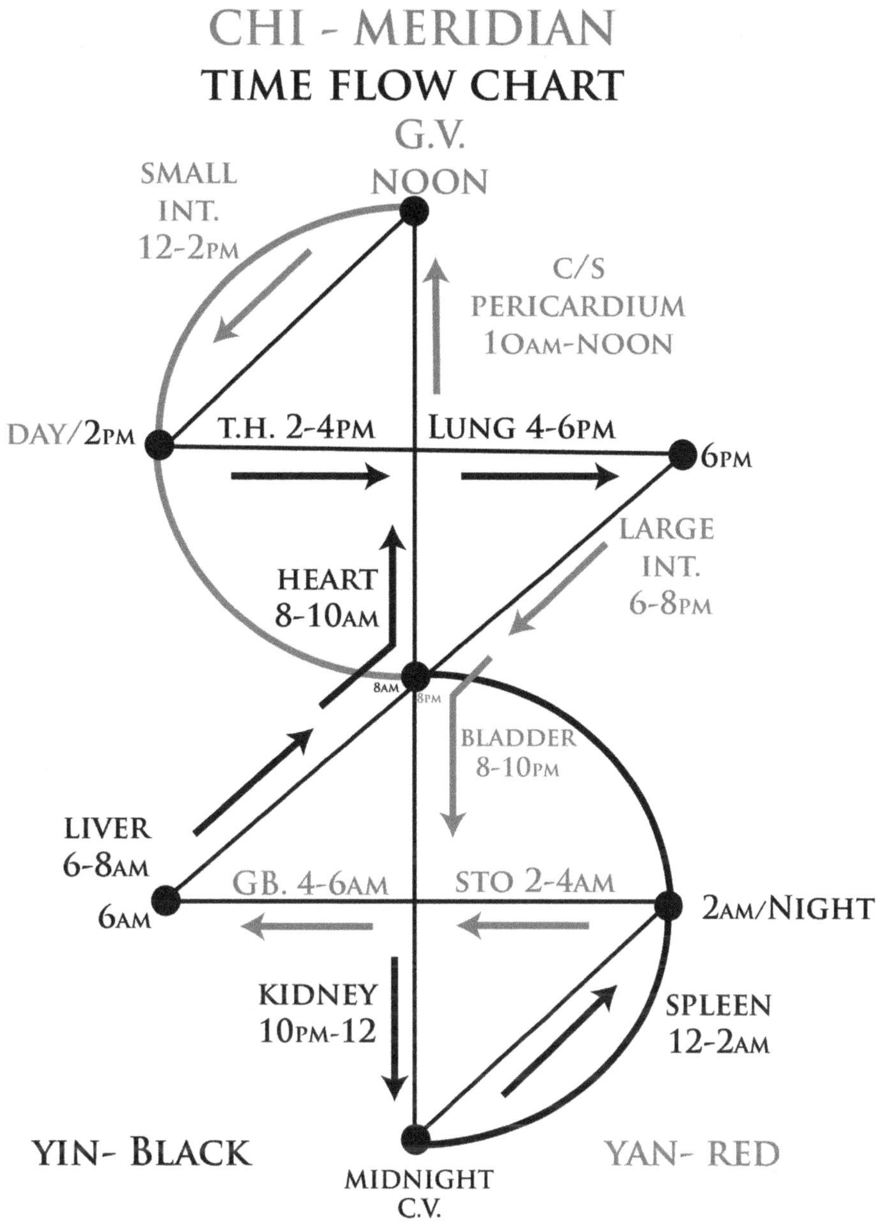

CHI - MERIDIAN
TIME FLOW CHART

G.V.
NOON

SMALL INT. 12-2PM

C/S PERICARDIUM 10AM-NOON

DAY/2PM

T.H. 2-4PM

LUNG 4-6PM

6PM

LARGE INT. 6-8PM

HEART 8-10AM

8AM

8PM

BLADDER 8-10PM

LIVER 6-8AM

6AM

GB. 4-6AM

STO 2-4AM

2AM/NIGHT

KIDNEY 10PM-12

SPLEEN 12-2AM

YIN- BLACK

MIDNIGHT C.V.

YAN- RED

© 2013 DR Harry R. Elia

The Great Season Circle Chart

The great season circle chart is an illustration of the circulation of energy of the 7 Elements during the course of a year, matching up the elements and meridians to the months and the seasons of the year. Just like the Chi time chart shows ideal energy times during completion of an entire day, the great season circle chart shows ideal energy times for each element during the course of an entire year. Matching up your activities to the lower, middle, or high times of the year's energy can be beneficial to making plans and fulfilling achievements. The outside circle shows the overall energetics of any particular time of year. During the winter months, you will see that energy is in its most still time. If you were to be in nature at that time, you could appreciate the stillness of the winter months. To be one with nature means to accord your activities with the energetics of each time or segment of the year. For example, the winter months are for contemplation, gathering your energy, and expending as little energy as possible. To go against the natural flow of energy of the year is to go against the Tao. "Anything which goes contrary to the Tao ceases to exist," as stated in *Tao Teh Ching*. Is it any wonder why the biggest flu season is in the beginning weeks of December? In November, we should be slowing our activities. We should be gathering our energy and expending less during the winter months. But we do not alter our work or daily schedules to be in tune with the shorter days. We even "adjust time" with daylight saving, adjusting nature to fit our schedules instead of the other way around. Modern man, in his modern "wisdom," is also hectically preparing for the big Christmas and holiday season, having more office and personal parties and of course eating more sugar-laden food and drinking more alcohol during this time. Instead of following the course of reducing our energy output, modern man goes against the grain, weakening his body and making it easier for colds and flu. It is a fact that all viruses and bacteria work much better in the warmth than in the cold. So why is the worst flu time in the cold? It is because we go against nature, and we create weakness. Overactivity and exhausting our energy in the time where we should be saving it, coupled with the emotional stress of the season and the cold weather (which increases the need for our body to spend more energy to keep warmer), all helps create our "flu season."

Our ancestors who lived an agrarian culture were much more in touch with nature. The yearly circle is similar to the growth of our crops, planting in the spring months, allowing for full growth during the summer, and harvesting in the fall, only to retreat to the "death" and stillness of the winter. New Year's is the worst time to make resolutions. It is a perfect time for reflections and thoughts of the New Year, but there is no spare energy in the winter. So with little energy, New Year resolutions fall short. The energy of creation and planning is more suited to the early spring and spring months just like planting. You would never plant in the winter. The Water Element months of December and January are for reflection, conservation of energy, and stillness.

The Earth months of February and March are not that much different. There is however a sort of energy vibration in the months of February and March. You can feel the Earth starting to change, even though there is little difference to actually see. This is the time to begin planning. Start to harness some of that Earth energy and to get ready for the coming spring explosion. During the spring months of April and May, all the stillness and energy gathered in the Water months, combined with the vibration and changes of the Earth months, will culminate in the explosion of spring. April and May are the time when there is maximum growth among Earth's plants and trees, and these are the Wood months. This rising energy continues to its zenith of growth, activity, and warmth in the Fire months of June and July. There are weddings, graduations, and family outings. The days are longer giving us more time for activity. The sun's energy around us is at an all-time high. The next two months of August and September should be a slight decline in energy. However, it is much like cresting a mountain and starting down the mountain. As you start down the mountain, it seems easier, and you seem to have much more energy than you had when climbing to its crest. The months of August and September are filled with activity. These Air months are associated with the brain, a fitting time for the start of a new year of school with his promise and high mental energy. The Air Element is connected to the brain as an organ. Our mental activity energy is at a high, leading up to the months of Metal, October and November. The Metal months are a time for culmination of your yearly activities into their "fruitful" climax, just as the coming harvesttime is culmination of the year's crops. The overall energy should start to decline from the summer activity. The Metal months include many awards ceremonies and activities that recognize your yearly accomplishments, culminating in what should be a reflective and grateful November and Thanksgiving, with energy starting to slow down in preparation for the winter stillness of Water.

The month of your birth may be a very telling indication of your personal challenges. Just as in the ideal time of day on the Chi time chart, your month is the ideal energy for that element. It can affect you in a Yin or Yan way. Let's take the example of my birth month of May. Looking at the 7 Element Chart, you will see that the month of May corresponds to the Wood Element and the liver organ. The core issues of this element are fairness, responsibility, and righteousness. The life areas are job career, material wealth, individual achievement, and individual growth. Like myself, if you are born in the month of May, these issues and areas will be both extremely easy and exemplify who you are, or they may be the life challenges that you need to work on (Yin or Yan). For me personally, the issue of fairness has always carried a lot of weight with my psyche. It is an issue that in the past was extremely troubling to me until I learned to let go of the concept that "life is supposed to be fair" and learned to deal with life's realities, fair or not. The ages of the Wood Element are approximately 7 to fourteen, where traits of responsibility individual achievement and growth are formed. In my family, I was the middle child between an older (six years) brother and younger sister. My father was excellent in building things and fixing things around the house, but he always did the projects with my older brother as I was usually too young and just got in the way. I spent those years in total play. My only responsibility was schoolwork, and that came easy to me. Missing out on some of the responsibilities, house chores, and jobs that should have been mine has led me to be a person that always wants to play first and work later. I have to consciously force myself to do the things that I don't want to do before doing the things I want to do. Procrastination is also my middle name. I have struggled with material wealth along with doing things in my career that should have been done years before. My older brother, on the other hand, is quite successful both career wise, financially, and knows how to fix things around the house.

Take a look at the main issues, emotions, life areas, and belief systems of your birth month element and see what your relationship to those things are. Also, look at the other side of the chart to see if the organs, systems, and areas of the body of your element have any special meaning to your health. If they seem not to be problems at all and in fact are the "good" parts of your personality or makeup, then look to the element, which is your element's opposite. In the opposite element, you may find your life's challenges. The opposites are Water/Spirit, Earth/Air, and Wood/Metal.

THE GREAT SEASON CIRCLE

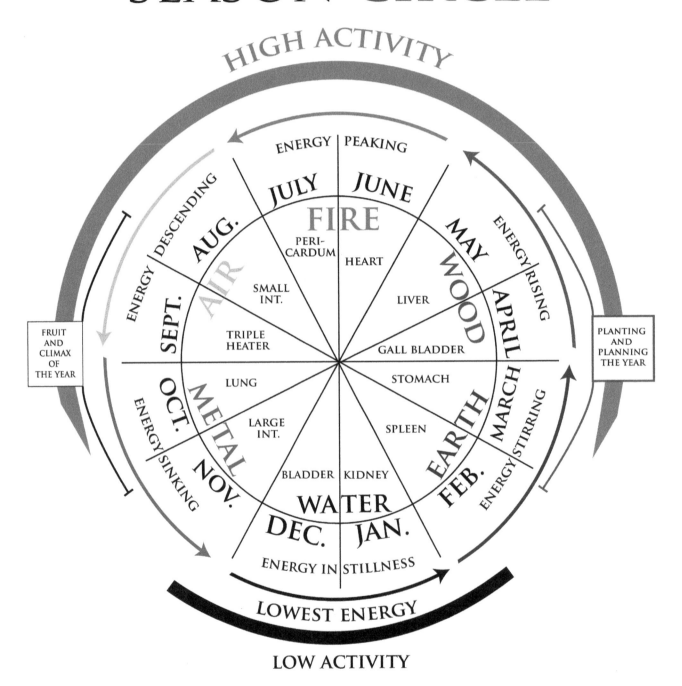

Great season cycle chart

PART II

Healing Yourself

CHAPTER 4

The 7-fold Path to Health and Longevity

In healing yourself, you must first make a decision to *change*. As my healing mentor, Dr. Victor Frank, would say, "If you keep doing what you've always done, you'll keep getting what you've always gotten, *make a change*." If you're concerned about being healthier, your path must be to change. The conscious thought of changing your life and your lifestyle is the first step to being healthier. The true ancient Chinese saying from the *Tao Teh Ching*, number 64 is "A journey of a ten thousand leagues starts from where your feet stand now." So the "first step" is your conscious decision to change. The direction and focus that you direct your mind will influence the Lifeforce Chi body in that same direction. Having a health crisis is like being on a runaway train heading for a cliff. It is not good enough to just close the windows, put earplugs in, and continue to enjoy the ride. You must *drastically change the track* to avoid the cliff. The more serious your health crisis, the more you must change and the stricter you must be in your lifestyle.

Many scientists have studied and tried to create markers for longevity. Most of their work concerns the genetics of mankind. Genetics are only a prediction of your life's *potential* longevity. Using genetics as an indicator of longevity also assumes that the circumstances of food, Air, Water, chemical pollution, and other environmental and emotional factors are exactly the same. Change those factors and increase, circulate, and balance your Lifeforce Chi body and *all bets are off*. This is borne out by an example of a couple that both passed their hundredth birthdays. When the best geneticists exhaustively studied their genetics, it was found that they had some of the worst genetic cancer markers. The male's genes for colon cancer were among the worst. Yet besides one small patch of slow-growing skin cancer, he was alive and healthy at one hundred six. The woman's genes were even worse. If she had taken the test when she was in her thirties, it would have suggested that she remove her breasts because her cancer markers for breast cancer were so significant. Yet these two people survived past one hundred and thrived, regardless of their genetic markers.

There are quite a few examples of pockets of intrinsic people around the world who outlive their modern brothers and sisters and do not have the use of any modern medical or technological "advantages." I have also studied, practiced, and witnessed personally a man named Kwan Sai-hung, who at ninety years old has the facial skin of a baby and is strong in both his body and his mind. Most people in our society that reach ninety are frail and dependent on drugs and artificial means to keep them alive. Kwan Sai-hung is a lifelong practicing Taoist who spent many years on the mountains of China as a Taoist monk and martial arts practitioner. He maintains the "bull-like" strength of men much younger than he into his ninth decade.

I believe as the ancients did that man's longevity potential ranges from one hundred to one hundred fifty years. What we do to our Lifeforce energy and to our physical body reduces that to fifty to seventy years. If we can "turn back the clock" concerning pollution and nutrition and practice ancient virtues and exercises, we can truly extend our genetic predictions. I have briefly outlined 7 areas that if worked on and improved will benefit not only longevity but allow you to enjoy the miracle of your physical and immortal Chi body while you live. The remaining chapters of this book will give you detailed breathing and Chi-Gung exercises.

This book is loaded with information and practices to help you improve your health; however, you must make a conscious effort to change and work daily on the practices that are outlined here. Health, longevity, and being "young when you are old" are all within *your* power.

The 7 Fold Path to Longevity

I. The Ancient Arts of Taoism
   a). Chi-Gung, Tai Chi, meditation
   b). Taoist thoughts on serenity, sex, virtue, and a balanced life

II. Food and Nutrition
   a). Eliminate modern processed and denatured food
   b). Clean the digestive tract and detoxify the liver
   c). Eliminate refined sugar
   d). Food combining and gluttony (overweight)
   e). Juicing and raw vegetables
   f). Whole food supplementation

III. Emotions
   a). Balanced emotional energy
   b). Letting go of the past, unbalanced belief systems, and past hurts
   c). Being present

IV. Air
   a). Breathing, increasing oxygen, and circulating Chi
   b). Clean, Air, trees, and pollution
   c). Chi-Gung and 7 Element Lifeforce Breathing Practices (this chapter)

V. Exercise
   a). Move the Chi
   b). Hard (ballistic) exercises in youth and; soft Eastern exercises for aging youthfully
   c). Walking, the best exercise

VI. Water
   a). Pure, clean Water
   b). Hydrate the system
   c). Water and hydration enhance Lifeforce body communication

VII. Be in Harmony with Nature and Love Yourself
   a). You are the CEO of your body; direct your body and energy
   b). Connect to the rhythms of nature
   c). Open your heart and love yourself and others

1. Ancient Taoist Way of Health and Longevity

> For to be overdeveloped is to hasten decay,
> And this is against the Tao,
> And what is against Tao will soon cease to be.
>> —Lao Tse (John C. H. Wu, translator), *Tao Teh Ching*, number 30

I have placed the "Way" first in my list because I believe it is the most vital pathway to health. The Taoist philosophy of moderation and balance is important to all 7 of the paths to health. The ancient Taoists were masters of longevity. The Taoists thought that longevity was a prerequisite for spiritual growth. Taoist immortality was a long and arduous task, which required time to accomplish. Practicing Chi-Gung, breathing exercises, Tai Chi, meditation, and other Taoist practices, along with Taoist philosophy, helps circulate and balance the vital Chi Lifeforce. Balancing your Lifeforce will increase your vitality and health because the Lifeforce Chi body is the *directing* force for the physical body.

Working on focus and synchronization of the physical body, the energetic body and the mind, through stillness and moving practice, will enhance and balance your Lifeforce. The advantages of Taoist Chi-Gung are powerful antidotes to the sickness and diseases of our modern culture. We now have more diseases than ever in the history of man. We know that longevity has not increased more than a few years in the past few centuries. Remember, it is the birth-death rate reduction from 29 percent to less than 1 percent that raised the longevity average statistics from about forty to seventy. In 1850, if you made it past forty years old, you could expect to live to average sixty-five years. You also would have lived a heartier and healthier life. The ravages of modern diseases like diabetes and cancer were extremely rare before the 1880s. We now have a plethora of autoimmune diseases unknown before the turn of the century (1900). Amyotrophic lateral sclerosis, multiple sclerosis, myasthenia gravis, lupus, rheumatoid arthritis, psoriasis, and also the epidemic of autism, allergies, and asthma, which have become the everyday realities of our modern existence that were not the realities of our forefathers.

> Commitment
> Rice suffers when it is milled.
> Jade must suffer when it is polished.
> But what emerges is something special.
> If you want to be special too,
> then you must be able to stick to things,
> even when they are difficult.
>> —Deng Ming-Dao, *365 Tao: Daily Meditations*

In the later part of this his book, we will focus on 7 Element Chi-Gung, which is based on the *I Ching* and the 7 Element Principles. If you were to make just some of the lifestyle changes in this chapter and faithfully practice a few of the breathing and Chi-Gung exercises for one hundred days, you will change your health and life for the better. Remember, it is not the degree of complexity of your practice but the diligence and the regularity of your practice that is the key to changing and improving your health. The balancing and unity of body, breath, and mind makes Chi-Gung practice the most powerful exercise you can do. The following practices in the next two chapters will give you a simple pathway to improving your health. The practices range from simple and elemental to moderately complex. What you choose to do is not as important as how faithfully and regularly you practice.

When Spirit takes command, the body naturally follows it, and this arrangement benefits all three treasures. When the body leads the way, the Spirit trails along, and this damages all three treasures.

—two-thousand-year-old Wen Tzu classic*

Moderation and balance is a Taoist foundation. Keeping all the parts of your being—physical, energetic, and spiritual—in balance is essential to health. Overextending any part of yourself takes you out of your center and thus is contrary to the Tao. Anything that is not in keeping to the Tao will not last long. The physical body is essentially important to your health. It must be nourished with life-giving food. It must also be exercised to maximize its efficiency and circulate blood and Chi. The energetic parts of you are just as important if not more so. Balancing your emotions, having a loving and positive outlook, practicing virtue just because you are inherently virtuous, and giving service to your fellow man are also essential parts of keeping yourself in balance. Practicing the art of Chi-Gung helps bring together the physical material and energetic spiritual parts of your being. Excess in any areas of your life destroys your balance and hinders your Lifeforce. This includes sexual excess. Which brings us to the Taoist views on sex?

Sexual Alchemy

All the best medicines and good food in the world cannot help one achieve longevity unless one knows and practices the Tao of Yin and Yan.

—Ko Hung

The Taoists revered sexual energy as a powerful physical force. This powerful energy could be transformed to spiritual energy and power. There were two schools of thought concerning sexuality. One was the solo path, and another was called dual cultivation. The solo path was one of celibacy, keeping the virgin sexual energy of youth and transforming it into energetic spiritual power and balance. Many Taoist monks were brought to the mountains during their preteen years of nine to twelve. They were trained in celibate practice, some even being celibate their entire life. Master Kwan Sai-hung is one such person, spending his youth and young adulthood in the sacred Chinese mountains where he was immersed in practice of the Taoist arts and keeping totally celibate. It is important to mention here that celibacy is not just repressing sexual ideas and thoughts completely. In fact, complete repression of sexuality can lead to a loss of sexual energy and cause other psychological problems. The Taoist monks were taught ways to recycle the sexual energy, bringing this powerful energy around the body to replenish all the organs, especially the brain. This path is not an easy one to undertake. Understanding this, the Taoists have another path to work with this powerful energy. In dual cultivation, the energy of man and woman are exchanged, and both partners can circulate and derive energetic benefit from their sexual union.

Female sexual energy was compared to Water, with male sexual energy being associated to Fire. Females also have more abundant sexual energy. Like an ocean, they can draw on their sexual energy without much loss. Being more Yin, the lower physical energy is much more abundant in females. This is evident in the fact that females can support a life inside their womb. I believe this is also the reason why in every culture, females traditionally outlive their male counterparts. Most sexual practice is concerned with men. This is because men's sexual energy can be drained and exhausted. Being like Fire, when it rages, it tends to burn out. So it is important that man burns his Fire slowly and smoothly. The image of a kettle of Water over Fire is often used as a Taoist example of the two sexual energies. The Water in the kettle signifies a woman and the Fire a male. If the Fire flashes and burns very hot but soon dies out, then the Water will just be lukewarm. If on the other hand the Fire burns slow, steady, and long, then the Water will eventually come to a boil. This arrangement will cause a rising steam (increasing spiritual energy) and become useful for cooking or making tea (increased physical energy). Thus, sexual union can become beneficial to both parties physically, emotionally, and spiritually. Training to retain emission as a male is imperative to hold on to vitality. It will also help keep a male's libido and sexual energy strong into old age.

As we mentioned before, women's sexual energy is compared to the ocean. Once the floodgates are open, you can draw from the ocean, and although it can be diminished, it will be difficult to drain. Man's sexual energy is compared to the oil in a lamp. Draw on it too much and it will run out at some point. There are many books on retaining, exchanging, and circulating sexual energy. This topic is far more extensive than can be covered in this book. However, some of the breathing practices in this chapter and in the advanced breathing section may be helpful to you in using sexual energy for health. If you're interested in a more in-depth study of the subject or seriously pursuing using your sexual energy for health and spirituality, the following books may be helpful:

> *Healing Love through the Tao* (There is a male and female version) by Mantak Chia
> *The Tao of Health, Sex and Longevity* (Part II, "The Tao of Sex," chapters 6, 7, and 8) by Daniel P. Reid
> *The Sexual Teachings of the Jade Dragon* by Hsi Lai
> *The Sexual Teachings of the White Tigress* by Hsi Lai
> *Ancient Lovemaking Secrets*
>
> —James W. McNeil
> *The Journey toward Immortality*

The majority of the information in these books concerns itself with the dual cultivation of male and female sexual union. Most of us find ourselves already having had sex or being in a current sexual relationship. There is very little written instruction about undertaking the solo path. You would have to research and connect to traditional Taoist monks like Kwan Sai-hung for that type of instruction. Solo or dual cultivation is entirely up to the individual. You will be better served by the practice that aligns with your philosophy and abilities the best. Both sexes can benefit extensively from the knowledge and practices of the above-mentioned books and thus use the powerful sex drive for Love, increased health, and spiritual growth.

Virtue

> What is meant by this?
> To practice virtue is to selfishly offer assistance to others,
> giving without limitation one's time,
> abilities, and possessions in service, whenever and
> wherever needed, without prejudice concerning the
> identity of those in need.
> If your willingness to give blessings is limited, so is
> your ability to receive them.
> This is the subtle operation of the Tao.
> —*Hua Hu Ching: The Unknown Teachings of Lao Tzu*, number 4

Those who want to know the truth of the universe should practice the four cardinal virtues.

The first is reverence for all life; this manifests as unconditional Love for oneself and all other beings.

The second is natural sincerity; this manifests as honesty, simplicity, and faithfulness.

The third is gentleness; this manifests as kindness, consideration for others, and sensitivity to spiritual truth.

The fourth is supportiveness; this manifests as service to others without expectation of reward.

The four virtues are not an external dogma but a part of your original nature.

When practiced, they give birth to wisdom and evoke the five blessings: health, wealth, happiness, longevity, and peace.

—*Hua Hu Ching: The Unknown Teachings of Lao Tzu*, number 51

The best way that I have to explain what virtue means is to compare it to what we call unconditional Love. To me, virtue means the unconditional Love of all people, all of nature, and also the unconditional Love of yourself. Unconditional Love opens us up to our spiritual potential. Connecting to unconditional Love will Fire up the Spirit in all of us. Loving all people, nature, and ourselves taps into the ocean of Love that is inherent in us all. It is not the right and wrong righteousness of dogmatic religious zealots nor allowing others to manipulate, step on us, and use us but feeling to the core that Love is the calling and *purpose* of our human being existence. Connecting to this core purpose is like turning on the furnace of our home; it warms not only the inside but also offers warmth and sanctuary to all that enter our home. Connecting to the good inside of us may not bring us commercial riches and wealth nor make us famous or successful. However, it can bring peace, happiness, and harmony to our lives. It also protects and develops the spiritual part of our being. It will make our friends and family glad that they knew us, and it is the greatest power of transformation.

What is well planted cannot be uprooted.
What is well embraced cannot slip away.
Your descendants will carry on the ancestral sacrifice for generations without end.
Cultivate virtue in your own person,
And it becomes a genuine part of you.
Cultivate it in the family,
And it will abide.
Cultivated in the community,
And it will live and grow.
Cultivate it in the state,
And it will flourish abundantly.
Cultivate it in the world,
And it will become universal.
How do I know about the world?
By what is within me.

—Lao Tse, *Tao Teh Ching*, number 54

It is my firm belief that human beings are inherently good. If we could get to the very core of our physical, energetic, and spiritual existence, then we would understand the very nature of the Love that is inside of us. We do not just Love; we become Love. This is not to say that there are not corrupted evil people in the world. There definitely are. However, those people have connected themselves to greed, selfishness, and egocentric activities. They see life as a struggle to get what they want and happiness as in the having of things and material wealth. They do not see their connectedness to all mankind and all of nature. They are only concerned with their physical being and their accumulation of wealth and power. Much of what has happened to them since their birth and their familial training have left them out of touch with the core of Love that they possess. The hardships of survival in the poor and the lore of material wealth of the rich sometimes blocks out the Love we are all capable of. In the end, it will be Love that leads us to the pathway of peace, happiness, and harmony. I once heard it said that "a person's challenge in life is the valiant struggle of a spiritual being in a nonspiritual world."

Yes, the attraction of physical pleasure and egocentric accumulation are strong and powerful drives, and all of us have to pay attention to our physical and material survival. But our pathway to true virtue starts by knowing what is enough, learning to enjoy what we have no matter what it is, and giving of ourselves to our fellow human beings unselfishly and without expectation of reward. With unconditional Love, we not only elevate our own Spirit but we may be able to elevate the loving spiritual core of those around us.

II. Food and nutrition

> The True One trusts the natural development of events. He does not bring what is artificial into the realm of the natural.
>
> —Hua-Ching Ni,
> *Attaining Unlimited Life: Teachings of Chuang Tzu*

Food is the fuel for the physical body. The choices you make will end up giving the body more energy or causing the body to lose energy in detoxification and sickness. Remember, it is the Lifeforce in the food that you eat that is important. Your body is not a chemistry lab. It is a living, breathing embodiment of Lifeforce. Yes, the building blocks of the physical body are complex chemicals, but it is the Lifeforce energy that is the underlying all-intelligent force that animates, moves, and creates those chemicals. Biochemicals and DNA are useless without the Lifeforce that creates, animates, and directs them.

Changing what you eat can be the best and fastest way to improve health. You have the choice over what you put in your mouth. Refined sugar and overeating can be very addictive problems. You must find strength and the determination within yourself to change your eating habits if you are to be healthy. If you are having trouble with that, then getting help from an outside source—such as a nutritionist, alternative doctor, or therapist—may be necessary. But remember, *real change* is the only way to significantly change your health.

a. Eliminate all processed and refined food

> In Tao, what is natural and beneficial is right.
> What is artificial and harmful is wrong.
>
> —Hua-Ching Ni,
> *Attaining Unlimited Life: Teachings of Chuang Tzu*

Your liver must detoxify every molecule of any substance that is not found in nature or not in its natural form. Every year, hundreds of new chemicals are created for the food industry. The human body must deal with this onslaught of man-made chemicals. We cannot escape all the toxicity around us. The easiest way to reduce the overwhelming chemical toxicity is to keep from putting toxic chemicals in your mouth. Individually, you may not have control over the pollution in the Air, but you can make a choice to rid yourself of the chemical toxicity in the food you eat. If it is in a box and came from a factory and not directly from a farm, *don't eat it*. If it is a mass-produced commercial product, you can be assured that the original ingredients are so removed from their natural state and so many chemicals have been added in that this "food" no longer has any nutritional value. When you are in the womb, you get your sustenance from your mother. After birth, you get sustenance from Mother Earth. If we take Mother Nature's life-giving substances, rearrange them, take nutrients out, put chemicals and preservatives in, and add synthetic vitamins, that creation is now an abomination of nature, and your Lifeforce will reject it.

I have recently heard a doctor on TV use the word "Frankenfood." His name is Dr. Michael B. Ward, a fantastic Chiropractor and whole food nutritionist, nicknamed the "Blood Detective" for his groundbreaking success in treating autoimmune diseases with whole food nutrition. You can contact him at his Web site at www.intmedny.com.and pick up his new book, *Frankenfood*. This word aptly describes many of the foods that are on our tables now. What if we take apart your body into small parts and then reconstruct those parts back together, adding things that were mechanical and unnatural in the process? Would it still you be *you*? Could we ever truly get back any of the Lifeforce essence that was originally your body? Of course not. Why do we think that we can take apart an organic full-of-life food, then attempt to reconstruct it with artificial flavoring (chemicals), preservatives (which are poisons), synthetic vitamins (also inert inorganic chemicals), emulsifiers (more chemicals), and parts of other foods that were not parts of the original natural life-giving food and think that we have created something that will benefit the body at all? Remember, your Lifeforce is a superintelligence and knows if a substance is natural or doctored. Just because the single synthesized chemical vitamin is put into the product, that does not mean that your body will use it. You would be better off adding grass seed to a food product then adding synthetic chemical vitamins.

Let's discuss vitamins. In nature, *all* vitamins are extremely complex combinations. For example, there are four main tocopherol compounds in a natural organic vitamin E complex. There are also many cofactors along with those four tocopherol compounds when vitamin E is naturally (cold processed) and directly from nature. Real vitamin E from nature includes four tocopherols, plus xanthine, selenium, and lipositols (sometimes called tocotrienols), at least eight compounds in all. It is also a "living entity" in the proper balance that nature supplied it. The Food and Drug Administration considers using only one of those four tocopherols (usually alpha) as vitamin E. That means that a labeled vitamin-E-fortified food may be missing many of the compounds found in a natural vitamin E source. Giving your body high amounts of only a small synthesized fraction of vitamin E is like saying your body needs a complete working computer—hardware, software, power source, and keyboard to function properly—and someone sends you one hundred keyboards and nothing else. Can't make much use of it, can you?

Modern science sees nutrition as simple chemistry, one single compound affecting another. The human body is millions of times more sophisticated and complex than that. The whole natural compound in its natural state is what works. It's like taking the steering wheel out of a car and expecting to drive. You are more than simply chemistry.

When the Lifeforce Chi body encounters a "fake," extracted, or synthetic single chemical vitamin, it is viewed as an "outsider" and must be detoxified. This is not even taking into account the hundreds of pesticides, preservatives, hormones, additives, and antibiotics that are in the modern processed food we consume today. Keeping all your food organic as much as you can is one of the easiest steps to help your body stay pure. Remember that toxic chemicals *are* cancer. Any amount of poison in the food you eat is a problem for your body, and that problem is cumulative during the course of your lifetime.

b. Clean your digestive system

Eating unnatural processed food and overeating will clog and interfere with the digestive process. Some scientists believe that many people have three to five pounds of undigested material in their digestive systems at all times. If the engine of your car is clogged with gunk and the timing is off, no amount of perfect fuel will make it run better. But if you clean and time your engine then add the perfect fuel, your car will run with maximum efficiency. Finding an alternative healer, Chiropractor, or nutritionist who can put you on a digestive cleanse that fits your needs will start you off in the right health direction. A liver detoxification program may also be vital to your maximum physical function. The Standard Process Company has an excellent twenty-one-day "boot camp" liver and stomach detoxification program. I have used this program successfully with many of my nutritional patients looking not only to lose weight but also to increase their health. You can contact www.standardprocess.com for information about a health care provider near you that offers this program or contact my office.

c. Eliminate refined sugar

I have already discussed the problems that refined sugar causes in the body (see glitches in chapter 2). Remember, *refined sugar is a drug, not a nutritional food.* None of you would give your young children strong caffeine, smoke cigarettes at the breakfast table, or sprinkle a little cocaine on your kid's food. But sugar-laden cereal, chocolate breakfast treats, candy bars, cupcakes, and a million other foods with added refined sugar are staples of the American diet we feed to children every day. Eliminating refined sugar from the diet will take a load off adrenaline stress, help the immune system, and add energy to the body in a few short weeks.

d. Food combining and gluttony

> If you look at people, they all seem to be in good health and free from sickness, but in reality, they have in their bodies the roots of illness which have not yet developed. It is regrettable that they only look for pleasures without realizing their mistakes and errors. They do not know that illnesses are caused by excess of food, drink, and pleasures. Their health declines, but they are not aware of their foolishness. When they get ill, they look for medicine when it is too late. They do not realize that inner ailments are latent in their bodies, and when the latter manifest, it is (sometimes) difficult to cure them.
> —Lu K'uan Yu, *Taoist Yoga, Alchemy and Immortality*

One of the ways to help increase digestive function is to adhere to ancient food combining principles. There are many types of food combining programs. The basic premise that you must keep in mind is that meat (heavy proteins) and starchy carbohydrates do not digest together well. Yes, the meat and potatoes may fill your belly and "stick to your ribs," but it means more work for your digestive system. The reason behind this is that protein takes a *very* acidic stomach to break it down while starches dilute the stomach acid, so complete digestion is hindered. The digestive system is like a self-cleaning oven. If it is on and nothing is in it, then it will clean itself. When you continue to overload the stomach, it backs up and jams up. Protein digestion takes a high amount of hydrochloric acid and complex enzymes to break down fully. Carbohydrates on the other hand are mostly digested in the mouth, and when they hit, the stomach may decrease stomach acid. So when done together, the two work against each other, slowing down and inhibiting a full and clean burn up of the material.

Contrary to popular belief, the most common digestive problem and cause of acid reflux is *too little* stomach acid, *not* too much. The Yin-Yan digestive balance is that the stomach must be highly acidic, the mouth slightly alkaline, the colon slightly acidic, and the tissues of the body even or slightly alkaline. Over time, with age and stress, the stomach acid level goes down along with the body (liver and pancreas), producing less enzymes to help break down food. To digest protein, you need high stomach acid. The reduction in stomach acidity, along with the reduction of enzymes to break food down, leaves undigested food in your stomach too long, causing acetic gas to build up. This gas from undigested food is the real culprit in acid reflux problems. By completely shutting down the acid of the stomach, you stop the pain but cause undigested food to enter into the intestines, reducing absorption of nutrients and causing other bowel problems in the long run. There is also recent documented study showing the "purple pill" and other acid reflux remedies can cause osteoporosis after three to six months of use. Seeing a qualified alternative doctor or practitioner who understands these digestive principles and uses digestive enzymes and possibly a substance called Gastrex by Standard Process for the pain will help your digestive problems and get you off lifetime damaging drugs. This balance maintains healthy and complete digestion.

Do your own experiment. If you are fairly healthy (*no serious digestive problems*), just eat meat, fish, chicken (protein), and vegetables at all meals for a while, eliminating *all* refined sugars (all sugar, except unadulterated fruits), processed carbohydrates, and milk and dairy products. *Remember*, this is a suggestion only. If you have any food allergies or digestive diseases at all, *please* seek some professional nutritional guidance. If you are able to follow this plan, your digestion will improve, and you will have more energy and possibly even lose some weight. Combine this with the information on processed foods at the beginning of this section and you're on your way to not only a healthy digestion but also possibly a better weight. I have personally gone from two hundred ten pounds to one hundred eighty pounds (my college weight of thirty years ago) by following that plan for six months. *No* pasteurized dairy products, *no* processed carbohydrates (processed bread, pizza, pasta), *no* refined sugar, and correct food combining as much as possible. I also did a Standard Process detoxification to start, along with a parasite cleanse. My health changed. My blood pressure of which was once two hundred over one hundred dropped into normal ranges (without drugs), and I have maintained my ideal one-hundred-eighty-pound weight for over ten years now.

The Magic Pill

Every few months, you will see advertisements for the "newest scientific breakthrough" to lose weight. A new pill, usually taken once a day, will "melt" away the fat and shed pounds of weight off you. You won't have to change anything. No exercise, no diet, just lose weight. The latest of these discoveries is green coffee beans. They supposedly work so well the pounds will just "fly off." By the time this book is published, no one will be talking about green coffee beans. Once the advertising campaign has sold millions of dollars of green coffee beans, the parent company will be off on its next million-dollar scam. This is also true of the vitamin-of-the-month club. A company will spend dollars on research creating a need for a vitamin, then sell you a cheap synthetic form of that chemical (real vitamins are highly complex, low-potency compounds direct and unspoiled from nature) to amass a fortune and go to another "need" a few months later. Remember, in our capitalistic society, 90 percent of science is bought and paid for by the company or group that stands to make a huge profit from it.

Medical doctors are now offering hormone therapy for weight loss. The plan is to gerrymander hormone balance from the outside in to manipulate the weight. Chemicals, hormones, and drugs that manipulate the body from the *outside in* are doomed to fail because once they are discontinued and no longer used, that patient must still make the lifestyle changes and solve the original cause of the problem; otherwise, real change cannot happen. Staying on drugs and hormones makes you a drug addict, and as most of the scientific follow-up studies have shown, being on drugs and hormones for the long term inevitably will give you long-range, long-term negative side effects. Do you remember the big mistake of female hormone replacement used as a standard medical procedure for over thirty years until the long-range studies came out showing it caused a much higher percentage of cancers after years of use?

There is no easy way. There is no magic pill or secret to health. The secret to changing your health is mindful effort and attention to changing the things that are causing the problems in the first place, which is your lifestyle. Take nourishment and sustenance from the Earth with real whole organically grown food and whole food supplementation. Exercise the mind, body, and spirit. Work on and develop your inner journey to find balance and peace within. The magic pill lies within you.

Gluttony

> To the Taoist, excessive eating and drinking is a sign of unrequited sexual desire… The end result of either excessive eating or emission (sexual) is loss of vital energy.
> —Stuart Alve Olson, *The Jade Emperor's Mind Seal Classic: The Taoist Guide to Heath, Longevity, and Immortality*

> It was our belief that the Love of possessions is a weakness to be overcome. Its appeal is to the material part, and if allowed its way, it will in time disturb the spiritual balance of the man.
> —Ohiyesa Wahpeton Dakota, *Indian Spirit*

Because something is abundant does not mean that we should completely consume it. Knowing what is enough is very powerful. We have been blessed and gifted with an abundant Earth. Running through the Earth's bounty like a pig at a trough is not the way to appreciate our bounty. Destroying Earth's bounty because it is in our way or just because we can is gluttony. When it comes to food, there is also a time when enough is enough. In America, most of us have access to abundant food. The ability to stop eating is important. There are more diseases from excess than from not enough. In the nineties, there was a study comparing the digestive health of students at Mamaroneck High School (an affluent New York school) to the children that were begging on the streets of Calcutta. The scientists were astounded to find more overall stomach problems and more severe digestive disorders in the well-off kids from Mamaroneck High School. The beggars on the streets of Calcutta were starving and had other disease problems due to poverty, but they were better off as far as digestive problems than the fast-food overfed, more affluent Americans.

Overeating and overindulging are many times bigger problems than not having enough. Gluttony connects to the "me first" syndrome of our overindulgent, materialistic society. The physical brain craves more of everything. When our brain connects to material things, pleasure, and excess, it gives these things power over us. We must continue to remember that our thinking physical brain should be under *our control.*

Gluttony also rears its ugly head in the way we treat our environment. It is again a "me first" attitude. We forget that the wealth of the Earth should be treasured, respected, and shared. Personally, we must use only what we need. We should be eating for the energy of our body and the increase of our physical energy to fulfill our lives' purpose, not the overindulgence of our egocentric self.

Start in small ways. Eat slowly and enjoy each bite. Push away seconds. Don't load your plate like it is your last meal. Eat to increase your energy, not to stuff every cell of your body. Moderation becomes the key philosophy. This philosophy can help you in all stages and places in life. Gluttony with food, sex, or owning material goods will always cause problems in the harmony of your physical energetic spiritual self. Remember, it was Jesus who said, "It would be easier to put a camel hair (camel hair being extremely thick) through the eye of a needle than for a rich man to get into heaven."

Juicing and Raw Vegetables

The energy of life is more completely contained in raw vegetables than in any other food. However, if you have spent a good deal of your life eating the Standard American Diet (SAD), you will have to make the transfer from bad to good slowly. Your digestive system is adaptive and will try and adjust to any food, no matter how bad. It will also prepare enzymes as best it can to digest that food. When you change, there will be an adjustment period. Also, the rich enzymatic full-of-life vegetables that you eat will help the liver and may start a natural detoxing process that may be uncomfortable for a while. If your bowels have been unhealthy for a long time, start with cooked vegetables as raw vegetables exercise the colon and other parts of the digestive system. This exercise that fiber-rich foods do is beneficial to the digestive system. But if yours is weak and overloaded for a long time, it will be like making an older person with pneumonia start a strenuous exercise program. Allowing your system to adjust slowly to the strenuous exercise to your colon caused by high-fiber and raw food will be beneficial. Also, if you are suffering from any debilitating digestive disease, please consult your medical doctor and/or a qualified nutritionist before changing your diet drastically.

Another way to enjoy the powerful life-giving energy of organic vegetables and fruits is juicing. It is my opinion that juicers using the whole fruit or vegetable like the "bullet" among others saving all the nutritious substance are better. But all types of juicing can aid the increase of live-giving energy for your health. There are many sources of good juicing practice. Don't be fooled by commercially made juices and smoothies as they are usually concentrated, can contain chemical additives even though they claim to be "natural," and sometimes are made with pasteurized milk and refined sugar. Making your own fresh organic vegetables and fruit juices with *nothing* artificial added is a great way to energize your health.

Drug Therapy versus Whole Food Nutrition Support

"Beating a dead horse."

I want you to imagine that you're a small delivery business over a hundred and twenty years ago. One horse and one carriage would make up your daily delivery business. Imagine if you will, that it was important for your income that the deliveries were made on time. One day, you noticed that your faithful horse was slowing down on the delivery run. This was starting to cause the deliveries to be late and negatively impacting your income. You could start whipping the horse to make him go faster. That would temporarily solve your dilemma and get your deliveries done on time. But what do you think would happen? You would probably have to whip the horse more and more. If this continues, at some point, you would be "beating a dead horse." Never did you try and investigate *why* the horse was slowing down and never did you try to strengthen the health of the horse. For example, was the horse sleeping at night? Disturbances in your barn could be keeping the horse up at night. Did you think to search the route to see if there was something that was disturbing or scaring the horse causing it to slow down? Maybe blinders or earplugs would help? Did you investigate whether the horse was sick or was he eating properly? Did you research food or supplements that might strengthen the horse? Did you search for ways to change the delivery schedule to possibly give the horse some rest in between? I know what you are thinking; maybe the horse was getting old. But even if that was so, doing the above-mentioned things may have helped the horse function closer to one hundred percent. No, you didn't think about that at all. You took the easiest route and just beat the horse. Never searching for *the cause* of the problem and never were you concerned about the long-term effects of your actions.

When you manipulate the "numbers" with drugs, you are essentially doing the same thing. In our pharmaceutical-based medical modern society, the underlying cause of our problems is never sought. We use drugs to manipulate and push our organs to function at a higher rate, bringing our numbers, whether they are blood pressure, cholesterol, or any others, into what we conceive the norm to be. There are already some studies showing that manipulating the numbers with drugs alone does not make a person healthier.

We take the easy way out, "whipping the horse" unconcerned without any thought to the cause of our problem and without any thought to the *positive changes* we should make in our lifestyle, as our lifestyle is probably the cause of the numbers being off the first place. We make no effort to relieve the stress on the organs nor do we make any attempt to help strengthen the organs themselves. Natural organic whole food supplement is how you give the organs of the body what they need to strengthen and function. Manipulation with drugs from the outside in may solve the immediate problem but is a far cry less productive if true health is your goal. Giving the Lifeforce and physical body the proper matrix to flourish can help organs naturally function better. Yes, drugs do solve immediate problems quickly, but they do not solve the cause and, taken long-term, almost always cause negative effects on the body. Yes, if you destroy an organ, crisis care may dictate that you use drugs to help you in your predicament. But drugs in any form do *not make you healthier*. We have been taking cholesterol drugs since the early eighties and blood pressure medication even longer. We spend millions on research, and we have developed tremendous technological surgeries. However, the *rates* of heart disease, cancer, autoimmune diseases, and allergies continue to soar past epidemic proportions. Long-term changes in your lifestyle, nutrition, exercise, emotional balance, and whole food nutrition can help make you healthier.

Remember, if you are facing a serious or life-threatening disease, *please* contact your medical doctor. They are the experts in crisis care. If however you are interested in better health through nutrition, then the following contacts may provide some helpful information.

Web sites:

www. westonaprice.org
www.standardprocess.com
www.localharvest.org
www.mercola.com
www.eatwild.com
www.seleneriverpress.com
www.michaelgaeta.com
www.advancedhealingcenters.com

A *must* read for anyone interested in the historic negative changes in the natural nature of food and vitamins is *Going Back to the Basis of Human Health* by Mary Frost.

Other great books on the subject are:

From Soil to Supplement by Royal Lee D. D. S., who is the genius behind the Standard Process products

The Cholesterol Myth by Uffe Ravsnkov, MD

Empty Harvest by Bernard Jensen DC and Mark Anderson

Another source of good nutrition advice is to order the *Health Alert* by contacting Dr. Bruce West by letter at 30 Ryan Court, Monterey, California. 93940.

Other sources include www.mediaded.com for books like:

The Commercialism of Childhood

Do the Math

Feeding Frenzy

The World According to Monsanto

Also, feel free to contact me for further information or care at my Web site, www.advancedhealingcenters.com or by phone at 201-599-0881.

III. Emotions

I have often said that it would be easier to separate our heads from our bodies than to separate our emotions from our lives. Emotions are a vital part of who we are in this human experience, and it is our emotions that make our human experience unique. Emotions are energy in action. Energy builds up in the Lifeforce Chi body and must be dissipated or circulated. This will happen in a Yan or Yin way. The over emotion will trigger actions of the physical body and force us to act on that emotion (Yan way). The Yin way is for the bottled-up emotion to turn inward and affect us internally, which will also injure our being. Both ways damage the Lifeforce Chi body, then the physical body and are negative to our overall health.

What can we do about it? I have a patient who once retorted to me that "I'm Italian; I can't help it." In some ways, he was right. The problem is not with our emotions but the buildup of unnecessary energy and the "overaction" or internal anxiety caused by that buildup. Why do we overreact? Why are we all a little "Italian"? We over energize and overreact to an event because that event has somehow connected to our personal files, belief systems, or core issues. For example, if you're someone who has a core issue about fairness, then when something in life trips that fairness switch, all hell breaks loose. We all have developed belief systems, most of which were formed between ages zero and 7 (and possibly past lives). We further develop them, positively or negatively as we grow. If our lives' circumstances reaffirm our formed belief system, whether they are in reality true or not, that belief becomes bigger and more powerful. When connected to a current event, something someone says, etc., the reaction is usually inappropriate and larger than it should be. It doesn't matter if we punch that person in the face or we internalize and feel bad inside; we have lost control of our physical and/or emotional body. The loss of control and overaction is what is damaging to our being.

Emotions are like Fire. If we control Fire, we can use it for our benefit. We can cook and heat our homes, and it becomes a positive element in our lives. However, if the Fire gets too big and is not controlled, then it will have destructive power and burn down our home. Emotions are the same. If they are channeled in a positive venue and they are not oversized and out of proportion, we are relatively emotionally stable. We cannot deny our emotions. We must feel them and "sit" with them. It is our reaction or overreaction that causes our troubles. Measured and reasonable reactions are a valuable part of our lives.

If you have an overemotional reaction to a situation, it is caused by what I call emotional cords. As an example, suppose you are playing a beautiful melody on a guitar. That would be an example of a positive harmonious emotion. Now take that same melody and hook up the guitar with a cord connecting it to a speaker as big as your house. The ensuing noise would blow out your eardrums. It is the same guitar and melody; only now the cords have connected it to something in your past, a belief system, or core issue; and it has caused that reaction to be greatly overblown and negative to your health.

To help you be emotionally in balance, you have to find a way to "cut the cords." Remember that the cords are connections to your personal files. They are part of *you*, and it doesn't matter what someone else has done. You will solve the problem by working on *you*. The first thing you can do to disconnect the cords is to fully realize that "it's not personal." Whatever the event or statement, you must disconnect it from "your story" and your ego. An event or negative remark is just that. Don't take it inside. Don't connect it to your insecurities, your fears, and your unworthiness.

I was Catholic as a young child, and during Lent, it was a tradition that there was always a large Lent candle, which was kept lit on the altar at all times. What if someone left a door open and a wind cycled through the church and blew the candle out? The candle represents to me your inner self. If the doors of the church can be selective and let the people in but close when the wind howls, then the candle will always give off its glow. We must not allow events or people to invade us and extinguish our light.

> That is why we must remember the sanctity of our own souls. Our thoughts are private. As long as we are determined, evil cannot sway us. People think that others can read minds or that the gods watch our every movement. No master, no psychic, no God can enter our inner gate if we choose not to let them in.
>
> —Deng Ming-Dao, *365 Tao: Daily Meditations*

Disconnect the stressors from your personal story and personal files and you are taking the first steps to emotional balance and control. It will take some work on your part. You must start to identify core issues and belief systems that you have developed. You must be introspective and focus on *why* you have this reaction. Knowing yourself will allow you to exert some control when a stimuli (event) starts to make your "blood boil." Understanding that this is "your issue" and a belief system that is just in "your head" and not necessarily true progresses you in pulling the plug and disconnecting from your "emotional cord."

Look at the belief systems and core issues on the 7 Element Chart. Depending on your emotional condition, you may need a qualified therapist or shaman to introspectively help you balance your emotional self. There is an old Taoist saying (there always is) that states, "It is better to be in the center of the boat." This means getting close to the railing may be exciting and nice to see things, but if a wave or storm comes, you will be thrown overboard. In the center, you will always be stable no matter what befalls the boat. Emotions are part of you, to be felt and realized. If you can keep in the "middle of the boat" and not overreact, then your physical and Lifeforce Chi body will not be injured, and the positively realized and channeled emotions will increase your health.

Past Hurts

Past hurts can be obstacles to our emotional balance and our overall happiness. These hurts can be inflicted by acquaintances or more damaging if inflicted by the people who are closest to us, friends, family, even our parents. There are many harmful and hurtful situations that we may experience as young children, young adults, and even into our adult years. These situations are almost like wounds to our emotional self. If they come from loved ones and parents, it's as if you were getting stabbed in the back with a knife, and it can be just as painful and damaging as if it was done physically. These past incidences and hurtful things can stay with us our whole lives. They become blocks for emotional balance and our overall happiness. My favorite Taoist writer, Deng Ming-Dao, puts these past hurts in an interesting light.

> You hurt me years ago;
> My wounds bled for years.
> Now you are back,
> But I Am Not the Same

In the past, warriors fought by striking the same points that acupuncturists use. One famous swordsman nearly died in a duel in which his opponent attacked him in such a way. After that, the swordsman became a wanderer and tried to renounce the martial life. Years later, his enemy found him and challenged him to a duel again. They fought. In the first flurry of blows, the aggressors step back in surprise. The swordsman smiled and said, "I have trained for twenty years to move my vulnerable spots." With that, he was finally able to triumph.

Spirituality is a process of inner healing. The wounds of the past can be the greatest obstacles for self-cultivation unless we find them all and heal them. The task can take years, but we must accomplish it.

In many cases, our wounds were inflicted by other people enemies. This is subtle. Our enemies can be others on the street or people much more intimate with us: parents, teachers, siblings, Lovers, and friends.

> If we move away from such people and succeed in our practice, they will have no chance to come back in our lives. How can they? We changed whatever made us vulnerable in the first place.
>
> —Deng Ming-Dao, *365 Tao: Daily Meditations*

So you see, it is by our own self-development and our "licking our wounds" and moving on that we conquer the past hurts that have been inflicted on us. Just like the warrior practices and works harder to eliminate his vulnerable places, we must change and not allow others to stab us with their swords of hate, jealousy, and envy. We also cannot allow past hurts to keep us stuck in an endless cycle of hate or regret. Like the warrior, we must develop, practice, and change ourselves so we no longer are the vulnerable victims of someone else's misdeeds and hate.

Another way to heal past hurts and reduce their impact on us is to see them as challenges that we *had to have* to become the person we are. See it as a lesson that you had to learn. Envision the people that have done hurtful things to you as your teachers that helped you change, overcome, and be a stronger you. Many people have turned around the hurts from their parents in their childhood by becoming the best parents they can be in their adulthood. They learned from the hurts of their past and *did not* pass those hurts on to their children. You will never have complete closure or satisfaction from past hurts. However, emotionally painful situations and people in your past can be conquered by you being the best person you can be. Conquer that hurt by loving and becoming the opposite of the people who have hurt you.

> Markings in clay disappear only when the clay is soft again.
> Scars upon the Self disappear only when one becomes soft again.
> —Deng Ming-Dao, *365 Tao: Daily Meditations*

A third way to help your emotional stability is to "go into your heart." Establishing a "soft" heart and filling your being with unconditional Love will soften and reduce the scars of the past. If you become hard, rigid, and hateful, the scars of the past will increase in their power over you. Only through softness and forgiveness can you overcome and reduce the power of past hurts. Remember, the whole reason you are here on this planet is to experience, share, and give Love unconditionally. It is through unconditional Love that you conquer all. Love the people close to you but also Love your enemies.

One of my favorite Taoist quotes echoes this theme.

> The Sage has no interest of his own,
> but takes the interests of his people as his own.
> He is kind to the kind:
> He is also kind to the unkind;
> For Virtue is kind.
> He is faithful to the faithful;
> He is also faithful to the unfaithful;
> For Virtue is faithful.
>
> —*Tao Teh Ching*, number 49

It is by loving unconditionally that we can transcend our circumstances. Love is the connecting force between the two powers of heaven and Earth. It lies between the Earthly material "po" spirits and the "hun" or heavenly spirits. You are never wrong when you truly Love. This must be real and unconditional Love, not infatuation and the "Love then hate" that we see in our modern-time TV and movies. Remember the ending of the original *King Kong* movie. The main character ends the movie by saying, "It was beauty that conquered the beast." I don't believe it was just beauty. I think it was "Love that conquered the beast." So too can Love conquer your beasts.

There are many self-help books that can be extremely helpful in developing and maintaining your emotional balance. The following books have been extremely helpful to me and may offer key insights for you to establishing emotional balance:

The Power of Now by Eckhart Tolle

The New Earth by Eckhart Tolle

all the books written by Dr. Wayne Dyer

All Your Prayers Are Answered by Dr. Sam Menaham

Zero Limits, the Secret Hawaiian System for Wealth, Health, Peace and More by Joe Vitale and Ihaleakala Hew Len

One of the most powerful practices that I know of is to spend as little as fifteen quiet minutes every morning reading something inspirational. The morning time is the most powerful time for all practice. Instead of reading the newspaper, which is filled with shocking, fearful, and sensationalized material from around the world just to keep your interest, spend fifteen to twenty mindful minutes reading and thinking about your day's purpose. Every day, I read a few passages from ancient Taoist and inspirational texts, digest them, and "sit" with them for a few minutes. This practice has kept me focused on the positive, inspiring me to look for true meaning and to strive for a purposeful loving day, even in the hardest emotional times. Here are some additional books that may be helpful in your positive life's journey:

365 Tao: Daily Meditations by Deng Ming-Dao

Hua Hu Ching: The Unknown Teachings of Lao Tzu by Brian Walker

Law of Attraction by Michael J. Losier

books and tapes by Dr. John Demartini

books and tapes by Deepak Chopra

IV. Air

There are three levels of breath: the physical, the energetic (Lifeforce Chi body), and spiritual. The first is purely a chemical and physical change. When we breathe in, oxygen is distributed throughout the cells of the body, allowing for cellular respiration, and carbon dioxide is exhaled as a waste product. Oxygen is vital to our body's normal function, but it is only one part of what breathing does for us. The second part of breathing is energetic. Fresh Air (unpolluted) has a negative ionic charge. The body tissue is positively charged. When you inhale and exchange Air, negatively charged Air passes through the positively charged body, giving off absorbable energy (Chi). To illustrate this ionic exchange theory, let me ask you a question: If you're driving at night and start to get drowsy, what you do? Open the window. Why? The Air inside your car still has plenty of oxygen in it. You won't pass out even if you are in the car for hours or even days. However, the Air is stale and not charged because you have already taken all the charge out. When you open the window, charged "fresh" Air is let into your car, and the energetic exchange tends to wake you up.

Why do people get drowsy in a full auditorium? Unless the auditorium has a fresh Air exchanger or ionizer in their air-conditioning units, the amount of people breathing the Air won't completely take all the oxygen, but they will take out all the charge in the air. There will be plenty of oxygen, so no one will pass out from oxygen starvation, but there will be no viable Chi left in the air.

Why do people vacation at the shore and in the mountains? In the mountains, the Air is less polluted, and the increased number of trees helps charge and rejuvenate the Chi of the air. Breathing freshly charged and less-polluted Air increases the body's energy and is partly responsible for that "refreshed" feeling a vacation can give you. At the ocean, you are close to the coming together of two powerful forces: the ocean and the land. The dynamic variant of energy of these two forces charges the ionic charge of the sea Air and again allows for a "refreshing experience." If it was just time off from your job that helps recharge you, then both of these vacations would be just as refreshing as sitting in your house or apartment with the same time off. But we all know that that is not true. Our ocean or mountain vacations help pump us up with energy, fresh charged Air, and Chi.

Pollution molecules are large and positively charged. Thus, they "soak up" the negative ionic potential of fresh air. Polluted city Air has much less energy in it then than open-country fresh Air filled with nature's energy-charging trees and greenery. Another difference between our Air now and the Air of the past is the decrease in the amount of oxygen of our modern air. Due to pollution and the reduction of trees and open land, the oxygen content of our modern Air has declined. It is estimated that the Air during the 1850s had 32 to 36 percent oxygen makeup. That percentage has dropped to about 19 percent (almost half) in our modern-day atmosphere. Working together to clean our Air is not just a good thing but an essential necessity.

The Air we breathe makes a difference in our Lifeforce and physical body. Treating pollution as just something we have to deal with in our capitalist society is like playing Russian roulette with your own family. Remember that lung cancer was almost unheard of as a cause of death before 1900. It is now the leading cause of death. In fact, cancer is a disease that is probably ten times more likely since the twenties.

My father, John Rocco Elia, was a good, hardworking, and very wise man. He once said something I will always remember. He said, "It is our job to make the world a better place for the people who come after us." Ignoring the specter of pollution and hiding behind rhetoric and capitalistic politics is damning the future of our kids and grandkids. No matter what your politics, creating a cesspool for our children and their children to live in just does not make sense.

Chi-Gung
New breath,
fresh, clean, full.
Starting at the source,
filling the body with spirit.
Life in all the cells,
vibrating and oscillating
with the universe.

—HE

Chi-Gung breathing is a vital exercise that will not only draw energy into the Lifeforce Chi body but can also help refine and circulate the Chi energy through the Lifeforce Chi body. By changing your breathing patterns alone and breathing fresh charged Air, you will undoubtedly increase your Lifeforce and your health potential. Besides the added potential of connecting and charging your Lifeforce with fresh Chi-packed Air, there is a second way to draw energy into your Lifeforce body. All living things, including plants and trees, have Chi energy. Shamans from the dawn of time have been able to connect to the energy or "spirits" of the animals and all the living forms of nature around us. Connecting and "bathing" your Lifeforce in the Lifeforce of another living entity can increase your energy and health. Anyone who has taken a solo walk early in the morning in quiet Woods can "feel" the energy around them. Even things we call inanimate objects—stones, Earth, Water, mountains, etc.—have intrinsic energy or spirit.

The last part of breathing is the spiritual part. When you draw in breath, you draw Air and energy through your immortal Chi Crystal or Lifeforce Chi body. I believe the Lifeforce body is a crystalline structure. With each breath, we draw in the universal God energy through our own Lifeforce field and into the physical body. With each exhale, we send our inner energy back through our energetic field and out into the universe. If the structure of our immortal Lifeforce Crystal is balanced, open, and loving, then universal energy can come through it on inhalation and light up the physical body with Love, light, and perfect messages. If our physical body is pure and filled with Love, our exhale goes out through the immortal Lifeforce Crystal (Lifeforce Chi body) and sends peace and harmony out to the universe. Any imbalance or negative emotion affecting the structure of the immortal Lifeforce Crystal will cause the incoming universal energy to be distorted and create a "shadow" in the physical body. Any toxin or impurity in the physical body reflects back and distorts the Lifeforce Crystal, which when reflecting our energy back out to the universe gives off a scattered and negative energy. You are different with each inhale and exhale. You are changed either positively or negatively with each breath in, and you have the power to change the universe positively or negatively with each exhale.

Chi-Gung can be a pathway for positive change in your energetic and physical bodies. Chi-Gung focuses the body, breath, and mind in unison. This causes a cessation of thinking and creates a meditative state that allows for the influence of the higher spiritual mind to be realized and experienced. This focused or "empty" mind along with the postures and breathing techniques makes Chi-Gung the most powerful exercise for health, longevity, and the development and balance of the Lifeforce Chi body.

V. Exercise

A moving door hinge never corrodes.
Flowing Water never grows stagnant.

—Deng Ming-Dao, *365 Tao: Daily Meditations*

We have already mentioned the value of Chi-Gung, which is more than a mere exercise. It is a moving meditation, where mind, body, and breath become one. The final section of this chapter and chapter 5 will describe and show you 7 Element Chi-Gung in full detail. I feel that Chi-Gung is the most beneficial exercise you can do, but by no means is it the only beneficial exercise. All exercise has benefits for the body. However, when you use Eastern philosophy of slow, smooth, and soft, you maximize your exercise by focusing and coordinating mind, body, and breath.

All exercise moves Chi by increasing blood circulation. Where blood goes, so does Chi. So this means that all Western exercise will help improve your health. What is the best exercise for you? Besides Chi-Gung and other Eastern exercises, your choice of exercise really depends on you. What is your age? If you are young (twenty-five or younger), competitive exercise or sports, lifting weights, and ballistic-type exercise may be fine for you. As you get older, you must morph from "warrior to sage," meaning you must adapt your exercise to your capabilities and your needs. Doing maximum squats with maximum weight is fine for a football player or for a high jumper, but at sixty years old, it may be too much pressure on your joints for your own good. Running is a great exercise, but long miles of running year after year may tax your joints and body too much. Remember the ancient Greek that ran the first marathon and fell dead right after it. You must always use the Yin with the Yan. If you lift weights, you must also stretch to keep the joints loose and open. Remember, tight muscles and joints block and slow down the vital Chi Lifeforce that runs through all the parts of your body. The looser and more open your joints are, the easier it is for Chi to flow through.

I believe in our later years that stretching and "soft" exercises should make up 50 percent of your exercise regiment. This strategy is borne out by the strength, flexibility, and youthfulness of the Taoist masters I have personally witnessed who have never lifted a weight or run a marathon. So open joints and good range of motion should be one of the goals of exercise. Yoga, stretching, Tai Chi, and other "soft" exercises should make up some part of your daily routine and your health regiment.

Moving the blood and increasing circulation and heart function helps the health of the whole body. Walking is one of the best time-honored exercises. It moves the blood, and because it is soft on the joints, it can be done at any age. In our modern society, many people feel that walking may "take too long." We are always after the quickest and most efficient exercise, and sometimes we miss the point. Walking uses the whole body; it also allows you to commune with your surroundings. You can absorb the sights, smells, and energy of everything around you. Walking in nature bathes you in the charged Air and energy of trees and greenery helps you absorb the Chi that nature has to offer. Remember, it is not what you choose to do but how many days in a row you do it. Working out for two hours once a week is not as good as doing fifteen minutes of exercising every day.

One of my favorite Taoist sayings is "Anything that you do one hundred days in a row changes your life." So pick an exercise program that you like. Take a class at first if you need to. It will force you to be regular, and then you can do the same or a shortened version of your class at home. If you pick something you really like, it will be easier to continue over the long haul. In making exercise part of your lifestyle, you will increase your health and the function of the two bodies.

VI. Water

Being hydrated is an essential need for the body. Dehydration will work to destroy organ function. The first organ to be affected by dehydration is the gallbladder. Dehydration and the toxic processed diet full of trans fats that makes up the mainstream American diet is why gallbladder removal one of the top surgeries in America. The next organ to be affected is the heart. Hydration is vitally necessary for the whole body. It is my opinion that the instantaneous message system of the Lifeforce Chi body is affected negatively by dehydration. Just like electricity travels better through Water, the sophisticated sound-light vibrations of the Spirit body message system functions better when the body is hydrated.

What Water should I drink? Water is a spiritual substance. It cannot be made "better" or improved on. That's like saying, "I know more than God." All the "new" Waters sold with synthetic vitamins and chemical flavors are abominations of nature, and most are detrimental to your health because of the sugar, chemicals, and added synthetic vitamins. Tap Water, on the other hand, has its own problems being full of man-made chemicals and toxins. There are multiple studies showing higher than "safe" levels of all sorts of chemicals and drugs in our drinking Water. It would be in your best interest to have filtered Water for drinking and bathing. Remember, your skin absorbs your bath and shower Water. There are many places to purchase Water and shower purifiers. Check out the Web site www.eWater.com for great shower filters and other interesting Water products. As far as drinking Water, it must be highly filtered. Water should be a pure substance, but ground contaminants and pollutants, such as heavy Metals and a multitude of poisons, are found in most modern Waters used for drinking and washing.

Water also easily holds the frequency of thoughts and emotions. Water and food can be energetically charged with your thoughts of Love. Taking a few minutes to bless, charge with Love, and be thankful for each meal is a simple way to maximize your food and Water benefits.

How much Water? The benchmark I have used in practice is one quart per fifty pounds of body weight. Your personal needs may vary depending on your health as well as your salt intake and eating habits. Eating a processed, high-salt, high-chemical diet may require more hydrating Water. If your diet leans toward vegetables as a main source of nutrition, your Water needs may be somewhat less. There is no need more important in our body than adequate Water hydration. Remember, Water hydrates; all other fluids may not. Things that are high in refined sugar in any form will actually dehydrate the body. I have found in my practice that hydration is inversely proportional to sugar sensitivity. A diet high in refined sugar intake will adversely impact the hydration of the body. This can be proved repeatedly through Applied Kinesiology testing.

When I was a young boy, I loved football and watched any game that I could. Back in the sixties, you never saw a football player come off the field with a cramp. Now modern football players who have far superior physical training are cramping up all over the place on any hot day. The reason is that they are trying to hydrate with sugar-loaded drinks. Back in the sixties, the only thing on the sidelines was Water. Even in the hottest days, there was no cramping. Sugar-laden drinks not only glitch the Lifeforce Chi body, but they may also interfere with hydration of the body. Water is what your body needs to hydrate, nothing else.

As a society, it is essential that we work together to have clean, unadulterated Water for the generations of our children that come after us. Water is a God-given gift. Allowing harsh toxic chemicals to be put into the Water we wash with and drink is insane. Dumping millions of tons of plastics and garbage in our oceans is demented. Regardless of your conservative or liberal politics, making the Earth's Water a cesspool of toxic chemicals serves only to deny health to our children's children. It is time for us as a race to wake up and start the process of making good unpolluted Water a birthright for those who come after us.

VII. Be in Harmony with Nature

> When you are in harmony with the Way, heaven is gentle.
> —Stuart Alve Olson, *The Jade Emperor's Mind Seal Classic: The*
> *Taoist Guide to Health, Longevity, and Immortality*

In this last section of hints for your health and longevity, we must discuss your connectedness to all things. You are a part of nature. In our modern city environment, we are sometimes cut off completely from nature. We can adapt and get used to this aberrant condition, but it is not in our best healthy interest. City dwellers run to the mountains and beaches for holiday. Small grassy city parks fill with people on a weekend and window boxes full of flowers hold testimony to the needs of the city dweller for nature. Artificial light, TVs, and computers create a fake world and keep us up all night with electronic excitement. We fall out of rhythm with the sun, the moon, and the Earth. No matter where you are, you are connected to this Earth with its rhythms and cycles. Being in a natural environment with Earthly rhythms and traditions is healthy for us as humans. We should all be farmers, and at one time in our history, most of us probably were. Farming follows the rhythms of the seasons and the Earth firsthand. Working outdoors in the fresh, charged country Air and literally having our hands in the dirt connects us to the Earth. But alas, we are where we are. To help our health and longevity, we must try to stay in step with the rhythms of nature the best we can.

The 7 Element Chart in this book has a circle of the seasons, which can help you expend or save your energy to match the patterns of the year and nature. Following the patterns of energy of the Earth and the universe is beneficial to your health. Even in the most crowded city area, we must find a park or small backyard to practice our Chi-Gung to absorb even a little of nature's Chi. The rhythms of the day must be kept, so we sleep when it is appropriate and rise in daylight.

Feeling your own body's fatigue point and stopping helps save precious Chi. This fact is most important in preventing a disease state. The leftover energy we save will become healing energy. If you run the human system to the very bottom of the energy tank and hit the "wall of fatigue," you are ensuring your weakness, depleting immunity, and robbing your body of the healing and balancing power it has. I often preach to my patients the 75 percent rule. When faced with a health problem, you must save and store at least 25 percent of your energy for healing. The more severe the health crisis, the more energy that must be shifted to the healing process. No matter how sophisticated your computer is, without any "juice," it cannot work.

This brings up another important health tip: *listen to your body*. When the "oil light" of your body goes on, don't just keep driving. Take a few minutes each day to evaluate how you feel. Meditate on it. If it is not good, you must start to do something to change it *right now*. Waiting and hoping it will go away will not suffice. Spend a little time in meditation about your body and your energy field every day. "See" if anything needs attention and make a plan to work on it. *You* can direct your body's energy. You are the CEO of your body's seventy trillion cells. What happens when the big boss shows up on the assembly line? That's right, everyone "hops to" and at least looks like they are busy working. You are the "big boss" of your body plant. Direct it. Meditate and send gold or white balls of light to any place in your body that needs it. *You* have the power.

The last tip of this section is to Love yourself. We are all different. If you were to compare, there is always someone stronger, better looking, or more successful than you. There are also people weaker, not as attractive as, and less successful than you. In comparing, we always put ourselves down. You are God's individual creation. How can that be bad? You have positives and negatives just like everyone else. You are a unique creation. There is no one exactly like *you*. Comparisons to others are self-defeating. You must learn to enjoy who you are. Celebrate your differences and your shortcomings; without them, you would not be you. Remember, your worth as a human being lies in your unlimited capacity to Love. Search your heart. Practice unconditional Love, the only real power. Unconditionally Love yourself and all the creations of the Great Spirit. Your heart holds an ocean of Love that cannot be emptied in one thousand years. Open up the dam. Let your Love flow outward no matter what the situation you find yourself in. Remember, Love is the Fire of transmutation, taking the physical action and turning it into spiritual tribute. Loving and accepting who and where you are right now can charge the seventy trillion cells with the healing power of creation.

Breathing for the 7 Elements

> During the span of our life, our breath constantly rises upward, until at death the breath finds itself in the throat, not in the lower abdomen as it was during childhood. When young, our cheeks are reddened, joints slightly bent the bones soft, the body is warm, and the breath is natural and concentrated in the abdomen. As we get older, our cheeks pale, joints stiffen, bones become brittle, the body chills, and the breath is concentrated in the chest. The Taoists seek to reverse this and return to a more natural state of health and vitality.
>
> —Stuart Alve Olson, *The Jade Emperor's Mind Seal Classic: The Taoist Guide to Health, Longevity, and Immortality*

Breath literally *is life*. Breathing affects us on all levels. The physical body draws life-giving oxygen from each breath. Every cell uses the vital oxygen for energy. Many studies have drawn conclusions relating to the amount of oxygen we breathe. The more oxygen entering into the physical body, the healthier the cells. However, there is an equally important function of breathing; it also pumps bioelectric energy into the Lifeforce Chi body Crystal.

The physical body is positively charged. Fresh Air is negatively charged. When you breathe Air in, the resulting clash of charges gives a bioelectric energy boost to the Lifeforce Chi body Crystal. When I coached high school wrestling, I would often urge a wrestler to take a short walk outside the gym and take some deep breaths just before his match. I knew that because of the amount of people in the gym, the Air would have oxygen but be devoid of its bioelectric charge. Taking a few deep breaths of fresh charged Air would bring up the wrestler's energy.

The third and vital role of breathing is that it is a bridge that connects the physical and Lifeforce Chi body Crystals to the universal God energy. Your physical body and your Lifeforce energy Crystal change with each breath. Breathing in passes universal God energy through the Lifeforce Chi body Crystal and into the denser physical body Crystal. The more positive or balanced your Lifeforce Crystal is, the more positive and harmonic the messages will be that run your physical body. Exhaling positive, unconditional Love energy from your physical body will help balance the Chi body Crystal and in turn give out to the universe more Love energy. This last phenomenon is one of the reasons that breathing and meditation practices can be so powerful in changing the Lifeforce Crystal and thus changing your health.

Breath is also the force that first connects us to the universal God energy. It is the start of our journey as human being on this planet and in this dimension. It is also the ending. When breath stops, the physical body separates from the Lifeforce Chi body, which holds our consciousness or what some would call our soul. The physical body stays in this world and disintegrates, and the Lifeforce Chi body and consciousness goes on to another world or dimension.

Why use different breaths?

> To exhale from different organs, cleansing the old and inhaling the new,
> to move like a bear and stretch like a bird.
> These are the activities of those who conduct the breath throughout their bodies,
> who practice stretching exercises, develop their physiques
> and seek longevity.
>
> —Taoist saying

There are some powerful and wonderful reasons to do 7 Element Breathing. The first is that developing and exercising different muscles of the diaphragm can lead to an increase in oxygen capacity, which means more oxygen to your cells. Another important reason is that diaphragmatic breathing changes the pressure in the abdominal and the pleural cavities. In essence, becoming a "second heart" as the Taoists would say. The diaphragm contraction helps the heart pump blood to the lower half of the body. A third reason is that developing and coordinating the different muscles and areas of breath allows for combinations and advanced Chi energy movement through breathing exercises.

In 7 Element Breathing, we develop different parts of the diaphragm, ribs, and lungs, using them individually and in unison. This helps us use the whole lung tissue for breathing. What if you only use your right arm and kept the left one in a sling? After a while, the muscles of the left arm, shoulder, and side would atrophy. Your body would become imbalanced. The stagnation of no movement would begin to affect the blood circulation and eventually the cells of the left arm. This decrease in energy circulation could eventually lead to diminished immune response and more chances of disease and problems in that stagnant side.

Suppose we use that same principle of stagnation and apply it to the lung tissue. Using one type of breathing all the time exercises and uses only one area of the lung tissue. The other areas can become stagnant. The lungs must regularly detoxify a massive amount of pollution and chemicals. Spreading around the job to the whole lung could reduce the likelihood of toxins building up in one area of the lungs. I have no hard-research proof to this next assertion, but it seems logical to me that if the whole lung tissue is used for detoxification of Air pollution and cancer-causing chemicals, it may reduce the buildup or overwork in one area of the lung, thus being a possible help in the prevention of lung cancer, the leading cause of death in America.

There are two more powerful reasons to practice 7 Element Breathing. The first one is that each individual breathing practice is elementally and energetically connected to an organ system, energy meridian, emotion, etc. (see the 7 Element Chart). By practicing the specific elemental breaths, we can work to strengthen and balance the specific organs, glands, meridians, and emotions that need our attention. The organ systems serve as great energy junction boxes of the Lifeforce Crystal, and disease is usually connected to one or more of these junction boxes being overloaded or drained. Coupling the breath with specific Chi-Gung stances and movements, we can affect significant positive changes to these organ systems and help heal specific areas of our body.

The second reason is the full development and control of the powerful diaphragm muscle. Developing and coordinating the diaphragm increases our breath strength, aids the heart in pushing the blood, maximizes oxygen capacity, alkalizes the blood, and allows us to change the subtle energies of our being. The culmination of 7 Element Breathing practice is the ability to circulate Chi through the microcosmic orbits. This information is found at the end of this chapter.

The Diaphragm

To understand the different breaths, we must first look at the body's breathing muscle, the diaphragm. The diaphragm is a large, complex, conical-shaped muscle structure that separates the abdominal cavity from the pleural or lung cavity. It resembles a large circular tent and has three main parts.

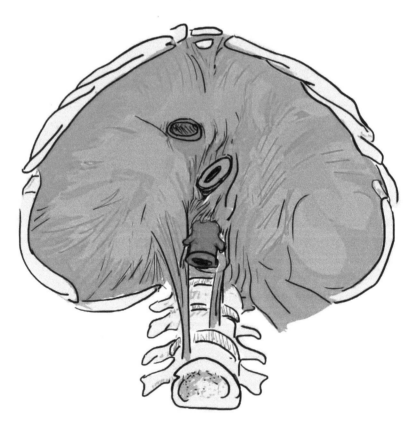

Illustration 25

The anterior or forward part attaches just behind the lower one-third of the sternum. The sides (two sides, making it really four parts) of the diaphragm adhere to the ribs all around. The posterior attachment is multifaceted and attaches to the lower thoracic and the upper one, two, and three lumbar vertebra. There are large central tendons that attach all this muscle in the center, giving the diaphragm its tent-like appearance. When we look at the diaphragm from the front, it has a smooth double hump shape with the heart filling the upper central area.

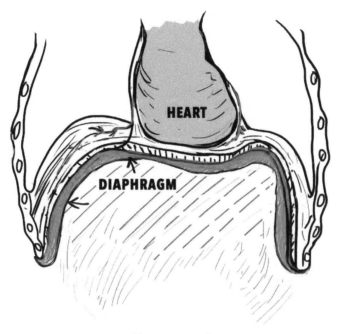

Illustration 26

From the side, the diaphragm has a unique upside down "hooklike" appearance due to the front attachment being higher than the back attachments.

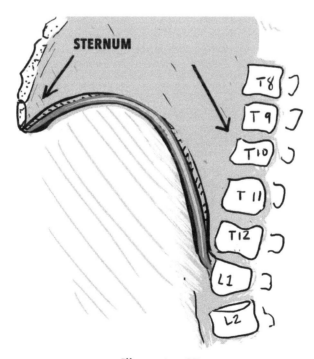

Illustration 27

The unusual shape and diversity of the diaphragm is very important to its function. The shape and complexity of the diaphragmatic muscles gives us the ability to breathe in different ways. There are three different diaphragmatic breaths. Combined with three types of breathing that use rib cage movement, we have six different breaths altogether. All breathing can be classified into two different focuses: the warrior's breath or the scholar's breath. The warrior's breath functions mainly to revitalize the body with energy and Chi. It is powerful and more forceful. Used in concert with the healing sounds and focused on one specific element, this type of breathing can energize a body area or function. The warrior's breath can also be used to clear and cleanse an area or element of the body. The scholar's breath is slower and gentler. It is a more meditative type of breathing, which when combined with visualization can be a powerful tool in healing a body system or element. Some elements and breaths lend themselves more to one type or the other, but both warrior- and scholar-type breathing can be used in each of the 7 Element Breaths.

As we begin to discuss the breathing pattern for each of the elements, please remember that some of the breaths will be easy for the beginner to learn, and some of the breathing techniques will take time and practice to master. Being disciplined to your practice will pay off in health benefits, as you will be able to energize, move, and balance your Chi with 7 Element Breathing techniques. Here are the 7 breaths with organ, gland, and elemental connection.

Seven Element Basic Breathing

To understand the universe, you must study and
understand these things...
Sixth, the Six Breaths wind, cold, heat, moisture, dryness, and
inflammation—which transform the climate in the internal organs.
—Brian Walker, *Hua Hu Ching: The Unknown Teachings of Lao Tzu*, number 61

Element	Character	Alternate Name	Organ Gland
I. Water	Cold	Back or reverse breathing	Kidneys, adrenals, bladder, sex organs, Reproduction
II. Earth	Moist	Belly or abdominal	Spleen, pancreas, stomach digestion
III. Wood	Dry	Side-rib breathing	Liver, gallbladder Detoxification
IV. Fire	Heat	"No breath"—all breaths	Heart, thymus (in between Yin and Yan) Circulation
V. Metal	Inflamed	Upper-back breathing	Lung, thyroid, skin
VI. Air	Wind	Chest breathing	Brain, pituitary Nervous system
VII. Spirit		Side abdominal breathing	Chi body, pineal

I. Water Breathing

The breathing related to the Water Element is back breathing. This type of breathing is sometimes called reverse breathing, as it is the opposite of the well-known belly or abdominal breathing. In water or back breathing, the abdomen is drawn back and folded inward, and the lower spine moves backward. This backward movement of the abdomen and lower spine combined with the compression of the smaller front section of the diaphragm opens up the lower anterior portion of the lungs and compresses Chi backward to the kidneys.

INHALE

Illustration 28

Done in the warrior's way with sound, this breath is an excellent strengthening or cleansing practice. It can be used as a good start to any Chi-Gung or regular exercise workout. When used in the warrior fashion, it compresses Chi in the kidneys and the adrenals. It can be used along with exercising the anal and perineum locks to increase sexual vitality. It can have a compressive effect on the large intestines and force movement and energy flow in those areas. Water breathing can be combined with the ancient Taoists sound "choooo" upon exhaling for more cleansing power, or it can be done silently and slowly in the sage way to strengthen and balance the adrenals.

Directions on Water Breathing

Sit with the spine straight on the edge of a firm chair.

Note: (All breaths can be done in the cross leg seated position on the floor. They can also be done in the standing postures found later in this book, but beginners may be more successful starting in a sitting position on a firm chair). Place your feet flat on the ground, bending the knees about ninety degrees. Always place the tongue to the roof of the mouth and inhale and exhale though the nose.

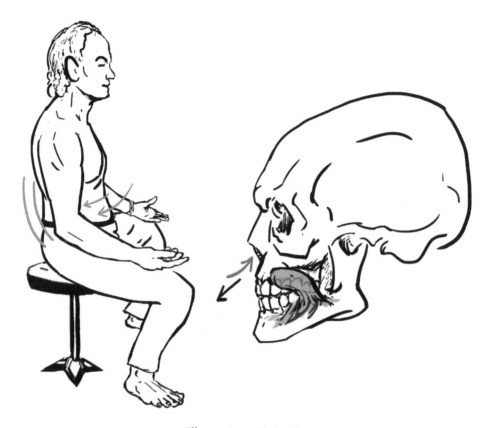

Illustrations 29 & 30

Hands can be on your knees palms down or cradled in your lap or in any comfortable position as long as the elbows are down and the shoulders are relaxed.

Now slowly pull the abdomen back, relaxing and moving the lower back posterior. To start, just move the back posterior and forward again, bending the lower spine backward and folding the abdomen inward a few times. Doing this to start will loosen the lower spine, which is necessary to accomplish the Water breath. Now focus on pressing the sternum down, folding in the stomach area, and moving the spine back, allowing Air to come in. Remember, when you contract the diaphragm, there is no need to "pull" the Air in. You are at the bottom of a "sea" of air. If you change the inner compression by contracting your diaphragm, Air will rush in just as sure as Water will rush in if you were in a car in the bottom of the ocean and you opened your window. Try to relax your chest and use just the compressive force of the front of your diaphragm and the movement of your back to allow Air to rush in.

When learning all the breaths, there is a tendency to have heavy muscular effort. But in time, you would like to have the breathing be almost effortless. Remember also to try and keep inhalation and exhalation smooth and even. There is a general tendency to breathe in slow and exhale fast. Placing the palms of your hands back against the kidneys will allow you to feel the compressive Chi being forced back. This particular breath is very essential in building the kidney Chi, increasing sexual energy, and clearing the energy for other exercise. All breaths should be done in cycles of three, nine, eighteen, thirty-six, or eighty-one. Practice this breath as much as you can before moving on.

Water breath review:

Part 1

In an upright sitting position, move the lower spine backward folding the abdomen inward. In the beginning, do this a few times without concentrating on breathing to loosen up and stretch the spine in preparation for practice.

Try not to drop the head too much.

Part 2

Focus on depressing the sternum down and contracting the front part of the diaphragm, allowing Air to rush in. Remember, in practicing these breaths, there should be little or no sound unless you are using the healing sounds on exhalation.

Return the back and the abdomen to the normal spine straight position. Allow the inhaled Air to be released smoothly. As you increase your practice, there will be less body movement and more isolated diaphragm movement.

In all 7 Element Breathing, the tongue should be held lightly against the roof of the mouth, and inhalation and exhalation should be done through the nose unless you are using a healing sound. This will help slow the breathing down. Remember, start your practice with inhalation and exhalation being even, slow, and smooth.

Locks

There are three locks: anal, abdominal, and neck. These locks are used to hold Chi in after inhalation. They help consolidate and compressed the Chi internally. In most practices, they are released upon exhalation, but in some, they are held slightly even in exhalation. The locks can be used differently with different practices.

Anal Lock

The anal lock is performed by tightening the external and internal anal sphincter muscles. This is a "pull up" action on the urogenital diaphragm. You will also tighten up the buttock muscles. At first, you will be tightening the external anal sphincter. Then as you continue to internally "pull up," you will feel the internal anal sphincter contract. These locks have a myriad of health advantages. Doing this exercise can help reduce night urination and incontinence in many cases. It strengthens the urogenital diaphragm and may also help keep the uterus in good position. It will strengthen and compress the inner organs with Chi.

Inguinal or Perineum Lock

The inguinal lock or sometimes called the perineum lock is performed by pulling in and up on the very lowest part of the abdominal muscles that attach right above the pubic bone. Tightening these muscles at the culmination of inhalation will keep the lower part of the inguinal section of the abdominal muscles healthy and in shape. When performing the inguinal lock, males should feel a draw up of their testicles. Females should concentrate on feeling a tightening or "pull up" of the outer vaginal lips.

Neck Lock

The neck lock is performed by slightly tucking the chin in, usually at the end of inhalation. This should be a smooth and gentle move without tremendous muscular effort.

Do not bunch up and tighten the shoulder and neck muscles. Keep them relaxed.

Power Practice

Using the Water breath (also called the kidney breath), breathe in and out a few times. At the end of your next inhalation, hold the breath and apply the anal lock and the inguinal lock. Maintain the inhale for a few seconds at first, building up over time. Repeat this often as it will build and strengthen with time and practice. By using the water or kidney breath, you can charge the adrenals, kidneys, and sexual organs. The two locks help compress and focus the Chi in the areas of the sexual organs and the kidneys. This practice can be powerful in restoring core Chi energy to the body and increasing sexual energy. It is also extremely helpful in strengthening the urogenital diaphragm and helping bladder or urinary issues.

II. Earth Breathing

The Earth breath is by far the most popular meditative breath. It is sometimes called belly or abdominal breathing. It is also one of the best breaths for increasing oxygen capacity. As water is the spark of life, Earth is its matrix and nurture. Earth breathing promotes long slow inhalation and exhalation. Professional singers have long known about this breathing because it allows them to sustain and hold notes longer.

Directions on Earth Breathing

The sitting posture for this breath should be the same as was described for Water breathing. Sit at the edge of the chair, spine straight and head up. Your feet should be flat on the floor, knees at ninety degrees. To perform Earth or belly breathing, you must first compress the larger back lower portion of the diaphragm. To do this, the abdomen or belly must protrude forward.

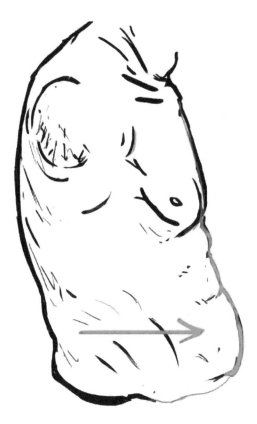

Illustration 31

Pushing the belly forward opens up the larger back and lower portion of the lungs. The Chi or energy moves to the belly and digestive organs. Since the lungs are bell shaped and the diaphragm attaches lower in the back, this breathing brings oxygen to the larger lower back area of the lungs and can greatly increase oxygen capacity and Chi gathering. In the beginning, place one or both of your hands on the abdomen at your umbilicus. Focus on the *dan tien* area completely. Try to keep from raising the chest along with the belly. Concentrate solely on your abdomen, pushing out on inhalation, leaving the chest still through the breathing process.

Earth or belly breath is the foundation for meditation in many ancient traditions. This breath lent itself to more use as a scholar or meditative style due to the large intake of oxygen and Chi, which enables the practitioner to slow down the breath and even pause in between breaths.

Earth Breath instructions:

1. Assume the sitting position, spine straight, feet flat on the floor, hands resting in the lap, elbows down, shoulders relaxed. Focus on pushing the belly out without trying to "pull in" air. Slowly expand the belly forward, contracting the back part of the diaphragm, and allow Air in, breathing through the nose. Remember, the chest should not rise at all; focus only on the movement of the abdomen.
2. Hold the breath for a second, then allow the abdomen to slowly come back to its original place, again exhaling through the nose.

Slow down the process as much as is comfortable and remember that meditation and breathing practice have a reverse tolerance: the more you practice, the less time it takes and the easier it is to receive benefits.

III. Wood Breathing (Side-rib Breathing)

Wood breathing is a fantastic compression breath. It uses the side and back of the ribs to open and close, pressurizing then relaxing the liver, spleen, and pancreas. The liver houses the blood and passes on its energy to the heart. Wood breathing is an excellent morning exercise. The Wood time is four o'clock to eight o'clock in the morning, which coincides with the sunrise and the heightened energy transfer of the Earth as the Yin (night) passes into the day (Yan). Doing Wood breathing at this time helps the smooth transition of energy and blood to the heart and cardiovascular system after a night of rest and slower circulation. This type of breathing uses a movement of the ribs laterally and posteriorly, which opens up the lower lateral sides of both "wings."

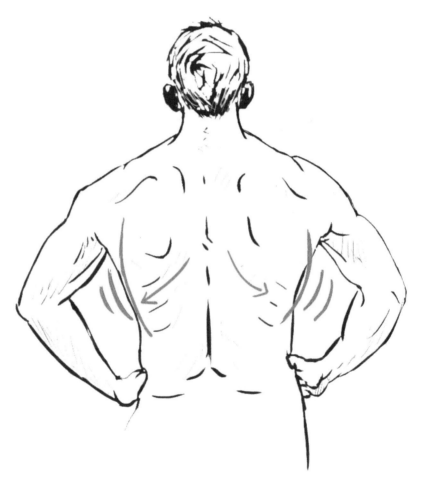

Illustration 32

Wood breathing is considered a rib type of breathing due to the fact that rib cage movement is the action that opens up the lungs for air. Small parts of the upper and outer diaphragm are used, but the main action comes from rib movement. This is the only Yin type of rib breathing, and as such, it is the most generative of the rib breathing types. Be careful to slow down as Wood breathing can generate a lot of heat and uses a lot of muscle energy.

Directions for Wood Breathing:

1. Assume the sitting position. In the beginning, you may place your thumbs at the edges of the lateral rib cage to focus on the proper rib expansion (lateral and posterior).

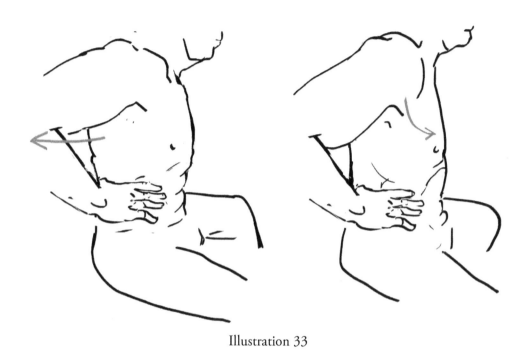

Illustration 33

Rib or Wood breathing is not a common technique, so we are starting in this position to help you concentrate on the outward and backward motion of the rib cage. Be aware that this movement is slight, and even after practice, it may only move an inch or two. If you are tight in the middle and lower back, this breathing type will be hard at the beginning. Once you have practiced and mastered it, your back muscles will be looser and more open. Try not to raise the shoulders at all as this is a common mistake and takes away from the proper practice. Sitting in front of the mirror might be helpful in the beginning. Please note that this type of breathing is not commonly taught and may take some practice to master. Once you have the idea, it can be helpful to assume the Wood breathing position, which is "prayer hands" while sitting, with the elbows slightly forward and the chest slightly concave.

Illustration 34

Direction 2. Inhale and move the ribs out and back slowly.

Direction 3. Exhale allowing the ribs to go back to their original position.

Remember to slow it down, as the muscular effort of rib breathing tends to make you want to go faster and faster. The Taoist's sound for the Wood Element is sshhhhh.

IV. Fire Breathing

Fire breathing is split up into two parts: *yin Fire* and *yan Fire*. *Yin Fire* is the cessation of all breathing. This is the space between Yin and Yan. *Yan Fire* is the use of all breaths together or in a pattern. We will discuss *yin Fire* now and save *yan Fire* for the end when all breaths are taught.

Yin Fire Breathing (Power Practice)

Because the heart is the pathway to spirituality, so the Fire breath is the way to spirit. Yin Fire breathing, which I sometimes call tranquility meditation, is the cessation of breath, meaning the space between inhalation and exhalation or the space between the Yin of inhale and the Yan of exhale. This space between breaths is a uniquely powerful place to stay, even for a few seconds. As my first Taoist teacher Ron Diana often said, "Between emptiness and form, there is Chi; between Yin and Yan, there is spirit." So it is in between the breaths that stillness and emptiness allows us to be aware and be in contact with our spiritual self. For this practice, any of the breathing methods can be used, but Earth or belly breathing is probably the best for beginners. The important thing is to develop your diaphragm and breathing muscles so that you can have long, slow, and smooth inhalations and exhalations. The ability to increase your lung capacity allows you to "sit" in between breaths longer and longer. This practice can be used any time and can settle your Spirit and enhance awareness.

True ch'i (breath) lies within emptiness, which is the breath of neither inhaling nor exhaling.
> —Stuart Alve Olson, *The Jade Emperor's Mind Seal Classic: The Taoist Guide to Health, Longevity, and Immortality*

An ancient immortal said: "Men are subject to birth and death because they breathe in and out by the nostrils and mouth; if they (practically) cease breathing, they will realize immortality." For if the practiser (almost) ceases to breathe, he will achieve major serenity.
> —Lu K'uan Yu, *Taoist Yoga, Alchemy and Immortality*

Directions:

Sitting comfortably in an upright position, use any of the 7 Element breaths to inhale slowly and full and exhale long, smooth, and soft. The inhalation should always be as long as the exhalation. The best breaths for beginners starting this practice will be Earth or belly breathing. Establish a smooth and slow rhythm. After nine full breaths and exhalations, just pause and stop your breathing altogether. Breathing is an automatic and a voluntarily controlled activity. There will be an automatic drive or want to take another breath. Calm your mind and allow your body just to sit in that place between the breaths. You will have enough oxygen if you have been practicing and developing your breathing muscles. You may have to overcome the natural urge to get more Air in. By doing this, you overcome anxiousness about breathing, which is one of the positive aspects of this practice. If fear or anxieties are some of your core issues, then this exercise will help. Anxieties only add to the unsettledness of your spirit. Conquering this anxiety to breathe leaves you with a peaceful and spiritual feeling. You obviously can only sustain this "in between time" for a limited time. Your body will eventually need to breathe. Conquering the fear of no breath and the relaxation found in between Yin and Yan can be extremely peaceful and spiritual. After a good amount of breathing practice, with just one to three deep breaths and exhalations, you will be able to sit comfortably in this position for thirty seconds to a minute. This will calm your mind and hopefully help connect you to your spiritual self.

VII. Spirit Breathing (Side Abdominal Breathing)

(Please note we are preceding in the same order as energy goes though the body. See the time chart.)

The Spirit breath expands the body in all directions. It is the Yan abdominal type breath and capable of high-volume capacity for oxygen and Chi. The control needed to push the center of the diaphragm down will allow for a later, powerful type of breathing I call the immortal breath. Control of the diaphragm to do Spirit breathing is the beginning to a more esoteric ancient Taoist breathing technique called turtle breath. Like turtle breathing, Spirit breathing allows Chi to fill the belt or extraordinary meridians. These meridians are related to the spiritual aspect of the energetic man. The center of the diaphragm lies underneath the heart. So by depressing the center, you may also activate a pumping aid aspect to the heart.

Spirit breathing directions:

Sit in a comfortable upright position either on a chair or with your legs folded under on the floor. Concentrate on the lateral parts of the lower abdominal area. Focus on depressing the center of your diaphragm and extending the lateral (side) aspects of the lower abdomen. This may take some concentrated effort and practice on your part. As with all 7 Element Breathing techniques, with time and patience, you open the door to using your breath to heal your Lifeforce. Although it is simple, nothing is easy without practice. Don't be discouraged initially, as all these breathing techniques are simply skills just like riding a bicycle. With time and a little bit regular of practice, they all will be accessible to you. Upon full inhale, allow your eyes to roll to the top of your head. The forcing of the diaphragm directly down and the rolling and concentration of energy rising to the top will expand the body and energy field in both directions.

VI. Air Breathing (Chest Breathing)

This is the easiest breath for most Westerners as it is the breath most of us use all the time. Air breathing or chest breathing uses the chest muscles to raise the front of the rib cage and allow the upper front part of both lungs to fill with air.

Illustration: chest breathing

The air breath can be very useful in "clearing out your head." In our culture, the brain and our thoughts are almost synonymous with our self-image. We live basically in our heads. A deep chest breath with a forceful exhalation and the sound "heeeeeee" can help you move the energy from your head.

Direction for Air Breathing:

Assuming a comfortable standing or sitting position in a chair on the floor, allow your chest muscles to raise the chest slowly. Full inhalation should feel as if the chest is expanded and as full as possible. When you have reached full inspiration, allow the muscles to relax and the chest to sink back to release the air. There is a tendency to breathe in slow and out fast. Except when noted, there should always be a balance between inhalation and exhalation. For example, if you are doing the cleansing practice mentioned above, then exhalation is quick and forceful. Only do cleansing practice for a few breaths to avoid getting dizzy. Slow, even rhythmic air (chest) breathing is the goal.

V. Metal Breathing (Reverse Chest Breathing)

The Metal breath is probably the least known and practiced of all the 7 Element Breaths. Metal breathing focuses on the upper back and the upper back part of the lungs, an area almost never used in common methods of breathing. Metal breathing is shorter and is harder to draw big volumes of oxygen due to the bell shape of the lungs and the smaller area at the top. However, using an area of your body that is never used and stagnant can only help overall health. Metal breathing is a posterior rib type of breath, and as such, it does not lend itself well to long, slow scholarly-type meditation. It can be tremendously useful with stuck emotions, and it is helpful in releasing grief, sorrow, and sadness, which are the emotions of the throat area and the Metal Element. In learning the Metal breath, it may be helpful to sit in a backless chair (stool) or a chair that only has support at the lower lumbar area. This will allow you the freedom to move the upper back.

Metal Breathing Directions:
Sitting comfortably with hands slightly clenched in fists on your chest, keep the elbows and shoulders down and relaxed. Now push the upper back posterior or backward as you slightly concave the chest. The head and neck will move forward and slightly down. The hands will help you concentrate on pushing the upper back backward.

Metal breathing illustration

135

If your trapezius muscles and upper back are tight as is the case with most people, you will find it difficult to relax and move the upper rib cage backward. Placing your thumbs on your shoulders and doing big circles with your elbows is a good way to move and stretch out the tight muscles before attempting Metal breathing. Continue to stretch and work with this breath. One of the benefits of this type of breathing is that it will help loosen and soften up the tight muscles and stress of the upper back.

Work at the individual breaths until you feel a level of muscle control and ability to stop one and start another. Practice the breaths in the 7 Element energy cycle of Water, Earth, Wood, Yin Fire (pause), spirit, Air, Metal, and Yan Fire (another pause) before beginning again at Water. This practice alone will help you learn all the breaths but more importantly coordinate and move energy through the Lifeforce body.

VIII. Yan Fire Breath (All Breaths)

The Yan Fire breath can actually be done two ways. One way is to do the breaths individually in the 7 Element sequence. That sequence is Water, Earth, Wood, Yin Fire (pause), spirit, Air, Metal, pause again, and start over. Coupling each breath in order with the still postures found in chapter 6 is a tremendous practice for moving energy around all 7 Elements.

The second way to do Yan Fire breath is to do all the breaths at once. That means expanding all parts of the diaphragm and all parts of the lungs at once. You must be able to do all the individual breaths reasonably well before undertaking this and the other advanced breathing practices that are in the later portions of this chapter.

Benefits of the Individual 7 Element Breaths

I. Water

Strengthens the kidneys and bladder. Tightens the urogenital and diaphragm. With the two locks, it is the basis for "shutting the gate" and avoiding male sexual emission (see *Taoist Secrets of Love: Cultivating Male Sexual Energy* by Mantak Chia for the full up-draw practice). Helps replenish weak adrenal energy. Can help foster willpower and perseverance. Can increase the tone of the lower or inguinal part of the rectus abdominis (lower inguinal part of the abdomen) and keep organs of the pelvis from prolapsing.

Simple Energy Meditation:
While doing the Water breath as slow and even as possible, focus your mind on drawing the raw powerful energy of the Earth through the bottoms of your feet. Focus on the bubbling spring point, K 1 (under the foot) and draw the energy up the legs and back on inspiration. When at full inspiration, contract the anal and inguinal locks, packing Chi into the kidneys.

II. Earth

Strengthens the stomach and spleen organs. Improves digestion. Helps foster motility of the small and large intestines, aiding the bowels. Can be used for meditations of all types. Helps increase oxygen capacity with practice. Can increase abdominal muscle tone

Sample Meditation: Sit comfortably and begin belly breathing. Allow the breath to be slow, smooth, and even. After practicing and developing the diaphragm muscle, slow the breath down and use less muscular force so the breathing is more natural. Focus your attention and create a circle around the abdomen with the umbilicus in the center, bringing into the circle images and energies of all your loved ones, both family and friends. Reach out energetically with kindness and concern for all those in your family circle. Connect with the warm energy of all your loved ones. Feel that energy reflect back to you, giving you a warm, contented, full-belly feeling. Continue connecting to the warm energies in your energetic circle of loved ones, bathing the abdomen and stomach with warm Earth energy.

III. Wood

Invigorates the liver and gallbladder organs. Helps push blood from the liver. Liver breathing takes muscular effort and can create a helpful heat and compression in the liver, gallbladder, pancreas, stomach, and spleen.

Done between the hours of six and eight o'clock in the morning, it can be helpful in aiding the heart and circulatory energy. Can help in detoxification of the physical body. Can also be helpful in metabolism and digestive breakdown.

Sample Meditation:

Sit comfortably and develop a slow and smooth rhythm with the Wood or Liver breath. Imagine the entire body being filled with the beautiful green color on inhalation. Continue to fill the entire body and energy field with a beautiful shade of green. Now on each slow exhale, imagine the green color draining from the top of your head down as if your body was full of Water and you pulled the plug and allowed it to slowly to drain. As it drains from each area, "see" it leaving that area pristine and clean of all toxins. As that green color drains down the rest of the body and goes down the soles of feet into the Earth, it carries with it all the toxins, poisons, chemicals, and stress that are inside and around your body, leaving bright beautiful healthy cells in every part of your body.

VI. Yin Fire

Following the Yin Fire practice of breathing in, then exhaling, and staying still, keeping in the middle of the breaths is one of the best practices for stillness of the mind, calming anxiety, and connecting to the Lifeforce Chi body.

Sample Meditation:

Sitting comfortably using any of the breaths you choose (Earth or immortal breaths that is listed under advanced breathing in this chapter work best for this meditation) allow your breath to become even, smooth, and slow. After a series of breaths, exhale slowly and just stop. Focus on the complete stillness and peace in this powerful place between breaths. Sometimes you may get to a place where you feel that your individual self is almost nonexistent, completely still, and void.

VII. Spirit Breathing

Develops the seldom-used center tendon, muscle portion of diaphragm. Increases Lifeforce energy to the belt meridians. Fosters increased spiritual energy. Promotes calmness and insight

Sample Meditation:

Sitting comfortably or standing in the Spirit posture (see chapter 6), begin to use the Spirit breath slowly and smoothly. Always keep inhalation and exhalation even. After you have established a rhythm, start to focus on the expansion of both sides of your abdomen. As your body expands out, focus on the energy field around it. Imagine this energy field getting larger and stronger around your whole body. With each inhale, see the field gets bigger. Continue your breath and pump power into the energy field all around your body. At this point, see a gold or purple color or any color that you associate with strength. Fill the energy field with that color. Now focus on your energy field and see it as a suit of armor, protecting you from all negative energies and diseases. Build a suit of Lifeforce armor that will protect you against anything.

VI. Air Breath

Helps clear the mind. Can increase brain energy and brain Chi Good cleansing breath for mental activity. Helps distribute Chi and mental energy to the body

Sample Meditation:
Assume a comfortable position. Sitting, standing, or lying on your back, use your chest muscles to raise the chest for inhalation and allow the chest to sink on exhalation. Slow the process down, keeping the inhalation and exhalation even. There is a tendency with the air breath to inhale deeply and exhale short and hard. You must slow it down and make it even. With eyes closed, concentrate on the upper half of your body. See the thickness of the energy around the head, the countless minutia of thoughts and worries. Focus on this denseness in the upper half of the body on inhalation, and on exhalation, pull the cloud or energy down the body. At the end of inhalation, pull in the inguinal area slightly as to focus this energy into the *dan tien*. Continue this process until you feel the head and upper part of the body clear of any heavy, dense, and negative energy. Cycling the energies down to the *dan tien* will transform them. If they are heavy, negative ones, allow them to exit the energy field.

VII. Metal Breath

Helps energize the immune system. Helps thyroid and thymus function Loosens tight trapezius and upper back muscles. Good for releasing emotions of grief and sadness

Sample Meditation:
Sit or stand comfortably and slowly compress the chest while inhaling to the back of the lungs. As you inhale, concentrate on the tightness in the upper back muscles and focus on allowing them to soften and open. Feel the tightness of emotion held in the chest, and on exhale, allow that tightness and stuck energies and emotions to release forward into, through, and out of the Lifeforce body to dissipate and be recycled by the universe. It is beneficial to exhale slowly while visualizing the release of stuck negative energy. Continue until you feel an opening and looseness in the chest and back muscles along with a release of emotions. As in all of the rib breathing practices (Wood, Air, and Metal), try to slow the process down as much as possible.

IV. Yan Fire

Using all the 7 Element breaths in sequence will move Chi through all parts, organs, and elements of the body in a way that will increase and circulate the Chi. Using all breaths at once maximizes oxygen potential and can invigorate the whole body. This breathing can increase oxygen capacity and work all the muscles of the diaphragm and the ribs. It also (using all 7 in sequence) can circulate the vital Chi Lifeforce.

Advanced 7 Element Breathing

A note to readers: Before reading and trying the practices in this section, make sure you have a solid understanding and ability with all the breaths taught so far. Practice the breaths in the sequence of Water, Earth, Wood, Yin Fire, Spirit, Air, Metal, Yan Fire, and back to Water. In this way, you will start to help circulate Chi through the Lifeforce body. Before moving on to this section, you should be able to go from one breath to another easily and comfortably. You may also consider the option of moving on to chapter 5 at this point where the basic breaths can be put together with still postures and movement or returning to the advanced breathing after chapter 6. The option is yours.

The Microcosmic Orbits and the Immortal Breath

The microcosmic orbit is a basic and extremely powerful Taoist meditation. It centers on using the mind to move energy around and through two of the major acupuncture pathways. These pathways are commonly called the conception vessel and governing vessel or *ren mai* and *do mai*. The governing vessel runs from the tip of the coccyx up the midline and spine of the back over top of the head down to the upper left. The conception vessel runs from the lower lip down the midline of the front of the body and ends at the pubic bone. It is a common practice while breathing and meditating to focus on the major points using your mind to move Chi up the back over the top of the head and down the front returning to the *dan tien*. There are many great masters far more advanced than myself that have written and taught this powerful meditation. Those of you who are interested can read *Awaken Healing Energy through the Tao* by Mantak Chia as a good source of learning the microcosmic orbit practice. It is my assertion that by developing and practicing the 7 Element Breaths, you can combine breathing with the focus of your mind to lead energy through the microcosmic orbits.

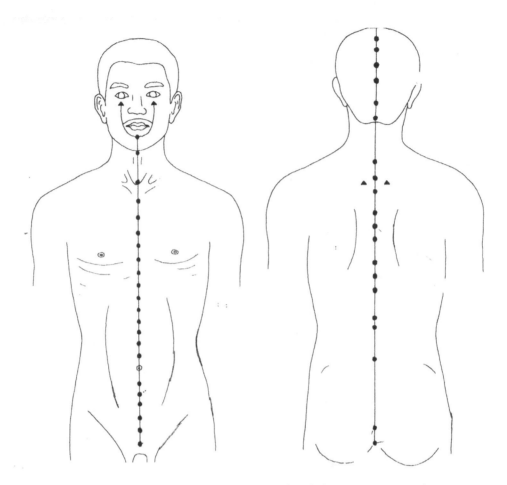

Illustrations of the conception vessel and the governing vessel

I. The posterior microcosmic orbit practice

Moving energy through the microcosmic orbit of the Lifeforce Chi body takes a concentrated effort of both breath and mind. It may seem extremely difficult, but in reality, once you apply yourself with some regular practice, you will have success invigorating your Lifeforce Chi body. I believe that the microcosmic orbit is a physical example of the Tai Chi or Taoist symbol in reality. When positive and negative energetic forces, like two opposing winds, meet each other in equal force and at the same place, there is very little movement of energy. When two forces come together but one force slides under or around and the other force moves over or around in the opposite direction, a whirlwind is created. This is exactly like the creation of the most powerful atmospheric forces of tornadoes and hurricanes. The swirling action magnifies the strength of the forces. It also sets up a sort of self-propelling phenomena. This magnification and ability to self perpetuate power is the reason I feel the microcosmic orbit is such a powerful practice to invigorate the human body's energetic Lifeforce Chi body.

Directions

Assume a comfortable sitting position on the floor or on a chair. If on a chair, move to the very front edge so that there is space between your back and the back of the chair. Now perform the Water breath pulling energy up and backward and use the two locks (anal and inguinal) to help draw back energy. Focus your mind on the *ming men* point at the third lumbar vertebra (see below illustration). Do not fully inhale. Inhale slightly and use the movement and your mind to move energy to the *ming men* spot. Now *continue* to inhale using the Wood or ver breath feeling the movement outward and backward of the lower rib cage and focus your mind to bring energy to the *Chi chung* point (T 11, see chart). Continue your inhale with the Metal breath and focus the mind on the *gia pe* point between the shoulder blades. Now look upward with your eyes (lids still closed) and focus your mind to bring the energy past *yui gen* (jade pillow) up to the crown or *pai hui* point. Feeling the energy above the crown of your head, imagine igniting a bright light above your head. At this point, as a beginner of this practice, you would roll the eyes down, swallow, and exhale focusing your mind on bringing the energy down the front of the body. So the practice would look like this:

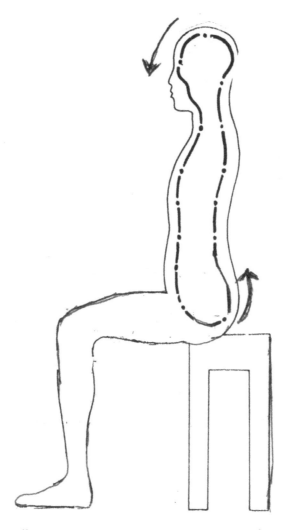

Illustration part 1: Posterior microcosmic orbit

Part II Advanced practice

In time, when you have complete control of all breaths and can extend your inhale, you can perform the following. After you have brought the energy to the *pai-hui* or crown above the head, light the light, and swirl eyes around in a circle nine times to the right and six times to the left. Then continue your inhale using the Air breath (chest), then the Earth breath (belly), and finally the Spirit breath (side abdomen). At this point, you would swallow and pull up a hard on the two locks, anal and inguinal, compacting the Chi in the *dan tien*. Hold for a few seconds then exhale the chest area first, the abdomen second. This practice requires you to have full physical control over the three diaphragmatic and three rib breathing forms. Practice and control of the muscles will allow you the oxygen and time to complete the whole cycle in one inhale. Remember, each breath cannot be forced, and your inhale should only be 20 to 40 percent with each type of breath and not to full capacity. Each breath must be shallow and soft. With time and practice, you will be able to reduce forceful muscular effort. Once you are able to complete the cycle on inhalation, then locking the Chi in the *dan tien*, just short sessions of this breathing will recharge, circulate, and perpetuate Lifeforce Chi energy.

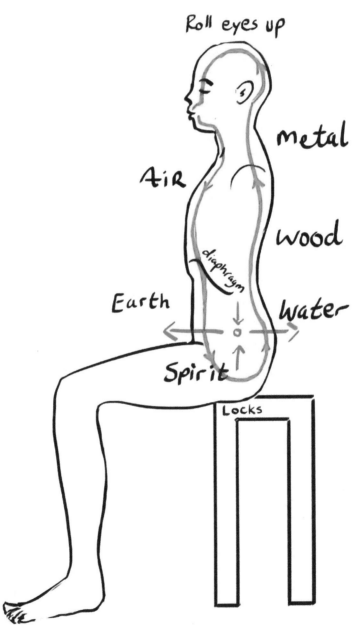

Illustration: Posterior microcosmic orbit using 7 Element Breathing A part 1and B part 2

The Immortal Breath

The immortal breath uses all muscle parts of the diaphragm: front, back and two sides. It is basically putting the Water, Earth, and Spirit breaths together, thus expanding the diaphragm in all directions at once. If you have practiced the individual breaths, it should be easy to put these three breaths together simultaneously. Focus on driving the center of the diaphragm downward. With practice, try to eliminate strenuous muscle effort and make the breaths smooth and comfortable. This breath is sometimes called true breath and has other names in some Taoist texts. This breath is excellent for pumping up the Lifeforce and for any type of meditation.

III. The central microcosmic orbit

There is a second and extremely powerful practice that can allow the Yin energy to rise up the central channel of the body to the crown, join with descending Yan energy from the heavens, and travel back down the center again, circulating and connecting the two halves of your being, Earth and heaven or Yin and Yan. To use this practice, you must become familiar and proficient at all the 7 Element Breaths and the immortal breath (which was discussed previously). Within a short time of diligent practice, the energies of the universe will be at your direction and will add to your health and well-being.

Directions

Sit comfortably and relaxed with your back straight, head up, shoulders and arms relaxed, and hands clasped in your lap in any way comfortable to you. Close your eyes and place the tongue against the roof of the pallet (as in all microcosmic breaths). Breathe through the nose in both inhale and exhale. Start with some smooth and gentle immortal breaths (Water, Earth, and Spirit at the same time), filling up only to about 40 to 60 percent capacity. Remember, try to reduce the muscular effort and make the breathing soft and smooth. Now inhale with the immortal breath using all the diaphragmatic muscles (front, back, and two sides) but only to about 40 to 60 percent capacity. Then start to expand all three of the rib breaths: Wood, Air, and Metal. As you breathe, imagine the energy of the Earth flowing through the bubbling spring point (K 1 bottom of the foot). Again, do not expand to 100 percent capacity. You will feel the energy and Chi rise from the *dan tien* from the lower immortal breath to the higher chest breaths. Focus your mind on this energy moving up the center (spine) of the body and rising to the top. As you expand the ribs laterally and the chest front and back, the oxygen and Chi will move up the body. Employ the two locks, anal and inguinal, as you expand the upper Element breaths (Wood, Air, and Metal). This will help energy rise to the top. The muscular contraction helps push the Chi up. Then bring the energy to the top of the head by rolling the eyes up and using your mind to push the Chi to the crown. Hold the total inhale and locks for just a second or two and imagine the energy of the heavens descending down to your crown. Now begin your exhale by rolling the eyes down and mentally seeing the energy drop down the central channel (spine). Exhale the chest area first, then diaphragmatic or belly area second. Make sure your exhale is through the nose and make it slow and smooth. The exhale should be relatively close in time to your inhale. When exhaling, envision (and later feel) the energy descending down the central channel. As you finish your exhale, relax the anal lock but hold or increase the inguinal lock to pack Chi into the *dan tien*.

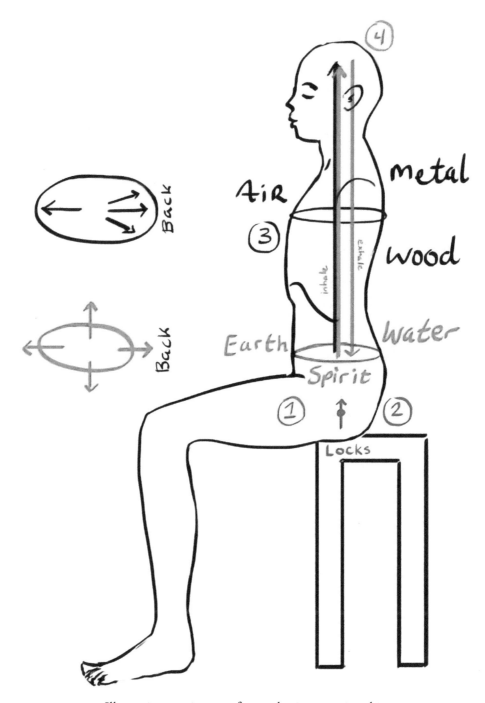

Illustration or pictures of central microcosmic orbit

Conclusion

These two breath meditations are powerful Chi movers and refiners. They are advanced but can become easily accomplished with practice. It is easier to learn from direct teaching rather than from a book, but outlined in this chapter is all you need to know. Your breath is literally your *life*. It is a pump for the Lifeforce energy. It does not need equipment and can be done anywhere there is fresh air. If you have difficulty or questions, please contact me at the e-mail address or phone number that are at the end of the book.

CHAPTER 5

7 Element Chi-Gung

Putting Breath Together with Stillness and Movement

I. Standing Practice

There are two types of ancient practices to generate life-giving Chi: Nei-Gung and Chi-Gung. Loosely translated, Nei-Gung means "internal" practice and usually includes breathing, meditation, and relaxed stillness. Chi-Gung may be thought of as all-energetic generating practices and also includes movement. In the first section of this chapter, we will explore the practice of stillness.

How can stillness generate energy you ask? Standing in stillness is probably the most powerful of all the ancient practices. Chi is always circulating, and the Lifeforce Chi body and the physical body structure is always vibrating or oscillating. By standing in stillness, you can remove tension and stress that can block the subtle but all-powerful Lifeforce, allowing Chi to move freely throughout your physical and energetic bodies. The mind will be the driving force. Singly focused, the mind will help direct the Chi. Taking even a few minutes away from your daily activities for a Chi-Gung routine will reduce your daily stress. When you are still and without thought—save only the focus on your body, breath, and energy—you can connect and be one with all the energy around you. Your individual *story* with its injustice and pain is removed from your shoulders, even if it is just for a short time. For that short time, your whole body can breathe and vibrate in sync with the universe. This may sound difficult and unattainable, but I promise you it is the easiest of all the physical, energetic, and spiritual practices. If you can shut down the physical brain by focusing on your body and breath, you will be transported for a short while to a lighter place where stress does not exist. By removing the interference of your stress *story*, your body and Chi will be free to circulate. Energy from the surrounding trees, plants, Air, and even cosmic energy from space will be able to penetrate your relaxed body.

When the muscle fibers of the body are tight and contracting, these fibers shorten and widen or get fatter.

Illustration of muscle cells, normal and contracted

This closes down the gaps between the cells, which are vital to live transport. When the cells are relaxed, there is space between them for fluid movement (lymph) and Chi movement.

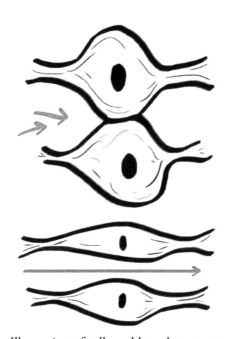

Illustration of cells and lymph passages

This tiny space also allows for the free flow of energy. Tightness and stiffness block not only lymph flow but also vital Chi. The more relaxed a person is, the more energy he can absorb from the universe. Athletes in any sport understand that the tighter they are, the less power they will generate. Watch a baseball player up at bat. He is constantly moving his arms and trying to keep his hands relaxed before the pitch. He knows if he is too tight, his movement will be stifled and his power diminished. All martial artists are well aware of the soft and flexible state that is necessary before any powerful strike or kick. By standing still, you are actually cultivating internal energy and internal strength. Instead of using energy as movement does, you're actually generating and circulating internal energy.

7 Element Standing Practices

In the beginning, stand in each posture as long as you feel comfortable. While you are standing, focus intently on your body position. Shift your position slightly to alleviate any tightness, pain, or uncomfortable feeling. We will begin with the nine simple postures. Use the appropriate breath for each of the 7 Elements in each position. This is a good way to continue to practice the 7 Element Breaths from Chapter 4. It is also a very powerful beginning practice for any workout or just for the start of a productive day. In the beginning, just standing a few minutes in each posture will be helpful. In time, increase the amount of time you spend in each position. Use the 7 Element Chart to connect each posture to the area you wish to focus on, either physically or emotionally. You can focus on one posture if those emotions, core issues, physical glands, or organs need help.

Performing the postures in sequence is a powerful practice that will help energy flow through the whole body. The proper sequence is Water, Earth, Wood, Yin Fire, Spirit, Air, Metal, Yan Fire, and then returning to Water, the beginning. Water is our starting and ending posture due to the fact that it is in Water (embryonic fluid) we all started this life. This is the order I will teach you the standing postures. Learning the standing postures will create a foundation that you can build on for other more advanced practice. These postures should be combined with the specific breathing techniques for each element already discussed in chapter 4.

Getting Started

All standing practices must have a solid base and lower body posture. It is a solid lower body Chi-Gung posture that will enable you to stand for longer periods of time. In the Chi-Gung posture, the sacrum and buttocks are slightly tucked under to straighten the lower spine out. This is accomplished by slightly bending the knees so the knees are approximately over the ball of the foot but no farther. Basically, it is like "sitting" into your standing posture.

I. Yin Water posture: "Cradle the Chi" (use Water breath)

Illustration of Yin Water posture

Stand with the arms down, shoulders relaxed, palms face up as if holding a pot of Chi at the *dan tien*. Elbows are slightly bent, and shoulders are down and relaxed. Hands are at the *dan tien* level (halfway between the pubic bone and umbilicus). Eyes can be open or closed or 90 percent closed, whichever feels better to you. Be careful not to drop the head and shoulders forward in this position and keep the back straight and shoulders and arms relaxed. Use the Water breath, breathing back to the kidneys and include the anal and inguinal locks as discussed in chapter 4.

Remember, the Water breath will increase kidney energy along with the adrenals and the bladder. It is excellent for bringing up your overall energy, increasing sexual energy, helping your willpower, and can be very helpful in urinary problems of cystitis or bladder incontinence.

Sample Meditation for the Water Posture

Assume the Water posture position. Focus on straightening the spine and having the body feel comfortable and relaxed while still erect. Keep the shoulders back and relaxed. Start drawing the abdomen back and allowing the lower back to open. In the beginning, this posture and breathing method will use a lot of muscular effort and some movement. As you practice, you will come to use less muscle effort and more of your mind's concentration to move the Chi. Focus on the bottoms of your feet, pulling Chi from a deep-Water pool under the Earth. Draw the energy up through the bottoms of your feet, through the legs, and back to the kidneys with each inhalation. Then as you exhale and relax slightly, tuck the inguinal area in to pack the Chi into the sexual organs. Imagine and create a small black pearl in the *dan tien*, filling it with the deep-Water energy from under the Earth (if black has a negative connotation for you, use any color that is positive for you). See it pulsate and get stronger with each inhale and exhale. Concentrate your mind to keep the level of energy constant. Then with each inhale, increase the power and strength of that pearl. Continue to breathe, feeling the strength building up in the kidneys, adrenals, and sexual organs. As energy gathers, pack it into the kidneys, adrenals, sexual organs, and the *dan tien*.

II Yin Earth Posture: "Supporting the Heavens"

Stand with feet shoulder width apart, slight bend in the knee, back straight, and sacrum tucked under. Elbows are at the side in contact with the body and hands extended slightly to the side with palms up as if you were holding a sword and presenting it to the emperor. Use the Earth or belly breath, inhaling slowly and exhaling slowly in an even smooth rhythm. Your thigh muscles, not your low back, should hold your weight. As in all breathing practice, keep your tongue against the roof of your mouth, breathing in and out through your nose.

Earth posture illustration

Sample Meditation

The Earth Element is connected to motherhood and family. After you have regulated your breath into a slow smooth rhythm, close your eyes and imagine a circle that your palms are holding up. Feel the Chi between the palms and fingers. In that circle, imagine an image of all those close to you. Envision all your loved ones, those here now and those that have passed on, in a connected circle that you hold up with your palms. Connect them energetically to one another and then connect them to you. Be thankful for any Love and support they have provided. Also, be thankful for the lack of support if that was the case, because it "pushed you out of the nest" and to your own lessons of strength and independence. Feel and project your own energies of Love, warmth, and forgiveness. Allow the circle that connects them and you to get stronger and brighter. "Listen" for subtle messages that your loved ones may have for you. Continue to breathe in Love and connect it to that circle of loved ones. After you feel the strength of that circle and its connection to you, you can bring the images of all your loved ones inside the belly, holding them forever in your being.

III. Yin Wood Posture: "Stand like a Mountain, Grow like a Tree"

Stand with feet shoulder width or slightly wider apart, knees slightly bent, sacrum tucked so that the lower spine and abdomen are straight. In the Wood posture, the weight is slightly to the ball of the foot and not toward the heel like the last two postures. The arms are out to the side, and there is a slight separation from of the arms and the body at the armpits. The palms are down with the pointer finger up slightly from the other ones. Make sure your head is straight up as if a string is pulling it to the heavens. Although the arms are to the side slightly, the shoulders must be back and relaxed. In this posture, you should feel an upright strength. Think of the power of a mountain or tree as you stand.

Wood posture illustration

Sample Meditation

Using the Wood or liver breath, work on having your inhalations and exhalations be totally even and smooth. There is a tendency with the Wood breath, because it is a rib type breathing to shorten the inhale or exhale and to speed up the breathing rather than slowing it down. As your breath is slow and even, start to focus on the spot to the middle of the foot or at the ball of the foot. The pressure in the stance is on the ball of the foot, so focus on the "bubbling spring" point just lateral to the ball on the bottom surface (plantar). Feel the strength of the lower body as solid as the rock of a mountain. Now slowly and gently "grow" the head upward, straightening out the spine. Focus on the strength of the lower body and the openness and freeness of the upper body. Growing out of the Earth, Wood is strong at its base and flexible at its top, just like a tree. Focus on the Yin energy coming from deep in the Earth through the bottom of your feet and up to the solar plexus. Allow that energy to spread to the top of the body, just like the roots of a tree draw the Water from deep in the Earth all the way out to its leaves. You may focus on the emotions of anger, frustration, jealousy, and resentment, pulling those energies from deep in the liver area where those emotions are stuck, then pushing them out through the hands back into the Earth to be recycled and changed. Focus on forcing the heaviness of anger and frustration out of the body into the surrounding and vast universe. Be like a tree that absorbs the carbon dioxide and pushes oxygen out to the surrounding universe. Releasing anger to the universe is like washing the dirt from your body in the ocean; the body is cleansed, and the vast ocean will accept and change the dirt, much like the vast universe will take from you your anger and frustration and transform it from negative to positive. Continue to focus on the cleansing power of this meditation. Pull the energy from the Earth to the liver and the solar plexus with big green Wood energy that will cleanse and push from the body impurities and negative emotions.

IV. Yin Fire Posture: "Hug the World"

This posture is sometimes known as the horse stance or hugging the tree stance in traditional Taoism. This is one of the most powerful postures for allowing healing Love energy to permeate your being. Place your feet slightly wider than your shoulders, then tuck in the sacrum, flattening the belly and the lower spine. With a slight bend in the knees, feel the weight of the body toward the back and heel of the foot and slightly to the outside of both feet. Bring the hands up to chest (heart) height, palms facing inward, the elbows slightly bent and slightly lower than hands. Your arms and hands should form a circle. Make sure to relax the shoulders and allow the arms to sink into the shoulders so there's no tension in the shoulders or the upper back. The palms of your hands should feel as if they are holding a loved one close, the fingers spread comfortably.

Front illustration of yin Fire posture

Sample Meditation

When beginning, the belly breath or Earth breath can be used in this posture. As you become more experienced with 7 Element breathing, this posture lends itself well to the tranquility meditation and/ or the immortal breath described in chapter 4. Again, allow the breath to be even and smooth. When you have created a soft, smooth breathing rhythm, start focusing your mind on the power of the bottom half of the body. Yin Fire is the culmination of all the Yin power, physical structural and solid. However, this raw essence energy must be transformed with Love to be fluid enough to flow upward and connect to spirit.

In this posture, focus on the Love and connection to all things in your life, including your loved ones and all the things of the Earth around you. Connect and give thanks for all the relationships in your life, both good and bad, as they have helped you grow spiritually. "Hug the world" means Love your physical life and body and all your worldly relationships. Allow your heart to be open. Let your Love flow freely to all you contact, both friendly and unfriendly. Open your heart and envision lines of energy flowing in all directions from your heart to all those in your life. Then connect those loving lines to all of nature that is around you. "See" all the people of the Earth connected with your Love. Focus on your oneness with all living things. Love your whole world and hold everyone and everything in your loving embrace.

VII. Yan Spirit Posture: "Hold Heaven in Your Gaze"

The Spirit posture takes the great arm circle of the Yin Fire posture and brings it overhead. The head, neck, and upper back must be open to allow the circle to rise. The hands are kept very loose with the arms sinking into the shoulders to avoid neck tension. The eyes should look into the sky above the hands, "gazing into heaven." It is very important to sink the arms into the shoulders and the shoulders into the trunk keeping the upper back loose and open during this posture. The eyes can be partially or totally open. The bottom half of the body is in the same posture as all before.

Note to reader: In this position, keeping your hands above your head, even if you follow the instructions, may be difficult to hold for long periods of time for some of you. So adjust yourself in your stance properly but understand also that it is fine to spend less time in the Spirit pose than in the other postures.

Illustration of the Spirit Posture

152

Sample Meditation Spirit

Spirit is our undeniable connection to the heavens. It connects us to the subtle but powerful great universal energy that some might name God or the Tao. This posture should foster gentleness and a light, airy feeling of attachment to the higher realms of subtle power. Using the Spirit breath, allow the breath to become smooth, even, and slow. Focus on a tiny bit of white energy sinking from the heavens through the crown and into the center of your brain. This powerful energy illuminates the crystal pineal gland in the center of the brain. Imagine a globe of rainbow colors spreading throughout the whole body from that center. Feel that tremendous rainbow energy affecting and illuminating every area and every cell of your body. Bring that multicolored crystal light to all parts of the body. Feel all the cells of your body vibrating with a higher spiritual and heaven-sent energy that invigorates and strengthens the whole physical body. Then imagine that glow extending around your body with a beautiful blinding white light of energy encircling your whole being. Continue to pump energy from above into that beautiful shell of white light that surrounds you, making it stronger and brighter until it lights up all things.

VI. Yan Air Posture: "Control the Mind, Direct the Body"

The Air posture has the arms and hands at the eye level. Holding the "tiger mouth" circle of your hands right at the eye level, you must make sure again to relax the arms into the shoulders and the shoulders into the body. The "tiger mouth" is created by bringing your thumb and pointer finger together to create a half circle. The elbows are bent about ninety degrees, and the forearms are almost directly vertical. The feeling of the posture is as if you are looking through binoculars seeing the world clearly. The eyes again should be open and focused strongly one object in front of you or partially open to dull your ability to focus on any one item intently. Remember, in this posture, keep your head up and over the spine and not lean the head and shoulders forward. You can bring the circle of your hands as close together or as far apart as feels individually comfortable to you. Remember to keep your shoulders back and relaxed; otherwise, you will build tension between the shoulder blades. As one of the more Yan Elements, air postures do not lend themselves to being held for extremely long times. Use the air or chest breath in this posture.

Illustration of the Air Posture

Sample Meditation

In human existence, the brain and mind are very important. They are the directing forces of the body's actions. Without direction or control, the mind becomes a toolbox for self-destruction. However, when the combination of compassion from the heart and the connection of oneness with all things from the spirit, the mind becomes the force behind the creation of beauty. Use this posture to organize your focus in life. See your actions as positive forces in your life and the lives of others. By focusing intently, clear the brain of its mess. We hold way too much useless information in our brains, stuff that clogs up the focus and function of our lives. Use the Air or chest breath and clear the brain of junk. With each inhale, fill the head with gold energy, and with each exhale, see a clearing wind blowing out all the useless junk and allowing your brain and mind to be clear and focused. With pure focused thought, there is perfect action using little energy but leaving nothing undone.

V. Yan Metal Posture: "Thunder and Lightning"

The Metal posture brings the hands down farther from the air posture, so the elbows and upper arms contact the chest, forearms being directly vertical. The palms face each other but are turned slightly outward at about a forty-five degrees angle. Bring the wrists slightly closer together, as if you were to hold your hands wide to shout. The body again is up right, legs slightly bent, sacrum tucked so the belly and low back are straight and weigh more to the ball of the foot than the heel. It is up to you in this posture to decide if your eyes are wide open and focused, half opened, and glazed or fully closed, whatever is comfortable to you. The breath is the Metal breath expanding the upper back backward, compressing the chest and allowing Air to reach the back upper part of your lungs. There is always a slight amount of movement in the upper body to accomplish this breath, so it does not have the perfect stillness of other postures. However, like the Metal Element, it lends itself to expression and speech. In this element position, you can use sound. As you exhale with your mouth, say a long "aaaahhhhhh" sound and end that sound with a short "uuuummmmm" sound.

This sound does not have to be loud but should be sustained such that you feel the vibration in your chest, throat, and heart.

Illustration of the Metal Posture

Sample Meditation and Thoughts

Metal is the symbol of man's creation. If it is the culmination of development and balance of the previous six elements, then the creative power will be positive and add to the beauty of the world. During this posture, focus on how you can contribute Love and kindness in the coming day's activity. See yourself as a positive force for good and a small piece of the valiant effort to be spiritual in a world devoid of spirituality. Your voice is your tool for your Love and compassion to infect the world. Breathe slowly in and exhale steady and strong saying "aaaahhhhh-uuummm." This can be as soft as or as loud as you need to. Make the "aaahhh" sound last as long as you can, then close your mouth, and make the "uuummm" sound continue. Feel the vibrations of your heart and chest emanating out to the universe. Feel the power of the vibration in your chest. Focus on spreading the limitless Love that you are capable of to everyone and everything.

VIII. Yan Fire Posture: "Embraced the Universe"

The Yan Fire posture brings the hands and arms out and open. Palms are up, and the chest is wide and open. The body's weight, as in all Yan postures, is more to the ball than heel of the foot. The head is up, the eyes open. The upper back and spine are slightly extended (back).

Illustration of the Yan Fire Posture

Sample Meditation and Thoughts

The Yan Fire heart message is the same as the Yin Fire message of Love, compassion, and connection, except on a larger scale. In this posture, you are vulnerable to the flow of the universe. You freely connect and give yourself up to that flow. Be open and a malleable to the will of the universe and your own path or Tao. Like a leaf in the wind, you float on universal energy to land exactly where you are now, which is exactly where you need to be. Using all six breaths together at once (explained in chapter 4), you expand out to the universe in all directions. Open and be aware of where the universe needs you to be and what it needs you to do.

IX. Yan Water Posture: "Return to Stillness"

The finish for the basic meditation and stillness postures is the Yan Water posture. This is very similar to many ending poses in the martial arts and Chi-Gung practices. The hands go down with the palms facing down and into the body, with the thumbs and forefingers forming the heart at the *dan tien* level. The elbows are very slightly bent with the shoulders down and relaxed. The spine returns to normal straight posture, and the head is directly over the spine with the eyes straightforward. The weight is again slightly to the ball of the foot.

Illustration of the Yan Water Pose

Sample Meditation and Thoughts

In the final posture, we return to Water. We finish where we started, in stillness. From the void comes existence, and from existence, we return to the void. In this posture, focus on the energy you have created and circulated due to your practice. You should be able to notice the Chi in your hands and arms. Feel that energy pulsating and sinking into the *dan tien*. Use the Water or kidney breath and remember on exhale to tuck the inguinal area in slightly to pack Chi into the *dan tien*. Be still in between breaths, savoring the stillness of your existence and the peace of being between Yin and Yan.

7 Element Long Chi-Gung Practice

Please don't be discouraged by the word "long." This practice does not have to be exceedingly long. If you are pressed for time, you can complete the cycle and gain benefit in as little as twelve to fifteen minutes of focused practice. Remember that in this practice as in *all* practices, the most crucial point is how many days of the week you practice. Fifteen minutes a day, six to 7 days a week is better than one hour once a week. As in any practice or discipline however, the more time you work, the greater the benefits to your physical body and Lifeforce Chi body.

Starting Water Chi-Gung

Assume a proper stance, sacrum tucked under, back and belly straight, knees slightly bend. Hands and palms down in front of the body about waist high, elbows bent. Then extend the palms to the left. When extending the arm, the elbows should not completely straighten out, keeping a slight bend, which will keep the shoulders and arms relaxed. As the hands extend the left, shift the hips to the right.

Picture 1

Bring the hands close to the body as the hips start to shift to the left.

Picture 2

Continue to rotate the hips to the left and extend the hands to the right.

Picture 3

Continue to rotate the hips and the arms in opposite circles.

Picture 4

As you move, focus internally on the joints of the body. Allow the joints to open and relax. Extend that relaxation to the muscles. Start to "see" your body as Water—smooth, open, and fluid. Make sure you slow the movement down. As any time you move in a circle, there is a tendency to go faster and faster. Continue to focus internally, relaxing and softening the joints. Your hips should move, and the arms should follow. You may imagine that you are in the ocean, slowly moving with the rhythm of the sea. Your eyes may be in three positions: closed, part way open as you can see only the ground, or all the way opened but focused on one spot in front of you. Once you are relaxed, you will start to feel the Tai Chi of the movement. Meaning, your hips will start to move before your arms have completed their movement. When the hips move and start their rotation before the arms finish moving, you are moving in two directions at once. Continue in this movement and "Water" feeling for as long as is comfortable, then start to shorten the circle of movement. As you shorten the circle, you will notice that your arms and hips will go back into sync, and your body will be going in one circle. Make the circle smaller and go slower until you reach the center. When your body is still at the center, close your eyes and feel the Chi continue to swirl around the body

Picture 5 (still pose)

Next, extend the arms to the right side and begin the process of Water Chi-Gung to the other side. The movement and instructions are the same, just to the opposite side. Continue about the same amount of time until you arrive at the same still posture as the last picture. Now you are ready to move to the Earth Chi-Gung.

Earth Chi-Gung

From the still pose, hands form fists, fingers up. And you draw the fists back to the body as you breathe with the belly (Earth breath). As your fists draw back, shift your weight slightly to the ball of the foot.

Picture 1: Earth Chi-Gung

As the hand are drawn under the armpits, they open, palms up, and continue around in a circle to from under the armpits to the front of the body to form a circle with the "tiger mouths together." The weight is slightly shifted to the heels.

Earth picture 2: hands under the armpits

Earth picture 3: finished movement with tiger mouth circle

Begin the movement again. The lower body Elements are slightly more Yin and the upper body Elements slightly more Yan, but all elements have a Yin and Yan in them. The Earth Element represents motherhood, family, ethnicity, etc. Mothers can be strong and fierce in defending their offspring but also tender and soft in loving their children. The beginning of the Earth Chi-Gung has strength with clenched fists, inhalation, and movement to the ball of the foot befitting Yan while the completion of the circle and the exhale should be soft and feminine. As you practice, feel the shift in energy from the beginning of the movement compared to the end of the movement. The circles of this movement represent the circle of the Earth. Shift the body slightly forward and then back with the inhale and exhale. Continue the movement with focus on the hard and soft feelings of both parts of the movement until you are ready to move to the next Chi-Gung.

Wood Chi-Gung

From the end of the Earth Chi-Gung, rotate the circle upward to the solar plexus (beginning of the rib cage) as if holding a challis. Inhale (Wood breathe) and slightly shift the weight of the body to the heels.

Wood picture 1

Now begin your exhale, shift the weight to the ball of the foot, and allow the hands to separate and finish slightly out to the sides with the pointer finger extended. The hands are at the waist and out from the body, and you should feel a little space between the body and the arms.

Wood picture 2

From this position, inhale and repeat the process.

Wood Chi-Gung is simple yet powerful. Focus on the forward and backward shift in motion in rhythm with the breath. The ver area is the great cleanser and detoxifier of the body. As you breathe in, focus on energy rising up the legs. Green is the Wood color. See that color filling up the body from bottom to top. As you exhale, see that color descending as if a plug was pulled and the green color descends back into the Earth, leaving the cells clean and vibrant in its wake. Use the Wood breath and slow the movement down as much as you can. Because of its simplicity, your mind may begin to wander and want to do something different or more exciting. Remember, *you* need to focus and harness your mind to do as you want. Focus internally on the subtle rhythm of the rocking motion and the smoothness of the movement.

Yin Fire Chi-Gung

From the Wood position of hands out pointer finger extended, bring the hands together in front of you fingers pointing to the Earth.

Yin Fire picture 1

Now as you inhale using all breaths at once, bring the "prayer hands" up the center of the body and turn the fingers to the heavens as you pass the heart.

Yin Fire picture 2

Continue to raise the prayer hands to the heavens with your inhalation.

Yin Fire picture 3

Now separate and turn the palms of the hands outward in a downward arc as you begin a long slow exhale.

Yin Fire picture 4

Complete your exhale and return to starting position with hands down, palms together, and fingers pointing downward.

Yin Fire picture 5

This Chi-Gung is good for opening up the heart. In the beginning of the movement, you should bend the knees slightly, lowering slightly toward the ground. As you pull the hands up the body and inhale, straighten slightly with weight shifting from the heel of the foot to the ball. You can imagine pulling up Water or energy from the Earth, bringing it up the body to the top and as you exhale, feeling the energy cascade down and around the whole body. This Chi-Gung should open the chest and shoulders. Smiling as you move should help the heart open. Continue for as long as you choose before moving on to Spirit Chi-Gung.

Spirit Chi-Gung

To make the transition from Yin heart Chi-Gung, start at the beginning of your exhale.

Spirit Chi-Gung picture 1

Now from this position, twist the upper body to the left and push the right hand to the heavens, palm facing the ceiling with fingers pointing backward. Look to the heavens and finish your exhale. At the same time, push the left hand in the opposite direction (down to the Earth), palm also down but fingers pointing to front. Stretch and push the hands in opposite directions with almost full weight on your left side and the left knee bent slightly. The right heel will come off the ground but maintain a firm contact with the Earth and the ball of the right foot, and as you stretch and expand, inhale with the Spirit breath.

Spirit picture 2

Now rotate the hands down, palms toward each other as you rotate the upper body back to center, exhaling as your hands travel down.

Spirit picture 3

Cross the palms in the center and reverse the movement pushing the left hand to the heavens, the right hand down, rotating the upper body to the right, and sinking the weight to the right foot, lifting the left heel but keeping good contact with the right ball of the foot and the Earth, as you stretch and expand breathe with the Spirit breath.

Spirit picture 4

Reverse the process and continue as long as you like. With Spirit Chi-Gung, you should be able to experience the feeling of expanding your body in all directions. With the Spirit breath, you expand to the sides charging the *dai mai* or extra meridian. You are stretching both arms, hands and palms in opposite directions, and the body is twisting and changing weight side to side. Focus on this expanding feeling on inhalation and the energy created when the palms face each other and cross on exhalation.

Air Chi-Gung

To transition from Spirit to Air, we start at the full inhalation and maximum expansion part of the Spirit Chi-Gung.

Air Chi-Gung picture 1
(Spirit Chi-Gung to the left)

Move the right hand down, palm facing away and across the face as you twist the body to the right side. The left hand moves lower across the waist palm also facing away from the body. Start to shift your body weight to the right by shifting your hips to the right.

Air Chi-Gung picture 2

Now continue to "push the air" to the right side as you continue to shift your weight and rotate your hips to the right. Your weight will be more on the right foot, and you can lift your left heel as we did in Spirit Chi-Gung but always keep the ball of the foot in solid contact with the Earth on the side of less weight. Your hands and head should be directly to the right side with hands closer together, palms facing toward the rear.

Air Chi-Gung picture 3

Continue the movement until your hands are behind your body. Your head should be turned all the way to the right with your eyes looking at your hands.

Air Chi-Gung picture 4 (facing backward)

From this position, start to shift your body back to the left by rotating your hips to the left. It is important that you make sure you initiate the movement back to the left with your hips first. In this Chi-Gung, the hips move first, and the hands follow. Hands will change top to bottom with the left hand across the face and the right hand at the waist level, both palms facing away from the body.

Air Chi-Gung picture 5 (beginning push movement to the left)

Continue to "push the air" and move to the left as you exhale. Remember, the hips lead, and the body follows. Continue to the left and begin the cycle again.

With air Chi-Gung, we should try to be like a tree in the wind, the top half of the body has loose and fluid movement while the trunk or lower half of the body twists and moves less. Unlike a tree however, our movement and power are generated from the hips and the shifting of weight from the bottom up, with the branches and leaves (upper body, arms, and hands) following the shift of the lower body and hips. Focus on the fluidness of the movement and look at your hands, paying attention to the smooth shift of weight and change of hands. This movement is called "pushing the clouds." Inhale with the air (chest) breath as you sink and turn backward and exhale as you push across the front. With your exhale, you may choose to make the "whoosh" sound. The fluidness and breathing should help clear the mind if you can fully focus on the feeling of the movement.

When you feel you have stayed "in the wind" long enough, you can start the transition to the Metal Chi-Gung by shortening and slowing the movement little by little. Bring the movement to the front of the body, so you are now not twisting backward but staying in the front and going side to side.

Air Chi-Gung picture 6

Continue to make the movement slower and smaller (as you did with Water Chi-Gung) until your hands are chest high at the center of the body. Now you are ready to shift to Metal Chi-Gung.

Air to Metal picture 7

Metal Chi-Gung

Start by pulling the hands to the chest as you breathe with the Metal breath (reverse chest breath). The hands should be facing each other in open and very loose fists. Your weight should shift back to your heels as you breathe and draw your hands to the chest, elbows into the body.

Metal Chi-Gung picture 1

Reach full inhale and pause for a second and start the sound "ssssss" (as if letting Air out of a tire) and finish the sound with "shoooooo" (like saying shoe but drawn out) as you let your arms and hands completely relax and drop down. Your hands show swing back and forth slightly by themselves. Let this natural movement continue as you also continue your exhale and return the upper body to a straighter stance.

Metal Chi-Gung picture 2

From this position, draw the hands back up to the first Metal position and star your inhale and the movement again from the beginning.

Metal Chi-Gung represents the Metal area of the throat and upper chest along with the lungs. Our lungs perform the vital act of breathing, taking in what we need and letting go of what we no longer need. Life is very similar. We take in and covert what we want and need, but too often, we hold on to and don't let go of what no longer serves us. As you breathe in and then exhale, focus on the relaxation of the body, the involuntary movement of the arms, and the feeling of "letting go." Focus on the "things," both physical and emotional, that you need to let go. Continue as long as you need to.

Yan Fire Chi-Gung

From the resting exhale phase of Metal Chi-Gung, circle both arms outward and upward in a great arc. Inhale as you raise the arms up and out using all breaths at once.

Yan Fire Chi-Gung picture 1

Continue the great arc and your inhalation until the hands touch high over the head, palms together.

Yan Fire Chi-Gung picture 2

Now bring the "prayer hands" down together, touching the lips (upper and lower) as you start your exhale.

Yan Fire picture 3

Continue to exhale and turn the fingers and hands downward with the heels of the hands in contact with the body until the fingers and hands point downward and rest below the hips. Sink slightly to the ground by bending the knees slightly. Your exhale should be completed, and your eyes and head should be focused downward following the hands.

Yan Fire Chi-Gung picture 4

You are now ready to start the movement over opening the hands and arms to the outside and beginning to raise them and inhale.

Yan Fire Chi-Gung is the second heart Chi-Gung. Because the heart is the great connector, Lifeforce rises up through the heart on the way up and goes back through the heart on the way down. Both Fire Chi-Gungs are great for opening the heart. If there is sadness, do just both Fire Chi-Gungs together to open the heart. In Yan Fire Chi-Gung, we are "grabbing" and pulling all the energies of the heavens, the stars, planets, sun, moon, and the entire universe into our bodies, bringing it down though our bodies and into the Earth. We become conduits for the great powers of the heavens and the Earth.

Focus and feel the power of the universe coursing through and down your body. Continue as long as you feel comfortable doing.

To transfer to the final Chi-Gung, change the final exhale part of Yan Fire Chi-Gung and separate your hands as you exhale, moving the hands down with the palms facing the Earth and the fingers pointing to one another, hands slightly away from the body.

Yan Fire Chi-Gung picture 5

And Yan Fire Chi-Gung picture 6

Yan Water Chi-Gung

From the above position of the last picture, keep the fingers pointing to each other with the palms to the Earth and rotate them to the outside, moving your hands in a circle to the outside. As you begin the circle, move the hips backward and inhale using the Water breath.

Yan Water Chi-Gung picture 1

Complete the outward circle as you exhale and bring the hips forward to meet the hands.

Yan Water Chi-Gung picture 2

Your body and weight should shift slightly from heel on inhale and backward hip movement to the ball on exhale when the hips come forward and meet the hands. This movement should be fluid and rhythmic but slow. As you relax into the movement, you will feel the urge to slightly sway side to side. This is the beauty of Yan Water Chi-Gung, it is fluid and slow movement in three directions, forward and backward, side to side, and in a circle. It is called "smoothing the pond," the idea being to circulate all the Chi created around the body. Keep the rhythm slow and focus on relaxing the joints and muscles.

Continue as long as you wish. When you are ready to finish, allow the hands, palms up, to cross in front of you. Then with a big inhale, circle the arms upward (identical to the beginning of Yan Fire Chi-Gung) and meet the fingers overhead.

Finish picture 1

Finish picture 2

Now begin to exhale, bringing the hands down, fingers pointing to each other, and palms facing the Earth.

Finish picture 3

Continue your exhale and move the hands down to the final resting position.

Finish picture 4

Close your eyes and remain in this position for a few moments. Focus and feel the energy of your palms. Pay attention to the area of the body that vibrates. Focus for a few moment internally and feel the energy and Chi of your body. When you are ready, breathe deeply, exhale, and open your eyes.

Thank you. You have completed the cycle that is the 7 Element Chi-Gung. With time and practice, the health benefits and relaxation will grow and grow. Learning from this book is not as easy as learning in person. But with continued practice, you will begin to "feel" the movements, and they will become full of life and as familiar as an old friend.

Good luck on your journey.

PART III

Healing Others

CHAPTER 6

Using 7 Element Healing for Healing Others

Each healer is simply a conduit between the person needing to be healed and all of life.
Healers are bounded by the degree of their own consciousness.

—Stephen Lewis

Using 7 Element Healing for Healing Others

The 7 Element concepts can help you enhance your own health and the health of others. The main concepts of balance and the laws of relationship between the organs, systems, glands and meridians can be used with any healing modality or technique. Understanding full versus empty and support versus direction dispersal, you can work to balance the energetic Lifeforce Chi body and thus change the physical body. The categories and parts that belong to each element—organ, gland, meridians, system, purpose, emotion, etc.—from the 7 Element Chart can help you focus on the elements and areas that you may need to balance. Using the 7 Element laws drawn from universal principles (see chapter 3 and later in this chapter), you can use the healing techniques that you know to help others.

Before you attempt to help others, you must work on developing and improving your own health. Chapters 4 and 5 of this book includes a variety of practices to increase your own health. To heal, your health does not have to be perfect, but you must however be on a path of healing, self-discovery, and self-development. Your compassionate heart must be open. Your mind and character must be in an open and "soft" state. Your physical and energetic bodies must also be soft, open, and compassionate to serve as a conduit for universal energy.

The most important characteristic of the healer is commitment to his or her patient. The investment in their patient's well-being and having an open, loving, and accepting heart are vital. Yes, a healer must be smart and a good technician, but your heart is the most powerful healer. If I were looking for a doctor or healer for myself, I would be most impressed by that healer's investment and dedication to *my* health, meaning his or her intensity when it comes to my individual situation. You do not need the "best" doctor; you need the doctor or healer that is "best for you." And as far as I'm concerned, that is the doctor who is open, loving, and totally invested in helping provide a *pathway* for me as his patient to better health.

In modern medicine, most physicians connect to their brain to help a patient, but true healing cannot happen unless a physician connects to his own heart. Yes, mental ability is important, and some diseases and symptoms can be helped by remembering symptoms from your studies in school, checking the Physician's Desk Reference for the proper drug, and making a prescription for the patient. However, the life-changing experience that takes a patient from ill health to good health must come from the mind *and* the heart. The patient may not always follow the pathway to health, but it is the physician's job to point the way, not to just take care of the symptom. It is the physician's task to work on the *cause* of the current problem. Many times, just alleviating the prominent symptoms may allow the underlying condition to grow more powerful. The doctor or healer's directions and advice may go completely unheeded by a lazy patient. But working to *wake up* a patient to the cause of this problem, the changes in his lifestyle that are necessary, and the future care and attention to his health are vital for the overall patient's health and happiness, which is that patient's inherent health potential.

It is also very important to acknowledge that healing is a partnership. No healer or doctor can help you if you are not willing to help yourself. I see so many modern-day patients nowadays search and go to various doctors to have them "solve my problems." Many of these patients never lift a finger in changing their life or working positively toward their own health. I have been able, in my practice, to eliminate serious anaphylactic peanut allergies in children through 7 Element Lifeforce Healing without shots or drugs. The first step is to remove all refined sugar from the diet (see glitches later in this chapter), only to have the parents say things like "you mean no more cupcakes or cookies?" It was as if I had told them something that was so bizarre and impossible, and they were weighing the effort of change against the health of their child. Doctors and healers are your guideposts on your own healing journey. It is very hard for them to "carry you on their backs." You must try at least to walk or crawl the path to your own health. One of my healing mentors, Dr. Michael Gaetta, once said, "You can only help someone as to their *response*, not their *need*." Only patients willing to participate in their own health journey can truly heal.

Communicating with the Lifeforce Chi Body

Learn all you can, then forget your learning.

—Lao Tse, *Tao Teh Ching*

If you only practice what has been taught to you, you can only go as far as your predecessors. If you take what has been taught to you as a launching pad, then you can discover new realities of your own being.

—HE

We have already discussed the fact that the physical body is the supporting structure for the Lifeforce Chi body, and the Lifeforce Chi body is the directing factor for the physical tissue. Diseases may start in either body and will affect both. If we pollute the physical body, we may disrupt, short-circuit, or glitch the Lifeforce Chi body. If the Lifeforce Chi body is short-circuited or glitched and out of balance, then the signals to the physical tissue will be altered in a negative way, allowing disease and dysfunction. Many types of alternative healers have been helping people for millennia by connecting to and balancing their patients' Lifeforce Chi body. The whole science and art of acupuncture is founded from the ancient Taoist principles and is a practice of balancing the Lifeforce Chi body. Modern-day alternative Chiropractors have used Applied Kinesiology, Total Body Modification, and other techniques to help balance the Lifeforce Chi body of their patients and thus have solved many disease riddles that were unsolved by traditional science. Sophisticated master Chi-Gung healers have used their own Lifeforce to balance the Lifeforce of others for centuries. These ancient techniques, combined with their modern-day counterparts, are the secret to unlocking the questions and mysteries of health that we seek. By using techniques that focus on the Lifeforce of the patient, we have a chance to heal and eliminate baffling diseases of the physical body. By regularly doing practices of meditation, specific breathing practices, Chi-Gung, martial art practices, yoga, and other mind (spirit)-body energy endeavors, we can strengthen the Lifeforce Chi body and avoid disease and disability. Focusing and helping change and balance the Lifeforce Chi body is the pathway for solving and preventing the ravages of disease. Check your medical textbooks; a good 80 percent to 90 percent of all diseases known are listed as *idiopathic—meaning, there is no known cause*. We know what's happening and what areas are affected, but we don't know *why*. The whys lie in the subtle but all-intelligent Lifeforce that has been blocked, exhausted (weakened), or confused (short-circuited).

There are more than a few ways to communicate with the Lifeforce Chi body. No way is better than another; it depends on the ability and the connection of the healer to his pathway or "language," which will ultimately yield success in communicating with the Lifeforce Chi body. I have worked with healers or intuitives that can actually "see" disturbances in the Lifeforce or aura of a patient. Many alternative healers have developed their own way to communicate with the Lifeforce Chi body. The method is not really important; it is the ability and the heart of the healer that will make it successful. I have worked for many years with the art of Applied Kinesiology muscle testing and have used that along with Total Body Modification reflexes and my own 7 Element Lifeforce Healing principles to not only communicate with the Lifeforce Chi body but to help it balance and function normally. The following section of this book is my personal journey and focus in healing. My purpose in writing this section is to assist practitioners to better help their patients through the principles of 7 Element Lifeforce Healing, regardless of their healing discipline or their means of communication with the Lifeforce Chi body.

> Modern medical health science is the practice of categorizing and standardization. The human being experience is uniquely individual. Unless diagnosis and treatment is individualized when it comes to health care, science will be woefully inadequate.
>
> —HE

My work is an eclectic practice drawn from my own thirty years of healing practice. It can be taught and learned, but the instruction would be easier to grasp as a one-to-one or in a hands-on seminar setting. Even if you are not interested in learning my individual healing practice, the principles of 7 Element Lifeforce Healing outlined in this chapter and book can be used by the individual and the professional practitioner to improve health. The laws of dispersal (or direction) and support apply to the fundamental function of the Lifeforce Chi body and the energetic organ system and meridian balance. I will step by step explain the 7 Element Lifeforce Healing System in this chapter. It is my hope that you will be able to take the principles and/or the specific techniques and use them for your benefit and the benefit of others.

Using Muscle Testing to Communicate with the Lifeforce Chi Body

Muscle testing has been used as a test for muscle strength since the turn of the last century (1900). Kendall and Kendall organized and outlined specific tests for each individual muscle in their text in 1952. In the early sixties, a visionary chiropractor named Dr. George Goodheart made a revolutionary discovery. He connected specific muscle testing not only to joint function and spinal subluxation but also to visceral organ function. With this discovery, he created a research group called the International College of Applied Kinesiology (ICAK). Since the sixties, many chiropractors and other types of healers have been using muscle testing in their technique systems. These include T.B.M. (Total Body Modification), behavioral kinesiology, bioenergetic synchronization technique, and neuro emotional technique, to name a few.

As with all great discoveries however, it has also fostered commercial and negative uses too. There are people who use muscle testing to sell products, prove their point, and have ulterior motives when doing muscle testing. Any tool, even a strictly scientific one, can be doctored to fit the needs of the tester and falsify an outcome. Even the gold standard scientific double-blind testing can be set up to give the results the "scientist" wants to get. We just have to look at modern drug companies who do trial after trial changing the parameters of each trial until they get the desired result and throw out all the "bad" trials and the complacent

Food and Drug Administration who allows a drug on the market without making a company publish *all* their research, not just the good information. A recent study in a new minor surgery technique for back pain serves as a prime example of science for profit. A new patented technique was being tested with back pain patients whose pain and problem made them candidates for back surgery. It was touted that this new technique would save patients from costly and extensive back surgery. The trials were run in a narrow six-month time frame. In that six months, the results were extremely positive, and this new patented therapy was on its way to making boatloads of money for its founders. However, one of the medical doctors, who had ten of his patients in the study, realized that from six to nine months after the procedure, six of his ten patients had severe back pain again and, as a result, had to undergo the surgery that this new procedure was supposed to avoid. When he reported the information on his patients to the company doing the research (who stood to make monetary gain from the new technique), he was immediately sued. All because he reported true results that were outside the strict six-month test period. They also filed complaints of malpractice to the medical board against this doctor. So much for "real" unbiased investigative science.*

How many times does a drug company get to market fully tested and sanctioned by the Food and Drug Administration, only to be rapidly pulled in its first few years because of serious and even deadly side effects? Drug companies use the narrowest parameters when doing clinical trials. They are concerned with the profit they are going to make and *not* on the real science of finding a cure. They "test" using the healthiest weight-proportioned test subjects they can find to minimize the drugs' possible side effects. Any detriment from strict parameters is thrown out of the trial. So when the drug hits the market and is prescribed to a seventy-year-old patient on five different medications, that patient and others drop dead from side effects, and all we can say is "oops."

Another inside fact in the drug business is that drugs are deemed effective and marketable when their testing shows them to be just 5 percent better than the placebo in double-blind tests. Just think about what this means. All a drug has to do to get approved is to be 5 percent better than a placebo. That means that the science behind a drug shows that it is possible that an approved drug may only help 5 percent better than a placebo for the people who take it.

So those of you who doubt the ability of muscle testing to be "scientific" have only to look at the practitioner and determine their sincerity, dedication to their craft, and whether or not they can be swayed by overriding monetary or ego concerns.

Quoting Dr. Walther in *Applied Kinesiology: Volume 1*, "Kinesiology, then, means the study of the principles of mechanics in anatomy in relation to human movement. The term 'applied' puts into perspective this utilization of kinesiology. According to Webster [*Webster's Dictionary*], the first definition of 'applied' is: 'Put to practical use: engaged in for utilitarian or contributory purpose...'" So to me, Applied Kinesiology means the use of muscle testing for learning information about the body. It is my personal contention that Applied Kinesiology in the hands of a virtuous practitioner, one who is not into his own ego but is connected to his heart and to the Love of his patient, can open a window of insight into the balance and function of not only the physical body but also the Lifeforce Chi body.

Muscle testing can become a sacred communication between the doctor and patient. Applied Kinesiology muscle testing can also give subclinical information about a patient. For example, when a standard blood test shows liver enzymes positive, it literally means that the liver is starting to fall apart and that a disease process is already underway. Most medical tests are designed to show when diseases are actually in progress. The greatest benefit of muscle testing is in its ability to help prevent disease. It is possible for a good muscle tester to find subclinical problems, which if taken care of may actually prevent the disease process from happening. Modern medical science is set up to be disease oriented, not health oriented. Finding a way to see problems coming and change course to avert the disaster is a better way to safeguard your health.

The Science and Art of Muscle Testing

Here are some of the basics needed to muscle test. There are many different ways that practitioners may use muscle testing. There are also different techniques involved depending on the practitioner. What I'm explaining here is the way I have used muscle testing to communicate with the Lifeforce Chi body. It is not the only way muscle testing can be used. Remember also that muscle testing is a skill and an art that needs to be practiced, honed, and polished. The more practice, experience, and focus you have in muscle testing, the greater your ability will become.

Four Cardinal Principles of Muscle Testing

I. Intent
    a. a clear mind
    b. an open heart
II. Muscle testing procedure
III. Connection to the Lifeforce Chi body
IV. Learning to read the muscle testing results

I. Intent

a. A clear mind

In communicating with the Lifeforce Chi body, you must maintain a clear and open mind. Your physical thinking brain must be quieted. To quiet the mind, you must have complete focus on the task at hand and go into an "allow" state. Your thinking brain must give way to your intuitive nature. There's a great old Taoist quote, "You cannot think your way to heaven." The thinking brain is necessary and will try to poke into your mind, but your testing must be of a pure and focused energy.

b. An open heart

If you have unconditional Love (virtue) for your patient or subject, no egotistical ulterior motives, and you sincerely practice and develop your skill, then the information you receive from your testing can be counted on.

II. Muscle testing procedure

How you do the muscle testing is extremely important. As a practitioner, you want to use as little force as possible. This is due to the fact that you may be seeing many patients in a day and may cause repetitive movement injuries for yourself. You must also be careful in your muscle testing not to unduly stress the muscles or the joints of your patients. Any individual muscle test can be used, and muscle testing can be done in any position: supine, prone, sitting, or standing. Some positions are better than others, depending on the individual patient and doctor. I feel personally that the best position for testing is when the patient is lying supine on a low table or Chiropractic table in front of the doctor who is standing. I also suggest the anterior deltoid muscle as the best muscle test in this position. We will start with this position and this muscle; however, there are many muscles and positions that can be used for testing. The best book on all the individual muscle tests is *Applied Kinesiology: Volume 1*, by David S. Walther.

Directions:

With the patient supine on a low-lying table or bed, have them straighten out the arm to be tested, locking the elbow and having the arm at a forty-five degrees angle or less in relationship to their body. (See illustration 1.)

Either arms of the tester or patient may be used. This is just a matter of comfort and preference. The tester stands at the side of the patient directing a light but steady force in the direction seen in illustration above. If there are no problems, then the patient should be able to "lock out" (stop) against the light pressure of the tester. The lock out is very important. The arm may move slightly until the deltoid muscle recruits enough fibers to stop the pressure of the tester. As a tester, once you feel the lock out stop, do not continue and try to overpower the patient. The lock out is what you as a tester is feeling for. The ability to lock out or to have a muscle continue to move under your pressure are your two potential outcomes. A muscle that locks out is a normal response, meaning that the body can recruit 100 percent of the muscle fibers with no inference, also meaning that there is no disturbance in the Lifeforce. A muscle that does not lock out means that there is a distortion in the Lifeforce and less than 100 percent of the muscle fibers can be recruited or it is a positive response to a doctor-intentioned question.

So:

1. if the muscle locks out:
    a. there is no disturbance in the Lifeforce
    b. there is a *no* answer to the intentioned question
2. If the muscle does not lock out:
    a. there is disturbance in the Lifeforce or normal function
    b. there is a *yes* answer to the intentioned question

A normal muscle should be able to recruit 100 percent of its fibers to stop the slow steady pressure of the test. If the Lifeforce is disturbed or the brain attacked in some small way such as quickly waving your hands near the eyes of the subject, the muscle cannot call into play 100 percent of its fibers. When the muscle can only recruit less than 100 percent of the fibers, it will appear to the tester as weak and not be able to lock out. So Applied Kinesiology muscle testing is not a test of strength but a test of the body's ability to call into play 100 percent of the fibers of that particular muscle.

At this time, it is vitally important that the tester make sure that the subject being tested does not recruit other muscles by changing body position. For example, when testing the anterior deltoid, if the subject bends his elbow even slightly, he will be recruiting other muscles besides the anterior deltoid. A patient may also recruit other muscles in this test by inwardly rotating and slightly lifting the shoulder from the table. Once the body gets the ability by position to call into play other muscles, then it becomes impossible to read the lock out of a single muscle. It is vital in muscle testing to be testing only one individual muscle. Any recruitment by changing body position will void your ability to test the subject. Also, the forty-five-degree angle or less is also important in isolating the anterior deltoid in this test.

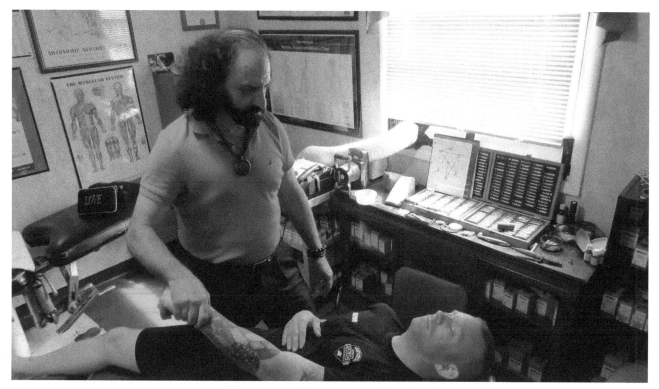

[Illustration of the anterior deltoid test]

III. Connecting to the Lifeforce Chi body

There are a few ways to make sure you are connected to the energetic body of the patient and that your muscle testing will be reliable. I suggest you use one of these methods or one of your own to start the muscle testing procedure. The idea here is to make sure that your testing will give you reliable results with this patient.

1.   Fist in the chest

The heart area is the most sensitive of the human body. We know that in 7 Element Lifeforce Healing, the heart is the connection between the spiritual and material parts of our physical body. It is the bridge between the top and bottom of the physical body, making it the most sensitive part of the physical body. A fist is a representation of aggressive force. Placing your fist on the chest in the heart area of a patient will interfere with the full hundred percent signal of any intact muscle. This is a sign that shows the patient's body is working the way it should.

2.   Body, heart, spirit

As a sign that I am connected to the patient, I will touch the center of the forehead and then the chest (heart) of the patient and then touch my head and heart, asking the intent question, "Am I in connection with this patient's Lifeforce Chi body?" Immediately after this gesture, the muscle will test "weak." (Remember, it is not weakness. It is a loss or interference of 100 percent signal to the muscle, but we will use weakness meaning that the muscle does not lock out, as a positive or yes.) This is an indication that you are connected to the patient's Lifeforce Chi body.

3. You may use the above two methods or design your own. Simply asking the intentioned question "Can I work with this patient?" or "Is this patient open to healing?" and testing the muscle before you start with the patient is necessary to assure your proper results. Another simple way to make sure your testing is true is to have the patient say, "My name is (whatever his name is)" and test the muscle. Since the patient saying his real name should not disturb the Lifeforce Chi body, the muscle will stay strong. If the patient says a fake name, that should cause a weak response as it is a lie, and a lie is a disturbance of the Lifeforce Chi body. You can develop your own way that makes sense to you and works for you to make sure you're in contact with the Lifeforce Chi body when starting your testing.

4. What to do if the following happens:
a. You cannot find any intact muscle, meaning a muscle that is strong or hundred percent innovated to start. This is usually the result of one or two things:

1. The person is dehydrated. This happens quite often. Have the patient drink at least a half to a full glass of Water and then start your testing again.
2. The muscle you have tested is itself having a problem, or the joints associated with that muscle are compromised in some way. If you know Applied Kinesiology, then you can fix the errant muscle or joint. If not, you must find another muscle that is "strong in the clear," meaning the muscle locks out without any problem or intention question when testing to start.

b. What should you do if the muscle that you are testing continues to always lock out, even when you placed the fist in the chest and have asked questions about your connection? Although this does not happen often, what it means is that the person is "locking you out" and overriding your testing with their determination, and sheer will not be read. This usually happens more with men than women. I believe this is because of the same reason men are less likely to ask for help or directions; they don't ask for help easily as they consider it a weakness. This is opposite but similar to what we talked about for practitioners in the first paragraph. Your mind must be open and compliant; otherwise, your testing will not be reliable. In this case, it is the patient's mind that is not opened to healing. If the patient's mind is a closed trap and is focusing their determined energy on blocking you, you can try a Total Body Modification trick called "macho." This is where you take your thumb and rub the center of the forehead vertically three or four times. Then retest the fist in the chest, and the muscle should be "weak." If not, rub the forehead a few more times, which should now help you overcome patient resistance and get a reliable muscle testing read. Also, make sure the patient is not altering their position and recruiting other muscles. You can also speak to the patient and ask them to join you in this joint healing endeavor. Their conscious, out-loud statement of allowing you to read them may also change being shut out.

IV. Reading the muscle testing results

Gaining experience or as the great samurai Miyamoto Musashi would say, "*migako*" or "polishing" your skill is vitally important to your ability to read your muscle testing results. It may take some time and patience to learn this valuable skill. Your pressure when testing must be slow, smooth, and steady. There will be some patients who will be extremely easy to read and others who may prove very difficult. I believe this is because of your overall connection to that patient. With time, even difficult patients will become easier to read. You must perceive the difference between a muscle that can lock out and a muscle that, although has strength, does not have full signal and does not lock out.

There are two ways that I use muscle testing. The first way is to place items, usually frequency vials, on the heart area of the patient and simply test any intact muscle (one that is "strong in the clear"). You can use any substance. For example, if the person is allergic to apples, placing an apple or a piece of an apple on their chest and simply testing and intact muscle will let you know whether the apple has disturbed the Lifeforce Chi body or not. In our food allergy testing, we get a little bit more involved and sophisticated than that, but basically if a person is very allergic to a substance, putting it in the sensitive heart area will disturb the Lifeforce and cause the muscle testing to be weak. This will also work with Dr. George Goodheart's technique of therapy localization. In this technique, you place your hand or the patient's hand on a part of the body or on various organ reflexes, and if that organ is not in balance, it will disturb the Lifeforce and will cause a weak muscle test. I also place my own hands in the various fields of the 7 Element-*I Ching* Crystal around and over the patient (see the 7 Element Chart) and test the muscle to find what element is out of balance.

The second way that I use muscle testing is to intentionally ask a question and then test the muscle. I usually do my intentioned questions silently in my own head. The reason for this is I do not want to influence the patient's active brain. However, I have found in my work that saying the question out loud or saying it to myself really doesn't make a difference in the muscle testing. So for example, you can also combine both methods by holding the adrenal reflex points (see Total Body Modification Chart or any reflex chart you know and use) and testing an intact muscle. If this shows a weak muscle test, you know that particular reflex organ or system is out of balance. You would then keep the hand on the reflex and ask an intention question, such as "Is the energy here empty?" or "Is the energy here blocked or full?" You can then use the 7 Element Chart and Elemental Laws to support or disperse the energy of that organ to help balance the patient. Later on, I will show you how to find out *why* that element organ or system is out of balance using the fields of existence.

Finding the Imbalance

There are many ways to find imbalances between one of the 7 Element organ systems and another. I have used Applied Kinesiology muscle testing and applied it to the 7 Element Lifeforce Crystal. Asking the right questions with the sincerity of compassionate intent, it is possible to discern a patient's imbalances. After the imbalances are discovered, the Elemental laws and laws of energy transfer can be used with any energy method to help solve the balance problem.

7 ELEMENT LIFEFORCE HEALING

SPIRIT

AIR

METAL

YAN FIRE

FIRE

YIN FIRE

WOOD

EARTH

WATER

© 2013 DR Harry R. Elia   [Small seven element crystal illustration]

Elemental Laws

Support
Water supports Earth.
Water supports Wood.
Earth supports Wood.
Earth with Fire supports Metal.
Wood with Fire supports Air.
Wood supports Spirit.
Air supports Water.
Spirit supports Fire.

Directs or Disperses
Spirit directs or disperses air.
Spirit directs or disperses Metal.
Air directs or disperses Metal.
Air directs or disperses Earth.
Metal directs or disperses Wood.
Metal directs or disperses Water.
Earth directs or disperses Spirit.
Water directs or disperses Fire.

7 Element Laws of Energy Transfer

1. Single-element support
    Use stimulation of the problem element to supplement and balance that element (7 Element Crystal).

2. Law of support
    Stimulate the support element to bring up the energy in the element that is empty or under energize (7 Element Crystal).

3. Law of dispersal
    If an element is full or blocked, stimulate the element that disperses it (7 Element Crystal).

4. Law of two to one
    To balance an element that is over- or under energize, stimulate its support and its dispersal elements simultaneously (7 Element Crystal).

5. Law of opposites
    If an element is over- or under energize, you can balance it by stimulating its opposite element on the time chart (7 Element Crystal and Chi-Meridian Time charts).

6. Law of energy time shift
    If an element is blocked, stimulate the next element on the time flow chart to "drag" energy from the blocked element (Chi meridian time flow chart).

7. Law of Fire.
    You can enhance the support or dispersal by simultaneously stimulating Fire element with the support or dispersal element (7 Element Crystal Chart).

Upon discovering what element organ system is depleted and what element organ system is full or blocked, you can use the elemental laws and the laws of energy transfer to help balance the system.

So to start identifying the main problem area that a patient presents, I can place my hand in the element area around or over the body at that point and test the muscle. Using the 7 Element-*I-Ching* Crystal from the chart and imagining it over the patient, I then continue to place my hand over each element area. For example, if I place my hand directly above the inguinal or pubic area and the muscle tests weak, that means there is a disturbance in the Water Element. With my hand in the area, I asked if the element is energetically full (blocked) or empty. I can then check the various parts and reflexes of the Water Element. These parts would include the adrenals, kidneys, bladder, ovaries or testes, lumbosacral vertebra, etc. by using the Total Body Modification, Applied Kinesiology, or whatever reflexes you may know. For example, if after these two steps are completed you find the adrenal reflexes to be weak, you can use any support techniques you know or muscle test nutritional support. I would use the Total-Body-Modification-specific spinal tapping to bring up the energy of the adrenals.

The next step in using 7 Element Healing is to discover a reason for the organ or gland to be weak or overused. Having the patient hold the reflex, touch the area, or put his hand in the area representing that element, I would now use a flat hand palm down and place it over each element area while I test the muscle again. This is called "fields of existence" and is covered a little further on in this chapter. To better understand the process, we must first explain the hands madras that can be used by the practitioner for receiving information in 7 Element Healing.

Chi Hands

1. Sword hand
   Two fingers out with the thumb, ring, and pinkie clasped (illustration)
   Used to locate organ or element disturbance (high or low energy)
2. Glitch hand
   Five fingers and thumb together (illustration)
   Used to locate Lifeforce glitches (see later discussion of allergy elimination)
3. Flat hand palm down
   Used for locating overall energetic disturbances of the Lifeforce energetic field or "fields of existence" (see later)
4. Divining rod hand
   Fist palms down with first two fingers pointing and spread
   Used for determining a structural disturbance joint muscle spinal subluxation
5. Flat hand palm up
   Back of the hand over the body
   Used for determining systems disturbance (see Total Body Modification techniques)
6. Chi hand
   Soft fingers, palm inverted, and wrist slightly bent
   Used for determining overall energetic Lifeforce disturbance in that area
7. Spiderman hand
   Pinkie, forefinger, and thumb extended with ring and middle finger touching the palm near the wrist
   Used for determining if a section of portion of work is done when the two extended fingers are in contact with the chest of the patient while testing the muscle. The weak muscle indicates that you are done with that portion of work, and you can move on. You should also check the Total Body Modification blocking procedure at this time.

Additional Hands

a. Empty fist
   Ring the fingers and thumb together forming a circle and place it over the element or organ- Used for indicating a *serious* disease or *serious* energetic disturbance of an organ gland system.
b. Flat hand, palms down, and fingers spread wide
   Used for a general area of the body, for example, over the abdomen for all digestion organs.

These are hand positions that I have used, putting them in the area of the element, then muscle testing to see if placing that hand madras in the specific area changes the muscle test. For example, I would place the sword hand into the energy field usually a few inches above the body of the patient in each of the 7 Element areas, and if the muscle test was positive (waver in the muscle), I would know that that element organ system is out of balance. Then asking the intention question with my hand in the same place, "Is it full or empty?" Then search for a second location for the element that has the opposite imbalance. This would give me the basic energetic imbalance. There are some classic imbalance couples, which relate to various energetic or disease patterns.

Common Energetic Imbalances

Any two elements or more can be imbalanced. Whenever one element is blocked, another element will be weakened or lacking in energy. Just like a river, if we damn up one area, the downstream area will become dry. Remember that the key to health is balance. If we can imagine a circle with strings attaching across in all directions, much like an American Indian dream catcher, then also imagine that pulling the circle at any spot will distort the balance of all areas. There will be a major disruption in the point where you are pulling and also a major disruption in the area across from the area being pulled. These are the two dynamic imbalances. However, imbalance may affect more than one area. In fact, imbalance in one area will affect the whole system to some degree. Determining the major imbalance, which organ system is full and which organ system is empty or weak, is the first goal of understanding the energetic imbalance of your patient. The following imbalances are some of the most common that I have found in my time in practice. They represent a good portion of the problems that are presented to me by my patients. They are *not* however all the possibilities, as you may discover any imbalance in two organ systems or imbalances in more than two organ systems. Allow your compassionate intuition and your muscle testing to guide you.

1. Full Air and empty Water

This imbalance is one of the most common that I find with my patients. It is what I usually refer to as the "Western person head," meaning that the head (Air) or brain is full and the energy of the adrenals and Water Element is empty. In our Western world, we worship the brain as the sole representation of our being. We are inundated with facts, trivia, and visual excitement. Much like an overly strong sun, we dry up the Water, and the focus of energy is taken from the *dan tien*, adrenals, kidneys, etc. This results in many "tired" syndromes. Although there may be other causative factors for the following conditions, this imbalance can be the imbalance of chronic fatigue syndromes, exhaustion, and even depression syndromes. It may also signal primary adrenal problems. In my experience, our modern lifestyle destroys and uses up adrenal energy. All the coffee, five-hour energy drinks, and synthetic supplements only compound the problem. The adrenals want to have smooth full energy. When the adrenals are treated like a yo-yo, exhausting them and then pumping them up with stimulant, they will deteriorate rapidly. Besides balancing the energetics, many of these patients will need whole food supplementation along with deleting from their diets refined sugar, coffee, strong spices, and other processed carbs. If the adrenals are wiped out, reeducating the neurotransmitter relationship between the pituitary and the adrenals is also an advanced technique that I have used in the past with success (see neurotransmitter technique later in this chapter). You should also check the rebooting section that follows.

This imbalance is also common with acute or chronic sinus infections. Weak adrenals (Water Element) along with a full or blocked Air Element can be a sign of a sinus infection or allergies. Remember, a full adrenal energy plays a big part in having a strong immune system.

Treat by stimulating the Spirit Element (Spirit disperses Air; Air then can support Water) body points, organ reflexes (pineal), meridian points, Chi-Gung healing head positions (see later chapter discussion), or any technique you may know.

2. Full Metal and empty Water

Full Metal and empty Water most commonly represents some type of respiratory, throat, or head infection. Although our immune system is in every part of our body, including all digestive organs, spleen, lungs, thymus, tonsils, and even in all the cells of your body, the Metal Element is the energetic commander of the immune system. Finding a full Metal Element is a good clue that there may be any type of acute respiratory invasion. In cases of chronic problems like emphysema or complete shutdown of the immune system, the Metal Element would be the one to show up weak or blocked.

The combination of full Metal and empty Water Elements is consistent with burnt-out or tired adrenals, which are our energetic "SWAT team." We pull energy from the adrenals to support the immune system in times of crisis, like when invading viruses and bacteria are present. Strong adrenal energy pumping up your immune system power is usually your best weapon against communicable diseases.

This imbalance is also found again in primary adrenal problems. Modern lifestyle have left the adrenals burnt out by no sleep, overwork, and a poor Standard American Diet. Many alternative practitioners will agree that burnt-out and drained adrenal energy is a cornerstone of patient problems they see. This imbalance, with an overload of the Metal Element, usually also means the thyroid is being overburdened. The thyroid and adrenals work together for overall body energy and production of hormones. When a person burns out their adrenal energy, the first reaction is low adrenal and overloaded or sluggish thyroid. Since most physicians do not test for adrenal insufficiency but do have blood tests for thyroid sluggishness, it is a common mistake to treat the thyroid with hormone therapy. I do agree that with modern atomic radiation exposure and electromagnetic radiation, there are primary thyroid problems, but it's been my experience that it is more common for the adrenals to be the prime problem. Tired adrenals overload the thyroid. If we have two people working on the job of energy in the body and one of them takes sick or stops working, the healthy person still at work has to do both jobs, working doubly hard. In time, the working person (thyroid) will also slow down. Wiped-out adrenals will often in time create a sluggish thyroid. Treating the thyroid especially with hormones (see treating a wild animal in chapter 4) will give temporary help but not solve the primary adrenal stress problem in the long run.

Treat and support adrenals, energetically and nutritionally. Check to see if this is a primary adrenal problem (ask the Lifeforce). Many doctors make the mistake of treating only the slowed-down thyroid with hormone drugs, which will help in the short run but fail in the long run since it is the adrenal stress that is dragging down the thyroid function. Again, if two oxen (adrenals and thyroid) are yoked together pulling a cart side by side and one ox gets injured or slows down, the other ox has to work twice as hard, and in time, it will also slow down. Treating the healthy ox for fatigue will help in the short run, but the situation will degenerate again as the healthy ox cannot do double the work for long. You must solve the problem of the injured ox (adrenals) for the pair to function normally.

This imbalance responds well to treating the Air Element (brain reflexes, small intestines, and triple warmer meridians), as the Air Element is the director or disperser of the full Metal Element, and it is also the supporter of the Water Element, a perfect single treatment for this imbalance (see 7 Element Chart).

With this imbalance, also check for type of respiratory problems: possible cold, flu, bronchitis, pneumonia, etc. Upper respiratory infections are also common with this imbalance. Use the techniques you know for the specific respiratory problem along with whole food supplementation and herbal support. If I can aid you in the specific treatment protocols, you can contact me directly at the number and address at this book's end. Remember, these are just the most common imbalances. There could be many others depending on the individual patient. Ask the Lifeforce using the 7 Element Crystal, hand positions, and fields of existence for the answers.

3.   Weak Air Element and Full Earth Element

The imbalance of weak Air Element and full Earth Element almost always points to some digestive disturbance. Any time the Earth Element is full, it is a hint about digestive sluggishness. This could cover a multitude of digestive problems: ileocecal valve or irritable bowel syndrome, bloating and gas problems,

problems with the sigmoid colon, ranging from simple diarrhea or constipation to colitis, hiatal hernia, acid reflux, and problems in digestive breakdown, absorption, and the digestive flora. Use whatever method you know to discern the specific problem. Standard Process has many whole food prescriptions for helping with digestive issues. Again, if you need more details on my own differential diagnosis, contact me.

Another possibility is stomach flu, ulcers, or other infections of the stomach and intestines.

Emotionally, a sluggish or full Earth element can point to emotional disturbances related to family members or people close to the patient. It is also related to a patients' relationship to the family or being a parent. For example, a woman reaching her late thirties and wanting to have a family and children may fear her time running out or any parent having trouble with the enormity of parent responsibilities. Using the fields of existence and the 7 Element Chart will lead you to these imbalance problems.

Treat energetically. Stimulating and supporting the Air Element will disperse the Earth Element energies (air or wind blows and disperses the sand). Other options can be found in the law of energy transfer chart mentioned earlier in this chapter.

4.   Empty Metal and full Wood

The elemental imbalance of weak or empty Metal and full Wood can point to various things. The first and most common one I think of is an emotional distortion created by anger and/or frustration, which builds up and jams the liver and Wood energy. In our society, this is a common problem. Anger and frustration block the liver energy. Later in this chapter, I'll present the 7 Element Emotional Technique, or you can use any emotional technique or way you know of to defuse anger and frustration. Remember also by using the Metal Element areas like communication, expression (speech and song), and creativity, you can dissipate or "cut" Wood.

Besides Wood Element ver emotions, this imbalance may also be also involved in the physical toxification of the liver. Our modern existence forces our livers to spend most of their energy in detoxifying environmental chemicals. Heavy Metals, solvents, neurotoxins (bug sprays), and a host of other inorganic nasty chemicals assault the liver every day. Alcohol and prescription drugs will also tax the liver physically and energetically. In the past (about one hundred twenty years ago), all the liver had to do was just the job of creating over fifty thousand biochemicals for the body and performing over thirteen thousand biochemical reactions for the body. There was *no pollution* then. Now three thousand five hundred new chemicals assault us every year. Remember, your liver has to detoxify *every* molecule of man-made poisons that enter the body. This has added a tremendous amount of additional work for the livers of modern man. The liver is the body's chemical factory. Our modern lifestyle has more than quadrupled the liver's workload by adding the new job of constant detoxification. This harsh and toxic chemical overload of the liver can lead to other problems like allergies and skin breakouts that may signal a time to do a physical liver detoxification. There are many liver detoxes. The best program I have found is the Standard Process detoxification program, which you can explore by contacting www.standardprocess.com and finding a physician in your area that administers the Standard Process detoxification program.

This imbalance is also where we might find primary thyroid deficiency. Remember to remove glitches of the thyroid (explained in the allergy elimination technique later) if they test positive and always try whole food nutrition and dietary changes as a solution before drugs (whole hormone therapy).

This imbalance or any full Wood ver energy can also commonly signal gallbladder problems. Remember, the two organs most affected by dehydration are the gallbladder and heart. The Standard American Diet or "sad diet" puts a lot of pressure on the gallbladder too.

Treat physically. Liver detox or gallbladder clearing and detox. *Treat energetically*. Clear anger and frustration (emotional techniques).Since Metal disperses Wood and is weak, you must support Metal with the Earth Element, both energetically and nutritionally, so Metal can disperse and balance the full Wood Element.

5.   Empty Metal and full Water

It is very unusual for the Water adrenal and kidney energy to be full. In a healthy vibrant person, this may be true, but in seeing patients, I more often find that kidney and adrenal energy are usually low due to stress and other factors. When the Water energy is full with the patient, it can be an overactive adrenal energy causing hyperfunction before the adrenals crash and show low energy. This is common with kids on sugar. Their overabundant young Lifeforce added to the pumped-up energy of refined sugar can give them over-stimulated adrenals. This may also be prevalent in severe fear syndromes especially with younger patients, as the overwhelming fear has not drained the adrenals yet. Also, patients facing big changes in life—such as divorce, moving, changing jobs, etc.—can increase the adrenal energy in the short run.

This imbalance sometimes can show up in kids with immune deficiency problems. These are the areas I would research first in patients with this kind of imbalance.

Treat physically. If sugar shows up when testing (research the Total Body Modification sugar protocol), patients must remove refined sugar completely from their diet and overcome their sugar addiction. This is vital especially with children and is again the first step in the allergy elimination protocol.

Patients must also be coached in finding balance in their life between activity and restorative rest. Breathing exercises to help circulate their Chi may also be helpful in these cases.

Treat energetically. If fear is the cause of this imbalance, refer to the 7 Element Emotional Technique that is described later in this Chapter.

Since Metal is the director and disperser of Water, the Metal Element must be supported nutritionally and energetically. Energetic treatment that supports and strengthens the Metal Element organs or glands, the main ones being the thyroid and lungs, will help establish balance. Supporting the Earth Element will also increase Metal strength as Earth supports Metal.

6.   Full Earth Element and empty Water Element

As always, when you find the Earth Element full or blocked, you must research digestive disturbances of the three parts of digestion: breakdown, absorption, and elimination. Coupled with depleted Water or adrenal energy, it will result, at the bare minimum, to sluggish digestion. There could also be other digestion problems that may be serious such as colitis or irritable bowel syndrome, reduced stomach acid, bowel toxicity, or parasites.

Emotionally, the full Earth Element can signal emotional stress with worry, anxiety, or guilt and problems that center around family, close friends, and close relationships.

Be sure to also investigate primary adrenal depletion also with this imbalance.

Treat physically. If this pattern is found, you must investigate and solve the physical digestive disturbance it may cause. I would suggest starting with alternative digestive treatment including dietary change, food allergy elimination (see later in this chapter), restoring the acid-alkaline balance of the digestive system, and using whole food nutritional support. Don't forget to advise your patients about reasonable exercise and being hydrated as both of these things help stimulate better digestion function.

Treat energetically. As Air directs Earth and supports Water, stimulating the Air Element reflexes, body points, or meridian points, etc. along with energetic treatment will help establish energetic balance. Pituitary support with nutrition (Pituitrophin PMG by Standard Process) has been extremely helpful in some of these cases (Air directs Earth).

The Three Diamonds, Twelve Triangles, and the 7 Fields of Existence

We exist in interwoven layers and parts. There are layers to our spiritual energetic bodies (Lifeforce Chi body) and our physical body. Understanding these parts of the whole is helpful in determining the "whys" of health imbalance. Up to now, we have used muscle testing and the 7 Element Principles to determine energetic imbalance. Using the fields of existence, we may be able to determine the source of an Element organ system disruption and the cause of that imbalance. The following diagram explains the major areas and parts that need to be searched to find the cause of Element organ system dysfunction.

FIELDS OF EXISTANCE

THE WHY OF IMBALANCE

SPIRITUAL
1. LIFE'S HEAVY QUESTIONS
2. LIFEFORCE FLOW (BLOCKED AT 3 BURNERS)
3. PINEAL, CRAMMS, CEREBRAL SPINAL FLUID

MENTAL
1. BRAIN & MIND
2. BELIEF SYSTEMS
3. PINEAL

EMOTIONAL
7 ELEMENT
EMOTIONAL TERM

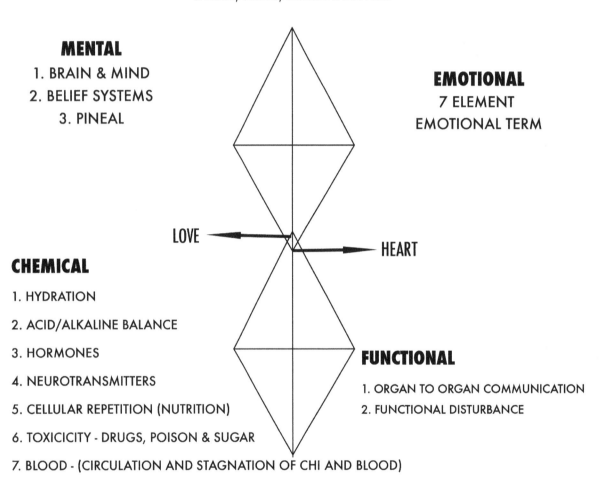

LOVE ← → HEART

CHEMICAL

1. HYDRATION

2. ACID/ALKALINE BALANCE

3. HORMONES

4. NEUROTRANSMITTERS

5. CELLULAR REPETITION (NUTRITION)

6. TOXICICITY - DRUGS, POISON & SUGAR

7. BLOOD - (CIRCULATION AND STAGNATION OF CHI AND BLOOD)

FUNCTIONAL

1. ORGAN TO ORGAN COMMUNICATION

2. FUNCTIONAL DISTURBANCE

STRUCTURAL

1. PHYSICAL BODY BLOCKAGES
(SPINE, JOINT, MUSCLE, FACIA)

2. FEAR SYMPTOMS (EXTREME)

3. ANYTHING THAT SHAKES YOUR LIFE FOUNDATIONS

4. EXTREME SUGAR

As you can see, the Lifeforce Chi body or spiritual energetic half of you corresponds more closely to the upper (more Yan) half of the body. It has three areas: spiritual, mental, and emotional. The physical body is more connected to the lower (more Yin) half of the body, which also has three parts: chemical, functional or communication, and structural. In between and connecting the two halves of the body is the heart. The physical organ, the heart represents the physical body, and the phenomena of Love represents the spiritual energetic portion of you. Placing a soft flat hand, palm down into the energetic field in each area about an inch or two above the body can signal you as a physician to the layer or part that is the cause of the imbalance.

For example, you would start by using the sword hand (first two fingers extended from the fist) and discovering a full or weak element or organ system and then asking full or empty. Then you can then have the patient keep their hand in contact with that reflex and place your flat hand, palm down, into the various fields of existence areas over the body but in the Lifeforce (one to four inches above the area). Finding one area that interferes with muscle signal (weak) will indicate what part or layer of this patient is the cause of that organ system problem. For example, if the flat palm in the area of the emotional field of existence (over the left shoulder area of the patient, Metal area) causes a positive muscle test (weak muscle), then you know that emotions is one of the causes of the adrenal draining or pumping-up problem. Using the 7 Element Principles, you can determine what emotion (see the 7 Element Chart) is causing the disruption. You could then use any emotional technique you know or the 7 Element Emotional Technique discussed a little later in this chapter to help balance the emotional drain of the adrenals.

Using the fields of existence, it may be possible for you to determine the causes of your patient's dysfunction. Let's explain each field so that you may have a better understanding of how to use this in determining the cause of the patient's imbalance. All the information discovered below will be related to the organ as long as your hand or the patient's hand is kept on the organ point or reflex throughout the procedure.

VII. Spiritual

Located above the head or forehead of the patient, the spiritual layer or part concerns itself with core issues, life areas, and belief systems of the Spirit Element. These may include the patient's deep questions about spirituality, their purpose in life, seeking peace and harmony, religious doubt, and their overall ability to receive joy and be happy. The Spiritual Element deals with our sense of oneness and connectedness with all around us, so someone that feels totally disconnected and at odds with themselves and life may show problems in the Spirit field. I have found this to be the case with older patients who have just retired or changed their role in life. A mother who now has children and grandchildren who are not close by and feels she no longer serves her motherhood purpose may have disturbances in the Spirit Element. If it is appropriate (if you have developed a trusting relationship with this patient), you should delve into these questions verbally with your patient. This can also happen to younger people who are facing a big change in career or a big change in their life such as marriage or divorce. Helping a person focus and come to grips with the opportunity of change can aid your patients in reducing the energy-draining effects of this type of stress.

VI. Mental

The mental part or layer of the spiritual energetic body can be searched by laying the flat hand, palm down in the general area between the head and neck on the patient's right side, the doctor's left side. The mental layer deals with the brain and mainly with the patient's concerns with control issues. I find it often when a patient feels like their life is out of control. Organization and problem solving is sometimes a pathway for these patients to feel a little bit more in control of what's happening to them. Control issues are very common when this field tests positive. They must also understand that control of the external world may be frustrating, but the pathway to solving their problems is to work on their own control and self-development. Use the other core issues, life areas, and belief systems from the 7 Element Chart to better define the problem.

V. Emotional

The emotional field area is to the patient's left side (doctor's right) in the area of the Lifeforce field between the head and shoulder. Getting a positive muscle response here (weak muscle is my signal) means that emotional turmoil or overemotional energy is one of the draining or blocking causes of whatever Element or organ system you have already found to be weak or blocked. The 7 Element Emotional technique can be used to determine the emotion and the life area causing the emotional disruption, and you can follow the treatment mentioned or treat the over emotion in any other way you may know.

7 Element Emotional Technique

Prerequisite Steps

1. Locate the full or empty (weak) organ system.
2. Keeping the patient's hand in contact with that system reflex and then test your flat palm though the field of existence, and if there is a positive response in the emotional field (to the patient's left between the head and shoulder area), then you can continue to the emotional technique.
3. Keeping the patient's hand on the positive organ reflex, find the emotion by addressing the 7 Element areas with the sword hand, intentionally asking what element is indicated (refer to the 7 Element Chart).
4. Then muscle test and ask the Lifeforce which emotion is the problem. For example, if there's a positive emotional Wood Element test (sword hand in the Wood Element area), then intentionally ask with muscle testing which emotion: anger, frustration, resentment, or jealousy. Let's say anger is positive.
5. Next, using the sword hand again, go through all 7 Element Areas and intentionally ask what area of life is this emotion caused by (see 7 Element Chart). For example, in asking what area of life you get a positive at the Earth area (to the left side of the patient's trunk), then you know the anger has to do with something connected to family (this may be concerns with close friends or others close to you but also may be your relationship to family, concerns of a woman who is deciding whether she wants to have children or not, or concerns of a "black sheep" son's relationship to family).
6. Next, form a statement bringing these two things together in a general fashion. For example, have the patient say, "I release all anger with regards to family." If this statement, said out loud by the patient, causes a weak muscle test, then you know you have at least one emotional cause of the original organ weakness or fullness.
7. Fix the organ reflexes of original organ system, in this example, the liver (I use Total Body Modification reflexes; you may use any method you like), and also the organ reflex of the emotion if they are different (you may also use the anterior and posterior universal reflexes noted later in this chapter). Then have the patient repeat the statement, "I release all anger with regards to family" again out loud, and the muscle test will no longer show positive.

In doing this work you are basically moving the present energy and not solving the patient's emotional problems. However, it helps balance their energy for the time being and is a good opening to get them to realize the effects that this emotional disturbance is having on their organ systems. Encourage them to formulate plans or affirmations to defuse the over emotion. Remember, the areas of life are general, which is good because you will cover the emotional problem without the patient having to be specific or totally divulge their problem. If the patient is willing, you can further delve into details of the emotional disturbance to help that patient or just move the energy and allow the patient to do the inner work in private.

IV. Heart or Love

This area of the fields of existence is the area that comes up the least with patients and rightly so. Disturbances in this area signal severe problems either physically or energetically for the patient. The heart is the center of the body. It reacts to imbalances of the other six elements. Imagine a ball in the center of six other balls all connected by strings. If I pull on one of the outer balls, the balls of the outer circle are disturbed; but the center ball, the heart, is also pulled out of the center. The greater the stress or blockage (pull) of an imbalanced element, the more the heart energy is pulled out of center. The physical heart is a reactor to stress and to disturbances in the other element's organ systems.

Problems of the liver's ability to detoxify and coordinate the balance of the body's chemistry causes the buildup of plaque in the blood vessels. The failing energy of the kidney can also cause increases in blood pressure and congestive heart failure (one of the leading causes of death from many critical conditions). Pancreas failure and diabetes put tremendous stress on the heart and the blood vessels. Finding imbalances in this field of existence may be a signal to you as the practitioner or friend to have the patient checked out by a cardiologist if he is not under care already. Remember, solving the imbalance problems of the other six elements and helping the patient with nutrition, exercise, detoxification, Chi-Gung, Nei-Gung, and emotional balance will all help the heart, but finding this element to be the main problem is a serious signal to you the practitioner.

The emotional part of this field of existence usually deals with the patient's main Love connections in their lives. This could be a romantic or spouse relationship or a direct family relationship: mother, father, brother, sister, and children.

III. Chemical

The chemical field of existence is part of the physical body triangle and is tested by placing flat palm down (toward the patient) in the Wood Element area to the right side of the patient's trunk over the liver area. If this yields a positive test, then one of the causes of the organ system deficiency or overload is due to physical body chemistry. I have isolated 7 different areas of chemical imbalance and have made a personal system of finding what chemical imbalance is affecting the patient. In this work, I use frequency vials (see Total Body Modification seminars), but you may find other ways to confirm the chemical imbalance. The following is my personal chart of how I asked the body questions starting from one to 7 about the chemical imbalance of the organ system we are working with from the start. These questions are asked intentionally with muscle testing.

Chemical Imbalance Areas

1. Hydration

If the body is not properly hydrated, there will be chemical interference in organ system function. You can ask this question directly with intentionally muscle testing the Lifeforce. If hydration is an issue, have the patient drink at least one glass of Water immediately to increase the accuracy of your muscle testing.

Also, advise the patient to begin daily hydration with Water. Remember, Water is your best hydrator; there is nothing better. Please advise your patient to stay away from any types of vitamin Waters or sports hydration drinks, as they are loaded with chemicals and refined sugar, which will reduce their hydration properties. Remember, sugar sensitivity and hydration work in reverse proportion. The more refined sugar, the less hydrated; the less refined sugar, the more the body hydrates.

2. Alkaline-acid balance

This can be muscle tested or the doctor can use a simple saliva pH test. Our Standard American Diet is a diet that causes the tissues of the body to become more acidic. There are many studies showing a connection between an acidified body tissue and disease. There are three ways to advise your patients on changing and balancing their body. Food is one way. Reducing or eliminating acidifying foods—such as coffee, refined sugar, refined carbohydrates, and overabundance of meats and grains—is a way to change the acidity with food.

A second and complementary way is to have the patient fully hydrate by drinking adequate supplies of Water. Also, taking a half to a full teaspoon of baking soda in a glass of Water once or twice a day (muscle test this out for each patient) will also help alkalize the body.

A third way to alkalize, which can be used in conjunction with the other two methods, is to do breathing exercises. Using the Earth or belly breath regularly will help the body to alkalize. Studies in India showed that doing fifteen minutes of this type of breathing exercises will increase oxygen capacity 10 percent and alkalize the body.

Remember, the body has a Yin and Yan acid-alkaline balance. The tissues of the body is slightly alkaline or slightly acidic depending on the area: the mouth slightly alkaline, the stomach extremely acidic, the bowels slightly acidic, and so on. Eating acidic foods (sugar and refined carbohydrates) *decreases* the stomach acid, increases the mouth acidity, and decreases the bowel acidity. All pH balances in the body are related and inversely proportional.

3. Sexual hormone imbalance

The third chemical possibility with a patient is hormonal imbalance. The main hormones to check are estrogen, progesterone, and testosterone. These can be checked by placing frequency vials in the area of the *dan tien* and muscle testing. Once you have found the hormone that is out of balance, you can use the 7 Element Hormonal Technique to balance.

7 Element Hormonal Technique

1. Find the hormone that is out of balance by placing each hormone vial—estrogen, progesterone, and/or testosterone—in the *dan tien* and muscle testing. Keep that vial in place for the whole procedure (W).
2. Have the patient place their hand on the adrenal cortex reflex (fingers on either side of the belly button) and muscle test (W).
3. Fix the adrenal cortex. Use Total Body Modification vertebra 7, 9, 11 or universal reflex test (becomes strong S).
4. With the patient still holding the adrenal cortex reflex, have the patient place three fingers of their other hand on the thyroid (see Total Body Modification Chart, thyroid reflex) and test (W).
5. Fix the reflex (tap C 4 three phases of respiration Total Body Modification or anterior universal reflex test (S).

6. With the patient holding both reflexes, adrenal cortex, and thyroid, the doctor places his hand on the pituitary reflex (thumb and forefinger on both sides of the bridge and the nose) and test. You can use a leg muscle (W).

7. Fix the pituitary reflex (pull up the bride and occiput on three phases of respiration (see Total Body Modification Chart) or use universal reflex fix.

8. Have the patient pick up the hand on the lower adrenal cortex reflex and then put it back down and retest (W). Fix the adrenal cortex reflex again and test (S).

9. Now have the patient pick up the hand on the throat (thyroid reflex) and then put it back down on the reflex. Retest (W) and fix the thyroid reflex again and retest (S).

10. Now the doctor picks his hand off the pituitary reflex and then replaces it. Retest. If it is strong you are done. If it is weak, redo the pituitary reflex.

11. Block the patient (Total Body Modification) or have the patient take a few deep breaths with their eyes closed.

Remember to check all three hormones and consider nutritional support or hormone imbalance. One or more of the following Standard Process herbal or nutritional support may be helpful: Symplex F, Organically Bound Minerals, Blackcurrant Seed Oil, Chaste Tree, Femco, to name a few possibilities. Send an e-mail or call me with questions.

4. Neurotransmitters

Neurotransmitters are powerful amino acid chains and enzymes that communicate from brain to tissue of the body and from organs and glands of the body to other parts of the body. They also help in the production of hormones that signal body action. Many of the neurotransmitters are found in the central nervous system; however, there is neurotransmitter production and function in many parts of the body. For example, it has been estimated in studies that 90 percent of serotonin is produced and used in the small intestines. The use and production of neurotransmitters is still not understood with complete certainty by currant scientific ability. In my work, I use energetic frequency and harmonization processes and focus on the energetic body rebalancing these powerful and important neurotransmitters and hormones. So if a flat hand over the liver area gives you a positive or week muscle test, you must then ask which of the chemical areas are affected. If it comes up neurotransmitter (number four), then you can use the following outline procedure.

The 7 Element Neurotransmitter Harmonization Technique can be extremely helpful in turning on organs and glands that have been shut down by overuse and Lifeforce Chi body confusion. My first success in using this technique was with a patient whose adrenals were affected after she was given a double dose of steroid drugs for a condition that she had. For months after the double steroid medical treatment, this patient was emotionally distraught, crying at the drop of a hat, and nervous and fearful, which was not at all her normal personality. The disturbance caused her adrenals to bounce up and down like a yo-yo. Once we cleared the drug glitch (see glitches under allergy elimination), we had to perform the neurotransmitter harmonization with the adrenals on a few visits until her adrenals and emotions returned to a more normal and familiar level.

7 Element Neurotransmitter Harmonization Technique

Chart

Spirit: Glutamate, *N*-Methyl-D-aspartic acid, Substance P   Hormone: Melatonin

Air: *gamma*-Aminobutyric acid, Cholinesterase, Enkephalin   Hormone: Lutinizing

Metal: Calcitonin, Tyramine, Tyrosine   Hormone: Thyrotropin

Fire: Angiotensin2, Bradykinin, Histidine

Wood: Dopa, Dopamine, Choline

Earth: Cholestokiain, Serotonin, Somatostatin   Hormone: Gastrin

Water: Acetylcholine, Epinephrine, Norepinephrine   Hormone: Adrenaline

Initial Work

After finding a troubled organ, use the fields of existence to locate the cause. If it comes up in the chemical area (Wood area), then run though the chemical areas (see fields of existence chart). If that comes up as neurotransmitters (number 4), then use the neurotransmitters and hormone vials for that organ originally in question from the above chart and start the following procedure:

1. Place the three neurotransmitters vials over the affected area or on the heart. Muscle test will give you a weak reaction. Then stimulate the reflex points (or universal reflex) for the organ of the original problem organ element.
2. Retest should indicate strong. Now place the hormone for that area with the other vials and retest. This should give you another weak result. Restimulate the reflex points for the original organ of the problem element again (or universal reflex). This should result in a strong test.
3. Now check the pituitary reflex and fix if weak.
4. Remove all four vials for a few seconds, then replace them on the body, and retest the problem organ element and the pituitary reflex. This should again give a strong response.
5. Intentionally ask if there's anything else to do, then use Total Body Modification blocking, or direct the person to close their eyes and take three deep breaths while the vials are on the body.

5. Cellular nutrition

The fifth area to check in chemical imbalance is cellular nutrition. This means that one or more of the element organ areas need nutritional support. If this comes up, then ask with sword hand what organ system needs nutritional support. Use the nutritional support that you are familiar with to support that organ system.

6. Toxicity

The sixth area to check for in chemical imbalance is toxicity. If number six comes up in your intentional muscle testing chemical search, then you must find out what is the toxic substance that is causing the problem element organ imbalance. Depending on what problem element you have, the common areas to intentionally ask are:

Heavy Metals—usually found with liver (Wood) or pituitary (air)

Alcohol—usually found with liver

Prescription drugs—again usually found with liver (Wood) or pituitary (nervous system, air Element)

Recreational drugs—liver and pituitary or nervous system

Sugar—usually adrenals (Water) or pancreas (Earth) but can be any element organ

Metabolic poison—can be found with any organ but is indicative of liver toxicity

Use Total Body Modification harmonization process, nutritional support or cleanses, or any method you know to detox the body. Work with the patient to eliminate the toxic stress. Also, check glitches.

7. Stagnation of blood and Chi

This area is concerned with the blockage or buildup of blood in an area of the body. This buildup is sort of an internal energetic block, as blood reflects the internal Chi movement. I used the blood vial (Total Body Modification vials) to find the area of blood buildup. Then stimulate the reflex of that area (or any organ stimulation you may know, acupuncture acupressure, etc.) We can change the internal energetics. This buildup is commonly in the liver but can be in any Yin organ and can also be the result of past physical injury.

II. Communication and function

This field of existence area is located in the lower left quadrant of the patient's body (Earth Element area). This is indicated of some communicative functional problem within the body's elements, organs, and systems.

When this area shows up in examination, there are three areas that I will personally check. The first is communication between organ reflexes. For example, in working with the body, when I have found imbalances between two organ systems, I will test all combinations between those organ reflexes and fix them. If spleen and adrenals were the imbalance, I would run those reflexes in both directions, spleen first then adrenals, and fix, then adrenals and spleen and also fix in that combination.

The second thing I would do is to work to balance the over or under energy imbalance between the two organs that are in question. This can be accomplished by using the principles of the 7 Element Transfer Laws and the Chi-Gung Healing, which is noted later in the chapter.

The last area I would check in working with the communication and function part of the fields of existence is to use any functional connections or tricks that are specific to the organs involved that I've learned through my years of Applied Kinesiology and Total Body Modification. I challenge you, the reader and practitioner, to use your own imagination and open up your thought processes to whatever possibilities you can think of. Remember, this pathway through 7 Element Healing techniques is just that, a pathway with many things being specific and undeniably repeatable and other things being left for you to explore yourself for the benefit of the patient.

1. Physical body structure and physical body energy

This area of the fields of existence relates to structural or energetic blockages in the physical body. This will also show up when the physical body is extremely exhausted and drained of energy.

1. Structural balance

    Structural balance refers to a physical blockage in the body. These blockages can be in the muscles, tendons, or lymph. The spine, being the main physical conduit and body support, is often the culprit of energy blockage and physical imbalance. However, the other joints of the body may also block the physical energy. As a Chiropractor, this is the easiest part of my job with patients. I search the spine and find the deviations or subluxations and correct them. There are also simple methods for Chiropractors to adjust the other joints of the body. Massage, acupressure, or any method you may know can be used to free the body of physical blockages.

2. Energetic blockages

    Adjusting the spine and joints will clear most energetic blockages. However, certain areas of the physical tissue may also be dense and causing blockages of energy. Muscle testing with one hand and passing over my other hand, palms down fingers separated close to the body, I can detect blockages and energy into soft tissue. Placing my hands above and below the area and in contact with the body, I focus and concentrate, using my energy to alleviate these energetic blockages.

3.   Physical exhaustion

This area may also show when a patient's energy is completely drained. This is a time to discuss with the patient how he balances work and rest. Also, look into sleep problems (check adrenal and pineal reflexes together). If the drainage is not from the first two areas, sugar may be the culprit. I have found some patients who are "sugarholics" to have extremely drained their energy while examining this field of existence area. Run the sugar protocol (see Total Body Modification seminars) and get them off refined sugar.

Allergy Elimination

Allergies, asthma, and autoimmune diseases are rampant in our society. We have more diseases now than ever in the history of man. We fool ourselves by saying things like, "Well, in the past, they didn't live as long as us," or "They didn't know they had these diseases." I am positive that if anyone from the 1850s on up had cancer, diabetes, allergies, asthma, heart disease, and any of the autoimmune diseases we have now, they would have known and documented it. It was *not* the middle ages of medicine. We are only talking about one hundred to one hundred fifty years ago, not ancient time. And yes, modern Americans *on average* are living a few years longer. But the biggest change in longevity comes from a decreased birth death rate and the reduction of world war conflicts. The birth death rate was approximately twenty-nine per one hundred births even at the turn of the century in 1900. If we change that birth death rate to what it is now 1 or 2 percent, that would raise the average age of someone in the late 1800s from approximately forty years to sixty-five. So longevity statistics are an average statistic.

Contrary to many modern beliefs, there were people hundreds of years ago living to ripe old ages past a hundred years old. The difference is close to half of the population that never made it to forty years old. So if we take the birth death rate out, on average, we are living a little bit longer today, approximately four to ten years, but we are experiencing a significantly greater number of sickness and ill health than in the past. As far as longevity, people of our time are getting cancers, colitis, allergies, asthma, diabetes, multiple sclerosis, lupus, myasthenia gravis, and a host of other diseases in their twenties, thirties, and forties, hardly a longevity problem. Diabetes was nonexistent in the 1880s. Many of our modern diseases, including cancer, were ridiculously rare before 1900.

Let us focus on one of our modern illnesses, allergies. Allergies are at epidemic proportions in our modern society. This is to say that at least 29 percent of the population has them. More children are seriously allergic to peanuts and other common foods than ever in the history of our country. In our modern society, we accept allergies as the status quo. We treat the symptoms with drugs; most of these drugs with long-term use have negative effects. All disease is an abomination of normal function and life. The reason you still have your allergies is due to the fact that modern medical science does not know the cause and cannot answer the question of *why* you have allergies and someone else doesn't.

What are allergies? They are energetic disturbances of the Lifeforce. The Lifeforce is altered from its balanced natural state, causing you to react to normal frequencies (allergens) and trigger an unnatural immune response to a normal substance. This immune response to normal things is an abomination of function and *not* natural. Medical science would have you believe that allergies and disease are normal states of being. They are not; they are abominations of normal function. Allergies and many types of asthma are not normal. If we can remove the causes and rebalance the body, then we can eliminate allergies. Historically, it is hard to find evidence of allergies before the 1900s. And if we could find some evidence, we would still be hard-pressed to find the sheer numbers of allergies and the severity of allergies that is now part of modern human experience. Anaphylactic peanut allergies are many times more common now than they were even thirty years ago.

The changes in our lifestyle and in our environment are the causes of allergies. The truth is that allergies are malfunctions of the human "software" or Lifeforce. Let me share with you the best examples I can of this phenomenon. The best example is to equate the physical body with the Earth, and the Lifeforce Chi body with the atmosphere that surrounds the Earth. In dealing with the problem of global warming, let's for our example accept the major theory of greenhouse gases contributing to the warming of the Earth (which is the accepted principle of about 95 percent of research science). If we do things on the Earth and create pollution, the resulting pollution disturbs the atmosphere balance. Simply stated, the disturbance of the atmospheric balance takes the normal sunlight and increases it, causing the Earth to warm unnaturally. By the same token, if we pollute the physical body with unnatural chemicals, pesticides, preservatives, poisons, and many other types of toxic agents, even if we say those toxic substances are "within normal limits" (which means individually these poisons will not kill you immediately), we will disturb the function of the Lifeforce (atmosphere).

For our example, just imagine that we were unable to "see" the atmosphere and did not know it existed and we kept just researching inside and on the Earth (physical body) for the causes of global warming. No matter how hard we look inside and on the Earth, we would never find the *cause* of global warming. We would know it existed and have some data about it, but the *cause* would still escape us because we would have to research the atmosphere to find the cause. If we keep looking in the physical body for the *cause* of allergies, we will never find it because the cause is in the Lifeforce Chi body. This creates a problem for the scientific medical community that does not even have a word for nor any focus on the Lifeforce Chi body.

Put toxins and chemicals in the physical body that are disturbing to the Lifeforce and you create "glitches" in software that is your Lifeforce. Glitches are the malfunction of the Lifeforce, much like when spyware or malware clogs up the software of your computer. One of the problems with glitches is that they are just like spyware. You can get spyware on your computer and never notice anything for years. But as soon as you get enough spyware, the function of the computer will slow or a program will malfunction. I once had so much spyware on my computer that when I tried to use Google to find out information on a subject, my eBay account would come up. By looking at the screen, I had no idea how to fix that and no clues as to the *cause*. An experienced IT guy would go "behind my computer screen" and clear all the spyware out of the software, and the computer programs would function normally again. That is the answer to eliminating allergies. Rebalance and clear the Lifeforce Chi body of malfunctions (spyware and other garbage) and then harmonize the Lifeforce Chi body to the offending substance; then that normal substance (allergen) will no longer energetically and physically react with the physical body.

Another problem for the scientific community is that just like spyware, which is unpredictable in when and what functions it changes on your computer. Glitches in the human Lifeforce software are also unpredictable and highly individualized. This means that same exposure to toxic, druglike substances can glitch one person and not another. Also, the combination and amount of glitches may cause one person to be allergic to one substance while the same combination may cause different or *no* allergy reactions in another. This creates a problem for the standardization of allergies, which is the forefront of the medical research and focus. Allergy elimination is a totally *individualized* process, which is first dependent on clearing the malfunctions (glitches) of the Lifeforce Chi body.

Glitches

Glitches are damages to Lifeforce field that must be corrected before allergy elimination is possible. There are nine different glitches that I have isolated as root causes for allergies. Let me say at this time that much of this work is built on the works of others and draws heavily from Total Body Modification procedures developed by Dr. Victor Frank and others in the Chiropractic field. Using the following procedures,

I have been able to eliminate and/or improve most allergy conditions. I have even had success in treating anaphylactic peanut and apple allergies. But I am not alone in that ability. Applied Kinesiologists, Total Body Modification practitioners, and others in the field of alternative Chiropractic and energy healing have also had success in these areas.

To understand glitches, you must first realize that the physical body and the Lifeforce Chi body are inseparable. They work simultaneously. Unless you have done mediation, yoga, martial arts, and/or worked on your spiritual development in some way, you may not be aware of the Lifeforce Chi body. This does not mean that it does not exist. When the Lifeforce Chi body is in balance with Chi flowing and circulating in perfect balance, the physical body systems, including the immune system, function normally and at maximum efficiency. Any discrepancy in the flow, circulation, and balance of the Lifeforce Chi body will be reflected in discrepancies in the physical body. Vice versa if the physical body is damaged, overused, or poisoned with toxic chemicals, that damage will reflect to the Lifeforce Chi body. The Lifeforce Chi body is the directing force for the physical body, so this is why meditation, Taoist practice, and balanced emotions can trigger better physical body function.

A second thing to consider is that as a human being, you are a living organic, physical, and energetic organism. Your physical body and the Lifeforce Chi body are intrinsically connected to all the organic life of nature. Anything that is natural is natural for you as a human being. Yes, there are some natural poisons and dangers, but as an organic living being, your frequency is attuned to the natural. Anything that is inorganic is unnatural to the human being organism. Every molecule of the inorganic man-made substance is an aberration to the organic living entity that you are. This is why glitches happen. They are caused by bringing in unnatural or man-made chemicals, poisons, and drugs into a pure natural organic living being. Remember, in our modern world, 90 percent of the things we come in contact with were not in existence before the industrial revolution and the turn of the century, 1900. It's no wonder that the dramatic increase in our modern degenerative diseases—including cancer, diabetes, autoimmune diseases, allergies, asthma, and a host of other conditions—were not prevalent and definitely not anywhere near the sheer numbers that they are today. The constant assault of inorganic and poison compounds and the extra energy needed to detoxify every molecule of these poisons is the first step to acquiring many of our modern diseases. This battering and assault on our body leads to discrepancies and imbalances in our Lifeforce that are the foundation of allergies and other diseases.

The following is a chart that can be used to eliminate glitches as a first step in allergy elimination. The Lifeforce glitch phenomena and information was already discussed in chapter 2. This is a guideline for your use. Remember, any number of combinations may appear when working with a patient. Also, please remember that this is a *completely individual* process. Twenty people can be exposed to the same amount of toxic stress, but only one person may get glitched. You must work with each person as a separate individual and not connected to the genetics or familiarity of their families. Your patient has arrived at their disease by their own pathway, and you must work backward to untangle the disease (a saying by Dr. Victor Frank).

The chart below illustrates the most common connections that I have found in my thirty years of healing work. Glitches are found by placing the "glitch hand," fingers, and thumb together (see hand mudras earlier in this chapter) into or over the different 7 Element areas. Then with intention muscle testing, you can use the chart below to determine the Lifeforce glitch and the energetic correction. This chart is what I have found after years of practice, but it is just a guide, as there may be occasions when you may have to search further with your muscle testing. Once the glitch is determined, the second chart will aid you in energetically removing the glitch.

These charts are an amalgamation of my own work, but the spinal reflexes along with the sugar protocol and the vertebral reflexes for each organ are the work of Dr. Victor Frank and other researchers at Total Body Modification. I would advise any physician or healer who wants to work with allergy elimination to take at the bare minimum, the first two modules of the Total Body Modification procedures before undertaking any allergy elimination work.

Most Common

Glitches/Element	Organ Gland
7. Spirit/pineal	Neurotoxins
	Solvents
6. Air/pituitary	Neurotoxins
	Electromagnetic radiation (EMR)
	Heavy Metals
5. Metal/thyroid	Vaccinations
	Molds
	Electromagnetic radiation (EMR)
	Sugar
4. Fire/heart or thymus	Solvents
	Vaccinations
3. Wood/liver	Sugar
	Heavy Metals
	Solvents
	Neurotoxins
2. Earth/spleen	Sugar
	Molds
1. Water/kidneys or adrenals	Sugar
	Molds
	Solvents
	Neurotoxins

Chart#2

Glitches-   Organ - Correction   Systems-Correction

(tap vertebral levels with inhalation and exhalation)
1. Sugar   Thyroid   C-4   Immune; L-3, T-9, C-4
(TBM   Liver   T-2, T-5, T-8
PROCEDURE) Pancreas   T-5
        Adrenals   T7, T9, T11
2. Heavy metals   Pituitary (Traction   Nervous sys; L-3, L-5
        w/ vials   Glabellar and occiput
    3xs with respiration)
                Liver T-2, T-5, T-8
3. Vaccinations Thyroid C-4   Immune sys; L-3, T-9, C-4
        (use vials w/ vert. levels)   Thymus T-9
4. Solvents   Thymus T-9   Circulation; L-3, L-5; C-5
    (w/vials)   Liver T-2, T-5, T-8
        Adrenals T-7, T-9, T-11
        Pineal (Temporal pump
                3xs inspiration)

215

5. Molds   Thyroid C-4   Skin sys. L-3, S-3
        Kidneys T-1, T-5, T-8
        Spleen T-1, T-5, T-9
6. E.M.R.   Pituitary (Glabellar   Nervous sys, L-3, L-5
        traction)   or
        Thyroid C-4   immune sys, L-3, T-9, C4
7. Neurotoxins Pineal (see above)   Reprod. sys.,L-3, C-7, L-5
                              Pit. (see above)
        Adrenals T-7, T-9, T-11
        kidneys T-1, T-5, T-8
        Liver T-2, T-5, T*

Additional (not found too often
8. Pharmaceutical drugs Liver T-2-5-8 Immune sys.
        nervous sys.
        Repro. sys.
9. Emotions   Thyroid C-4   Any system

Once you have cleared all the glitches, you can proceed to the harmonization of the allergy with the Lifeforce Chi body. Depending on how confused or glitched your patient is will determine how long or how many visits it may take to clear all the confusion or glitches in the Lifeforce software. Remember, after a glitch is cleared and retested, have the patient lie still, eyes closed, and take a few deep abdominal (Earth) breaths or use Total Body Modification blocking procedures to save the glitch clear. The harmonization process that we will continue on to next, along with the above organ vertebral reflexes, is credited to Dr. Victor Frank and the researchers of Total Body Modification.

Allergy Harmonization Procedure

The following procedure is an energetic breakthrough from research of Dr. Victor Frank and the Total Body Modification researchers. After you have completely cleared all nine glitches and have rechecked to be sure they are clear, you can start the allergy harmonization procedure. Be sure to remind patients that going back on refined sugar is one of the easiest ways to reglitch the system and interfere with allergy elimination. The harmonization procedure is very simple. Because allergies are a disturbance between the allergen and the Lifeforce Chi body, which then becomes a chemical reaction in the physical body, the way to eliminate an allergy is to get the Lifeforce Chi body in harmony with the allergen. What we are essentially doing is helping the Lifeforce be energetically in harmony with the offending allergen. Because the Lifeforce Chi body is organ specific, meaning that the balance of the 7 Element organs or glands is of primary importance, then finding the element organ that is disturbed by the specific allergen and using the harmonization procedure with the organ or gland involved is how the harmonization procedure works.

Harmonization Procedure

Part 1

Step 1

Place the suspected allergen or frequency vial on the heart area of the patient and proceed to muscle test. If the allergen is disturbing the Lifeforce, it will cause a positive test or weak muscle test.

Step 2

Using the sword hand and placing your hand in the various areas of the 7 Elements and with intentional muscle testing, ask and see which corresponding organ or gland of that element is disturbed by the allergen.

Step 3

Using the Total Body Modification organ reflexes, stimulate the proper vertebral sequence relating to the organ or gland in question (see correction chart above). You may also use the universal reflexes (outlined later in this chapter) instead of the Total Body Modification reflexes or any other energetic strengthening technique you know for that particular organ. The following is the most common organ or gland and element connections for allergies.

Element	Organ or Gland
1. Water	Adrenals
2. Earth	Spleen
3. Wood	Liver
4. Fire	Thymus
5. Metal	Thyroid
6. Air	Pituitary
7. Spirit	Pineal

(Remember that these are just the most used organ or glands for harmonization for each element, but it can be any gland or organ related to the disturbed element.)

Step 4

After strengthening the organ reflexes, pick up the allergen from the chest for a few seconds and then re-place it on the chest and muscle test. The test should now show strong, confirming the harmonization is complete.

Part 2

Now use Goodheart's therapy localization technique. With the vial or allergen still on the body, have the patient place their fingers or hand on the allergy site, meaning if the patient gets a stuffed up head as their allergy symptom, have them place their hand on their forehead, then muscle test. If it is their eyes, have them touch their closed eyes with their fingers, then test. If the allergy symptoms occur in the throat, have them place their hand on the throat, then test, etc. For any positive test while the hand or fingers are touching the body part and the vial (allergen) is on the body (heart or neck area works the best for the placement of the vial or antigen), rub out the posterior universal reflex at the jade pillow (the space right under the occiput, acupuncture spot GV 16). Then retest. The muscle should show strong.

Final step

With the allergen or vial still on the body, check the reboot procedure (outlined later in this chapter) and fix any chakra that creates a weak muscle response.

This harmonization procedure seems easy and is very simple. Remember that you must clear the underlining glitches to make this harmonization process work to eliminate the allergy. Also, it has been my experience that you must test all possible allergens as the procedure seems to work the greatest after *all* allergens have been harmonized. There may be quite a few allergens that the patient does not realize they are sensitive to. I suggest any doctor who is serious about allergy elimination should take at least the first two Total Body Modification modules and work with the Total Body Modification vials and equipment.

When the patient comes in for a checkup visits, be sure to run through all glitches to make sure the patient is glitch free. Serious traumatic events or continuing exposures to toxic chemicals and refined sugar can set the patient back on an allergy path. It is my experience, however, that mainly refined sugar and electromagnetic disturbances commonly reglitch the patient. Please remember that all patients are individuals and must be treated *totally* individually.

Other Healing Helps

Anterior Universal Reflex Fix

The universal reflex fix is an easy and short way to correct any disturbed or short-circuited reflex. Fixing a reflex is like resetting a fuse; it will only temporarily fix a problem. You must discover the underlying causes of the overload (fields of existence, bad diet, etc.) or the overload will only short-circuit the fuse again. This reflex fix though will come in handy and shorten your search time. You may use this reflex instead of the Total Body Modification reflexes. You can stimulate the points by a circular rubbing with your fingers or rapidly tapping the points. Do them in the following order:

Point 1. Tap or circularly rub the jugular notch.

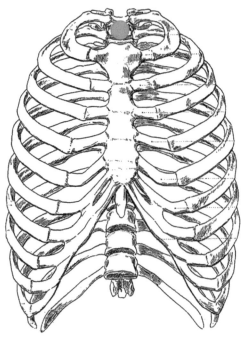

Illustration

Point 2. Tap or circularly rub the angle of Louis.

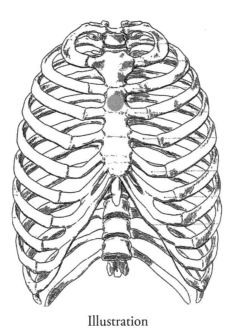

Illustration

Point3. Tap or circularly rub a point just below or at the tip of the xiphoid process.

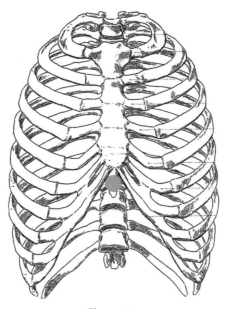

Illustration

Posterior Universal Reflex

The posterior universal reflex can be used to fix any out-of-balance reflex or organ dysfunction. Please remember that you are only fixing a fuse, and you must work on the reasons that caused the dysfunction. The posterior universal reflex is at the spot referred to in acupuncture as the "jade pillow" at the base of the posterior skull or occiput in the middle (which is G 16 on the acupressure charts)

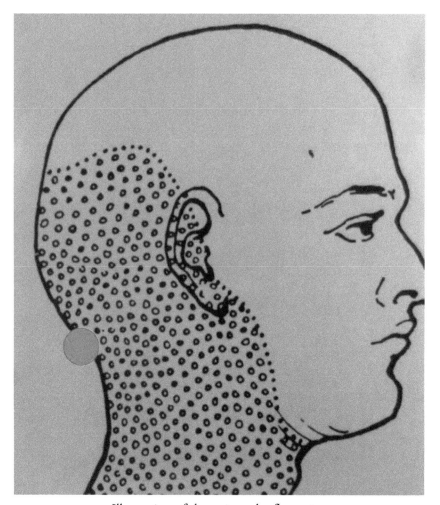

Illustration of the universal reflex point

Rebooting the Lifeforce

This is a technique that helps reset the different organ-specific areas of the 7 Elements of the body. This technique may be helpful for you as a precursor to starting with the patient or as an ending to your treatment. Basically, it is similar to rebooting your computer.

Step 1

Have the patient place their middle finger in the middle of the forehead (third eye) as you, the doctor, place the middle finger of your left hand at the jade pillow (the spot under the back of the skull at vertebral level C 1). If this causes a positive (weak) muscle test, then fix by circular rubbing the jade pillow area and placing your right hand above the forehead. Retest while touching the jade pillow and having the patient still contacting the third eye. Muscle test should be strong.

Step 2

Have the patient hold his thumb and pointer finger to the bridge of the nose (pituitary reflex). The doctor places his middle finger at the jade pillow. Then muscle test. If the muscle is strong, move to the next step. If it is weak, fix in the same manner as above by circular rubbing the jade pillow and placing the palm of your right hand over the forehead of the patient. Retesting should give you a strong muscle test.

Step 3

Patient now touches the throat with three fingers (thyroid reflex). The doctor then places the left-hand middle finger on the jade pillow. Test the muscle. If strong, move on; if weak, fix in the same way as above.

Step 4

Have the patient place their middle finger on the angle of Louis at the midsternal area. The doctor places his finger at the jade pillow. Test the muscle. If strong, move on. If weak, rub the jade pillow, then retest. The muscle should be strong.

Step 5

The patient now places the middle finger right below the xiphoid process. The doctor's finger stays at the jade pillow. Test the muscle. If it is strong, move on. If weak, rub out the jade pillow spot on the patient, then retest. The muscle should be strong.

Step 6

The patient now places their finger at the umbilicus. The doctor's finger stays at the jade pillow. Test the muscle. If it is strong, move on. If it is weak, rub out the jade pillow, then retest, and the muscle should be strong.

Step 7

The patient places his finger a few inches below the umbilicus on the *dan tien* area. The doctor's middle finger remains on the jade pillow. If the muscle test shows weak, rub out the jade pillow. Retest, and the muscle should be strong.

To the Reader

The above material is a synthesis of my study in Applied Kinesiology, Total Body Modification, my personal Taoist practice, and over thirty years of clinical experience.

I have outlined my work and experience in this chapter to open the door for you, the reader and/or practitioner, to explore new ways of helping others.

Please understand that although these healing techniques in the right healing hands can create miracles, they must be used along with modern medical practices, especially with truly sick patients. Modern medical practice is the best at crisis care. If your patient or friend is in crisis, medical care is *required*.

I have helped many sick and allergic patients with the work outlined in this chapter. It is my sincerest hope that this work will help others to a healthier and happier life.

CHAPTER 7

Healing the World

"Be victorious today over what you were yesterday; Tomorrow be victorious over
your clumsiness and then also over your skill. Practice what I have written without
letting your mind deviate from the way. One thousand days of training to develop,
ten thousand days of training to polish. You must examine this well."
—Miyamoto Musashi, Written this twelfth day
of the fifth month of the year of Shōhō (1645)

How do we change the world? We change the world in the *only* way we can, by changing and developing ourselves. We do not have the power to change others. We only have the power to change ourselves. As the wise and famous samurai, Miyamoto Musashi, commands us with his powerful words in 1645:

"Be victorious today over what you were yesterday."
Grow, evolve and make yourself a better person today than you were yesterday.
That in itself would be a great spiritual mantra to live by.
Every effort we make in physical, mental and emotional development,
Every second we spend working on our own "stuff,"
Every moment we spend in prayer, meditation and stillness,
Every time we touch the untouchable,
Every chance we have to practice unconditional Love,
Whenever we come to the realization of our own miraculous being;
These are the times that we contact the Shen (spirit) of our existence.
We can become a mirror of LOVE, PEACE, and HARMONY.
And in doing so WE CHANGE THE UNIVERSE.

My first Taoist teacher and dear friend Ron Diana once said, "You are vitally important to the evolution of the universe. You must be present and conscious."

When we seek to improve and spiritually develop ourselves, we add to the developing consciousness of the Earth and subsequently the universe. The path of self-development is our only path to change our world. The Taoists have a great concept in regards to human development. They believe that the physical body and health must be refined and purified; then the Lifeforce Chi body must be balanced and circulated, including emotional and mental development. When these two areas of our being, the physical body and the Lifeforce Chi body are refined, developed, and in balance, then the inherent *shen* or Spirit will appear. It is like saying that there is Fire in every piece of Wood. We can't see the Fire in the Wood but is inherently there. If the Wood is prepared by being dried first and then we light it, the Fire will consume the Wood, and the Wood becomes all Fire. There is Spirit inherent in all human beings; it is not always apparent. When we strive to develop ourselves in all directions—physical, emotional, mental, and spiritual—and we use the spark of opening our hearts and loving unconditionally, then the Spirit that is inside us will become apparent. We will become all Spirit just as the Wood becomes all Fire.

This self-development, self-evolution theme is echoed by Lao Tzu:

Would you like to liberate yourself from the lower realms of life?
Would you like to save the world from the degradation and destruction it seems destined for?
Then step away from shallow mass movements and quietly go to work on your own self-awareness.
If you want to awaken all of humanity, then awaken all of yourself.
If you want to eliminate the suffering in the world,
then eliminate all that is dark and negative in yourself.
Truly, the greatest gift you have to give is that of your own
Self-transformation.

—*Hua Hu Ching: The Unknown Teachings of Lao Tzu*, number 75

Everybody's life and "story" has its negatives, missed chances, and regrets. There is no perfect being on this planet. I always say, "We are all off the road and working to get back on the road." Even the Dalai Lama isn't always right down the middle of the white line all the time. He may not be as far off as most of us, but he too has to work to shift himself to the center. Many times in life, we feel as if we have gone off the road into a ditch. These are the times that take the most valiant effort to pick ourselves up and get back on the right path. But remember, the worth of a person is never measured when life is going their way and all is right in their world. The worth of a person is measured by their *actions* when everything in life has gone wrong, and they find themselves at the lowest possible place. It is when all seems lost that the worth of a person is measured: by what they do and how they move in a positive direction to right the ship and change their lives for the better.

There is no time limit to this spiritual quest. As long as you are alive, you can have spiritual growth and realization. There is no score being kept. You can lose ninety-nine battles but win the last one and have spiritual transcendence. I had a Catholic-school early upbringing. Most of it was scarily unspiritual. But I remember something that one of the brothers said that always stuck with me. He was talking to us; and he said that no matter where you find yourself, no matter how bad you feel, and even if you've committed some horrible criminal act, "there is a saint in heaven that was in that same place at one time." This was one of the truly spiritual and positive things that I can remember from my early Catholic education. It struck me that no matter where we find ourselves, if we can just turn and go in the right direction, we have the chance to add to the Love and positivity that our spirits were meant to be. I think that I will have on my tombstone the saying, "It doesn't matter where you are now, as long as you are going in the right direction."

There is *always hope*. There is *no* way to change the past. There is *always* a way to change your *direction* and move toward *Love now*.

Introspective

He knows men is clever;
He who knows himself has insight.
He who conquers men has force;
He who conquers himself is truly strong.

—Lao Tse, *Tao Teh Ching*, number 33

One of the keys to self-development is introspective, to look inside and see your strengths, weaknesses, and understand what you need to change to grow. Some of my best growth information came in long talks with my shaman, spiritual advisor, and best friend, Vincent Santo Ferrau. He would challenge me to look "inside" of my actions. He would encourage me to investigate the "whys" of what I was doing. To look deep inside my needs and discover what it is about me that continues to keep me stuck. We all need healthy doses of introspective time. Time to reevaluate our path in life, not to criticize ourselves for our shortcomings but try to investigate the reasons behind them. One tool for self- introspective is to look at the different stages or parts of your life and examine the main issues that continue to be the stumbling blocks throughout our lives.

Our human life here on Earth is a journey. That journey has stages. Each of these stages must be experienced and developed before moving on to the next stage and ultimately moving on from this life. If any stage is stifled or missed, parts of it must be revisited later in life to complete our growth. If we stay too long in any stage (get stuck), we will stunt our development. These tendencies will plague us until we conquer or complete them. The 7 Element concept can help us see our proper progression and our whole growth as a human being. It can also help us see where others may need help (notice I said help, not change others) on their journey. The first four stages are approximately 7 years in length; the latter stages can be four to 7 years. These are obvious approximations as no two-life journeys are exactly the same. Each stage has its priorities for growth, and they can be repeated in a higher form as we get older. The following is our life's' journey in the 7 Element perception:

Stage 1: Water (birth)
    Purpose: Survival
    Emotions: Fear
    Core issue: Change, support, will to live, perseverance
    Belief system: Life is safe, good, and positive or life is scary, bad, and negative. I want to live or I want to die.

The Water stage is the creation time. Is it time we spend in our mother's womb, encased in her "Water" (embryonic fluid). We are literally aquatic creatures at this time, breathing in Water as our Air, much like fish and amphibians. This stage includes gestation up to our birth where we "come out" to the world and take our first breath. Our first breath connects our being to the universe in our human duality existence of energy and substance. The experience of the womb and birth are well documented as possible causes for later actions. This stage will help determine our core or root belief system: "life is safe or life is unsafe and scary." This belief system may stay with us our whole life or be changed either way by the influence of our other element stages and experiences. This belief is vitally important to our overall positive or negative attitude toward life and health.

The Water Element and stage is also responsible for our survival instincts and can be influenced by the circumstances of our gestation and birth time. Perseverance and will to survive can be impacted by our fetal gestation and birth. Our core physical and emotional fortitude and strength is formed at this time, influenced by the "Yuan Chi" and genetic and personal energy of our parents. Our Yuan Chi or "Lifeforce battery" and longevity potential are formed in the Water stage. This is our potential longevity and not our actual longevity, which is influenced more by our actions and lifestyle.

Fear-related issues and issues of feeling unsafe and fearful of the world and the future are formed in the Water stage of gestation and birth. This instinctual fear or negative response to the questions of "Is life is safe or scary?" and "Is life inherently good or against you?" is a powerful force, positive or negative. It is important core issue in health and, if negative, can be a massive block to healing. The Water Element's kidneys, adrenals, bladder, and sexual and reproductive organs can be affected. This can cause low energy and depression, which are connected to the Water Element. The most important factor is the core belief system that life will be all right or life will be negative. Have you ever been around two people when a negative happens in their life? One person looks at it and says, "It will be all right; it will turn out okay." The other is convinced that "it was going to happen sometime" or "there's nothing worse than this" (no matter what this is). One is inherently positive, and the other is inherently negative. This issue is paramount in healing. One person wants to do whatever it takes to be healthy and sees their health problem as just an obstacle that they will overcome. Another gets a health problem, no matter how small, and sees it as the "end of the world" in some way.

Your parents' prenatal emotional relationship, mother's nutrition, the circumstances of your birth, and the makeup of your individual parents physically, emotionally, and spiritually will be a determining factor in your perseverance and your core positive or negative outlook on health and life. So it is in a person's best interest to have a secure, nonfrantic, nutritionally sound, and loving gestation and birth period to start out "on the right foot." You can check the belief systems and core issues or areas for each stage and part of the body on the 7 Element Chart. Also, understand that these core issues of each stage can be overcome or changed by self-introspection, personal development, and spiritual growth.

Stage 2: Earth (ages approximately zero to 7)
    Purpose: Nurture
    Emotions: Guilt, anxiety, and worry
    Core issues: Self nurture and nurture of others, abandonment, and family
    Belief systems" I am worthy of Love or I am not worthy of Love. I feel secure or I feel alone and abandoned.

The Earth stage is from birth to approximately 7 years of age. It is a time when we are bound to our family. Our lives are almost 100 percent dependent on our family connection. Our mothers are our most important influence, especially in the early infant years. Ethnic traditions are taught by example and because they are your family's way. Your family experience shapes much of your personality and many of your choices later in life. Your experience can make you a carbon copy of your parents, good or bad. It can also be a positive or negative influence in your parenting style when you have your own children. Later stages and life experiences can help you reverse a negative upbringing. Some people make it a goal to be better or different than the parents. The Earth stage is a nurturing stage, where you need your family matrix to help you grow physically and emotionally. Our concerns in this stage are usually self-centered. As babies, we cry out for food or when we need or want something. Our main concerns are of a self-centered, self-nurturing nature. During this stage, we often adopt our parents' mannerisms, actions, and ideals as our own. As with all stages, if we miss the nurture that we need at this stage or have negative imprints, we must later in life make changes related to our ability to nurture ourselves. For example, the Earth stage's purpose is nurture. We need to be nurtured and protected by our parents and our family unit. If our zero-to-7-year-old time is tumultuous, and we are also abandoned, or we miss the nurturing we need. We could take the direction of being "needy" and continuing to look for our "mother" in relationships and friends. The purposes, core issues, and belief systems that relate to each element on the 7 Element Chart will either be a strong point and easy for us or our weakness and our challenge.

We can be overmothered or "oversmothered" at this stage, which will also alter the normalcy of future relationships. Any abnormal or nonloving experience at this crucial stage can cause an over- or under- Yin or Yan personal problem in the future. By understanding what we should be receiving and connecting to any stage, we can then evaluate the causes and hopefully find the solutions to the way we feel and act. A poor or nonnurturing, nonloving childhood can cause you as a parent to react in a Yan or Yin way. As a parent, you may decide to right the wrongs of your childhood, bringing up your children in the exact opposite way you experienced in your childhood. Or your reaction may be no reaction, and you follow the same path as your parents, good or bad. Thus, an abused child can continue the abuse as parents or turn one hundred eighty degrees and try to rectify the abuse by acting in a completely opposite manner in bringing up their own kids. This sometimes causes parental overreaction. For example, if you were strictly disciplined as a child, you may not discipline your kids at all.

This stage is by far the most powerful in determining your personality and reactions. Events happening when you are zero to 7 years old take on a magical quality. The world is a tremendously big place to a small child. If you have moved away from your early childhood neighborhood and then returned as an adult, it will look tiny to you. In this stage, the world you see is not one of true reality but one of the fantasies of your perception. We truly believe in Santa Claus, the Easter Bunny, and monsters under our bed. We see the world through colored lenses that blur out some of the reality. Have you ever recalled a minor incident in your childhood that your parents don't even remember? Something they did or said that was insignificant to them but was monumental to you as a child. The world is "bigger than life" at this stage of development. That is why it is vitally important for parents to be mindful of the things they say and their discipline methods as they have a great impact on this stage of life. It doesn't matter the discipline method, as long as there is thought and purpose in it. The Love a parent feels is energetic and spiritual, and as long as a parent's Love is strong and unconditional, a child will know and feel it even when being disciplined. As a parent, you will never be in complete control of how your zero- to 7-year-old perceives the world. Inadvertent sayings and experiences will happen despite your best efforts, but the overall Love and support you give your child, balancing the urge to do everything for them versus helping them when needed, along with your true Love, will build a zero-to-7-year-old experience that will be the "Earth" that gives their later life grounding and centering.

Our psyche sometimes mixes things that don't match together or makes connections that are fantasy based in this stage but stick with us for life. Some of our belief systems are developed or fortified in this stage. Inadvertent connections between things that don't really connect in reality can even be the cause of sexual fetishes later in life. We have experiences that are not sexual but in this stage get connected to a sexual desire that we don't even realize as sexual. Distorted connections to inanimate objects or visual experiences may distort our natural reality-based sexual growth.

In this stage, it is important that we learn to be nurturing and caring, taking cues from our family's nurturing of us. These family lessons are paramount in our ability to nurture others and ourselves. For example, taking care of pets or learning to help care for siblings are important steps in our own ability to nurture others and ourselves as adults. The guidance that our parents give us in our own nurturing adventures will help formulate our nurturing ability, which is one of the core issues of this stage. Being taught respect, care, and helping a sibling creates valuable lessons for the zero-to-7-year-old experiences but, more importantly, adds to our positive adult relationships, parenting, and attitudes. It is easy to see that stability, Love, and nurture in this Earth stage play a vital role in the future of our adult personality.

What if our experience is opposite? If we don't receive the nurture, the learning to care for others, whether they are siblings or pets, how do we grow into loving spiritual beings? I believe that understanding the early influences on you and comparing what should have transpired in this stage allows you to make decisions in your adult actions that may be opposite of what your Earth stage experiences were. Thoughtful introspective without hate or blame can enable you to "right the wrongs" of your early childhood by embracing Love and learning to nurture yourself and others. This spiritual growth is much easier said than accomplished. I believe we need to see our life as a journey of growth. We must look at the experiences we've had, both positive and negative, as things we "needed" to have for this life's journey. Even having parents that may have been abusive or negative may be what we *needed* in this life to change ourselves to the positive.

I remember a television interview story told by a very old Kirk Douglas about his father who was mean, demanding, and always belittling him. Mr. Douglas decided in his life that he was going to be a success no matter what, just to spite his father's negativity and emotional abuse. With tears in his eyes from the pain of his early childhood, he was able to look at the rough and negative experience of his childhood as the thing that spurred him on to be the successful person he is.

Our experiences, both negative and positive, are our challenges to growth. As powerful as our Earth stage experiences are, spiritual introspective may be more powerful in determining major changes in our life that put us back on our path. Remember, it doesn't matter when we make a loving spiritual change to our being. It is important for us to look at our experiences as not just negative, hateful, unjust, and unfair or in a "why me" perspective but as challenges for us to overcome and in the process grow closer to our true spiritual potential. For those of us as myself, who have had stable, loving, and positive Earth stage experiences, it may be easier in some ways for us to face the challenges of our adult life, but all our pathways will always have obstacles and challenges for us to meet. Having introspective and knowing yourself and the relationship of your actions to your past experiences may give you guidance on your path through the journey of life.

Stage 3: Wood (ages approximately 7 to fourteen)
   Purpose: Growth
   Emotions: Anger, frustration, jealousy, and envy
   Core issues: Fairness and responsibility
   Belief system: I can or cannot handle the load (responsibility). Life is easy or I just can't win.
   Hard work is good or hard work is for fools.

From the ages of 7 to fourteen, we start to develop our own personalities. We are still connected and highly influenced by our parents and family mores, but we start to act and think in a more individual pattern. We also may take our family values and "go on the road" posing our parents' beliefs to teachers, fellow students, and others. Our sense of responsibility and individual achievement are developed at the Wood stage. We have jobs and functions in our family unit. Our relationships to the jobs or responsibilities at this time can shape our future work habits and our push or not for individual achievements in work, growth, and material attainment. As always, too much or too little strictness as far as responsibility in chores and work at this stage may have an opposite or the same response (Yin or Yan) that will reflect in our attention to responsibility. Being held strictly responsible at the Wood stage will reflect in our attention to responsibilities or our opposite rejection of our parents' strictness. Using myself as an example, I was a middle child with a brother who was six years older. My brother, being so much older than I, bore the brunt of family responsibilities, chores, and jobs. I was left on my own to play most of the time. When there was a major house project, it was accomplished by my father and brother working together. I was "too young" to be helpful. So I spent my time playing sports rather than fixing things or doing family jobs. The results were that my brother became an extremely responsible and financially successful adult. I have had responsibility issues and struggled financially most of my life. To this day, I have to force myself to work first and play later. I have to discipline myself to take care of the things I have to, before the things I want to. My only job during my Wood stage was to get good grades in school. Because of that, I did work hard at grades throughout my life and excelled at school. But ask me to fix the plumbing or complete jobs around the house and it always seems to be last on the list.

Achievement habits are formed in the Wood stage. Most teachers will agree that success at the second to fourth grade levels are vital to scholastic success in later grades. Our material values are also shaped at this time. Our sense of "mine" or "yours" and our monetary foundations happen during the Wood years. Our sense of power is also illuminated at this stage. Bullying is rapid through grades three to eight, roughly the

Wood Element years. This struggle for identity and power can create lots of tough memories and wounds to our psyche. During the Wood stage, there seems to be a struggle for identity, exploring "who you are." During this phase, groups form. When I was in school and later teaching, there were all sorts of different groupings: the "heads," the "jocks," the "nerds," the "hoods," the "popular girls," etc. Each generation may have different names for the grouping of kids during this stage, but the process is the same. All these focus us on identifying ourselves with something outside of our family, something that fosters our sense of who we are, even at the cost of our total individuality.

The Wood stage experiences will formulate our desire for growth in the academic, personal, and spiritual endeavors. We will actively pursue education, wealth, self-control, power, and yearning for spiritual growth; or "we will stay in our groove" and not push or reject going forward in any area. We may become avoiders of work or workaholics. Remember, the formulation of these stages will push us in a direction, but as full-functioning adults, we have the power to recognize and change the natural instinctive pull created by our element stage experience and go in a positive direction in our growth. That is the power of knowing ourselves and tracing our experiences, good or bad, throughout all 7 Element stages.

Stage 4: Fire (ages approximately fourteen to twenty-one, the turning point)
    Purpose: Connection
    Emotion: Love
    Core issue: Relationships
    Belief systems: If I Love I will be hurt or I will Love in spite of the possibility of being hurt.
    I am connected to all people or I am a separate entity not connected to others.
    All people are God's creation or people should be categorized and labeled.

The Fire stage is the time to "grow up." It is a rite of passage stage from childhood to adulthood. Almost all primitive and modern cultures had their adulthood rituals and rites at this time. From the years of fourteen to twenty-one, we are expected to go from very little responsibility to the rigors of being adults. From the 7 Element Chart, we can see that the Fire stage is connected to the heart. Its purpose is Love. It represents our connectedness to the people around us, to our whole environment, and to the world. It is in this stage that we make important connections to friends and members of the opposite sex. Our sexual feelings are awakened, and we explore romantic and physical contact with others. Many of the choices made in the Fire stage—the pursuit of education, job and career direction, a lifetime mate, etc.—direct the rest of our lives. The Fire stage is the most important stage of our 7 Element developmental journey. Just like our heart, opening to Love is the most important part of our spiritual journey. By design, it is also the turning point and the main downfall that plagues our modern society.

It is here, in the fourteen to twenty-one years, that most parents have competition for their parental responsibilities from TV and peer groups. It is also a vital part of this stage that we should learn reverence for all the Creator's creatures. To learn respect for the opposite sex. To not only connect with our peer group (friends) but also our parents, neighbors, younger children, and older relatives. You can see the problem here. A complete focus on our peer group without the connection of parental wisdom and spending time with younger and older people can create a focus on our self and our group that weakens our communal spirit and our tolerance for others and narrows rather than broadens our human experience. In ancient cultures and tribal communal living, this time was spent in mentorship. The child would study and follow older members of the tribe. He or she would be taught the necessities that they may need to grow. They would be taught not only survival skills of hunting, collecting and preparing food, and defending themselves but also be initiated and educated in the tribal views of sexual union and adult responsibility. In stark contrast, today is filled with violent video games, contests to see who can have the most sexual conquests and abuse girls, and a super push fill our material wants and to feel important and powerful. The first three stages are foundation, the walls, and a roof of our individual house. Now in the Fire stage, we decorate the inside and decide whether we will connect and invite others in with Love and hospitality or would turn our house into an ego cave for our own selfish desires and needs.

It is at this stage that we need our parents' guidance the most. We also need guidance from elders in our society. But instead, most parents allow children to grow up minus constructive adult contact and education. It is here where a good coach or teacher can have the biggest impact on a person's life, filling in for short period of time in a mentor's role.

Back in the 1970s, I was on vacation visiting in an extremely rural part of Virginia. One of the uncanny things I noticed was no matter where you went, you would run into *whole* families. All the family members went shopping together, went to movies together, and went out to dinner together, as a group, no matter how old the children were. High school students were with their parents as were younger siblings together for many, if not all, of their activities. I was taken back because where I came from, in a wealthier suburban area of New Jersey, packs of adolescents roamed malls as a group. Parents and adolescents were on different schedules doing different things at different times. It is important at this stage that we are taught by example to be good family and community members whether we are dealing with our little brother or sister, another adult, or an elderly person. Although peer group socialization is important, narrowing our experiences to just our peer group impedes our spiritual growth, our tolerance, and our ability to be open and loving to all.

Don't despair, as the Tao of our life will give us multiple chances to repair the damage and fulfill our element stage purposes later in life. The Ebenezer Scrooge story demonstrates that miraculous turnabouts can happen, but affording our children with full loving experiences according to the stages of development is a much easier way to ensure the spiritual growth of our world by helping positively develop each individual.

Love is the transitional transcending force. The first three stages of Water, Earth, and Wood are more about our physical and individual development. It is the Fire stage of Love and compassion that we transcend the physical by connecting to the Love of one another. This Love of others, Love of ourselves, and Love of our environment and existence will connect the physical and spiritual aspects of our being, and the *shen* or soul Spirit will become apparent. Connecting our children and young teenagers to the power of unconditional Love is a challenge for all parents, teaches, grandparents, and anyone else that has the opportunity to influence young adults. Showing young adults their connectedness to all people and their environment is crucial for us in developing a better world. It is not the power-ego development but willingness to foster harmony that will save our planet and our existence. Showing children the ripple effect of their actions, both positive and negative, will help them see that they are part of the evolution of their family, town, the country, the world, and the universe. They are not isolated individuals with the goal of having more "stuff" than anyone else, but they can be positive beacons of Love that will brighten others and in turn add more light to the world than darkness.

Stage 7: Fire to Spirit
(Stage 5 in energetic order)

Spirit
Purpose: Oneness, harmony, and peace
Emotion: Joy or shame
Belief system: I am one with all things around me: the Earth, the universe, God, Tao or I am disconnected and separate from all around me.

In Taoism, the heart is thought to be the seat of *shen* or Spirit. In 7 Element Lifeforce Healing, the heart and Spirit are closely aligned. The direction of the Lifeforce energy from the heart or Fire Element goes directly up to the Spirit Element. Water and Earth combine to give us Wood. When burned and transformed by the heat of the Fire Element, it becomes smoke, which rises to the heavens. The transformation of the more material and physical lower elements by the heart transforms them to spirit. The Spirit energy rises the highest then travels downward, enriching Air and Metal Elements and continuing downward to complete the cycle (see the 7 Element energy flow chart). This is why the Fire stage is so important. By teaching children to Love, share, and be in harmony with others and their environment, their physical material instincts can be transformed and infused with spiritual intent and action. At this crucial point in our development (Fire stage), we can transform our greed, selfishness, and self-centered actions into actions that not only help us but also add to harmony and peace in our world. It is so important to inspire our young people (fourteen to twenty-one years old) to be sensitive to all those around them and to see themselves as part of the whole community of humanity. Even in this stage of personal upheaval and finding direction in education, career, and socialization, young adults must have good examples and instruction on loving, being sensitive and aware of others, being part of a greater community, and connecting to all around them. The further stages of development of Air (balance rational thought) and Metal (expression) will be tempered with Spirit and the goal of harmonious actions that not only benefit us but also others and our Earth. This will cause the downward force of spiritual energy to control and balance the physical or material part of our being. We will act in coordination with all parts of our being—physical, energetic, and spiritual. The physical material ego needs will be in concert and balance with the spiritual communal harmonious soul.

The Spirit Element is like a wisp of smoke, just a hint of existence. It is a real entity but one that is hard to lay your hands on. The Spirit stage has no time. The Taoists feel that the *shen* or Spirit is housed in the heart. To me, it means that when the heart is open and loving unconditionally, the inherent Spirit of a person becomes apparent. It is hoped that some time in a person's life, their spiritual essence will be self realized. Sadly, many never realize their own spiritual core essence. In a perfect world, the Spirit Element would be recognized during or just after the Fire years of fourteen to twenty-one. This is why on the sacred mountains of China, the Taoists initiate monks at ten to twelve years old. They then study and practice until they are in their twenties, getting spiritual guidance at the perfect time. Too often, realization of our spiritual being waits until the decline of an aged physical body and the specter of death forces us to deal with our spiritual nature. It is easy to see how a person that gets true spiritual guidance (not religious dogma) at a very young age can balance their existence and make them a beacon of light for the world. The best and easiest modern example to see is the current Dalai Lama, who was engulfed the spiritual teaching of a nonviolent Buddhist nature from a very early age. He grew to a spiritual existence, and his whole life has become an example of Love and spirituality.

If we use the Fire Element stage to transcend our egotistical desires, then the following stages will be infused with the Spirit of Love and harmony. If we get stuck in any stage due to lack of Love, addiction to drugs, or any other emotionally stifling experience, then we are doomed to a stunted or delayed spiritual growth. And we may stay stuck in one of the physical or material "me" or individual stages. Even worse, if we bypass the Fire stage development of Love and connectedness to all, we could directly connect the Air Element (adult thinking brain) to our selfish physical needs. Connecting the Air Element (rational thinking brain) to any of the lower three physical or material or "me" stages and bypassing unconditional Love and our connectedness to all those around us is what creates the monsters of our time: the psychopaths and sociopaths who use their brains to calculate how to steal, rape, and kill, never connecting to their hearts or seeing themselves connected to their victims at all. The CEO workaholic who connects the Air Element (adult rational brain) to the Wood Element (achievement, material success) will work nonstop to fulfill egotistical greed goals, forgetting about compassion for their fellow man and unaware of the damage that their "take and take more" attitude and actions have on others, the environment, and even their own family life. If our adult actions are not filtered through the compassion of the heart and the connection and oneness of spirit, then they become selfish, physical, material, and egotistical purposes. They become the struggle for survival, kill first and often, or the hierarchy of power and dominance of the savage animal world, not the higher human capabilities of harmony, Love, sharing, and peace. It is imperative that the stages of heart and Spirit are not bypassed. If they are, they must be realized later in life; otherwise, a person will be devoid of real spiritual growth and his impact on his surroundings will not have the lasting positive effect of Love.

Stage 6: Air (ages approximately twenty-one to twenty-7)
    Purpose: Rational thought, organization, problem solving, and knowledge culmination
    Emotions: Hate, prejudice, and obsession
    Core issues: Control, judgment, and categorization
    Belief system: My life is in my control or my life is out of my control.

The Air Element stage is a culmination of our brain development. In this stage, we figure out what directions we want to go in and make decisions on what we are going to do with the rest of our lives. We continue with advanced studying, and if we are already working, we learn the inside facts and become knowledgeable about our jobs and careers. We make major life decisions about marriage, family, where to live, etc. If the other stages have been vetted with good experiences and good development, we can make crucial decisions using a developed thought pattern that is balanced with the first five Element stages. If we have had negative experiences or have been stuck in the other stages, our decisions will not have the light of wisdom intelligence and perfect action. Look back on your own twenties and see if the decisions you made at this crucial time were anchored in a stage development problem, lack of knowledge and experience, or were they the perfect decision for that time. This stage is truly decision time, and our brains have to be balanced with the proper temperament of the good experiences of the preliminary stages of Water, Earth, Wood, Fire, and spirit. This will allow us to make positive judgments for ourselves and for the good of others.

Too often, the Air Element is connected directly with one of the more material and physical elements of Water, Earth, or Wood. If a person's thinking brain (Air Element) is fixed and connected to the Wood stage and Element without the experience of compassion and awareness of those around them (Fire stage), their mind will focus exclusively on material goals of work, money, success, and achievement. This is fine if it is tempered with compassion and realization of others and the impact of your actions. If not, it can cause anything from a workaholic to a power-ego-driven-"any way to the top"-type person. It is a sad commentary, but it is my opinion that most of the current CEOs of major American corporations and pharmaceutical companies would probably sell heroin to four-year-olds if they could make a big profit and get away with it. The "me first" overachiever without any worry about others and the effects of their actions all point to unbalanced Air, Fire, and Spirit Elements.

In the physical body or in the Lifeforce Chi body, when elements are out of balance, they can cause malfunction and disease. If the stages of development of our life are out of balance or missed, they too will cause malfunction of our spiritual path and imbalance in our world and universe. The emotions of hate, prejudice, and obsession are all associated with the Air Element and Air stage. It is easy to see how warped or fragmented Elemental stage developmental experiences can cause an unbalanced Air Element. The brain's perceptions, without the temperament of the heart's Love and compassion (Fire Element), and the Spirit Element's oneness concept can lead to a cold, calculating thought pattern and actions that explain the holocaust and many other examples of man's inhumanity to his fellow man.

An overdeveloped or imbalanced Air Element is a common "Western" disease. In this part of the world, we are "all in our head." If we can think it up and do it, we do, never focusing on caring about the impact of our actions. The European philosopher Descartes is famous for saying, "I think therefore I am." Our Western world places an extremely high and exclusive emphasis on thinking and the brain as the epitome of human existence. "I think, I feel, and I am one with all things" should be the statement of human existence, bringing together a balanced human action. As a physician and healer, I am often confronted with patients who overload their brain to the exclusion of their physical body and feelings. This "all in the head" type of functioning dries out and depletes the Water Element, much like the sun absorbs Water from the Earth into the atmosphere. This type of imbalance can cause a decreased sexual energy and ultimately cause a "burn out" of the body. Since the Air Element supports the Water Element, an overused or blocked Air Element can cause a physical energetic drought. Adrenals and kidney energy will be weakened, which can weaken the entire body, including the immune system. The overwhelming amount of information and the constant thinking of solving our modern problems can cause a dearth of energy. Many people extend this by trying to figure out every future perceived problem to feel that they have complete control over their lives (control is the Air Element core issue). This "big head" syndrome is part of the modern-day stress that makes us vulnerable to disease. This is why meditation is so important and valuable to the Western mind. Meditation creates a state where the mind is cleared and in the long run controlled by the person, rather than being the controlling force. Just imagine the example of driving your car. The car is the physical and solid entity (physical body and physical brain). The person (you) is the superintelligent Lifeforce Chi body. When you get in your car, *you* decide where to go and direct the car's energy to *your* destination. The car does not drive you to where it wants to go. You direct the car's destination, not the other way around.

You should be the directing force over your physical body and your brain. The brain and body should not be running nonstop on its own accord. Meditation is the practice of calming and clearing the mind of chatter. With time, this practice will afford you control over the mind by being able to shut it down at will. This is especially helpful for good sleep but will also balance out the overwhelming stress of our modern existence. Remember, a little bit of peace balances out a lot of chaos. There are many meditation practices from different disciplines that all can be helpful. I recommend using the stillness breathing practice of getting between Yin and Yan (between inhale and exhale, tranquility breath) found in chapter 4 of this book.

5. Stage 5: Metal [ages twenty-eight to thirty-five]
(Stage 7 in energetic order)
    Purpose: Creativity and expression
    Emotions: Grief, sorrow, and sadness
    Core issues: Being true to yourself, expression or speaking out, and letting go
    Belief systems: It is okay to speak out and be my true self or I must hide my true self
    and hold my tongue.

Understanding the progression of stages and knowing the energetic pathway of the body and the universe leads us to the Metal stage.

CHI - MERIDIAN
TIME FLOW CHART

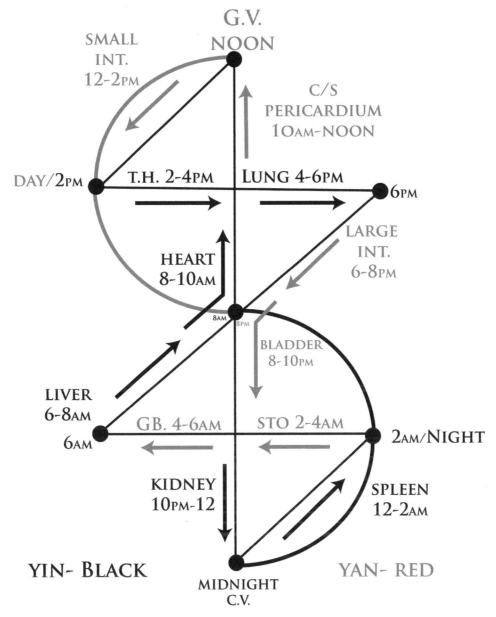

© 2013 DR Harry R. Elia   7 Element Growth and Energy Flow Chart

The Metal stage is the culmination of all six of the stages. It is our creative and expressive stage. Hopefully, we have benefited from good experiences and growth in all the other stages to allow our expression to be one that is complete, complex, and connected to our mind, Love, and spirit. The old adage of "think before you speak" rings true. Our expression in life should be a balanced culmination of all of "us," and it should connect to positive experiences in all the other six elements stages. The Metal stage is the time start to make a real impression in our world. We gain insight and knowledge in our chosen job or professional career. We are usually in a stage of parenthood, directing and contributing to our family unit along with our individual growth. Many decisions we make in this stage will set the course for the second half of our lives. There is also a time when we start to relive some of the other stages. We are parents now, hopefully learning and using our positive childhood experiences to be positive parents. Or learning from our childhood experiences to change our parenting skills in a more positive way. We may be involved in our children's activities revisiting positively but hopefully not reliving our own childhood activities. We will have many more opportunities to be loving and spiritual beings in this time, whether it be in our work, family, or community activities. For many of us, it is the time to grow and shine in the public eye. Directing communal activities, being part of business projects, or just contributing to our home, surroundings, and family's growth.

It is the time for our creative expression to be at the maximum. The different parts of us and our core issues and stages can be realized at any time, but with proper stage development, we not only have a positive balance but an ability to reach higher levels of spiritual growth in our later years. All other stage core issues may also coalesce in the Metal stage, meaning we may be forced by fate to deal deeply in all core issues and question some of our false belief systems. This may bring about heavy conflict and crisis at this stage. Divorce, job changing or loss, moving from one place to another—all forcing us to deal with our unresolved issues and fractured stage development. One thing I can assure you of is that any issues that you have failed to deal with or any parts of yourself that you have denied accepting will continue to be issues in your life over and over again. The journey of life will force you to look deeply, realistically, and lovingly at yourself. It will also bring up fractured and underdeveloped stages of your growth.

Life will also continue to make you deal with the things that you want to avoid until there is no avoiding them. That is why it is important to continually "look" at yourself. Look inside and behind the reasons for your actions. It is only in understanding yourself deeply and accepting yourself fully can you consciously ascend to what you were meant to be. Self-questioning, self-inspection, meditation, and realizing and loving what and who you truly are is the pathway to improving, developing, and realizing your true spiritual self. It would be wonderful if all the stages of our lives were perfect, balanced, and in harmony with our spiritual growth. However, that would not be human life. The human journey is fractured, incomplete, and ridiculously hard at times but also has moments of tremendous beauty and wonder. Our foundations are important. The better the foundation, the better chance for staying on the true path. But even with perfect stage development, there are no guarantees. A person with a good foundation may still end up in the ditch, and a bad foundation or fractured stage development doesn't mean failure. Your human story is up to you. Introspection and knowing fully and truly loving yourself is the opening door to your spiritual transcendence.

Being One with the Universe

> Heaven and Earth are the parents of all things. They join together as one body. When they part, it is the beginning of all troubles. If in one's life all three spheres—body, mind and Spirit—are in perfect balance, one is able to join in the larger flow of universal life.
> —Hua-Ching Ni, *Attaining Unlimited Life: Teachings of Chuang Tzu*

Energetically and emotionally, we can develop our connection to universal energy. To understand this process, we need to look at the energies of Heaven, Earth, and Man. Man finds himself between the two powerful forces of Heaven and Earth. The heaven or Spirit force of the stars, sun, planets, and atmosphere—with its clouds, rain, thunder, and lightning—radiates its power down to man. The forces of the Earth, Water, and Wood emanate from below.

Illustration: man between the powers of heaven and Earth

Inside of man, the two separate forces of physical and spiritual energy go in the opposite directions. The raw physical needs of survival and sex (Water), food (Earth), and material wants (Wood) are parts of the lower anatomy of man and draw the energy to focus in a downward direction. The higher aspirations of rational thought (air), creativity (Metal), and spiritual harmony and peace (spirit) are directed to the upper part of the body.

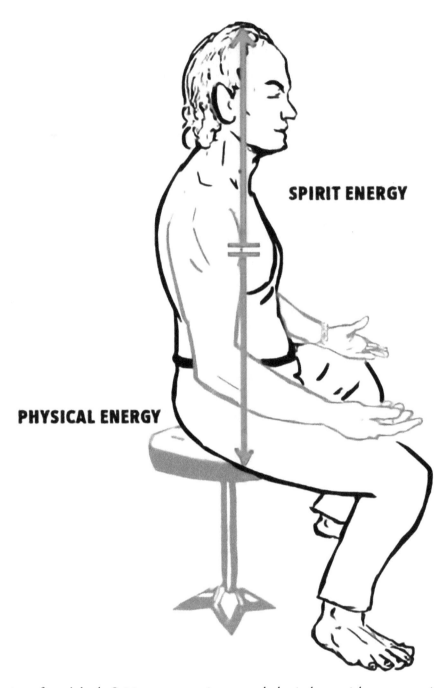

SPIRIT ENERGY

PHYSICAL ENERGY

Illustration of man's body Spirit energy moving up and physical material energy moving down

Putting these two pieces together, we see man's energy at odds and separate from the universal energies of heaven and Earth. How do we align our energies to the universe?

There has to be an internal shift to allow spiritual energy to descend and energy from the Earth to ascend so that we become not a separate entity but conduit for the energies of heaven and Earth. In the stillness of sitting or standing meditations, we can sometimes find a deep-seated relaxation that allows us a sort of void of the human energies, clearing the way to absorb energy from the heavens, the Earth, and all living things around us. Chi-Gung practices revolve around absorbing nature's bountiful energy. These are why the meditation and physical practices from all different masters from different parts of the world can achieve a balanced body and mind that allows for strong immune systems and physical strength without weightlifting and marathon running. There is a secret to achieving a oneness with the universe that lies outside practice and meditation. The secret is the human heart.

In the 7 Element concept, there are two parts to the Fire Element: Yin Fire and Yan Fire. In the universal picture, these two parts of the Fire element represent man and woman. In other words, there are also two hearts of human beings: the male or passionate heart and the female or compassionate heart. Each of us, both male and female, have both heart energies inside us. The Yan or male heart is the fiery single-purpose passion that drives strong and powerful action. The Yin or female heart is one of compassionate feeling for all those around us, which connects our actions to their impact on others. Both of these heart energies are important for human existence. However, whether we are male or female, we must have the Yin compassionate heart *rule* the Yan passion. When the Fire of passion consumes us totally, our actions are not always for the benefit of ourselves or others. Directed and dominated by the Yin compassionate heart, the fiery passion of the Yan heart becomes worthwhile positive action that benefits not only ourselves but also those around us. No matter how big a charitable organization gets, it must always keep its loving and giving (Yin passion) original principles intact and not ever lose sight of the original goals. We easily see this in positive early religious doctrine that in time is perverted to kill and torture in the name of God. By opening up our loving heart, we create a powerful vortex of energy within ourselves that is the first step to becoming one with the universe. When the Yin compassionate heart rules the Yan passionate heart, we redirect human beings' strongest and most focused power into alignment and harmony with universal energy. The Yin over Yan cycling of heart energy is at the center of the well-being of individuals and society at large. It is the first and most important step to aligning your human energy to the energies of the universe.

Illustration Yin over Yan heart

There are three main centers of the physical body: sometimes referred to as body below (physical), the mind above (mental and emotional) and the spirit middle (Love). Taoists sometimes called these the three burners. The upper center is more in contact with Heaven energies. The lower center is more in contact with the lower or Earth energies. It is important that we have the right configuration and balance of these centers to enable us to become conduits for universal energy. The most important one is the heart center as we have already discussed. But to be in a congruent flow with the Earth and Heaven energies, we must have the proper direction or Yin Yan balance of these other centers also. The upper center—which is made up by the elements of Spirit, Air, and Metal—must also, like the heart, reverse the flow and have Yin as its director. Let me explain this. Let's take the example of the human brain, which is part of the Air Element. Its functions include clinical analysis, calculating, problem solving, categorizing, rationalizing, storing information, and making judgments on our stored information compared to what we are presently conceiving. If this is not attached to a Yin perspective of softness and compassionate knowledge, tolerance for others, and of our connection to all things, then our brains become little more than computers, having no concepts or care about the positive or negative aspects or repercussions of our actions. We can easy look at our human history and see many examples of cold, calculating inhumane action. So it is important for Yin to also dominate Yan in the upper center or burner, making tolerance, adaptation to situations, and an understanding that rigid categorization and simple association does not begin to define the variations and beauty of human beings and existence. In order to flow and become a conduit for the heaven energies above, we must have open minds. We must allow our minds not to be rigid but ever flowing and open to new ideas, new concepts, and the opinions and thoughts of all people. We must be able to understand and accept, if not agree with, the views and opinions of others. Having Yin dominate the Yan of the mind and heart centers opens up our human existence to flow with universal spirit.

The lower burner or center must also change to pull energy up and reverse the downward flow and focus of the physical body. The lower center must have Yan as its directing force. Yan must dominate Yin in the lower center. This means thought, expression, and Spirit must be in direct charge of the powerful lower physical and sexual energies. When Yan dominates Yin in the lower body center, the resulting vortex will allow for the powerful Earth energies to rise up the physical body with control and proper direction.

When the three burners are properly aligned with Yin and Yan balance, the physical body and Lifeforce Chi body will become aligned with universal (Earth and heaven) energy. This will allow for a complete conduit effect, allowing the human body to be a cycling center for the energies of heaven and Earth.

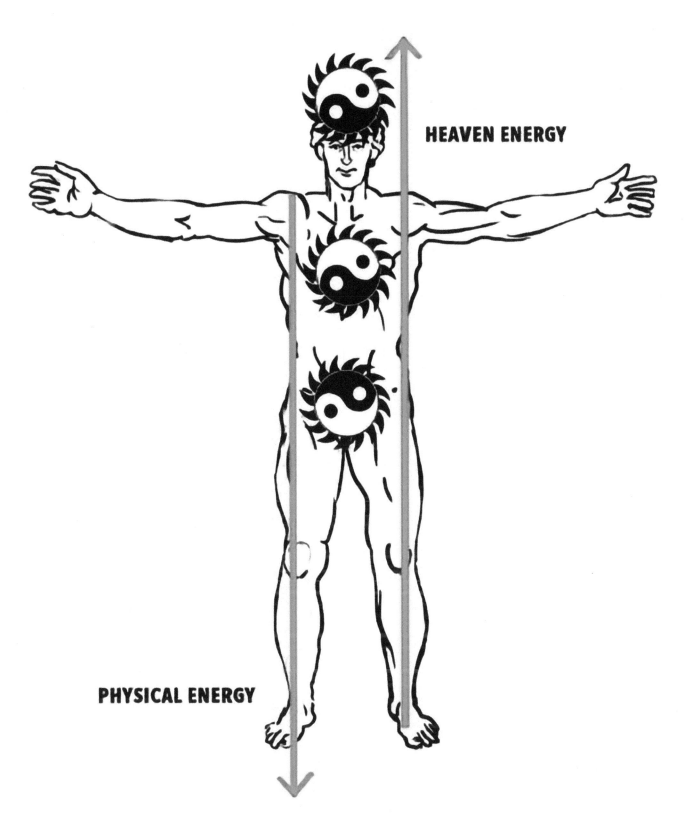

Illustration: three burners system and proper Yin Yan cycles, full page

This cycling energy is greatly enhanced by learning the basic Taoist meditation and practice of the microcosmic orbit. This basic practice is found in many Taoist texts and well described in books by Mantak Chia. The three microcosmic breathing practices at the end of chapter 4 in this book can also serve to help you align with the universal forces of heaven and Earth. Enhancing the circulation of energy through the microcosmic orbit practices, along with completely opening the heart, softening the mind, and being in control of the physical sexual, gluttony, and egotistical material excesses are two pathways to building harmony between you and the universe. The most important is practicing unconditional Love and opening your heart.

EPILOGUE

The day will come when,
after harnessing the winds, the tides, and gravitation,
we shall harness for God the energies of Love.
And on that day,
for the second time in the history of the world,
man will have discovered Fire.

—Teilhard de Chardin

Now is the universal time of Fire. Fire can be healing warmth or fiery destruction. Our universal Earth, as we know it, is at the Fire stage. Just like the stages of your human life, the Earth and humanity also has a journey in stages. The history of humanity has been through the Water, Earth, and Wood stages of development. Now is the crucial Fire stage. We will transform the culmination of the Water (survival), Earth (family and community), and Wood (growth: human and technological) to spirit, or we will self-destruct. We will burn with universal Love and light, or we will be consumed by darkness. We can take our progress as humans and forge it with Love and touch our spiritual selves. Now is the time of universal transformation.

The end of the Mayan calendar is no accident. It heralds a change into a new era, a shift into a new consciousness and action, where we will transform with the power of Love or we will be forced to transform with the Fire of destruction. Man's path has never been clearer. Give up the egocentric, selfish ways so that the whole world can enjoy harmony. Change, grow, and rise up to ride the wave of spirituality and Love or be crushed under the great wave of change. For thousands of years, we have conquered one another and caused mayhem and death in the name of God, country, power, hate, and prejudice. How long will it take for humanity to be concerned with getting along peacefully rather than aggressively, sharing rather than hoarding, loving rather than hating? In the past, we have had many transforming "lights"—the Buddha, Jesus, Lao Tse, and countless others. We have had some modern "lanterns" also. Among them are Mahatma Gandhi, Mother Teresa, Martin Luther King, and the Dalai Lama, to just name a few. They have all pointed to the "light" of nonviolence, Love, peace, and harmony. They all preached a simple mantra: *Love.*

Love is the saving grace of the human race. Having *Love* for ourselves, for all those around us, and LOVE for our planet and existence.

Be kind to the kind.
Be kind to the unkind.
For virtue is kind.

—Lao Tse

Love your neighbor as yourself.

—Jesus

If people were to regard other states as they regard their own,
and their neighbor as thy regard themselves,
then they would not attack one another,
for it would be like attacking their own person."

> —Mo Tzu, Taoist master, who lived approximately in 400 BC

True Love is boundless like the ocean, and swelling within one,
it spreads itself out and, crossing all boundaries and frontiers,
envelopes the world.
It is my firm belief that Love sustains the Earth.
There is only life where there is Love.
Life without Love is death.

> —Mohandas K. Gandhi

Darkness cannot drive out darkness;
only light can do that.
Hate cannot drive out hate;
only Love can do that.

> —Dr. Martin Luther King

Love and compassion are necessities, not luxuries.
Without them, humanity cannot survive.

> —Dalai Lama

The thought manifests as the word.
The word manifests as the deed.
The deed develops into habit.
And the habit hardens into character.
So watch the thought and its ways with care.
And let it spring from Love,
Born out of concern for all beings.

> —Buddha

Therefore, to those who want to know the way to deal with the world,
I suggest, Love People.

> —Chang San-feng, Taoist Master credited with creating Tai
> Chi Chuan, who lived approximately in 1400 AD

This simple mantra of *Love* is *the* solution for your life and the world at the same time. Start by completely loving yourself. *Love* all of *you*, *Love* what you perceive as the good and bad *you*. By loving, we transcend. Remember, you are precious in the eyes of God even with your darkness. Fill yourself with Love and light, and there will be no room for darkness. As Lao Tse said simply two thousand five hundred years ago:

Why not simply honor your parents,
Love your children,
Be faithful to your friends,

Care for you mate with devotion,
Assume responsibility for problems,
Practice virtue without first demanding it of others.
I call you to
Be the best brother or sister you can be,
Be the best son or daughter,
Be the best mother or father,
Be the best friend,
Be the best mate.
And also Be the best stranger that you can Be.
—*Hua-Hu Ching: The Unknown Teachings of Lao Tse, number 52*

I was in charge of and coached a lot of junior wrestling programs in my past. I directed many grade school programs starting from ages 7- or eight- to fourteen-year-old kids. Wrestling is a contact and tough physical sport, which has the added pressure of one-on-one combat. Eventually, when a brand-new young wrestler at 7 years old took the mat for his first match in a tournament situation with a gym packed full of people, the pressure of the physical combat and the one-to-one struggle in front of a crowd usually created some tears by the end of the match. Most of these very young wrestlers were too emotional to realize what the score was or even if they won their first match or not. Knowing this, I would lead up to matches by a little practice ritual. When running practices with the very young kids, I would train them to shout the following answers out. I would shout out, "What do we expect?" Their reply would be "to do our best." I would then reverse the statement and shout out, "Are you doing your best?" They would shout out "yes." Over and over during practice, I would try and let them know that it was not winning but doing their best that should be their focus. I constantly got them to shout it out as a team. When the first big tournament match came, I would be at the side of the mat for every new young wrestler. They would usually struggle in their first match, and of course, many of them would come off the mat with an emotional cry, win or lose. I would grab their head with my hands, look them right in their eyes to shock them, and say, "Did you do your best?" The prerecorded practice answer would come out "yes." "That's great!" I would shout. Then I would pick them up and hand them over to the older wrestlers who were also watching at mat's edge. The older kids would put the "newbie" on their shoulders and make a lap around the gym, bringing the new wrestler to the medal area, where there was always a medal or ribbon even if they lost. Between my excitement of them "doing their best," the older kids making a big deal about them, their ribbon, a hug from their parents, and something to eat from the cafeteria, their first match was usually a rousing success, win or lose.

I tell this story because at the end of our life, if you believe that, God will meet you or your life will be judged in any way. What will God say? Will He say, "Were you perfect?" "Did you always win?" "Did you never make any mistakes?" No, I think he will say, "Did you do your best?" What a great life it would be. What a great world it would be. Even if we started today just to do our best and be the best person we can be.

Open your heart to your friends *and* your enemies.
See peace, not war.
See oneness, not separateness
See harmony, not chaos.
Be the harmony.
Be the peace.
Be the Love.
Be the inherent spiritual being that you are.
May your inner path and journey lead you to LOVE, PEACE, AND HARMONY.